The Templars' Last Secret

The Templars' Last Secret

A BRUNO, CHIEF OF POLICE NOVEL

Martin Walker

Alfred A. Knopf · New York · 2017

THIS IS A BORZOI BOOK
PUBLISHED BY ALFRED A. KNOPF

Copyright © 2017 by Walker and Watson Ltd.

All rights reserved. Published in the United States by
Alfred A. Knopf, a division of Penguin Random House LLC,
New York, and distributed in Canada by Random House of
Canada Limited, Toronto, Penguin Random House Companies.
Simultaneously published in Great Britain by
Quercus Publishing PLC, London.

www.aaknopf.com

Knopf, Borzoi Books, and the colophon are
registered trademarks of Penguin Random House LLC.

Library of Congress Cataloging-in-Publication Data
Names: Walker, Martin, [date]—author.
Title: The Templars' last secret : a Bruno, Chief of Police novel /
Martin Walker.
Description: First United States edition. | New York : Knopf, 2017. |
"A Borzoi book."
Identifiers: LCCN 2016056366 | ISBN 9781101946800 (hardcover) |
ISBN 9781101946817 (ebook)
Subjects: LCSH: Police—France—Fiction. | BISAC: FICTION /
Suspense. | FICTION / Crime. | GSAFD: Mystery fiction. |
Suspense fiction.
Classification: LCC PR6073.A413 T46 2017 | DDC 823/.914—dc23
LC record available at https://lccn.loc.gov/2016056366

Jacket image: Ruins of Commarque Castle, Dordogne, France,
by Martin Beddall / Alamy
Jacket design by Stephanie Ross
Map copyright © 2012 by Jamie Whyte

Manufactured in the United States of America
First United States Edition

To Adele

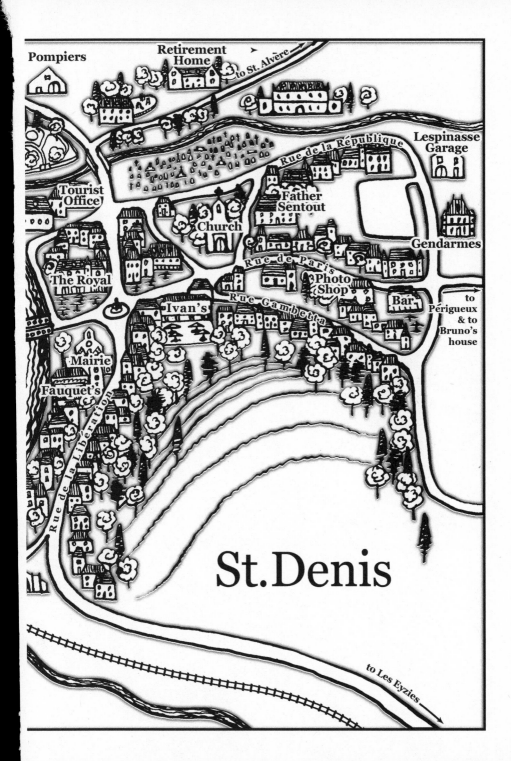

The Templars'
Last Secret

Chapter 1

Bruno Courrèges, chief of police of the small French town of St. Denis, awoke a few seconds before six, just as the dawn was breaking. His cockerel, Blanco, named for a French rugby hero, greeted the new day as Bruno donned his tracksuit and running shoes. The morning jog through the springtime woods around his home in the Périgord countryside was a delight as the sun cast long beams through the pale green of the new buds and leaves on the trees. The temperature was exactly as he liked it, not cold enough for gloves but crisp and fresh enough for him to enjoy warming up as he ran, his basset hound, Balzac, bounding along at his side.

Back at his home, its old stone walls glowing in the early light, Bruno fed his geese and chickens, watered his vegetable garden and took a look at the seedlings in the new greenhouse he had built from a kit. He placed his kettle on the stove for coffee and put one of his fresh eggs into a saucepan to boil while he checked his e-mails, then turned on the radio, tuned to France Bleu Périgord. He grilled the last half of yesterday's baguette, shared it with Balzac and sliced his toast thin so he could dip it into the egg yolk. The national radio news ended and shifted to the local news. At the third item, Bruno pricked up his ears.

Périgueux psychologist Marie-France Duteiller has filed a complaint with the procureur *on the slow progress of the investigation into allegations of pedophilia at a church-run children's home near Mussidan some thirty years ago. She claims that the inquiry led by Chief Detective Jean-Jacques Jalipeau has been "insensitive and dilatory" and has denied justice to the victims who accused several local notables of abuse when they were orphans at the home. Commissaire Jalipeau said last night that inquiries continued, although the investigation was highly complex and controversial, since the allegations depended on memories that had been recovered during hypnosis by psychologist Duteiller.*

His good mood of the morning evaporated as Bruno sighed in sympathy with his friend Jean-Jacques, known throughout the police as J-J. The investigation had been under way for months and evidently was not getting very far. This was unusual. Bruno might agree that at times J-J could be insensitive, but "dilatory" was one of the last words he'd use to describe the big, untidy man whom he'd come to admire on the occasions they had worked together. Such cases usually ended with a celebratory dinner, at which J-J played generous host, in recognition of the many times during the inquiry when he had lunched and dined at Bruno's table. J-J's cheerful personality matched his bulk, and he shared Bruno's fondness for good food and wine. Their warm relations had even survived a waspish newspaper cartoon after one recent terrorist case when Bruno had been portrayed as Astérix the Gaul and J-J as his gigantic and overfed friend Obélix. The cartoonist had come closer to reality when he portrayed each of them with a bottle of Bergerac wine, suggesting it was their equivalent of the magic potion Astérix swigged before battling the Roman legions. Above all, and unlike many in the Police Nationale, J-J did not treat a municipal policeman like Bruno as a lower form of life. He'd come to value Bruno's profound knowledge of the people of the commune of St. Denis, developed in part through years as an active member of the local tennis, rugby and hunting clubs. He accepted Bruno's idiosyncratic way of doing his job and recognized Bruno's role in ensuring that St. Denis had the lowest rate of reported crimes in the *département* of the Dordogne. Bruno in return respected J-J as a relentless detective with a deceptively subtle way of navigating the politics of policing in France. Whatever the radio might be reporting, J-J was old enough and experienced enough to take care of himself. If he needed Bruno's help, he knew he would only have to ask.

Bruno planned this morning to go first to the riding school of his British friend Pamela to exercise his horse, Hector, before heading for his office in the *mairie*. Perhaps on horseback he'd get some inspiration for a speech he had to give at a wedding at the end of the week. And perhaps I should think about getting some new clothes, Bruno thought as he scanned his wardrobe with the forthcoming event in mind.

Two-thirds of the hanging space was occupied by his official dress. There were police uniforms for summer and for winter, plus a full-dress parade uniform and an overcoat. At the back of the cupboard was a separate plastic bag holding his French army reserve uniform with its sergeant's chevrons, in which he was required to report if summoned back to duty. Hanging in the utility room, where he kept the washing machine and the secure cabinet with his guns, were a set of military camouflage that he used for hunting and the old army tracksuit he had just taken off to air after his morning jog.

Bruno had few civilian clothes. There was a dark blue wool suit he'd bought when invalided out of the French army after taking a sniper's bullet in his hip during a tour of duty in Bos-

nia. He'd long since lost the extra kilos he'd gained during his
months-long hospital stay and while convalescing, so it hung
loosely on him these days. A dark blue blazer and a pair of gray
slacks shared a wooden coat hanger. Khaki chinos hung with the
dark red jacket that he wore over his uniform shirt and trousers
when he wanted to look plausibly civilian. Its equivalent in black
was kept in his official van. A pair of jeans was folded on the top
shelf with his polo shirts, sweaters, his police képis and a blue
UN peacekeepers' helmet that he kept for sentimental reasons,
despite its dents and scrapes.

Anyone could take one glance at my wardrobe, he mused,
and tell the story of my life: the army and then the police, all the
signs of a man more at home in uniform than in civilian dress.
His modest collection of clothes suggested a man who was careful with his money, seeing no need to spend much on new garments when the French services took care of most of his needs.
His dark suit was timeless, of a classic cut, paying no regard to
the whims of fashion that dictated that this year trousers should
be tight and ties and lapels narrow.

He knew this was a sparse wardrobe, even for a country
policeman. I am a man, he thought, of little imagination and less
style; or perhaps I simply have other priorities. Bruno disliked
shopping for clothes, although he could spend many hours happily perusing hunting magazines for a new shotgun that he could
not afford or a new rod for when he went fishing with the baron.

The good thing about weddings, he thought, was that people
usually had eyes only for the bride. Nobody would care what he
was wearing; the dark blue suit would do fine. The ceremony
was to take place in the *mairie,* followed by a reception and
dinner for close friends at the National Museum of Prehistory
in Les Eyzies. The gallery of flints, with its life-size models of
early humans wearing skins and holding spears, might be considered an unusual place to choose. Bruno thought it very suit-

able, since bride and groom were professional archaeologists of renown. Clothilde, the bride, was the museum's senior curator, and her husband-to-be, Horst, after retiring from his university post in Germany, had joined the museum as an adjunct professor responsible for archaeological digs. Most of the guests were in the same profession.

Idly, Bruno wondered if they might offer the fashionable Paleolithic diet of nuts and berries, fruit and charred meats, instead of the more traditional wedding feast. No, he concluded. Horst might be amused by such a meal, but Clothilde was a sensible Frenchwoman—she would understand that when guests came to the culinary heartland of France, they expected the classic food of the Périgord.

As Horst's best man, Bruno was a little nervous about the speech he'd have to give. He would obviously be expected to make some reference to his friend's distinguished career in archaeology, before an audience that would include some of Europe's top experts in the field. On Bruno's bedside table lay the latest issue of *Archéologie,* a popular magazine that contained Professor Horst Vogelstern's latest article, comparing the various small statues of women that had been found at prehistoric sites across Europe.

Long before he had become Horst's friend, Bruno had subscribed to the journal, fascinated by the wealth of cave art and prehistory that surrounded him in the valley of the River Vézère. The cover of the magazine was arresting, a photograph of a woman fashioned from clay with gigantic hips, a prominent vulva and pendulous breasts. The caption was "Miss Europa, 25,000 B.C." This Venus of Dolní Věstonice, the place where she had been found in the modern-day Czech Republic, was the oldest ceramic known. It was just one of several illustrations accompanying Horst's fascinating piece.

Bruno had been intrigued to learn that just over a hundred

of these statues, known as the Venus figurines, had been found. They had mostly been made between 28,000 and 20,000 B.C., in the early Paleolithic or Stone Age, and had emerged in caves and graves scattered from Spain through France and Germany to Siberia and south through Italy and the Balkans to Syria and Israel. If there was one outstanding element that could be said to have connected our direct ancestors among early Stone Age peoples, Horst argued, it was their fascination with amply proportioned women. Usually between five and twenty centimeters in height, the figurines were the first-known depictions of any human form, and they were highly stylized. The women had with rare exceptions enormous breasts, buttocks and thighs, a swollen stomach and a prominent pudendum. Some had complex and carefully carved hairstyles, or perhaps headdresses made of small shells, rather like the one that was on display in the Les Eyzies museum.

Inevitably they had been seen as fertility symbols, since they focused so much on the female breasts and reproductive organs. Countless bookshelves had been written on these figurines and their role in prehistoric culture. There was speculation on whether they signified an early matriarchal society, in which female fertility was the great mystery and object of worship. Some feminist scholars interpreted this to mean that women had ruled the families and perhaps also the tribes. Most scholars, however, sought to place these Venus figurines into the mysterious context of prehistoric art in general. Some tried to discern timeless concepts of beauty and proportion from these limited and somewhat blowsy foundations. But all could agree that these figurines appeared to coincide with the explosion of human creativity, between the first great work of cave art at Chauvet in France, some thirty thousand years old with its extraordinary depictions of horses and other beasts, and the masterpiece of the Lascaux cave in the

Vézère Valley, some seventeen thousand years old. Chauvet and Lascaux portrayed almost exclusively animals. The Venus figurines were palpably human.

The sudden flowering of art in this period had long fascinated historians, wondering what creative magic had begun suddenly to touch our ancestors. Why were these supposedly primitive creatures suddenly inspired to start making an art that is instantly appealing to modern humans, who recognize instinctively an aesthetic sensibility akin to our own?

All this, Bruno told himself, provided excellent material for a lighthearted and slightly teasing speech to be made at the wedding. He could talk of Horst's lifelong fascination with the Venus figurines and the female form and his endless pursuit of perfection in the shape of Clothilde. That gave Bruno a theme that would flatter both bride and groom and refer to their common passion for prehistory. He would also suggest that this marriage of the Frenchwoman Dr. Clothilde Daumier and a German symbolized all that was best of the new Europe.

Jotting down these notes, Bruno felt a weight lift from his shoulders. He dreaded having to give speeches and as a result put so much effort into preparing them that his friends kept pestering him to speak. At least this one was now sketched out, though he knew a few hours of careful drafting still awaited him, part of a busy day ahead. He was due to give evidence before a tribunal in Sarlat at ten, so Bruno checked his appearance in the bedroom mirror, summoned Balzac from his morning patrol of the garden and was about to set off to the riding school when his phone vibrated. It was Ahmed, one of the professional firemen who led the team of mostly volunteer *pompiers* in St. Denis. As well as fighting fires, they also acted as the region's emergency medical service.

"We've got an urgent call to Commarque, that ruined château

off the road to Sarlat," Ahmed began. "A woman, possibly dead, fallen from the cliff or the castle wall. The guy who phoned it in runs the kiosk at the entrance, said his name was Jean-Philippe Fumel, and he'll be expecting you. Fabiola's on call today, and she's meeting us at the spot. Will we see you there?"

Bruno said that he would join them at the château and then called the riding school to say that duty called; he could not exercise Hector this morning. Pamela replied that she'd just heard the same news from Fabiola, and they'd expect him for the evening ride instead.

"Bisous," she said as she hung up. It always slightly confused Bruno when Pamela used this affectionate French term, which meant "kisses." Their affair had been over for some months, but the mutual attraction that remained reminded him that there was more than friendship between them. He had no time to think of that now. He phoned the *mairie* to leave a message explaining why he'd been called away. Then he thumbed through his phone's address book to find a number for the Count of Commarque, a genial giant of a man who had for the past thirty years mounted an ambitious project of research, restoration and public education at the grandiose ruin his ancestors had built. The count, whom Bruno knew from the rugby club, deserved to know of the accident and might have some useful background to contribute. It was not long after seven in the morning, so Bruno was not surprised when there was no reply. He left a message.

Before he left, Bruno checked his mailbox at the end of the drive, on which he had painted PAS DE PUB to tell the postman not to deliver the endless supermarket and other advertising brochures that would otherwise clog the box. There was a bank statement and a postcard from London showing an unimpressive modern building captioned as the police headquarters at New Scotland Yard. The message was simple: "Wish you were here instead of me. Give Balzac a big hug and a kiss from me, and a little hug for you."

It was signed with the single initial *I,* which meant "Isabelle," the woman who got away. No, Bruno thought, that wasn't right. When she left the Périgord for a high-powered job on the staff of the minister of the interior in Paris, she had wanted him to join her. But Bruno could never see himself in some cramped apartment in Paris with no garden, where it would not be fair to keep a dog, let alone his chickens. He knew he'd lose touch with all his friends and the hunting and tennis and rugby clubs and would miss the training sessions for the schoolkids that made up so much of his life. Now Isabelle had an even-bigger job coordinating French and European antiterrorist efforts. Balzac had been her gift to him when his previous dog had been killed, and these occasional postcards from foreign capitals always seemed more about Balzac than about him. Or perhaps it was just Isabelle's way of reminding him of what he was missing, not that he needed reminding. He sniffed the card, wondering if it were his imagination or if he really detected just a hint of her perfume. He offered the card to Balzac, who sniffed and gave a discreet but plaintive howl. Balzac missed her, too.

Chapter 2

Installing Balzac in his preferred place on the passenger seat, Bruno set off for Les Eyzies. He gave his usual wave of salute to the statue of prehistoric man on the rocky ledge above the town's main street. The statue symbolized the town's role as the center of prehistoric studies. After the first find of such remains during the construction of a railway, skeletons of people with much more modern skulls than those of the first Neanderthals were then unearthed in 1868. Called Cro-Magnon people after a local place-name, the skeletons emerged just as the arguments over Charles Darwin's theory of evolution were raging across Europe. So many visitors began to descend on the region that a new hotel, inevitably called the Cro-Magnon, was built to receive them. A flurry of archaeological investigations nearby soon established that the valley of the River Vézère was an extraordinary repository of human and prehuman remains.

Close to the first Cro-Magnon find was the Abri Pataud, a hundred-meter-long balcony in a great cliff where modern archaeologists had found traces of forty separate camps of nomadic reindeer hunters. These early humans had used local stone to build a rough wall on the rim of the balcony to form a sheltered room, and the animal bones left behind suggested it had been used for a prolonged period. The skeletons of a young woman and a newborn baby were found there, some twenty thousand years old. These bones were used as a model to construct a life-size statue of the woman, on display in the attached museum. Bruno had a great affection for this young mother, and it had been enhanced when he learned from Horst's article that another figurine, the Venus of Abri Pataud, had also been found nearby. She represented so much of what Bruno loved about this valley, the sense of history being so close that across two hundred centuries there had lived a girl here he might have loved. So he blew her a kiss as he drove past, heading toward another of his favorite sites, the medieval fortress of Commarque.

Perched on a rocky outcrop in the hills between the rivers Dordogne and Vézère, the half-ruined château was for Bruno one of the most impressive in the region. Unlike the famous medieval fortresses of Beynac and Castelnaud that glowered at each other across the Dordogne as they had during the Hundred Years' War between the English and French, Commarque was not on the standard tourist route. Its remoteness somehow added to its grandeur. The outer walls enclosed a large village that contained the remains of six grand houses, each inhabited in the Middle Ages by a different noble dynasty, while the Commarque family held the main keep with its high tower. Bruno had heard the ensemble described as a kind of holiday camp for the feudal elite, a place where they would gather for celebrations and feast days to scheme and plot and arrange marriages while enjoying the magnificent view over the valley of the River Beune.

Standing atop the tower one day, the Count of Commarque had told Bruno that its height had enabled his ancestors to see and signal to the town of Sarlat, twenty kilometers up the valley. In the Middle Ages, the trees, which later would cover much of the region, had been cut down to produce charcoal to feed the hungry furnaces of dozens of smithies and ironworks. The hills of the Périgord during that period had been covered with sheep rather than timber.

Bruno navigated the rough track down to the château entrance and parked. He let Balzac jump down from the police van, where the dog started sniffing his way around the area, as if recalling his previous visits and checking for any changes. The young man at the entrance kiosk looked startled to see a policeman arrive with a basset hound. He shook hands, introduced himself as Jean-Philippe and asked, "Sniffer dog?"

"The best," said Bruno, and followed him to the base of a forbidding cliff, where his friend Fabiola, a doctor, was waiting beside the corpse. Her examination seemed to be complete, for she was gazing upward, as though admiring the high walls and tower. At her feet lay the body of a middle-aged woman wearing a blue nylon tracksuit, one leg of which was almost ripped away to reveal a leg bent unnaturally in three places. Through the tear a broken bone poked through the skin, although there was little blood. Her heart must have stopped pumping when she hit the ground, Bruno thought.

He felt a wave of sadness, the sudden fall of silence and solemnity that always came upon him in the presence of death. Despite his years in the military and the nature of his work as a policeman, his duty to attend to traffic accidents and the natural deaths to which he was called, he never became accustomed to it. If he ever did, Bruno suspected that he would feel compelled to resign.

Standing there beside Fabiola, Bruno recalled that she'd once told him that at medical school she'd attended a compulsory lecture on death and its impact on doctors. Doctors in hospitals would attend hundreds, probably thousands, of deaths, but most of them would be strangers. Doctors in general practice would attend far fewer deaths, but the majority of them would be familiar, patients of many years, perhaps. Either way, the lecturer had said, the emotional toll would grow and weigh more heavily over time. Bruno closed his eyes briefly and then forced himself to look at the corpse.

The dead woman had dark hair cut short, a plump face that was markedly suntanned although it was early in the year and a livid scrape along one cheek. She was lying on her back, her head bent so badly to the right that her neck must have been broken. Her right arm was upraised and bent at the elbow, an old cow's horn close to her hand. Her other hand was resting on her stomach, which seemed an oddly peaceful pose for someone who had presumably fallen to her death. The foot attached to the broken leg was bare while on the other foot was a cheap running shoe rather than the specialized footwear used by rock climbers. Bruno looked around but couldn't see the missing shoe.

"She's certainly dead, so I sent the *pompiers* away. There was nothing for them to do," said Fabiola, after greeting him and then bending to caress Balzac, whose tail wagged furiously to express his pleasure at seeing her. The dog then took one cautious sniff at the dead woman's bare foot and then backed away and sat, looking at Bruno and waiting for instructions.

"She has a broken neck and broken leg, so it looks like a fall," Fabiola went on, her voice without emotion. "She has no identification that I could see, and you'll have trouble getting good fingerprints. Her fingers are scraped raw from the climb, but there's no obvious sign of foul play. I'd say she's around forty years old and considerably overweight, so I'm surprised that she was climbing a cliff like that."

"Would you have climbed it?" he asked, knowing that in her days as a student Fabiola had been a keen mountaineer.

"Not in the dark, I wouldn't," she replied, shaking her head firmly. "Even in daylight I'd want ropes and pitons before I tackled a climb like that. From her footwear, it looks like she didn't know what she was doing."

Bruno looked up at the sheer wall of rock face above the overhang. It soared some twenty meters before giving way to the stone wall and tower, which rose another twenty meters farther. The lower stretch of cliff contained a number of openings that Bruno remembered were troglodyte chambers. One of them had been a kitchen, and the others were storerooms and places where the families of château servants had lived. After the place was ruined and abandoned during the religious wars of the seventeenth century, people had still lived in the caves, and the Resistance had used them for shelter during the war. The caves were dry, and there was water nearby.

The count had told him that the entire rock on which the château had been built was honeycombed with caves and fissures, some of them containing evidence of human habitation dating back millennia. A famous stone engraving of a horse's head had been found in one of them, reckoned to be fifteen thousand years old. But what made Bruno step back in surprise was the sight of freshly scrawled letters high on the tower, in luminous paint of a reddish-orange color.

"*I-F-T-I,*" he spelled out the letters. "Does that mean anything to you?"

"I've been puzzling over it," said Fabiola. "See where the paint fades down and away just after the final *I,* as though she was starting a new letter, and that was when she fell. It could be an *L* or a *K,* a *Y* or even an *R.* I've no idea what she was trying to write. I was never much good at crossword puzzles."

"I can't think of any words in French that begin with *I-F* but I suppose it could be English," said Bruno. "And that looks like the same color paint on her hand. It's very distinctive."

"Yes, mixed with blood from her fingers. That cow horn beside her right hand is odd. Quite a coincidence for her to have fallen and landed right beside it, so the horn may have fallen from her pocket or it could have been placed there later. If so, someone else must have been involved. I had a quick look around, but I saw no sign of the spray paint she seems to have used. If you can't find the can, somebody must have taken it away."

"How long has she been dead?" Bruno asked.

"Not long, around three to four hours I'd guess. Certainly not more than eight, which means she was climbing at night. No sign of a flashlight; in fact, there's nothing in her pockets."

"Maybe she was climbing by moonlight. It's close to a full moon." Bruno kept a careful watch on the lunar calendar for his gardening. "I'll have to find out if it was cloudy. Anything from her dentistry?"

"Not that I could see, just a few standard fillings that could have been done anywhere in Europe, but you might want to ask a dentist. I'm almost done, just one or two more final checks, and then I'd better get back to the clinic."

"Anything about this that strikes you as odd, apart from the cow horn?" Bruno asked. He trusted Fabiola's expertise and her instincts.

"There are a couple of marks on her wrist and neck that aren't clear to me. They could be rope burns if she was climbing with one. But there's no sign of any rope or harness, and they could be marks from her fall. I know the police will take a good look at them, but I won't forgive myself if I miss something."

"Could I use your magnifying glass?" Bruno took it and bent to peer closely at the mark on the woman's neck and the ones on her wrist and forearm. He saw something glinting, two or three shreds of greenish-blue material.

"Could those be strands of nylon, perhaps from a rope?" he asked, passing her the glass.

She squinted. "Looks like that to me."

"That means she was almost certainly climbing with a partner who's disappeared along with the rope and the paint. Your death certificate had better say that she died in a fall, in possibly suspicious circumstances."

Fabiola nodded. "Other than confirming the nylon threads, I don't see the point of going to the expense of an autopsy."

"That will be up to J-J," said Bruno. "It's his budget."

As the region's chief detective for the Police Nationale, J-J automatically took over any suspicious death inquiry. Not that they were frequent. The number of homicides each year in the *département* was usually in single figures, and J-J almost always solved them, sometimes with Bruno's help.

"Good luck with identifying her," said Fabiola, closing her medical bag. "With luck you'll be finished in time so we can go riding together later. I'll leave the death certificate at the clinic for you to pick up, and I'll put down 'death by a fall, probably suspicious.' What I ought to write down is 'suicide by stupidity.'" She blew him a kiss by way of goodbye.

Bruno waved back as he pulled out his phone to call J-J and sent Balzac off to search. By the time he had briefed J-J, Balzac's bark signaled that he had found something. Bruno strolled a few meters along the base of the cliff to see his dog standing beside the dead woman's missing shoe. Stroking Balzac in appreciation, Bruno sent him off to search for any traces of the woman's scent. Then he went back to his van for binoculars and began to scan the cliff. About twenty meters above the fallen shoe and slightly to its right, he saw something glinting in the morning sun. It could be a piton, one of the metal supports that climbers hammered into cracks in the rock to support a rope. He'd leave that for J-J's people to examine.

Balzac barked again, this time from about a hundred meters away across the valley. His tail was stretched out flat, one paw raised, his neck lifted, the pose he assumed when pointing at game. Bruno walked across the turf to join him, feeling the ground start to become boggy beneath his feet as he neared the bank of the small River Beune, which here spread out into several sluggish streams. His dog waited with the dutiful patience of a well-trained hunting hound, his whole body pointing to the slope across the valley. It seemed that the dead woman must have come that way, across the watery meadow. Odd, therefore, that there had been no sign of mud on her legs or shoes.

Bruno returned to the body. Although J-J's team would doubtless take their own photos, he began taking pictures with his phone, just so he had a record and could start the process of identification. He started with a general shot of the location, used his zoom to capture the letters scrawled on the wall of the château and finally moved in for some close-ups of the face before examining the hands more closely. Good forensic work might get some partial prints, but mostly the fingertips had been scraped bloody.

Other questions nagged at him, beyond the obvious one. Did she fall or was she pushed? Why would anyone have wanted to climb the cliff? If she wanted to get inside the outer wall of the château, it would be easier to climb where it was lower. Easier still, he thought, to come from the opposite direction, along the ridge where the only obstruction was a crumbling wall. Had she been trying to get into the tower itself? Or was she simply daubing some unfinished slogan? Perhaps the count would know.

Chapter 3

The count appeared not long after Fabiola left, and found Bruno poking through the grass at the base of the cliff where Balzac had found the missing shoe. Balzac darted across to greet the newcomer, who bent to fondle the basset's long ears. The count, a tall man, rose to his full height as Bruno greeted him and began to explain what little he knew as they walked toward the body.

"I've never seen her before and I have no idea who she is, God rest her soul." The count's usually cheerful face was solemn as he stared down at the body, shaking his head. He raised his hand to his brow and crossed himself. Only then did he look up at the cliff looming above and stepped back in surprise as he spotted the large scrawled letters on the castle wall.

"What on earth . . . ?" the count exclaimed. "Is this supposed to be some kind of graffiti art? Was she painting these letters? It doesn't mean anything, not in any language I know."

"I was hoping you might help identify her or whatever slogan she was daubing. She's not carrying any papers and you can see from the state of her hands we'll have trouble getting fingerprints."

"I'm assuming she was one of the Templar enthusiasts. We've had trouble with them before, trying to break in and dig around into the morgue in Bergerac until we can identify her, and then it will be up to the next of kin. We'll check the missing-persons list, distribute a photo through the media, all the usual procedures."

The count nodded, looking down again at the dead woman. Suddenly he seemed to notice something. "That horn beside her hand," he said sharply. "Who put it there?"

"It was here when I arrived. I was going to ask the guy at the gate if he'd seen it, too. Why?"

The count was already striding back to the small hut, where Jean-Philippe was laying brochures, guidebooks and souvenirs on the counter. There was a smell of coffee in the air. As Bruno followed, he saw a machine steaming away at the back of the kiosk.

"No, of course I didn't put it there. Where would I have found it? The horn was lying by her hand when I first saw her," Jean-Philippe was saying as the count looked fiercely at him.

"Whoever did it, it's not funny," said the count. He pulled a guidebook from the stack, opened it to a page and handed it to Bruno. "Here, look at this. The Venus of Laussel, found just across the way."

It was a photo that Bruno remembered seeing in the magazine that carried Horst's article, one of a plump woman standing with an arm raised, holding the horn close to her ear. It might almost have been a telephone. The woman had no face; the stone above her chest had been eroded. But there was a suggestion of long hair on the opposite side of her head from the horn.

"It's the same pose," the count said. "That couldn't have happened by chance. Somebody who knows about the Venus of Laussel put that horn by her hand deliberately."

And she wasn't climbing alone, Bruno thought. He looked again at the photo. This Venus was not a statue but an engraving carved into the rock. There was no sense of scale, and Bruno asked what size it was.

the place. I invited some of them in to watch at the last archae
logical dig here, so they could be satisfied there's none of th
legendary Templar treasure here. I thought we'd seen the end (
them after that. I think I've got an e-mail address somewhere fo
the secretary of their association. Perhaps he might be able to
identify this unfortunate woman."

"Maybe this was an accidental fall, but some aspects are trou-
bling," Bruno said, explaining why he'd called in J-J and the
detectives. "It's not even clear how she got here."

"She could have left a car in the parking lot up the hill," the
count said. "I came here a different way."

"There was no car parked when I came and no car key in her
pocket."

"You'd better check the parking lot at Cap Blanc as well.
It's just across the valley, an easy stroll, although a lot longer by
road." He pointed and Bruno turned to look. It was the same
direction that Balzac had taken.

"I had no idea it was so close," he said. Bruno knew Cap
Blanc, a cave in which prehistoric people had carved bas-relief
sculptures of horses so lifelike they seemed to be walking out of
the wall.

"Just over there is the *gisement,* the rock shelter where they
found the Venus of Laussel," the count replied, pointing. "And
you know about the carving of the horse's head in the cave
beneath the cliff. There have been more important prehistoric
finds in this little spot than almost anywhere else on earth, quite
apart from the château. Listen, Bruno, I'd rather not have this
body here long. We have a group of schoolkids coming from
Bergerac later this morning. What are you planning on doing
with her?"

"Detectives from the Police Nationale in Périgueux are on
their way, so it will be up to them. I imagine we'll have to put her

"About half a meter tall. It was found here with several other engravings, all from the same period, about twenty-five thousand years ago," the count said. There had been another Venus, less well preserved, also holding what could have been a horn. It was called the Venus of Berlin because it had been sold to a German museum in 1912, where it was destroyed during the last war. But there was also an engraving of a much-slimmer young woman, seen from the side, and another of two women joined at the hip, one sitting upright, the other upside down.

"It's a real treasure trove," the count went on. "Alongside the two women was another engraving, *la femme à la tête quadrillée,* or the Venus with the net, since her head is covered in something that looks like one. If they'd left it all in place it would be one of the most important sites in France, but the collection was broken up, and the main engravings are now in the Bordeaux museum."

"Are they sure it was a horn?" Bruno asked, squinting at the guidebook photo. "It could be a big seashell."

"It could also be a crescent moon," the count replied. "There are thirteen vertical stripes on it, which could refer to the lunar calendar, and if these Venus figures are fertility symbols those stripes could be linked to the female menstrual cycle. We don't know. Some scholars suggest it might be one of the first-known musical instruments, perhaps a hunting horn."

"So do you still think the Templar enthusiasts are involved in this?"

The count shrugged. "Your guess is as good as mine, but the Templar people have been here several times, bringing metal detectors and spades to dig around. They're a menace, but any serious archaeologist is always welcome, they just have to go through the usual application procedures with the Ministry of Culture and the museum at Les Eyzies. We've got two or three who have been approved and are coming this summer, working under Horst's supervision. We've also got a seismic and radio-sounding team starting work to look for caves we haven't found yet. Clothilde arranged that."

"Tell me about these Templar enthusiasts and what they thought they were looking for," Bruno said, nodding his thanks as Jean-Philippe handed him a paper cup of coffee. "I know they were Crusaders, some kind of religious order in the Holy Land, but that's about all I do know."

The count grinned, looking almost boyish. "Have you ever crossed the Pont Neuf in Paris?"

Bruno nodded. "Both ways. Left Bank to Right Bank and back again."

"Then when you reached the island in the middle of the Seine, you went past the entrance to place Dauphine. Right at that spot was where Jacques de Molay, the last master of the Templars, was burned at the stake in 1314. It's also where he pronounced his famous curse on Philip IV and the pope and on the royal line of the Capetians. Before the year was out, king and pope were both dead, and the throne of France had passed to the house of Valois. The Templar curse had come true."

The king's excuse for their suppression, the count went on to explain, was the allegation that the Templars had become corrupted, indulging in witchcraft, sodomy and every other sin he and the pope could think of. The king's real motives were less high-minded; he feared that they were becoming a state within the state, and he wanted their lands and their money. Not long before, he'd embarked on a pogrom against the Jews in France, confiscating their wealth. Having spent that, the Templars offered the next available fortune.

"There's even a story," the count added, "that when the king was guillotined during the Revolution, nearly five centuries later, somebody dipped a handkerchief in the royal blood and called out, 'Jacques de Molay, you are avenged.' That was in the place de la Concorde."

"So the Templars weren't wiped out?"

The count shrugged. "A lot of the Freemason groups of the eighteenth century claimed descent from the Templars. Freemasons were for reform, a constitution, cutting down the power of the Church, all those Enlightenment causes. That's why several of the leaders of the American Revolution were Freemasons. Did you ever see an American dollar bill? It carries the eye in the pyramid, one of the symbols of the Illuminati, a Freemason sect. Curious, no?"

Bruno had over the years heard various conspiracy theories about the Freemasons, but this was a new one. He asked, "But why are people still so interested in the Templars?"

"It's the legend of lost treasure. The Templars were supposed to be very rich, which is why the king of France suppressed them and took all their property after the Crusaders had been driven out of the Holy Land. I'm no expert, but there's a very clever medieval scholar named Dumesnil who lives in Sarlat and has written a couple of books about them. I think he teaches at the lycée in Brive."

"And what have the Templars to do with your château?"

"It's a Templar site. When my ancestor, Gérard de Commarque, went off to the Crusades in the early twelfth century, he entrusted the place to the Templars."

"When did your family get it back?"

"Good question. Ownership became somewhat confused. But there's no doubt it belonged to us, although the counts of Beynac kept trying to take it over. Charlemagne gave the land around here to my earliest-known ancestor, Bovon de Commarque, for brave deeds in fighting off the Viking raids. You know they sacked Bordeaux and Bergerac and even the Abbey of Paunat, just downstream from St. Denis?"

Bruno nodded. "Looking for loot, just like King Philip and the Templars."

The count laughed. "You don't call it looting when the king does it." Thinking of the body, his facial expression hardened. "Sometimes I wonder if we don't have too much history here in France."

"Your family made a lot of it," said Bruno, trying to keep his voice neutral. As an orphan who had never known his parents, he'd always assumed that his own family had played humble roles in France's past. At best they had been poor peasants, dying young of disease or famine; at worst, they had been victims, foot soldiers or cannon fodder for the dreams and ambitions of the nobles. Bruno was a good republican, reckoning that despite the horrors of the Terror, the Revolution of 1789 had on the whole been good for France. The count had probably lost some of his forebears to the guillotine and may have felt differently.

The count looked at him sharply. "Your ancestors also helped make our history, one way or another. And mine at least had the good sense to look for wives elsewhere than their fellow aristocrats. That's probably why our line didn't die out. And I didn't inherit this place, you know. I had to buy it back."

"And you're doing well by it," Bruno said, and meant it. He admired the research and restoration work the count had carried out for three decades. "Where could I find this secretary of the Templar enthusiasts?"

The count pulled out a mobile phone and read out the name and number. "He's a pleasant-enough guy, if a bit dull, a retired civil servant who worked for the finance ministry. I imagine the Templars added some interest to his life. And here is that Templar scholar I mentioned, Auguste Dumesnil. I don't have his phone number, but for his e-mail put a dot between his names and just add @orange.fr."

Bruno thanked him, scribbling down the details in his notebook. "Can you think of any other reason than treasure hunting for the dead woman's presence here?"

"If she was climbing the cliff to the *donjon* wall, I doubt she was looking for treasure," the count replied. "There are easier ways to get into the courtyards, which is where the treasure hunters usually go with their metal detectors. And those who don't look in the courtyard concentrate on the caves beneath."

"So what might she have been looking for in the *donjon?*"

"I have no idea," the count replied, shaking his head. "Since we stabilized the ruins and began the restoration, the *donjon* has been very thoroughly examined as part of the rebuilding. There's nothing in the place, apart from the exhibition of photographs of various archaeological finds, and anybody can pay the admission and see those. Over the centuries since the wars of religion, it was thoroughly looted. Even some of the stones were taken for building. Maybe the graffiti was her only purpose and, if so, perhaps she wasn't climbing up but climbing down from the tower. Let's go up and take a look."

He unlocked the entrance gate to the château, and they climbed up the winding path to the *donjon,* the fortified keep where the defenders could hold out even if the courtyard had fallen to the attackers. The count's guided tour revealed nothing of interest, no furniture except for some display cases in an upper room showing the process of restoration. As they came down, Bruno saw J-J's car crawling carefully down the rutted road, followed by the crime scene truck.

Looking at his watch and saying he was expected in court, Bruno introduced J-J to the count, led the way to the body and pointed out the graffiti. "When I get back from court, I'll distribute the photos I've taken to the local media," Bruno said. "Anything else I can do, just let me know."

"We'll stay in touch," said J-J, looking up at the graffiti and scratching his head. "Any idea what the hell that scrawl could mean?"

"It could be English or some other language," said Bruno, shrugging. "I'm pretty sure it isn't French."

"I'll call you this afternoon, after what I imagine will be a difficult meeting with the prefect about this pedophile business," J-J said.

"Why is he involved?" Bruno asked. "It's a police matter."

Prefects were appointed by the president of France to be the representative of the French state in each of the country's 101 *départements*. Mainly concerned with ensuring the local governments operated in accord with national policy, prefects also took charge during national disasters and had a special role in coordinating the various arms of the police. Operational matters, however, were usually left to the police officials.

"He says it's a question of public confidence in the police."

"Are you getting anywhere with it?"

"Not really. It's a hell of a case, all happening thirty years ago. The three complainants have histories of mental illness, and their accusations come from what the psychologist treating them calls 'recovered memories.' In other words, they never mentioned being abused until this woman began working with them. We've tracked down and interviewed every one of the other kids at the home at the time, and not one admits to being mistreated." He looked up at Bruno. "You were in one of those church orphanages, weren't you?"

"Yes, but I was at the one in Bergerac. And I was only there for a few years before my aunt was able to take me in to live with her family. I was caned on the backside and had my knuckles rapped with a ruler a few times. But I was never abused sexually and didn't hear of anything like that while I was at the home. The worst thing that ever happened to me was when the priest said animals didn't have souls and so would never go to heaven. That broke my little heart. I'd have been about five at the time, and I've never felt the same about religion since."

J-J nodded. "It's a lousy situation and I'm in the middle, with all my detectives ready to go on strike if they have to do any more work on a case they think is a bunch of fantasies. But the magistrate in charge seems ready to believe anything this psychologist says and insists we keep up the inquiry. And the prefect's wife is just the same."

"What does Prunier say?" Bruno asked, referring to J-J's boss, the police commissioner for the region.

"He's tried to get the file closed, but the prefect won't hear of it, even though most of the other inmates at Mussidan don't believe it ever happened. It's just these three and one of the ex-nuns, who says there was a discreet policy not to leave a couple of the priests alone with any of the children. She's not the most reliable witness, since she became an alcoholic after she left the Church." J-J rolled his eyes. "She's another one being treated by this same psychologist."

"It all sounds pretty thin."

"Not to the investigating magistrate it doesn't. She's out to make a name for herself and thinking everything this psychologist says is gospel truth. Anyway, that's my problem. I'll call you after I see the prefect."

Chapter 4

Bruno reached the courthouse in Sarlat with a few minutes to spare but had to push his way through two small groups of demonstrators confronting each other on the steps. One was waving banners proclaiming membership in the CGT trade union, long linked to the Communists, while others held placards declaring NO SLAVE LABOR and chanting "Keep Sundays free." The other group, dressed in bakery white with flour smeared on their faces, was chanting "We want to work." The scene did not look angry to Bruno, and one of the trade union demonstrators, a man with whom he'd played rugby, greeted him and shook his hand. But Bruno reminded himself that you never knew where trouble might start.

Two of the town policemen kept a path clear for people to enter the courthouse but made no other attempt to interfere. Hugues and his lawyer greeted him with smiles of relief, although Bruno was only there to be a character witness for one of the hardest-working men he knew. Hugues had been born and raised in St. Denis but ran his thriving bakery business in a new development for light industry outside Sarlat. Bruno had known him as a teenager, learning the bakery business as an apprentice at Fauquet's. When his grandmother died, leaving her house to the family, Hugues had persuaded his father to sell it and invest the money in Hugues's plan for a bakery of his own. It had been the peak of the property market, just before the crash, and he took over the lease of a sleepy small bakery on the outskirts of Sarlat.

From the beginning, Hugues had big ambitions. He had enough money to install modern equipment and then pursued his belief that the baking industry was poised for a revolution. The tradition of small artisan bakers serving a static neighborhood clientele was already under threat from the supermarkets selling bread and cakes more cheaply. But Hugues reckoned there was another market to attack. He visited every hotel, restaurant and campsite in the area and offered to deliver them fresh breads and croissants every morning in time for breakfast. The goods would be free for the first week, and if they liked the products, they could sign a contract.

Supplying the hotels and campsites meant he had to deliver his goods seven days a week, and that was where Hugues ran into trouble. Under French employment law, a bakery was supposed to close at least one day a week to ensure that the employees had a day off. Hugues was proud of his employees and by now had opened a second bakery in Périgueux and was employing sixteen people, all of them earning above minimum wage with a profit-sharing bonus on top. The thirty-five-hour workweek was in force so he organized them on a shift system, which meant that every employee worked only five days each week, although the baking ovens were working flat out each day. In Hugues's view, he was in full compliance with the labor laws.

But that was not the view of the Clic-P movement, an alliance of labor unions in the retail and service industries that had launched a nationwide campaign against working on Sundays and late hours. Bruno understood the principle of their campaign, but could not understand why they had picked on Hugues and suspected that the local union leaders simply saw him as an easy target.

"I can't believe I'm facing a criminal record for delivering bread on Sundays," Hugues said. "Nor can the staff." He pointed to the group of employees outside who had rallied to support him, some still in the white aprons and hairnets they wore in the bakery.

"Will you really have to close down?" Bruno asked.

"No, because we have the second bakery. With each one working six days a week I can juggle things so we make bread every day," he replied. "But delivering to the Sarlat area from Périgueux and then from Périgueux to Sarlat just for one day a week each means I'll have to hire more delivery people. That drives up costs and I've already got to pay off a new bank loan for the second bakery. Not to mention the legal fees. What really annoys me is that the whole thing has become political. The unions are trying to get the left-wing mayors and councils to boycott my products, and the conservatives want to turn me into some kind of martyr. That's the last thing I want."

The case was called. A police tribunal was a relatively informal court meant to try minor offenses before a single judge aided by a legal clerk. Bruno's role was brief. He was called as a character witness who had known Hugues for ten years. Bruno praised him as a generous and kindly man always prepared to support local causes. At the end of each day, the last delivery of his drivers was to hand over that day's unsold bread to the Restos du Coeur, which fed the needy, and to other local charities. Hugues's lawyer then called three of Hugues's employees, each of them a union member and one of them a Socialist councillor, who praised their employer and his working practices. The problem, the lawyer suggested, was the careless phrasing of the law.

"It's clear that we are dealing with an exemplary employer

War Cabinet was its publication of official reports in 1917 and 1918, which gave an outline of its regular day-to-day procedure. Pertinent excerpts from the War Cabinet Report of 1917 are reprinted below.

✔   ✔   ✔

The most important constitutional development in the United Kingdom during the last year has been the introduction of the War Cabinet system. This change was the direct outcome of the war itself. As the magnitude of the war increased, it became evident that the Cabinet system of peace days was inadequate to cope with the novel conditions. The enlarged scope of Government activity and the consequent creation of several new departments made a Cabinet, consisting of all the Departmental Ministers meeting under the Chairmanship of the Prime Minister, far too unwieldy for the practical conduct of the war. It was extremely difficult for so large a body to give that resolute central direction which became more imperative the more the population and resources of the nation had to be organised for a single purpose—the defeat of German militarism. Even the development of a comparatively small War Committee did not entirely meet the needs of the case, as the final responsibility rested not with them but with the Cabinet.

With the change of government [*i.e.,* the establishment of the Lloyd George Ministry in December, 1916], therefore, a new method of governmental organisation was introduced. The system of the War Cabinet distinguishes between the body which is responsible for the supreme direction of the war and the Ministers who have charge of the great administrative departments of State. The general direction of the policy of His Majesty's Government during the war rests with the War Cabinet, whose members, with one exception, are relieved of the day to day preoccupations of administrative work, and whose time is, therefore, entirely available for initiating policy and for the work of co-ordinating the great Departments of State. . . . The only exception to the principle laid down above that the members of the War Cabinet should be free from administrative duties was in the case of Mr. Bonar Law, who filled the office of the Chancellor of the Exchequer, and one of whose principal duties was to act as the chief representative of the Government in the House of Commons.

The method of working the War Cabinet is as follows. At each meeting the Cabinet begins by hearing reports as to the progress of the war since the previous day. Unless it wishes to confine its deliberations to general questions of policy, it then proceeds to deal with questions awaiting its decision. As these questions in the vast majority of cases affect one or more of the administrative departments, almost all its meetings are attended by the ministers and their chief departmental officials concerned. The majority of the sessions of the War Cabinet consist, therefore, of a series of meetings between members of the War Cabinet and those responsible for executive action at which questions of policy concerning those departments are discussed and settled. Questions of overlapping or conflict between departments are determined and the general lines of policy throughout every branch of the administration co-ordinated so as to form part of a consistent war plan. Ministers have full discretion to bring with them any experts, either from their own departments or from outside, whose advice they consider would be useful. The extent to which this policy of inviting expert assistance is carried may be judged from the fact that from December 9th, 1916, to December, 1917, no less than 248 persons other than members of the War Cabinet and the Secretariat have attended its meetings. . . . Under this system the War Cabinet has held more than 300 meetings in the past year. This fact in itself indicates the great change which has taken place in the work of the Cabinet. . . .

Apart from the attendance of the Ministers in charge of the Departments concerned, certain other arrangements are made to ensure that the Government Departments are kept in close touch with the policy of the Cabinet, and, conversely, that the members of the War Cabinet are kept in touch with the policy and action of the various Departments. Minutes are kept of the discussions of the War Cabinet. Complete files of these minutes are sent to the Ministers most closely concerned in the conduct of the war. In addition, copies of the War Cabinet minutes affecting them are sent to all other Departments. Besides this, the Secretariat of the War

Cabinet are responsible for preparing weekly reports by arrangement with the Secretaries of State for Foreign Affairs, India, and the Colonies on the matters with which they are concerned. These reports are circulated widely to all Ministers. Conversely a number of the Government Departments render weekly reports to the War Cabinet and also to other Ministers who are concerned or interested.

The working of the War Cabinet cannot be fully understood without some reference to the Secretariat, which has come into existence in order to enable it to do its work. The Secretariat consists of the Secretary, Lieut.-Colonel Sir M. P. A. Hankey, and of ten Assistant Secretaries, with an office establishment located at 2, Whitehall Gardens. Under instructions from the Prime Minister the principal duties of the War Cabinet Secretariat are as follows:—

(1) To record the proceedings of the War Cabinet.

(2) To transmit the decisions of the War Cabinet to those Departments which are concerned in giving effect to them or otherwise interested.

(3) To prepare the agenda papers; to arrange for the attendance of Ministers and other persons concerned; and to procure and circulate the documents required for discussion.

(4) To attend to the correspondence connected with the work of the War Cabinet.

(5) To prepare the Reports referred to in the previous section. . . .

— Reading No. 22 —

LORD CURZON ON THE EARLIER CABINET, 1918[22]

In a debate in the House of Lords on June 18, 1918, Lord Curzon, who was spokesman in that House for the Lloyd George War Cabinet, made an instructive comparison between it and the earlier cabinet. His comments on the earlier cabinet, which are given below, reveal how unbusinesslike its procedures were.

Let me begin by asking, What was the old Cabinet system which the present Government was intended to replace? . . . My noble friends will bear me out when I say that meetings of the Cabinet were most irregular; sometimes only once, seldom more than twice, a week. There was no agenda, there was no order of business. Any Minister requiring to bring up a matter either of Departmental or of public importance had to seek the permission of the Prime Minister to do so. No one else, broadly speaking, was warned in advance. It was difficult for any Minister to secure an interstice in the general discussion in which he could place his own case. No record whatever was kept of our proceedings, except the private and personal letter written by the Prime Minister to the Sovereign, the contents of which, of course, are never seen by anybody else. The Cabinet often had the very haziest notion as to what its decisions were; and I appeal not only to my own experience but to the experience of every Cabinet Minister who sits in this House, and to the records contained in the memoirs of half-a-dozen Prime Ministers in the past, that cases frequently arose when the matter was left so much in doubt that a Minister went away and acted upon what he thought was a decision

[22] *Parliamentary Debates,* Fifth Series, House of Lords, XXX, 263-265.

which subsequently turned out to be no decision at all,
or was repudiated by his colleagues. No one will deny that
a system, however embedded in the traditions of the past
and consecrated by constitutional custom, which was
attended by these defects was a system which was des-
tined, immediately it came into contact with the hard
realities of war, to crumble into dust at once. . . .

— Reading No. 23 —

LORD BIRKENHEAD ON WOMAN SUFFRAGE, 1928 [23]

*The chief opposition to the Equal Franchise Bill of
1928 appeared in the House of Lords, where only a
minority really favored its passage. Lord Birkenhead,
who was a member of the Cabinet, was in principle op-
posed to the measure; but he urged its acceptance, arguing that the battle had already been lost when the
franchise was granted to women on a limited basis in
1918.*

It is worth while going into the history of this matter.
Through my own attitude in relation to it there runs
a golden vein of consistency which, inasmuch as it has
been much misunderstood, I take the opportunity of making once again very plain. I was against the extension of
the franchise to women. I am against the extension of
the franchise to women. I shall always be against the
extension of the franchise to women. There is not the
slightest inconsistency in my career in regard to it, nor
is there the slightest inconsistency in my standing at this
Box tonight and recommending this measure. . . . I

[23] *Ibid.*, LXXI, 251-254.

will make this matter of history . . . indisputably plain.
It was in the year 1918, after the War, that the disaster
took place. Had it not been for the War in my judgment
we should have continued successfully to resist this
measure for an indefinite period of time. But what happened? In that year, in which nearly everybody went
mad, when the phrases of President Wilson and his
predictions were translated into logical and mathematical
conclusions, and we talked of self-determination when
we made the Peace Treaty—it was in that year that a
discussion arose as to the extension of the franchise. . . .

Let me describe to your Lordships how gradually, yet
how inevitably, we descended the slippery slope. First of
all, it was not proposed that women should be included.
Then a member of the House of Commons, and an important one, said that whoever was included or was not
included, it was quite impossible to exclude from the
franchise the brave men who had supported our cause
in the field. . . , That argument in the spirit of the
moment was accepted with facile enthusiasm, and accordingly the soldiers were admitted, subject to the qualification of age and without reference to any other very
rigorous examination. Then another member of the
House arose and said: "If you are extending the franchise to our brave soldiers in recognition of their valour
on the field how about our brave munition workers,
many of whom would greatly have desired to serve in
the field . . . ?" That argument, too, was difficult to
resist when once you had yielded to the first. Then
an insidious and subtle member of the House said:
"How about our brave women munition workers?" and,
having once on principle yielded to the first argument, it
was absolutely impossible to resist the second. . . . The
moment . . . you had settled the principle that women
were to have votes at all it became a lost cause to argue
that there should be differentiation between people of the
same ages. . . .

— Reading No. 24 —

THE ABDICATION, 1936[24]

The Instrument of Abdication in which Edward VIII announced his irrevocable determination to renounce the throne was sent to the two Houses of Parliament on December 10, 1936. The text of his message, as it was presented to the House of Commons, is given below.

The Prime Minister (Mr. Baldwin) at the Bar, acquainted the House that he had a Message from His Majesty the King to this House, signed by His Majesty's own hand. And he presented the same to the House, and it was read out by Mr. Speaker as followeth, all the Members of the House being uncovered:

> Fort Belvedere,
> Sunningdale,
> Berkshire.

Members of the House of Commons,

After long and anxious consideration, I have determined to renounce the Throne to which I succeeded on the death of My father, and I am now communicating this, My final and irrevocable decision. Realising as I do the gravity of this step, I can only hope that I shall have the understanding of My peoples in the decision I have taken and the reasons which have led Me to take it. I will not enter now into My private feelings, but I would beg that it should be remembered that the burden which constantly rests upon the shoulders of a Sovereign is so heavy that it can only be borne in circumstances different from those in which I now find Myself. I conceive that I am not overlooking the duty that rests on Me to place in the forefront the public interest, when I declare that I am conscious that I can no longer dis-

[24] *Ibid.*, House of Commons, 318: 2175-2176.

charge this heavy task with efficiency or with satisfaction to Myself.

I have accordingly this morning executed an Instrument of Abdication in the terms following:—

"I, Edward VIII, of Great Britain, Ireland, and the British Dominions beyond the Seas, King, Emperor of India, do hereby declare My irrevocable determination to renounce the Throne for Myself and for My descendants, and My desire that effect should be given to this Instrument of Abdication immediately.

"In token whereof I have hereunto set My hand this tenth day of December, nineteen hundred and thirty-six, in the presence of the witnesses whose signatures are subscribed.

(Signed) EDWARD, R. I."

My execution of this instrument has been witnessed by My three brothers, Their Royal Highnesses the Duke of York, the Duke of Gloucester and the Duke of Kent.

I deeply appreciate the spirit which has actuated the appeals which have been made to Me to take a different decision, and I have, before reaching My final determination, most fully pondered over them. But My mind is made up. Moreover, further delay cannot but be most injurious to the peoples whom I have tried to serve as Prince of Wales and as King, and whose future happiness and prosperity are the constant wish of My heart.

I take My leave of them in the confident hope that the course which I have thought it right to follow is that which is best for the stability of the Throne and Empire and the happiness of My peoples. I am deeply sensible of the consideration which they have always extended to Me both before and after My accession to the Throne, and which I know they will extend in full measure to My successor.

I am most anxious that there should be no delay of any kind in giving effect to the Instrument which I have executed and that all necessary steps should be taken immediately to secure that My lawful successor, My brother, His Royal Highness the Duke of York, should ascend the Throne.

EDWARD, R. I.

— Reading No. 25 —

DINGLE FOOT ON THE POWER OF THE EXECUTIVE, 1937 [25]

On January 27, 1937, Dingle Foot moved in the House of Commons "That, in the opinion of this House, the power of the Executive has increased, is increasing, and ought to be diminished," a resolution paraphrasing a famous one introduced by a Whig member of parliament, John Dunning, in 1780, which had been aimed at the practices of George III. The two resolutions had very different fates; Dunning's was carried by a safe majority, while Foot's was not even debated.

It is very nearly 157 years since a Motion in these terms was last moved in this House. On 6th April, 1780, Mr. Dunning moved a Motion couched in similar terms with regard to the powers of the Crown. The dangers which we believe exist today are not dissimilar from those which existed then, but they come not from the Crown, but from the servants of the Crown. . . . There are two aspects of this subject to which I want to call the attention of the House. The first is the continuous encroachment of the Executive at the expense of the House of Commons, with the result that this House becomes more and more subservient to the Government of the day. The second is the attempt that has been deliberately made in Statute after Statute in recent years to invest Government Departments with completely arbitrary powers. Hon. Members will not be surprised if I have occasion to quote the words of the Lord Chief Justice [*Hewart*] . . . which he wrote in his book published eight years ago:

[25] *Ibid.*, 319: 1026-1033.

The old despotism, which was defeated, offered
Parliament a challenge. The new despotism, which
is not yet defeated, gives Parliament an anaesthetic.
The strategy is different, but the goal is the same. It
is to subordinate Parliament, to evade the courts,
and to render the will or caprice of the Executive
unfettered and supreme.

I have sat in this House for only five years, but even
during that time I do not think that anyone who has
followed our proceedings can have failed to observe the
increasing control of the Government of the day over the
business of the House of Commons. . . . I know that
it is inevitable in these days that we in Parliament should
delegate a good deal of authority to bodies outside, and
I know that we have to give Government Departments
considerable power to issue Orders, Rules and Regulations; but the feature of almost all Regulations, even
when they come under the review of this House and
require affirmative Resolutions, is that they cannot be
amended. We cannot do more than either accept or reject them as a whole. . . .

The only effective safeguard we have managed to
invent so far is the control of the courts of law. . . . It
is common knowledge that in a number of recent Statutes
there have been inserted Clauses which have been deliberately designed to give Ministers and their Departments arbitrary powers, and to prevent the courts from
inquiring into the legality of any Orders or Regulations
they may make. . . . I only want to submit that when
we give to a Government Department or a Minister
power to make Regulations and to deprive the courts of
the right to inquire into the authority or the legality of
those Regulations we are within measureable distance
of government by decree, and government by decree,
after all, is the hallmark of dictators everywhere. . . .

— Reading No. 26 —

THE EMERGENCY POWERS (DEFENSE) ACT, 1939[26]

Emergency executive action in the Second World War was provided for by the Emergency Powers (Defense) Act of 1939, which was somewhat modified by a second act in 1940. The government was given extraordinary powers, which were exercised through orders in council that in turn delegated powers to subordinate authorities, usually ministers. On this foundation was erected a structure of administrative legislation that touched every aspect of national life.

✔   ✔   ✔

Be it enacted . . . :—

1.—(1) Subject to the provisions of this section, His Majesty may by Order in Council make such Regulations (in this Act referred to as "Defense Regulations") as appear to him to be necessary or expedient for securing the public safety, the defense of the realm, the maintenance of public order and the efficient prosecution of any war in which His Majesty may be engaged, and for maintaining supplies and services essential to the life of the community.

(2) Without prejudice to the generality of the powers conferred by the preceding subsection, Defense Regulations may, so far as appears to His Majesty in Council to be necessary or expedient for any of the purposes mentioned in that subsection,—

(a) make provision for the apprehension, trial and punishment of persons offending against the Regulations, and for the detention of persons whose detention appears to the Secre-

[26] *Public General Statutes of 1939*, II, 1009-1010: 2 & 3 George VI, c. 62.

tary of State to be expedient in the interests of the public safety or the defense of the realm;

(b) authorise—

    (i) the taking of possession or control, on behalf of His Majesty, of any property or undertaking;

    (ii) the acquisition, on behalf of His Majesty, of any property other than land;

(c) authorise the entering and search of any premises; and

(d) provide for amending any enactment, for suspending the operation of any enactment, and for applying any enactment with or without modification.

(3) Defense Regulations may provide for empowering such authorities, persons or classes of persons as may be specified in the Regulations to make orders, rules and byelaws for any of the purposes for which such Regulations are authorised by this Act to be made. . . .

(4) A Defense Regulation . . . shall have effect notwithstanding anything inconsistent therewith contained in any enactment other than this Act. . . .

(5) Nothing in this section shall authorise the imposition of compulsory naval, military or air force service or any form of industrial conscription [*the Emergency Powers (Defense) Act, 1940, modified this section and expanded the power of the executive to issue regulations to include making provision for requiring persons to place themselves, their services, and their property at the disposal of the government*]. . . .

— Reading No. 27 —

LIVERSIDGE V. ANDERSON, 1942[27]

*The most important decision in the litigation that grew
out of Defense Regulation 18B, which was issued during
the Second World War, was in the case of Liversidge v.
Anderson. Robert Liversidge had been detained by the
Home Secretary Sir John Anderson in May 1940 under
Regulation 18B. Liversidge claimed that his detention
was unlawful and applied for particulars (a) of the
grounds on which the Home Secretary had "reasonable
cause" to believe him to be a person of hostile associations and (b) of the grounds on which the Home Secretary had "reasonable cause" to believe that because of
such hostile associations it was necessary to exercise
control over him. The case reached the House of Lords
on appeal in 1942; and in an almost unanimous decision
the Lords dismissed the appeal, holding that "reasonable
cause" was for the Home Secretary to decide and that
his decision was not subject to judicial review. Excerpts
are given below from the opinion of Viscount Maugham,
who agreed with the majority, and from that of Lord
Atkin, the only dissentient.*

✓   ✓   ✓

Viscount Maugham: . . . First, reg. 18B paras. (1)
and (1A), alike require the Secretary of State to have
reasonable cause to believe two different things. Taking
the first paragraph, he must . . . believe the person (a)
to be of hostile origin or associations, or (b) to have
been recently concerned in acts prejudicial to the public
safety or the defence of the realm. . . . Any one of these
various circumstances is sufficient to satisfy the first fact
which the Secretary of State must believe. . . . But then
he must at the same time also believe something very
different in its nature, namely, that by reason of the first

[27] *Law Reports*, 1942, 220-228.

fact, "it is necessary to exercise control over" the person in question. To my mind this is so clearly a matter for executive discretion and nothing else that I cannot myself believe that those responsible for the Order in Council [*Defense Regulation 18B*] could have contemplated for a moment the possibility of the action of the Secretary of State being subject to the discussion, criticism and control of a judge in a court of law. If, then, . . . the second requisite, as to the grounds on which the Secretary of State can make his order for detention, is left to his sole discretion without appeal to a court, it necessarily follows that the same is true as to all the facts which he must have reasonable cause to believe. . . .

Lord Atkin: My Lords, I have prepared an opinion which is applicable both to this case and to that of Greene *v.* Secretary of State for Home Affairs.

These cases raise the issue as to the nature and limits of the authority of the Secretary of State to make orders that persons can be detained under Reg. 18B of the Defence (General) Regulations, 1939. The matter is one of great importance both because the power to make orders is necessary for the defence of the realm, and because the liberty of the subject is seriously infringed, for the order does not purport to be made for the commission of an offence against the criminal law. It is made by an executive minister and not by any kind of judicial official, it is not made after any inquiry as to facts to which the subject is party, it cannot be reversed on any appeal, and there is no limit to the period for which the detention may last. The material words of the regulation are as follows: "If the Secretary of State has reasonable cause to believe any person to be of hostile origin or associations and that by reason thereof it is necessary to exercise control over him, he may make an order against that person directing that he be detained." They are simple words and as it appears to me obviously give only a conditional authority to the minister to detain any person without trial, the condition being that he has reasonable cause for the belief which leads to the detention order. . . .

It is surely incapable of dispute that the words "if A has X" constitute a condition the essence of which is the existence of X and the having of it by A. If it is a condition to a right (including a power) granted to A, whenever the right comes into dispute the tribunal whatever it may be that is charged with determining the dispute must ascertain whether the condition is fulfilled. In some cases the issue is one of fact, in others of both fact and law, but in all cases the words indicate an existing something the having of which can be ascertained. And the words do not mean and cannot mean "if A thinks that he has." "If A has a broken ankle" does not mean and cannot mean "if A thinks that he has a broken ankle." . . . "Reasonable cause" for an action or a belief is just as much a positive fact capable of determination by a third party as is a broken ankle or a legal right. If its meaning is the subject of dispute as to legal rights, then ordinarily the reasonableness of the cause . . . is in our law to be determined by the judge. . . . I proceed to show . . . that "reasonable cause" for a belief when the subject of legal dispute has been always treated as an objective fact to be proved by one or other party and to be determined by the appropriate tribunal. I will go further and show that until June or July of this year in connection with this reg. 18B, there never has been any other construction even submitted to the courts in whatever context the words are found. . . .

— Reading No. 28 —

WINSTON CHURCHILL ON THE WAR CABINET[28]

During the 1930's Winston Churchill, almost alone among British statesmen, recognized the threat to world

[28] Winston Churchill, *The Gathering Storm* (Boston, 1948), pp. 418-419. Reprinted with the permission of the publisher, Houghton Mifflin Company.

peace when Germany rearmed. He was brought into the War Cabinet of Neville Chamberlain directly after the outbreak of the Second World War; and when the latter resigned in May, 1940, Churchill became prime minister and continued as such for the remainder of the conflict. In the passage given below he made clear his objections to a War Cabinet on the Lloyd George pattern and thus indirectly explained the basis of his own.

✓   ✓   ✓

Newspaper opinion, headed by *The Times,* favoured the principle of a War Cabinet of not more than five or six Ministers, all of whom should be free from departmental duties. Thus alone, it was argued, could a broad and concerted view be taken upon war policy, especially in its larger aspects. Put shortly, "Five men with nothing to do but to run the war" was deemed the ideal. There are, however, many practical objections to such a course. A group of detached statesmen, however high their nominal authority, are at a serious disadvantage in dealing with the Ministers at the head of the great departments vitally concerned. This is especially true of the service departments. The War Cabinet personages can have no direct responsibility for day-to-day events. They may take major decisions, they may advise in general terms beforehand or criticise afterwards, but they are no match, for instance, for a First Lord of the Admiralty or a Secretary of State for War or Air who, knowing every detail of the subject and supported by his professional colleagues, bears the burden of action. United, there is little they cannot settle, but usually there are several opinions among them. Words and arguments are interminable, and meanwhile the torrent of war takes its headlong course. The War Cabinet Ministers themselves would naturally be diffident of challenging the responsible Minister, armed with all his facts and figures. They feel a natural compunction in adding to the strain upon those actually in executive control. They tend, therefore, to become more and more theoretical supervisors and commentators, reading an immense amount of material every day, but doubtful how to use their knowledge without doing more harm than good. Often they can do little more than arbitrate or find a

compromise in interdepartmental disputes. It is therefore
necessary that the Ministers in charge of the Foreign
Office and the fighting departments should be integral
members of the supreme body. Usually some at least of
the "Big Five" are chosen for their political influence,
rather than for their knowledge of, and aptitude for,
warlike operations. The numbers, therefore, begin to grow
far beyond the limited circle originally conceived. Of
course, where the Prime Minister himself becomes
Minister of Defence, a strong compression is obtained.
Personally, when I was placed in charge I did not like
having unharnessed Ministers around me. I preferred
to deal with the chiefs of organisations rather than
counsellors. Everyone should do a good day's work and
be accountable for some definite task, and then they do
not make trouble for trouble's sake or to cut a figure.

— Reading No. 29 —

THE PARLIAMENTARY CONTROL OF NATIONALIZED INDUSTRIES, 1950[29]

*On October 25, 1950, one of the first debates took
place in the House of Commons on the general administration and organization as a whole of the nationalized
industries. The excerpts given below are taken from
speeches by the Laborite Herbert Morrison and the
Conservative Sir Oliver Lyttelton, both of whom bring
out the difficulties involved in establishing parliamentary
control.*

[29] *Parliamentary Debates,* Fifth Series, House of Commons,
    478: 2795-2803; 2899-2905.

The Lord President of the Council [*Mr. Herbert Morrison*]: . . . When we set up a public corporation what are we trying to do? We are trying to get the best of both worlds. After all, that is half the art of politics, of Parliament and of public administration. . . .

We are trying to do this: First, we have a public concern . . . in which is invested the public ownership of certain economic undertakings, and there are channels of accountability, of Parliamentary argument and of discussion. Secondly, we try to graft on to that basis a commercial or business management capable of acting with speed, capable of rapid decisions, and a business concern which is in a situation whereby it can make mistakes from time to time without causing an immediate Parliamentary crisis or furore, or great criticism or embarrassment for the Minister.

. . . If we have a public corporation, in order to get the advantages of commercial management and in order to free it from other meticulous Parliamentary and political control, the House must take it that, in those circumstances, the details of Parliamentary questions and the details of Ministerial management, supervision and control have to be foregone. . . .

I mean that he [*the Minister*] cannot be held responsible for matters which he had no power to do. . . . Therefore the eligibility of the [*Parliamentary*] question depends upon the nature of the statute and the powers which the Minister has got, as to whether they [*sic*] are permissible or not. This sphere is pretty wide. It includes, for example, the appointment, salaries and conditions of service of board members; programmes of research and development; programmes of education and training; borrowing by the boards, which, I think, includes capital expenditure; the form of accounts and audits; annual reports; pensions schemes, compensation for displacement; and various matters concerned with consumer councils.

So that is the very wide sphere in which there is, or can be, ministerial responsibility, and within which questions can be put. . . .

Suppose we accept the "whole-hog" doctrine that a

Minister has to be answerable to Parliament for everything a board does, and that members of boards must be liable to be summoned before a Select Committee for annual examination at some length. The inevitable consequence follows that there will develop in the minds of the members of the boards, their officers and their commercial employees the same sort of spirit as in the Civil Service—that they will look over their shoulder and be exceedingly careful, because they may be pulled up by a Parliamentary question or by a Select Committee of the House of Commons. We shall have evolving within the management of these boards the same spirit that we have in the Civil Service, something that is quite good in its own sphere but that would not be good in the case of these boards.

Therefore, if the boards were functioning in a way that every action could be subjected to Parliamentary question, we should suffer in business efficiency. On the other hand, I do not want to go too far the other way. . . .

Mr. Oliver Lyttelton: . . . First of all, let us look at Parliamentary control. The plain fact is that the structure of government, considering the way it has arisen and the duties and responsibilities of this House, cannot be satisfactorily geared to a corporation engaged in day-to-day business. . . . We can patch up here and there by palliatives and mitigations, and try to get a little further away from the total absence of responsibility, behind which Ministers can hide if they so wish. In the long run we cannot gear a day-to-day business with a legislative assembly, and all attempts to do so are doomed to failure. . . .

. . . I turn, first, to the matter of accountability. I do not suppose that anyone who has thought long on the subject considers it other than a very intractable problem. . . . If the day-to-day administrative details are to be the subject of day-to-day questioning . . . then I give my opinion . . . that administration will become practically impossible. Apart from the time that would be spent in answering questions upon administrative detail, there is also the psychology which is built up. . . .

This psychology has many disadvantages in the ordinary administration of Acts of Parliament, but it would be quite fatal—and I think the Lord President agrees with me on this—if it were applied to national boards in day-to-day industry. It would act as a brake to the whole effort. If hon. Members ask the Minister of Transport why the cod on the 6.30 from Waterloo once again tastes like cold, damp cotton wool, the task of the right hon. Gentleman, which is clearly far beyond his or anybody else's powers already, would become quite impossible. I think this is common ground, but, on the other hand, and speaking more seriously, vast sums of public money have been invested in these industries. The idea of a Minister disclaiming responsibility for this investment is repugnant to the ideas of Parliamentary control of expenditure and cuts across the control of the purse which, both actually and historically, is the first sanction in the hands of this House. . . .

I find the subject a difficult one and I can do no more than suggest some steps towards a solution. I believe that Ministers have to accept responsibility for much more questioning upon these national boards and that they have to exercise the right, which they have, of not answering the questions if, in their judgment, these apply to trivial administrative details. The House of Commons will be an extremely good judge of whether this refusal is being used in the public interest . . . or as a cloak to conceal administrative incompetence. . . .

— Reading No. 30 —

THE ACT OF UNION, 1800[30]

The Act of Union, which went into effect on January 1, 1801, governed the constitutional relationship between

[30] *Statutes at Large*, XLII, Pt. II, 648-672: 40 George III, c. 67.

*Great Britain and Ireland for one hundred and twenty
years. Its major provisions are printed below.*

✟   ✟   ✟

Whereas in pursuance of his Majesty's most gracious
recommendation to the two houses of parliament in
Great Britain and Ireland respectively, to consider of
such measures as might best tend to strengthen and consolidate the connection between the two kingdoms, the
two houses of the parliament of Great Britain and the
two houses of the parliament of Ireland have severally
agreed and resolved, that, in order to promote and secure
the essential interests of Great Britain and Ireland, and
to consolidate the strength, power, and resources of the
British empire, it will be advisable to concur in such
measures as may best tend to unite the two kingdoms of
Great Britain and Ireland into one kingdom, in such
manner, and on such terms and conditions, as may be
established by the acts of the respective parliaments of
Great Britain and Ireland.

And whereas, in furtherance of the said resolution,
both houses of the said two parliaments respectively have
likewise agreed upon certain articles for effectuating and
establishing the said purposes, in the tenor following:

ARTICLE FIRST

That it be the first article of the union of the kingdoms
of Great Britain and Ireland, that the said kingdoms of
Great Britain and Ireland shall, upon the first day of
January which shall be in the year of our Lord one
thousand eight hundred and one, and for ever after, be
united into one kingdom, by the name of the United
Kingdom of Great Britain and Ireland. . . .

ARTICLE SECOND

That it be the second article of union, that the succession to the imperial crown of the said united kingdom,
and of the dominions thereunto belonging, shall continue
limited and settled in the same manner as the succession
to the imperial crown of the said kingdoms of Great
Britain and Ireland now stands limited and settled, according to the existing laws, and to the terms of union
between England and Scotland.

ARTICLE THIRD

That it be the third article of union, that the said united kingdom be represented in one and the same parliament. . . .

ARTICLE FOURTH

That it be the fourth article of union, that four lords spiritual of Ireland by rotation of sessions, and twenty-eight lords temporal of Ireland elected for life by the peers of Ireland, shall be the number to sit and vote on the part of Ireland in the house of lords of the parliament of the united kingdom; and one hundred commoners (two for each county of Ireland, two for the city of Dublin, two for the city of Cork, one for the university of Trinity College, and one for each of the thirty-one most considerable cities, towns, and boroughs), be the number to sit and vote on the part of Ireland in the house of commons of the parliament of the united kingdom. . . .

ARTICLE FIFTH

That it be the fifth article of union That the churches of England and Ireland, as now by law established, be united into one protestant episcopal church, to be called The United Church of England and Ireland; and that the doctrine, worship, discipline, and government of the said united church shall be, and shall remain in full force for ever, as the same are now by law established for the church of England; and that the continuance and preservation of the said united church, as the established church of England and Ireland, shall be deemed and taken to be an essential and fundamental part of the union; and that in like manner the doctrine, worship, discipline, and government of the church of Scotland, shall remain and be preserved as the same are now established by law, and by the acts for the union of the two kingdoms of England and Scotland.

ARTICLE SIXTH

That it be the sixth article of union, That his Majesty's subjects of Great Britain and Ireland shall . . . be entitled to the same privileges . . . as to encouragements

and bounties on the like articles being the growth, produce, or manufacture of either country respectively, and
generally in respect of trade and navigation in all ports
and places in the united kingdom and its dependencies;
and that in all treaties made by his Majesty, his heirs and
successors, with any foreign power, his Majesty's subjects
of Ireland shall have the same privileges . . . as his
Majesty's subjects of Great Britain. . . .

ARTICLE SEVENTH

That it be the seventh article of union, that the charge
arising from the payment of the interest, and the sinking
fund for the reduction of the principal, of the debt in-
curred in either kingdom before the union, shall continue to be separately defrayed by Great Britain and
Ireland respectively, except as herein-after provided:

That for the space of twenty years after the union
shall take place, the contribution of Great Britain and
Ireland respectively, towards the expenditure of the
united kingdom in each year, shall be defrayed in the
proportion of fifteen parts for Great Britain and two
parts for Ireland; and that at the expiration of the said
twenty years, the future expenditure of the united kingdom . . . shall be defrayed in such proportion as the
parliament of the united kingdom shall deem just and
reasonable. . . .

ARTICLE EIGHTH

That it be the eighth article of union, That all laws
in force at the time of the union, and all the courts of
civil and ecclesiastical jurisdiction within the respective
kingdoms, shall remain as now by law established within
the same; subject only to such alterations and regulations
from time to time as circumstances may appear to the
parliament of the united kingdom to require; provided
that all writs of error and appeals, depending at the time
of the union or hereafter to be brought, and which might
now be finally decided by the house of lords of either
kingdom, shall, from and after the union, be finally decided by the house of lords of the united kingdom. . . .

And whereas the said articles having . . . been
humbly laid before his Majesty, his Majesty has been
graciously pleased to approve the same; and to recom-

mend it to his two houses of parliament in Great Britain
and Ireland to consider of such measures as may be
necessary for giving effect to the said articles: in order,
therefore, to give full effect and validity to the same, be
it enacted by the King's most excellent majesty, by and
with the advice and consent of the lords spiritual and
temporal, and commons, in this present parliament assembled, and by the authority of the same, That the said
foregoing recited articles, each and every one of them,
. . . be ratified, confirmed, and approved, and be and
they are hereby declared to be the articles of the union
of Great Britain and Ireland, and the same shall be in
force and have effect for ever, from the first day of
January which shall be in the year of our Lord one
thousand eight hundred and one; provided that before
that period an act shall have been passed by the parliament of Ireland, for carrying into effect, in the like
manner, the said foregoing recited articles. . . .

— Reading No. 31 —

THE ROMAN CATHOLIC EMANCIPATION ACT, 1829[31]

*The Roman Catholic Emancipation Act of 1829
abrogated the old oaths and declarations which had made
it impossible for Catholics in the United Kingdom to sit
in parliament or hold office. Henceforth they could do
both by taking a special oath of allegiance which included the denial that the Pope or any foreign prince
had any temporal power in the United Kingdom. Catholics were expressly excluded from a very few offices,*

[31] *The Statutes of the United Kingdom of Great Britain and
Ireland,* LXIX, 49-51; 10 George IV, c. 7.

including that of the lord chancellor and of the lord lieutenant of Ireland; and under the Bill of Rights (1689) no Catholic could come to the throne. Excerpts from the Act of 1829 are given below.

✓ ✓ ✓

Whereas by various Acts of Parliament certain Restraints and Disabilities are imposed on the Roman Catholic Subjects of His Majesty, to which other Subjects of His Majesty are not liable . . . And Whereas by various Acts certain Oaths and certain Declarations . . . are or may be required to be taken, made, and subscribed by the Subjects of His Majesty, as Qualifications for sitting and voting in Parliament, and for the Enjoyment of certain Offices, Franchises, and Civil Rights: Be it enacted . . . That from and after the Commencement of this Act all such Parts of the said Acts as require the said Declarations, or either of them, . . . as a Qualification for sitting and voting in Parliament, or for the Exercise or Enjoyment of any Office, Franchise, or Civil Right, be and the same are (save as hereinafter provided and excepted) hereby repealed.

II. And be it enacted, That from and after the Commencement of this Act it shall be lawful for any Person professing the Roman Catholic Religion, being a Peer, or who shall after the Commencement of this Act be returned as a Member of the House of Commons, to sit and vote in either House of Parliament respectively, being in all other respects duly qualified to sit and vote therein, upon taking and subscribing the following Oath, instead of the Oaths of Allegiance, Supremacy, and Abjuration:

"I A.B. do sincerely promise and swear, That I will be faithful and bear true Allegiance to His Majesty King George the Fourth, and will defend him to the utmost of my Power against all Conspiracies and Attempts whatever, which shall be made against his Person, Crown, or Dignity. . . . And I do faithfully promise to maintain, support, and defend, to the utmost of my Power, the Succession of the Crown, which Succession . . . is and stands limited to the Princess Sophia, Electress of Hanover, and the Heirs of her Body, being Protestants;

hereby utterly renouncing and abjuring any Obedience or Allegiance unto any other Person claiming or pretending a Right to the Crown of this Realm: And I do further declare, That it is not an Article of my Faith, and that I do renounce, reject, and abjure the Opinion, that Princes excommunicated or deprived by the Pope, or any other Authority of the See of Rome, may be deposed or murdered by their Subjects, or by any Person whatsoever: And I do declare, That I do not believe that the Pope of Rome, or any other Foreign Prince, Prelate, Person, State, or Potentate, hath or ought to have any Temporal or Civil Jurisdiction, Power, Superiority, or Pre-eminence, directly or indirectly, within this Realm. I do swear, That I will defend to the utmost of my Power the Settlement of Property within this Realm, as established by the Laws: And I do hereby disclaim, disavow, and solemnly abjure, any Intention to subvert the present Church Establishment, as settled by Law within this Realm: And I do solemnly swear, That I will never exercise any Privilege to which I am or may become entitled, to disturb or weaken the Protestant Religion, or Protestant Government in the United Kingdom. . . . So help me God." . . .

V. And be it further enacted, That it shall be lawful for Persons professing the Roman Catholic Religion to vote at Elections of members to serve in Parliament for England and for Ireland, and also to vote at the elections of Representative Peers of Scotland and of Ireland, and to be elected such Representative Peers, being in all other respects duly qualified, upon taking and subscribing the Oath hereinbefore appointed. . . .

— Reading No. 32 —

CHARLES STEWART PARNELL ON HOME RULE, 1885 [32]

In his speech at Cork in January, 1885, excerpts from which are given below, Parnell called attention to Ireland's economic and political grievances. In words that were often quoted later he declared that, under the Union, Ireland could not ask for more than the restoration of an independent Irish parliament, but that no man had "the right to fix the boundary to the march of a nation."

We shall struggle, as we have been struggling for the great and important interests of the Irish tenant farmer. We shall ask that his industry shall not be fettered by rent. We shall ask also from the farmer in return that he shall do what in him lies to encourage the struggling manufactures of Ireland, and that he shall not think it too great a sacrifice . . . when he has to purchase anything, to consider how he may get it of Irish material and manufacture, even suppose he has to pay a little more for it. . . . We still [*shall?*] also endeavour to secure for the labourer some recognition and some right in the land of his country. We do not care whether it be the prejudices of the farmer or of the landlord that stand in his way. We consider that whatever class tries to obstruct the labourer in the possession of those fair and just rights to which he is entitled, that class should be put down and coerced, if you will, into doing justice to the labourer. . . . But I go . . . to the consideration of the great question of national self-government for Ireland. I do not know how this great question will be eventually settled. I do not know whether England will be wise in time and concede to constitutional arguments and meth-

[32] *The Times*, January 22, 1885.

ods the restitution of that which was stolen from us towards the close of the last century. It is given to none of us to forecast the future; and just as it is impossible for us to say in what way or by what means the national question may be settled, in what way full justice may be done to Ireland, so it is impossible for us to say to what extent that justice shall be done. We cannot ask for less than the restitution of Grattan's Parliament, with its important privileges and wide and far-reaching constitution. We cannot, under the British Constitution, ask for more than the restitution of Grattan's Parliament. But no man has the right to fix the boundary to the march of a nation; no man has a right to say to his country, "Thus far shalt thou go and no further," and we have never attempted to fix the *ne plus ultra* to the progress of Ireland's nationhood, and we never shall. But, while we leave those things to time, circumstances, and the future, we must each one of us resolve in our own hearts that we shall at all times do everything which within us lies to obtain for Ireland the fullest measure of her rights. . . .

— Reading No. 33 —

DOUGLAS HYDE AND IRISH NATIONALISM, 1892[33]

Irish nationalism in the late nineteenth and early twentieth century was encouraged by leaders like Douglas Hyde, who in 1893 founded the Gaelic League. His nationalism was cultural rather than political, as these excerpts from his speech in the previous year to the National Literary Society of Ireland show, but the distinction was difficult to maintain in practice, and some of

[33] Douglas Hyde, "The Necessity for De-Anglicising Ireland," *The Revival of Irish Literature* (London, 1894), pp. 117-161.

*his followers were members of the later Sinn Fein. Hyde
himself played no part directly in the struggle for Irish
independence of British control, but he was elected the
first president of Eire under its Constitution of 1937.*

✓ ✓ ✓

When we speak of "The Necessity for De-Anglicising
the Irish Nation," we mean it, not as a protest against
imitating what is *best* in the English people, for that
would be absurd, but rather to show the folly of neglect-
ing what is Irish, and hastening to adopt, pell-mell, and
indiscriminately, everything that is English, simply because it *is* English.

This is a question which most Irishmen will naturally
look at from a National point of view, but it is one
which ought also to claim the sympathies of every intelligent Unionist, and which, as I know, does claim the
symp....y of many.

If we take a bird's-eye view of our island to-day, and
compare it with what it used to be, we must be struck
by the extraordinary fact that the nation which was once,
as every one admits, one of the most classically learned
and cultured nations in Europe, is now one of the least
so; how one of the most reading and literary peoples has
become one of the *least* studious and most *un*literary,
and how the present art products of one of the quickest,
most sensitive, and most artistic races on earth are now
only distinguished for their hideousness.

I shall endeavour to show that this failure of the Irish
people in recent times has been largely brought about by
the race diverging during this century from the right
path, and ceasing to be Irish without becoming English.
I shall attempt to show that with the bulk of the people
this change took place quite recently, much more recently than most people imagine, and is, in fact, still
going on. I should also like to call attention to the illogical position of men who drop their own language to
speak English, of men who translate their euphonious
Irish names into English monosyllables, of men who
read English books, and know nothing about Gaelic literature, nevertheless protesting as a matter of sentiment
that they hate the country which at every hand's turn
they rush to imitate.

I wish to show you that in Anglicising ourselves whole-
sale we have thrown away with a light heart the best
claim which we have upon the world's recognition of us
as a separate nationality. What did Mazzini say? What
is Goldwin Smith never tired of declaiming? What do
the *Spectator* and *Saturday Review* harp on? That we
ought to be content as an integral part of the United
Kingdom because we have lost the notes of nationality,
our language and customs.

It has always been very curious to me how Irish sentiment sticks in this half-way house—how it continues to
apparently hate the English, and at the same time continues to imitate them; how it continues to clamour for
recognition as a distinct nationality, and at the same
time throws away with both hands what would make it
so. If Irishmen only went a little farther they would become good Englishmen in sentiment also. But—illogical
as it appears—there seems not the slightest sign or prob-
ability of their taking that step. It is the curious certainty
that come what may Irishmen will continue to resist
English rule, even though it should be for their own
good, which prevents many of our nation from becoming
Unionists upon the spot. . . .

But you ask, why should we wish to make Ireland
more Celtic than it is—why should we de-Anglicise it at
all?

I answer because the Irish race is at present in a most
anomalous position, imitating England and yet apparently hating it. How can it produce anything good in
literature, art, or institutions as long as it is actuated by
motives so contradictory? Besides, I believe it is our
Gaelic past which, though the Irish race does not recog-
nise it just at present, is really at the bottom of the Irish
heart, and prevents us becoming citizens of the Empire. . . .

What we must endeavour to never forget is this, that
the Ireland of to-day is the descendant of the Ireland of
the seventh century, then the school of Europe and the
torch of learning. . . . What the battleaxe of the Dane,
the sword of the Norman, the wile of the Saxon were
unable to perform, we have accomplished ourselves. We
have at last broken the continuity of Irish life, and just

at the moment when the Celtic race is presumably about to largely recover possession of its own country, it finds itself deprived and stript of its Celtic characteristics, cut off from the past, yet scarcely in touch with the present. . . . It has lost all that they [*past Irish heroes*] had—language, traditions, music, genius, and ideas. Just when we should be starting to build up anew the Irish race and the Gaelic nation—as within our own recollection Greece has been built up anew—we find ourselves despoiled of the bricks of nationality. The old bricks that lasted eighteen hundred years are destroyed; we must now set to, to bake new ones, if we can, on other ground and of other clay. Imagine for a moment the restoration of a German-speaking Greece. . . .

In conclusion, I would earnestly appeal to every one, whether Unionist or Nationalist, who wishes to see the Irish nation produce its best—and surely whatever our politics are we all wish that—to set his face against this constant running to England for our books, literature, music, games, fashions, and ideas I appeal to every one whatever his politics—for this is no political matter— to do his best to help the Irish race to develop in future upon Irish lines, even at the risk of encouraging national aspirations, because upon Irish lines alone can the Irish race once more become what it was of yore—one of the most original, artistic, literary, and charming peoples of Europe.

— Reading No. 34 —

ARTICLES OF AGREEMENT FOR A TREATY BETWEEN GREAT BRITAIN AND IRELAND, 1921 [34]

[34] *Parliamentary Papers,* 1921, Session 2, I, Cmd. 1560.

The Articles of Agreement for a Treaty between Great Britain and Ireland, signed on December 6, 1921 and subsequently ratified by the parliaments in both countries, brought to an end the era that had begun with the Act of Union in 1800. Pertinent excerpts are given below.

1. Ireland shall have the same constitutional status in the Community of Nations known as the British Empire as the Dominion of Canada, the Commonwealth of Australia, the Dominion of New Zealand, and the Union of South Africa, with a Parliament having powers to make laws for the peace order and good government of Ireland and an Executive responsible to that Parliament, and shall be styled and known as the Irish Free State.

2. Subject to the provisions hereinafter set out the position of the Irish Free State in relation to the Imperial Parliament and Government and otherwise shall be that of the Dominion of Canada, and the law, practice and constitutional usage governing the relationship of the Crown or the representative of the Crown and of the Imperial Parliament to the Dominion of Canada shall govern their relationship to the Irish Free State.

3. The representative of the Crown in Ireland shall be appointed in like manner as the Governor-General of Canada, and in accordance with the practice observed in the making of such appointments.

4. The oath to be taken by Members of the Parliament of the Irish Free State shall be in the following form:—

I . . . . do solemnly swear true faith and allegiance to the Constitution of the Irish Free State as by law established and that I will be faithful to H.M. King George V., his heirs and successors by law, in virtue of the common citizenship of Ireland with Great Britain and her adherence to and membership of the group of nations forming the British Commonwealth of Nations.

5. The Irish Free State shall assume liability for the service of the Public Debt of the United Kingdom as existing at the date hereof and towards the payment of war pensions as existing at that date in such proportions as may be fair and equitable. . . .

6. Until an arrangement has been made between the British and Irish Governments whereby the Irish Free State undertakes her own coastal defence, the defence by sea of Great Britain and Ireland shall be undertaken by His Majesty's Imperial Forces. . . .

7. The Government of the Irish Free State shall afford to His Majesty's Imperial Forces:—

(a) In time of peace such harbour and other facilities as are indicated in the Annex hereto. . . .

(b) In time of war . . . such harbour and other facilities as the British Government may require for the purposes of such defence as aforesaid. . . .

9. The ports of Great Britain and the Irish Free State shall be freely open to the ships of the other country. . . .

11. Until the expiration of one month from the passing of the Act of Parliament for the ratification of this instrument, the powers of the Parliament and the Government of the Irish Free State shall not be exercisable as respects Northern Ireland, and the provisions of the Government of Ireland Act, 1920, shall, so far as they relate to Northern Ireland, remain of full force and effect, and no election shall be held for the return of members to serve in the Parliament of the Irish Free State for constituencies in Northern Ireland, unless a resolution is passed by both Houses of the Parliament of Northern Ireland in favour of the holding of such elections before the end of the said month.

12. If, before the expiration of the said month, an address is presented to His Majesty by both Houses of the Parliament of Northern Ireland to that effect, the powers of the Parliament and the Government of the Irish Free State shall no longer extend to Northern Ireland, and the provisions of the Government of Ireland Act, 1920, . . . shall, so far as they relate to Northern Ireland, continue to be of full force and effect, and this instrument shall have effect subject to the necessary modifications. . . .

16. Neither the Parliament of the Irish Free State nor the Parliament of Northern Ireland shall make any law so as either directly or indirectly to endow any religion or prohibit or restrict the free exercise thereof. . . .

17. By way of provisional arrangement for the administration of Southern Ireland during the interval which must elapse between the date hereof and the constitution of a Parliament and Government of the Irish Free State in accordance therewith, steps shall be taken forthwith for summoning a meeting of members of Parliament elected for constituencies in Southern Ireland since the passing of the Government of Ireland Act, 1920, and for constituting a provisional Government, and the British Government shall take the steps necessary to transfer to such provisional Government the powers and machinery requisite for the discharge of its duties, provided that every member of such provisional Government shall have signified in writing his or her acceptance of this instrument. But this arrangement shall not continue in force beyond the expiration of twelve months from the date hereof.

18. This instrument shall be submitted forthwith by His Majesty's Government for the approval of Parliament and by the Irish signatories to a meeting summoned for the purpose of the members elected to sit in the House of Commons of Southern Ireland, and, if approved shall be ratified by the necessary legislation.

(*Signed*)

On behalf of the British Delegation.

On behalf of the Irish Delegation.

D. Lloyd George
Austen Chamberlain
Birkenhead
Winston S. Churchill
L. Worthington-Evans
Hamar Greenwood
Gordon Hewart

Art O Griobhtha
Michael O Coileain
Riobard Bartun
E. S. O Dugain
Seorsa Ghabhain Ui Dhubhthaigh

— Reading No. 35 —

THE IRELAND ACT, 1949[35]

The Ireland Act, 1949, snapped the last tie between Great Britain and the greater part of Ireland, now known as the Republic of Ireland. Though the final separation was accomplished with expressions of good will on both sides, particularly with regard to the problems of citizenship, the provision in the Ireland Act which reaffirmed the inclusion of Northern Ireland in the United Kingdom aroused deep resentment in Dublin. In the excerpts which are given below it will be noticed that a residence qualification for voting was reintroduced in Northern Ireland.

✓   ✓   ✓

Be it enacted . . . as follows:—

1.—(1) It is hereby recognized and declared that the part of Ireland heretofore known as Eire ceased, as from the eighteenth day of April, nineteen hundred and forty-nine, to be part of His Majesty's dominions.

(2) It is hereby declared that Northern Ireland remains part of His Majesty's dominions and of the United Kingdom and it is hereby affirmed that in no event will Northern Ireland or any part thereof cease to be part of His Majesty's dominions and of the United Kingdom without the consent of the Parliament of Northern Ireland.

(3) The part of Ireland referred to in subsection (1) of this section is hereafter in this Act referred to . . . as the Republic of Ireland.

[35] *Public General Acts . . . of 1949*, I, 364-369: 12 & 13 George VI, c. 41.

2.—(1) It is hereby declared that, notwithstanding that the Republic of Ireland is not part of His Majesty's dominions, the Republic of Ireland is not a foreign country for the purposes of any law in force in any part of the United Kingdom or in any colony, protectorate or United Kingdom trust territory, whether by virtue of a rule of law or of an Act of Parliament or any other enactment or instrument whatsover. . . .

6.—(1) Notwithstanding anything in the Representation of the People Act, 1948, a person shall not be entitled to vote as an elector at an election of a person to serve as a Member of the Parliament of the United Kingdom for a constituency in Northern Ireland unless he was resident in Northern Ireland during the whole of the period of three months ending on the qualifying date for that election. . . .

7.—(3) Save as otherwise expressly provided, this Act shall be deemed to have had effect as from the eighteenth day of April, nineteen hundred and forty-nine.

A SELECT BIBLIOGRAPHY

Adams, George B. Constitutional History of England, rev. by Robert L. Schuyler. New York, 1934.

Allen, Carleton Kemp. Law and Orders. London, 1945.

Anson, Sir William R. The Law and Custom of the Constitution. Volume I, ed. by Maurice L. Gwyer. Oxford, 1922; Volume II, ed. by A. Berriedale Keith. Oxford, 1935.

Bagehot, Walter. The English Constitution. The World's Classics. With an Introduction by the Earl of Balfour. London, 1952.

Butler, D. E. The Electoral System in Britain, 1918-1951. Oxford, 1953.

Campion, Lord and others. British Government since 1918. London, 1951.

Costin, W. C. and Watson, J. Steven. The Law and Working of the Constitution: Documents, 1660-1914. 2 vols. London, 1952.

Critchley, T. A. The Civil Service Today. London, 1951.

Curtis, Edmund and McDowell, R. B. Irish Historical Documents, 1172-1922. London, 1943.

Dicey, A. V. Introduction to the Study of the Law of the Constitution. Ninth edition. With an Introduction by E. C. S. Wade. London, 1939.

Emden, Cecil S. Selected Speeches on the Constitution. 2 vols. London, 1939.

Ensor, R. C. K. England, 1870-1914. Oxford, 1936.

Finer, Herman. The British Civil Service. London, 1937.

Hancock, W. K. and Gowing, M. M. British War Economy. London, 1949.

Jennings, W. Ivor. The British Constitution. Cambridge, England, 1950.

————. Cabinet Government. Cambridge, England, 1951.

————. Parliament. Cambridge, England, 1948.

Keir, David Lindsey. The Constitutional History of Modern Britain, 1485-1951. London, 1955.

Keith, Arthur Berriedale. The British Cabinet System, ed. by N. H. Gibbs. London, 1952.

————. The Constitution of England from Queen Victoria to George VI. 2 vols. London, 1940.

Laski, Harold J. Parliamentary Government in England. New York, 1938.

Le May, G. H. L. British Government, 1914-1953: Select Documents. London, 1955.

Low, Sidney. The Governance of England. London, 1919.

Mansergh, Nicolas. Ireland in the Age of Reform and Revolution, 1840-1921. London, 1940.

McKenzie, R. T. British Political Parties: The Distribution of Power within the Conservative and Labour Parties. New York, 1955.

Morris, Homer Lawrence. Parliamentary-Franchise Reform in England from 1885 to 1918. New York, 1921.

Mowat, Charles Loch. Britain between the Wars, 1918-1940. Chicago, 1955.

Muir, Ramsay. How Britain is Governed. London, 1935.

Namier, L. B. The Structure of Politics at the Accession of George III. 2 vols. London, 1929.

Ogg, Frederic Austin. English Government and Politics. New York, 1936.

O'Hegarty, Patrick Sarsfield. A History of Ireland under the Union, 1801 to 1922. London, 1952.

Pares, Richard. King George III and the Politicians. Oxford, 1953.

Porritt, Edward and Annie G. The Unreformed House of Commons: Parliamentary Representation before 1832. 2 vols. Cambridge, England, 1909.

Robson, William Alexander. Justice and Administrative Law. London, 1947.

Seymour, Charles. Electoral Reform in England and Wales, 1832-1885. New Haven, 1915.

Stephenson, Carl and Marcham, Frederick George. Sources of English Constitutional History. New York, 1937.

Wade, E. C. S. Constitutional Law. London, 1955.

Woodward, E. L. The Age of Reform, 1815-1870. Oxford, 1939.

INDEX

VAN NOSTRAND ANVIL BOOKS already published

who does not seek to flout the law," the judge finally declared. "I sympathize with him and wonder whether some members of the union, particularly those currently out of work, might want to ask their leaders whether their campaign against this particular bakery makes any sense. However, given the law as it stands, I sincerely regret that I have little choice in the matter but to impose the minimum fine of five hundred euros and order each bakery to close one day each week."

A bunch of media people were waiting outside the court talking to the two sets of demonstrators when Vaugier, the union representative, pushed brusquely past Bruno and Hugues to ensure he was the first to get to the microphones and proclaim the union's victory.

"This is just the beginning, and I warn other bosses who try to exploit our workers by making them work every day of the week that we'll be coming after them, as well," Vaugier announced proudly. A thin-faced man with close-cut gray hair, he was wearing a dark blue shirt and red tie and sported a Parti de Gauche badge in his lapel.

The local police had disappeared, and already a brief scuffle had broken out as two of Hugues's bakers advanced angrily on Vaugier to denounce him as a liar. Bruno took Hugues's arm in a tight grip to hold him back from the fray.

"Stay out of this and let your lawyer do the talking," Bruno told him. "Anything you say will make this worse."

Bruno tried to push Hugues off to the side but found the way blocked by a big man who was carrying a sign that said MAKE THE RICH PAY and chanting some slogan Bruno could not make out. He put out a beefy hand to grab Hugues's arm, but Bruno pushed it aside and tried to move on. The man began to bring his sign down on Bruno's head as someone else tried to grab his arms from the rear.

Bruno had learned about street brawls in the army and knew he needed some space, free arms and one decisive blow. He slammed one elbow back hard into the belly of the man behind him, raised his other arm to block the descending sign and then moved forward, raised his leg and slammed the side of his boot down hard, scraping it along the shin of the man before him. It did no permanent damage, but the pain was intense, and the man's face collapsed as he screeched and sank down to clutch his leg.

Bruno turned and pushed Hugues to get him clear, seeing two of the bakery employees suddenly surrounding them in support. Bruno looked back and heard the union leader, Vaugier, shouting about police brutality.

"Stop this now or you're next," Bruno shouted to him, feeling his blood rising. Then the trade unionist who'd greeted him stepped between Bruno and Vaugier, his arms outstretched and calling for calm, and the moment was over. Bruno thanked him and followed Hugues as the bakery workers dispersed. Then Philippe Delaron of *Sud Ouest,* the regional daily, came up to tell Bruno he had a good photo of the sign being aimed at Bruno's head, just in case he might need it.

"I've got a better photo than that for your paper," Bruno said, and told him of the dead woman and the graffiti that now desecrated the château of Commarque. In return, Bruno added, he'd expect a prominent placement for the dead woman's photo to help identify her.

"Thanks, Bruno. I'd heard about the dead woman from the *pompiers,* but the graffiti makes it a better story. Fluorescent-red paint, you say. And what is it, some kind of political slogan?"

"More than that, it's a mystery. Go to Commarque and take a look and see for yourself. Maybe your readers can work out what it means. And there's another mystery. The unknown woman wasn't alone. Somebody took away the spray can of paint and the climbing rope she was using. Your headline writes itself— 'Mystery Woman's Secret Slogan Defaces National Monument. Did She Fall or Was She Pushed?' "

Back in his office, Bruno e-mailed a description of the dead woman to other local newspapers and radio stations, along with an appeal for anyone who might have known or met her to call him. He looked at the photo of her face that he'd taken on his phone. She looked peaceful, and French law recognized no privacy in death. The priority now was to identify her, so he e-mailed the photo to the message network of *mairies*, tourist information offices and hotels in the communes up and down the valley. The kids in the computer club at the local *collège* had developed the system at Bruno's request. He then posted the woman's few details onto the missing-persons register, in the hope that some family member wondering where she might be would contact the police. Finally he called the number the count had given him for the secretary of the Templars' club, left a message asking for a call back and e-mailed him the photo, asking if he would share it with other club members. He was about to turn to the day's mail when the mayor called on the internal line and asked Bruno to step into his office.

He assumed the mayor wanted to hear about the unknown woman. Bruno left Balzac in his office, closing the door to stop the dog wandering into the kitchen in the hope that someone would give him a biscuit. He took his notes and a printout of the woman's face to the mayor's office. Bruno was surprised when the mayor introduced him to a young black woman whose perfume already filled the room with a powerful blend of musk and gardenias. She rose from the visitor's chair to shake Bruno's hand.

"Amélie Plessis," she said. *"Enchantée."*

She had a strong grip and wide shoulders, her hair had been

cut very short, and her black patent-leather shoes boasted perilously high heels. She had lively eyes with maybe a hint of mischief in them. Bright red lipstick and even-brighter blue eyeshadow combined with very white teeth to make Bruno think of the French tricolor. Amused by the thought and impressed by the self-confidence of the young woman, he smiled at her as they exchanged business cards.

"From the Ministry of Justice," she added, superfluously, since her card already explained her provenance. And so did her bureaucrat's uniform: black suit, knee-length skirt and white blouse. "I'm looking forward to our working together and learning about your philosophy of policing."

What on earth did that mean? He tried not to show his surprise. And why was the justice ministry sending someone like this down to St. Denis, rather than the usual pasty-faced clerk from Paris? And to work with him? What were her origins? Her accent was not entirely French; the vowels were a little too generous, the rhythm of speech bubbling rather than tinkling in the approved Parisian style. It was not quite Caribbean, not quite the accent of Quebec, not quite from Marseille, but had hints of all three. Her smile was perfunctory rather than genuine, not reaching her eyes. Bruno detected a touch of suspicion, or perhaps apprehension, in her gaze, as if she'd learned to be wary of policemen.

"Mademoiselle Plessis was telling me that the new minister is a great supporter of the municipal police as being much closer to the public than the gendarmes and with a more friendly image," the mayor said, one eyelid drooping in what might have been the ghost of a wink at Bruno. "But the minister needs some evidence that would allow her to act upon her belief, and we think you might provide it. Mademoiselle Plessis would like to accompany you for the next two weeks for a time-and-motion study, recording your work minute by minute throughout the day."

Bruno was speechless. A Paris bureaucrat at his side every moment of the day, recording everything he said or did? He felt his jaw dropping as he gazed helplessly at the mayor, wondering what on earth could have induced him to commit this act of betrayal to his faithful chief of police.

"I knew you'd like the idea," said the mayor. "And there'll probably be a security aspect to her work, given the opening of the new Lascaux museum later this year. Mademoiselle Plessis tells me that the president of the Republic is planning to attend. You've always been a great supporter of the village police and their local knowledge against the gendarmes who seldom stay long enough in one place to be useful. Now's your chance to prove it."

"Understood, Monsieur le Maire," said Bruno, trying to come up with an excuse that would extract him from this chore. "But now that we have such excellent relations with the new head of the *gendarmerie* here, those concerns have largely disappeared. As you told the local newspaper only last week, relations between us and Commandante Yveline are now exemplary."

"Yes, yes, but our guest has no time to lose. Perhaps you could escort her to the hotel where she'll be staying, and then come back here while she unpacks before taking her with you for the rest of the day."

Chapter 5

Bruno did as he was told, picking up the suitcase and leading the way across the square to the hotel, his mind reeling as he tried to pay attention to the young woman who insisted that he call her Amélie. She announced briskly that she'd recently graduated from magistrates' school and had been recruited by the ministry. Her family, she went on, came originally from Haiti, but she had been born on French soil, the island of Guadeloupe, after her parents had fled the corrupt rule of the Duvaliers. She had grown up in Marseille and won a scholarship to university in Montreal, sang in nightclubs to earn extra money, returned to France, joined the Socialist Party and decided on a career in politics via the law. She relayed all this in a walk of fewer than a hundred meters, leaving Bruno breathless by the sheer energy her stocky frame produced.

"How did you get the job in the ministry?" he asked when they reached the hotel and Amélie paused for breath. He was more interested in her singing but thought he'd better show polite interest in her career.

"I got to know the minister through politics. We're in the same branch of the party. I suppose you're on the right, given your mayor's politics. But I'll try hard not to let that shape my conclusions."

"I don't think party politics has anything to do with policing," Bruno said.

"Really?" she said, raising an eyebrow. "In my view everything is to do with politics."

He waited while she checked in, then walked back to the mayor's office, still thinking of some way to squeeze out of this absurd imposition. As if any policeman could ever act normally when his every moment was under the scrutiny of someone from the ministry!

He'd no longer be able to throw away after a quick glance the reams of paperwork that came from the ministry but would have to pretend to read the stuff, which would leave little time for any sensible work. Nobody would tell him anything with this young woman constantly at his side, scribbling notes on a clipboard. Fauquet at the café would shrink from passing on any choice item of gossip if he suspected for a moment that it was being recorded. Bruno's habit of stopping at various houses in the scattered hamlets that surrounded St. Denis for a small glass of something would be entirely misunderstood by the bureaucrats at the ministry.

Worst of all, it was just approaching that moment in late spring when the fish were rising and Bruno's garden needed maximum attention. People living in Paris would never understand that no country policeman would command respect if his vegetable garden were less than exemplary, or if he failed to demonstrate his skills at hunting and fishing and other rural pastimes. He'd have to think of a good excuse to give the mayor and rehearsed a couple as he climbed the stairs to the mayor's office.

"Much as I'd like to cooperate with the ministry, I honestly don't think I'm the right police officer . . ."

"Forget it, Bruno. It's settled and you can't back out. And if you can't charm that nice young woman who's still wet behind the ears, you're not the Bruno I know. Now go and take your medicine like a man."

Dismissed and admonished, Bruno turned to go, thinking at least that time spent with Amélie promised to be interesting, if exhausting. As he opened the door, the mayor said, in a kinder tone, "Look on the bright side, Bruno. When she logs all those drives you have to make, perhaps those idiots in the capital will finally realize that this commune alone is larger than Paris. And she's a protégée of the new minister. So she has *piston,* political influence. She's already on the executive committee of the Socialist Party youth wing and I know she's having dinner with the pharmacist this evening. So bear that in mind. A bright young black woman with a law degree and political ambitions is just what his party is hoping to publicize and promote. This young woman is going places."

The pharmacist was the Socialist Party chairman in the valley, who would doubtless be aware of just how much *piston* Amélie commanded. And since both Amélie and the mayor had now confirmed that the president of the Republic, a Socialist, would attend the opening of the new Lascaux museum, half the local Socialist Party would be angling for invitations. Bruno himself was interested to see the new project, which went by the name of Lascaux IV. Lascaux I was the original cave, discovered in 1940 and closed to the public in 1963 when their respiration and the bacteria they brought into the cave had combined to produce a white fungus that was damaging the seventeen-thousand-year-old paintings. Lascaux II, an exact and impressive copy of the two most impressive chambers of the cave, had been opened to tourists after it was completed in 1983. Lascaux III, a traveling exhibition of partial copies, films, fossils and audiovisual explanations, had been on display at successive museums around the world for the past five years.

The new Lascaux IV, at a cost of some sixty million euros, was designed to be a showroom for French technology to display a Lascaux for the twenty-first century, with a new copy of the entire cave as precise as modern computers could achieve. It was planned to include 3-D presentations, interactive demonstrations of how the images had originally been painted, comparisons with cave art from other cultures, prehistoric and more recent. Above all it was to allow more tourists to experience the cave than the thirty at most that Lascaux II could accommodate.

Promoted and pushed by a veteran Socialist politician of the region, with financial backing from the Socialist government, the project had become a political football, with opponents grumbling that the money could have been better spent elsewhere. Bruno disagreed. He had been so awed by his first sight of Lascaux, so struck by the realization that he would never again think of the people who had produced this masterpiece as primitive, that he wanted the whole of the human race to see the cave and be similarly moved. He had already attended meetings to plan the security measures for the grand opening.

Bruno collected Balzac and was about to cross the square to meet Mademoiselle Plessis when he was hailed by Father Sentout, the priest of St. Denis who followed the fortunes of the town's rugby team with the same devotion he gave to his dwindling band of worshippers.

"My dear Bruno, is there any progress on the dreadful pedophile business they were discussing on the radio this morning?"

"None at all, I gather. It's a difficult case, involving recovered memories many years after the events. Why are you interested?"

"The priest who has been accused of this, Father Francis. I knew him before his death when he was a colleague, another teacher at my seminary. This was after he'd been at Mussidan.

I find it impossible to believe he could have done such wicked things."

"He wouldn't have been the first priest to have gone astray like that."

"No, indeed, and that is a tragedy for the Church. But I knew Francis to have been a truly good man. Since he can't stand up for himself, surely his friends and those who knew him should try to defend his memory. Is there some way I and some other priests could give some kind of character reference to the police or the investigating magistrate?"

Bruno gave Father Sentout J-J's name and address at police headquarters in Périgueux and suggested he write a letter. Then he excused himself, since he saw Amélie emerge from the hotel. The priest laid a hand on Bruno's arm.

"Francis may be dead, Bruno, but for this unjust accusation to continue to sully his name would be an offense against God and man. You believe in justice on earth just as I believe in the ultimate justice of heaven. I know that you must understand that."

Father Sentout released his grip and Bruno said, *"A bientôt."* He could feel the priest's curious gaze follow him as Bruno crossed the square to greet the young woman on the hotel steps. She had changed from her suit into tight jeans over the same black shoes and now wore a black leather jacket over her white blouse.

He introduced her to Balzac, who was already charmed by the woman, and she seemed equally enchanted with the basset hound. She bent down despite the tight jeans and caressed the dog's ears. Balzac responded by leaping up to give her face a friendly lick. She laughed and gave him a kiss in return, on his head.

"Do you have any other shoes, suitable for walking in the

countryside?" he asked. "Not a lot of my time is spent on paved streets."

She darted back up to her room to change and descended in a pair of suede boots, with heels that were chunky and lower than the stilettos. He sighed, thinking it would be quite a challenge to persuade her to wear the spare rubber boots he kept in his van.

He escorted her back across the square to Fauquet's for a coffee and an attempt to lay down some ground rules. He'd try to get her to stay in the car, noting down simply that he was making inquiries, seeing confidential sources, following up reports of suspicious activity. He introduced her to Fauquet and the other regulars as a colleague from Paris. Not quite sure what to make of this, and clearly startled by Bruno's guest, they greeted her with reserved formality and quickly left the bar. Bruno was surprised they hadn't stayed long enough to ask about the dead woman. By now they must have heard the news from the *pompiers*. Fauquet turned his back in silence to make the coffees.

"This is the best place in the region for croissants," Bruno told Amélie. "Soon you'll be a regular customer, just like all the rest of us." He spoke too loudly for Fauquet to ignore him.

Suitably mollified, Fauquet put a complimentary chocolate biscuit onto each saucer and gave Amélie a croissant from the basket on the counter. "On the house," he said. "Just so you know Bruno is right about my baking. You going to be here long?"

The interviewing technique of the veteran café owner would put most policemen to shame. Before the croissant was finished, Fauquet had learned Amélie's name, her origins, her education, her current job and that her father was a teacher in Lyon. She had two elder brothers, one an engineer working at Air France and the other in the Ministry of Pensions, which established her in Fauquet's eyes as a respectable young woman from the profes-

sional classes, and thus a suitable if somewhat unusual adorn-
ment to his establishment. There was only one black resident of
St. Denis—Léopold from Senegal, whose market stall did a good
trade in African cloths and belts, carvings and bead necklaces.
Bruno was particularly fond of Léopold's two sons, stalwarts of
the *collège* rugby team and formidable tennis doubles partners.

Bruno steered Amélie out to the terrace where they could
enjoy the spring sunshine and Bruno could set his ground rules
away from Fauquet's ears.

"I started at seven this morning, with a callout to an unknown
woman who died falling from climbing a château wall. I'd just
returned when the mayor called me in to meet you," he began.

"Why was she doing that?" Amélie asked.

Bruno shrugged. "It was the middle of the night. She might
have been drunk. My first job is to identify her, which could take
some time."

"Was it an accident?"

"Possibly, but it's certainly suspicious. Someone else was at
the scene but disappeared before we got there. I'll take you there
now, if you like; it's on the way to colleagues I need to see in Les
Eyzies and Montignac. We may have to go door-to-door to show
photos of her. First, I'll call on the gendarmes to brief them. I can
introduce you at the same time."

He passed over to her one of the printouts from his phone
and a copy of Fabiola's death certificate, and then went into the
café to leave another printout with Fauquet. One of his customers might know the woman.

"The gendarmes are giving us trouble on this ministry project
I'm on," Amélie said on his return. "They don't want our team
monitoring them at all. They say we have no jurisdiction and
even if they wanted to cooperate it would make their work more
difficult."

"Have you tried seeing it from their point of view?" Bruno asked. "I have to say that it will be difficult doing some of my usual work with you alongside me, starting with seeing my confidential informants. And then there are people who are friendly and who offer me coffee and cakes or a glass of wine and who talk frankly about things they know but who would hate to be considered as informants in any sense. If I took you along, I could lose those contacts, and they make up the heart of police work here where it's all about knowing everybody."

"I don't want to make things tough, but I do have to do this job properly," Amélie replied, with a hesitant smile. "I suppose I don't need to put down names and addresses of confidential informants, or even to get close enough to listen."

"If I were to ask you from time to time, and told you what I was doing, could you stay in the van, out of sight?"

She looked unhappy at the thought of this, so he asked, "Do you have your terms of reference, some form of letter saying exactly what is expected of you?"

She pulled from her bag a transparent folder. The papers inside had the familiar red, white and blue diagonal stripes of the justice ministry across the top corner. The relevant letter of instruction told her "to accompany the officer throughout the working period and keep a detailed and timed record of the officer's work and movements, while staying as close as reasonable or possible without obstructing the policeman in the course of his duty."

Noting that phrase "throughout the working period" Bruno realized that he could operate in his usual way without Amélie outside the formal thirty-five-hour week he was supposed to work. But he pointed to the last phrase about "obstructing the policeman."

"As I read it, that means I can reasonably ask you to stay in the van. I'll try not to do that too often. And now, let's go say hello to the gendarmes, but I'll stop on the way at a company that rents out *gîtes* to tourists and give them a photo to show their staff. They may recognize the dead woman."

"I put her photo on Instagram and on Facebook while you were in the café, asking if anyone knew her," Amélie said casually. "That may help. I hardly ever use it these days, but I've got over fifteen hundred Facebook friends, and I asked all of them to share the photo, so that will be thousands of eyeballs for you. Even more on Instagram."

"You did what?" Bruno sat up in surprise. "I appreciate that you were trying to help, but you should have asked me first. I'm not sure it's a good idea to put a dead woman's face all over social media. What if a family member finds out that way? It would be quite a shock."

She shrugged. "Too late now, it's done. And I presume the priority is to identify her as soon as we can." She paused, looking at him coolly. "Or are you just covering your resentment at not thinking of it yourself?"

"I'd hope I'm more professional than that," he retorted, his tone crisp, and he realized he was glaring at her. He forced himself to soften his expression, aware that this was a professional relationship and he'd better make it work or the next two weeks would be miserable.

"The fact is I'm not very familiar with social media," he said. "We're not exactly at the forefront of the information age here in the Périgord. E-mails and searching the web are about my limit. Let's hope your idea works."

She surprised him with a quick grin that didn't reach her eyes. "And let's hope her nearest and dearest don't see it first. I can see that you might be right about that."

"And maybe it will work and we'll save a lot of time," he replied, hoping some kind of truce had been established.

"I couldn't find you on Twitter," she went on, not even looking at him, her face bent down over the screen of her phone as she tapped in some note or message. "And while the *mairie* has a Facebook page, the only reference it has to you is your phone number."

She put her phone into her bag and looked up at him. "That's not good enough, Bruno. I hope you understand the importance of social media in the future of policing. It's the way most young people communicate these days. I think my report had better recommend that we set up courses for you rural policemen on how to use it."

Bruno nodded politely, his heart sinking at the prospect. "Let's see how your Facebook inquiry works out."

Chapter 6

Traditionally the gendarmes of France had lived in military-style barracks. Founded after the French Revolution, the gendarmes were deployed almost as an army of occupation in rural areas, where the Church and the old ways remained strong, and distrust of the Revolution was fierce and sometimes violent. Gendarmes came under the orders of the Ministry of Defense and were a paramilitary force. They were never assigned to their home areas and retained a distinct separation from the communities they policed. Although a modest building, the St. Denis *gendarmerie* looked as if it had been designed to withstand a siege, and as with most such police posts, the yard and parking area behind it had long been sealed off from the public.

So Amélie expressed surprise to see the gates to the inside yard open and some young civilians playing a game of basketball with shirtsleeved gendarmes. She was even more surprised that the front door was wide open and the hallway decorated with colorful kids' paintings from the local grade school. Balzac trotted in behind them as if he owned the place.

"Not your usual *gendarmerie*," she said, sounding as though she approved.

"And not your usual commander," Bruno replied. "Her name

is Yveline and I think you'll like her. She was on the last Olympics field hockey team and she's well liked, even by the old guard among the gendarmes who were horrified at the thought of being led by a woman. Firm but fair, they say."

Sergeant Jules was at his desk, the very image of the old guard gendarme, big and burly with a craggy face that seemed to say he had seen it all twice before and wasn't much enjoying seeing it again. His grim exterior concealed a kindly nature and an affection for St. Denis that almost matched his devotion to the town's hunting club. Under some of the more rigid commanders of the past, Bruno had only been able to retain relations with the gendarmes by going through Jules. But the old sergeant was Yveline's greatest fan, and in return she had turned a blind eye to his skill at evading the regional headquarters' attempts to reassign him to another district.

He greeted Bruno and Balzac cheerily, but his eyes widened when Bruno introduced Amélie as a colleague from the justice ministry in Paris, here to pay a courtesy call on the commandant. Jules glanced with dismay at the paintings, which would doubtless strike any Parisian bureaucrat as too messy and informal for the authority of the *gendarmerie de la République*!

"We got permission from the general in Périgueux, a special exhibition," he stammered as Amélie stretched out a hand to him.

"I like it," she said. "It makes a nice change from those boring public-service posters you usually see in these places. And it's good to see your guys playing basketball outside."

Yveline came out with a welcoming smile and led them into her office where a pot of coffee awaited them, more of the kids' paintings on her wall. Balzac greeted her as an old friend.

"The mayor called to let me know you were on the way, and I'd like to add my own welcome," Yveline said. "As you know, our leaders in Paris have decided not to cooperate formally with your project, but that won't stop us helping as far as we can. I think it's a great idea, and Bruno is a very suitable subject for your work. We work closely with him and depend heavily on his local knowledge and friendships, something that we haven't always been good at."

"Perhaps at some point I could have a very informal and off-the-record chat with you about how you see the future of police-gendarme relations. You seem to have a rather refreshing approach," said Amélie.

"Maybe we could do it over dinner one evening at my place," said Bruno, remembering what the mayor had said about the need to win over Amélie and knowing that a good meal always helped cement relations.

"That's a good idea," said Yveline. "Bruno's a good cook, so we'll be in for a treat."

Amélie's face broke into a smile. "And if I'm with you, Yveline, perhaps we may be able to drink a little more wine than the regulations usually recommend."

"Maybe not if Yveline is driving," said Bruno, grinning. "I could pick you up at the hotel and then get the pair of you a taxi for the run back to town. We'd better not start this project with any embarrassments. How about tomorrow night at seven?"

In the hallway Philippe Delaron was photographing the display of paintings under Sergeant Jules's beady eye. Still focusing his camera, the *Sud Ouest* reporter spoke without taking his eye from his viewfinder. "Hi again, Bruno. Jules told me you were here. I sent in the photo from the château, and the picture desk likes the idea of asking the readers to solve the puzzle. Can you give me anything more on this dead woman, Bruno? Any idea yet who she is?"

Philippe turned and looked almost as surprised as Sergeant Jules had been to see Amélie.

"Well, hello," he said, sticking out his hand and giving her a smile of practiced charm that had secured him girlfriends in most of the villages up and down the valley. "And who might you be, mademoiselle?" Automatically, he raised his camera to take a snapshot, a trick that Philippe had found usually worked with girls before.

Bruno put his hand in front of the lens. "None of your business, Philippe," he said genially. A photo in *Sud Ouest* of Amélie visiting the *gendarmerie* might prove uncomfortable for Yveline. Philippe took it in good cheer; he and Bruno went back a long way. "And we have nothing new on the dead woman, which is why we're asking you to run the photo in tomorrow's edition."

"It's already up on our website," said Philippe.

"But the only people who read that are you and your competitors, and very occasionally me."

"So you're not Bruno's new girlfriend and you're obviously not under arrest, which means that you must be something official." Philippe was smiling at Amélie in his engaging way. "I'm Philippe, photographer and news reporter for *Sud Ouest,* a newspaper with a bigger circulation than *Le Monde*. And we're much more readable. Are you going to be in town long?"

"Stop it, Philippe," said Bruno. Amélie remained silent, her face expressionless. She seemed thoroughly unimpressed by Philippe's chatty attempts at charm, however well they might work on the maidens of the Vézère Valley. Good for her, thought Bruno. "This is police business. I'm taking her to the place where the dead woman was found."

"No point, nothing to see. I've just been there, and J-J's boys had already taken her off to the morgue, and the count was closeted with J-J. I got a quote from the guy in the kiosk selling tickets. So, the usual routine, Bruno, let me know what you can, when you can." He turned to Amélie and gave her a rather-more-sincere smile. "Don't let Bruno frighten you. He's got a heart of gold, really. He even kept me out of jail." He waved and disappeared.

"You seem to have a special relationship with the local press, even though he does overplay the role of the eager young news-hound," she said as Bruno led the way up the rue de Paris, Balzac at their heels. He'd intended to show her the old streets of St. Denis, the medieval houses and fountain. But Amélie had something else in mind.

"What was it that Philippe said about your keeping him out of jail?"

"I'd rather not arrest people if there's a better solution."

"Tell me the story, just for my own interest," she said.

"It was nearly ten years ago, not too long after I arrived in St. Denis," Bruno explained. "Philippe was in his last year at school, and along with three friends he'd stolen the car of an elderly British resident to go joyriding. They were going too fast, crashed it on a corner, abandoned the car and fled, wiping their fingerprints from the steering wheel, gearshift and door handles. They thought they were being very clever.

"I'd kept an eye on Philippe as a young screwup and managed to get some prints from the lever that adjusted the seat. I went to see the Englishman, then to see Lespinasse at the local garage, and finally I called on Pascal the insurance agent. All this was before I went to the Delaron house to inform Philippe and his parents that he was in deep trouble and that I'd be taking him to the *gendarmerie* to be fingerprinted."

"I thought you said you didn't like to arrest people," Amélie interrupted.

"The story doesn't end there," he replied. "The fingerprints matched, and Philippe was led down to the cells and left to stew while I had a beer in the nearby café with Sergeant Jules. Then I went down to Philippe's cell and asked who the other boys were. Philippe said nothing. So I named two of Philippe's usual cronies, one now a sous-chef at an up-and-coming restaurant in Bordeaux and the other who now works for a balloon ride business that's very popular with the tourists. The third name I kept in reserve. Philippe refused to confirm their names, which I thought decent of him."

"So he had not been formally arrested at this point," Amélie said. "That means you didn't have the right to take his finger-prints."

"Right, and that's why I said that I'd offer him a choice," Bruno went on. "I could call the *procureur* and let the law take its course. As for the alternative, the Englishman liked his wood-stoves. With the current price of firewood he was prepared to forgive Philippe if he and his pals came in person to apologize, supplied him a winter's worth of chopped firewood and under-took to wash and polish his car regularly for the foreseeable future. The insurance agent was prepared to forgo damages if the four joyriders over the coming year reimbursed his company the cost of the insurance payout. The *garagiste,* Lespinasse, was prepared to charge much less than his usual rate for the repair, since he and I both suspected that Lespinasse's nephew Maurice had been the fourth youngster in the car.

"So four fundamentally decent if mischievous youngsters had learned their lesson and been kept out of the criminal justice system. It was a solution that not only gave me pleasure," Bruno continued. "It also made me a number of friends, including Les-pinasse, Pascal the insurer and the kindly English math teacher who had retired in St. Denis."

"But that's exactly what a sensible cop ought to do," said Amélie. "Young boys are always full of piss and vinegar, but detention just makes them worse. Unfortunately that kind of a solution isn't available for most of the young kids picked up these days for smoking weed or shoplifting. Can I use that in my report as an example of local police solutions? I won't use your name."

"I suppose so. Philippe talks of it often enough," Bruno said. "You realize that it's almost impossible for a gendarme to do something like that. They just don't have the flexibility."

"How do you mean?"

"The gendarmes have been given targets for so many arrests, so many fines and traffic tickets issued. It's crazy. You don't judge a cop by how many people he puts in jail. I'd rather judge them by the ones they keep out."

"I agree," Amélie said, "but for that to work you need cops who know the local people. Now you know why I picked St. Denis for my research project."

He stopped in his tracks. "No, I don't know why you picked us. You didn't know that story."

"No, it was another one, about fraud in the truffle market that led to a big case on illegal immigration."

"Where on earth did you hear about that?"

"In magistrates' school. We had a visiting lecturer from Eurojust telling us about European arrest warrants and different styles of policing. She told us about the importance of our municipal police here in France and mentioned St. Denis as an example."

Bruno felt a lump forming in his chest. There could be only one Eurojust official who knew about St. Denis and the truffle business.

"Would that have been Commissaire Perrault?" he asked.

"Isabelle Perrault, that's right. You must know her. She said she used to be based down here. She's great, a real star."

He nodded, the sadness that thoughts of Isabelle summoned

mixing with pride that she had chosen to cite him as an example of local policing that she admired. The summer of their love affair was still the happiest time of his life, just as the weeks after her decision to move to Paris and pursue her career had been the saddest. A star indeed but not a lucky one for Bruno.

And with that, they reached the door to Ivan's bistro. The clock on the *mairie* was striking noon, which every good French citizen knew to be the signal for lunch.

Chapter 7

The price of Ivan's daily lunch menu had risen to fourteen euros, which was still excellent value for the soup, homemade pâté, main course, salad with cheese and dessert, with a quarter liter of house wine included. The bistro was full, and not only because word had raced around town about Bruno's new colleague from Paris. Ivan's place was a local institution and, thanks to his love life, Ivan's restaurant had steered the tastes of St. Denis in new directions. There had been all the variants of mussels, *à la Normande, à la crème, au curry* as well as the usual *marinière,* thanks to a Belgian girl he'd met on a beach in Ibiza and persuaded to return with him. When she stalked out and began walking with her suitcase to the station, the whole town had mourned with Ivan.

After a springtime break in Turkey, Ivan had returned with a Spanish girl for a memorable summer menu of paella, tapas and gazpacho. Bruno could still almost taste her dessert of *leche frita,* a rich creamy center encased in flour and beaten egg, fried and then dusted with sugar and cinnamon. A German girl had turned the entire valley into admirers of her Wiener schnitzel, which she served with a rich and slightly tart potato salad. Ivan's last holiday in Thailand and Malaysia had excited great expectations of curries cooked with coconut milk and lemongrass, which was what arrived, except that the girl had been Australian rather than Thai.

Ivan was currently living and cooking alone. Mandy, the Australian, had gone to her wine course in Bordeaux, and Ivan was back to serving his traditional cuisine of the Périgord, which he did very well. But even as they fell with pleasure on his soups and his roast meat and fowl, the diners would sometimes fall silent, a distant look appearing on their faces. Like hunting dogs on a scent, they would cock their heads as if thinking with nostalgia of the other cuisines they were missing.

And so when Ivan asked whether Amélie had enjoyed her meal and questioned her about her native cuisine, all other conversation ceased. When she said "Guadeloupe," the chorus of wistful sighs was like a tropical breeze wafting through the room. Dreams of fresh fish steaming over the embers of a fire on the beach as the Caribbean sunset blazed in the west convened Ivan's customers into the kind of spiritual union that Father Sentout's Sunday sermons seldom achieved.

"And what do you miss most about it?" Ivan asked.

"Epice," she said. "It's the classic sauce, made of stewed peppers and garlic, parsley, thyme and green onions. We use it in everything, but I like it best on rice and red beans along with my mother's chicken and cashew nuts."

Even though he had eaten well, Bruno felt his taste buds start to stir again, and around the room he saw others virtually licking their lips. Ivan asked, "Could you teach me how to make that?"

"You're a bad man, stealing my mother's secrets," Amélie said with a laugh, and the whole bistro chuckled with her.

One by one, they came up to be introduced: Rollo, the headmaster of the local *collège;* Dougal, the Scotsman who ran the agency for holiday rentals, along with Hubert, who ran the town's famous wine cave. It was Joe, Bruno's predecessor as town policeman, who lingered longest. He took Amélie's hand in his own gnarled paws and asked what wine the locals drank with Caribbean food.

"People drink rum, sometimes with cola, sometime with a squeeze of lemon juice. Here in France, my parents usually drink rosé in summer and red wine in winter."

Joe looked at the carafe of Bergerac Sec white wine that Ivan had served. He bought ten-liter boxes of Cuvée Roxanne from Hubert's cave, the same wine that Bruno usually bought in summer for everyday drinking.

"And do you think our local Bergerac would go well with your Caribbean food?"

"Very well," Amélie replied, smiling at the courteous old man.

"We'll have to start her education in our wines, Bruno," Joe said, and raised her hand to his lips before departing.

"That was quick. Your first day and you've won over half the town," Bruno said as they left, after an amiable dispute over the bill. Amélie insisted on buying lunch, saying she was being given a daily allowance for this mission, and it was only fair since she was dining as his guest the following evening.

"Now we'll head up the valley, since I have to see my two colleagues," Bruno said. He put Balzac into the back of his van and they set off. "You said you'd sung in nightclubs. What do you sing?"

"Anything at all," she replied. "I started in a church choir and had childish dreams of being an opera singer, but then I discovered Broadway musicals and jazz. Then my mom bought me an album of Ella Fitzgerald and I fell in love with scat, improvised vocals that use the human voice like an instrument."

"You mean like wop-bop-a-doo-bop?"

She laughed, a rich, comforting sound that warmed the heart and was so infectious that Bruno laughed in turn.

"Not really, more like this."

And off she soared, with an extraordinary cascade of sounds, not a single word to be recognized, only the pure, clear notes and syllables that seemed to mark the rhythm, almost as if they replaced the drums of a jazz combo. She went on with infinite variations until she sang the title of the song that Bruno had groped to recognize. It was "How High the Moon." He noticed that his fingers were beating time on the steering wheel, his head nodding in time with her music.

"That's wonderful," he said. "I used to wonder if it just meant the singer had forgotten the words."

"Not at all, it's about the creation of new sounds, new words, if you like. And it comes in different styles. Listen to Ella Fitzgerald sing scat and you can hear that she's catching the sound of the big band era in which she began her career. Listen to Sarah Vaughan and it sounds like one of the bebop jazz combos where she started out. Two women, two styles, but all scat, jazz for the human voice. People in the Caribbean have sung that way for generations, and some claim it began with slaves singing African dialects when they were brought across the sea. Who knows? But it needn't only be jazz. Listen."

She launched into a classic operatic aria, slow and evidently tragic, that Bruno half recognized. As she sang her invented sounds, he realized that it was not greatly different from hearing it sung in the original Italian, a language he did not know.

"That's from *Tosca*," she said. "An aria called 'Vissi d'Arte,' and when I hear it performed by Leontyne Price it sounds like scat to me. Or listen to Maria Callas sing 'Casta Diva' from *Norma* and it's the same. But that's not all I sing. Do you like Cole Porter and Irving Berlin?"

Without waiting for an answer she launched into "Cheek to Cheek," a song Bruno knew in a French version by Daniel Roure. Although she was a far-better singer, he began singing along, he in French, Amélie in English, until they stopped at the roundabout before Les Eyzies.

"Thank you, I enjoyed that," he said, driving on when the road cleared. "Normally I only sing for my dog. Or in the shower."

"I usually have to sing alone these days, so it's good to share it with someone. You can carry a tune well."

"Have you stopped performing?"

"Mostly," she said, and shrugged. "When I was at law school there wasn't time, except for parties, singing for friends. I'd love to keep it up, although I'm not sure it would do my career much good."

"We do free concerts on the riverbank in St. Denis during the tourist season, so if you ever want a vacation, all expenses paid and a modest fee for singing in the evening, we can sign you up right away. I organize the concerts and do the bookings."

"I'm flattered. It sounds like fun and it's something to add to my notes about your work as a policeman."

He parked the car in the shadow of a huge cliff towering over the long main street of Les Eyzies. As they climbed out, he pointed upward to where a giant statue of a man, done in primitive style, gazed out from a ledge in the cliff across the town and the river.

"That's our Cro-Magnon man, a symbol of all the prehistory we have within a hundred meters of where you're standing. I always salute him when I pass."

Louise Varenne, the town policewoman, was waiting for them at the *mairie.* She showed no surprise at Amélie's presence; Bruno assumed Sergeant Jules must have phoned ahead to tip her off. Bruno had introduced Yveline, Jules and his wife to both of his police colleagues up the valley over a barbecue of fresh-caught trout in his garden. It was the first time that Louise had met the gendarme *commandante* socially, and now they were on first-name terms, which did wonders for their cooperation. Food, Bruno believed, was a village policeman's secret weapon. The more people who came to eat at his table, the more he heard and learned and the more welcome he was in the twelve hundred households that made up the commune of St. Denis.

"I made copies of your photo of the dead woman and took it around the campsites, shops and cafés," Louise said after welcoming them, including Balzac. "No success so far except for the owner of the gas station who thinks the woman filled the tank of a silver Peugeot Traveller a couple of days ago. No credit card slip, though. She paid cash."

Bruno related what the count had told him about previous break-ins at Commarque. "Do you know of any Templar enthusiasts around here?"

"Dozens, after that spate of bestselling novels came out all about them," Louise replied. "I read some of them myself. But I don't think the craze lasted, except for people living off the tourist trade."

Half the shops in the region offered toy swords, plastic helmets and child-sized white surcoats emblazoned with a red cross. English tourists thought these items celebrated their warlike ancestors while all the others knew it as the sign of the Templars.

"Do you know anywhere that sells blue-green nylon rope or climbing ropes?" Bruno went on. "Dr. Stern found some strands on the body."

"No, but my brother's in the climbing club," Louise said, reaching for her phone and calling him to explain her query. She listened a moment, thanked him and said she'd e-mail him a photo of the dead woman in case she was known to any of the climbers.

"He says it doesn't sound like proper climbing rope, more like the cheap nylon stuff available in hardware stores. I'll let you know if anyone recognizes the woman."

Bruno thanked her and led the way around the corner to the museum, where he embraced the two women at the ticket desk, introduced Amélie and asked if Clothilde was in her office. They knew he was to be a *témoin* at Clothilde's wedding, and he was told to go straight up. Climbing the stairs, he was explaining to Amélie that Clothilde was one of the leading prehistorians in France, when he heard footsteps above him and a voice saying, "Stop it, Bruno, you'll make me blush. You'd better not put any of that flattery into your wedding speech."

A small powerhouse of a woman appeared, with fiery-red hair piled on her head and held in place with a pencil. She wore a green-and-white-striped man's shirt over black leggings. Reading glasses dangled from a chain around her neck.

"I hope I'm not interrupting," Bruno said, kissing her and introducing Amélie. "I need to pick your brains about a woman found dead beneath the cliff at Commarque this morning." He showed her the photo and explained that the count thought she might have been a Templar fan. And he asked about the pose that echoed the Venus of Laussel.

Clothilde shook her head at the photo. "I don't know her, but I can scan the photo and put it on my Facebook page. A lot of us archaeologists stay in touch that way. But I can't see an archaeologist climbing up something. We usually dig down."

"What about these letters?" He showed her his photo of the graffiti. "We think she was writing them in graffiti on the wall of the *donjon* when she fell. Do they mean anything to you, any language that springs to mind?"

"Sorry, no. But I can tell you it's not English." Clothilde turned to Bruno. "Oh, Bruno, did you know that the ground-penetrating radar and seismic team are coming this very week and working near where that woman fell? It's going to play hell with all my plans for the wedding. Horst and I will have to be there when they're working, so we may have to call on you to tie up various loose ends."

"I'd better ask the Police Nationale if they're still treating it as a crime scene, but whatever happens, I'll do my best to help out." He grinned at her. "You'll be pleased to hear that I've got my speech drafted. When does your *dame d'honneur* arrive?"

"Lydia Manners is flying in from London on Friday with her husband to be in time for the *dîner des témoins* at Laugerie Basse. They're opening the inside cave for us, and we'll dine in there. Her husband is English, a former soldier, so you and he should get on. She's American, but they live in Oxford where she works at the Ashmolean Museum. And don't forget you're organizing the bachelor dinner with Horst and his male friends on Thursday. And for God's sake don't let him drink too much."

"Have you heard of some Templar scholar in Sarlat called Dumesnil?" Bruno asked. "The count mentioned him as an expert I might consult."

"Dumesnil? You'll meet him at the wedding. Both Horst and I think the world of him. A brilliant man, he's written one of the few really good books on the Templars. He teaches history in Brive, but if you get a chance, visit him at home in Sarlat. It's like entering a medieval cloister, and he's said to follow the Benedictine rule, although he's not a priest."

"What's that?" asked Amélie.

"Monastic prayer discipline. Matins at midnight, Lauds at three in the morning, that kind of thing. If you ask me, he's slightly crazy, but brilliant in his way, of course. He could waltz into a job at any university in Europe, but he says that being a schoolteacher is his version of the public service of the rule. He's an odd duck, but he's very engaging at the same time."

"He follows the rule, but he's not a monk?" Bruno asked.

"No, nor is he a priest. Auguste claims to have no vocation, but if you ask me it's because they stopped holding services in Latin. He also helps with the choir at Sarlat Cathedral."

After more coffee with Clothilde, Bruno and Amélie headed up the main road to Sarlat, Bruno pointing out the various prehistoric sites and châteaux along the way before turning off to Cap Blanc to ask the staff if they recognized the dead woman. When he'd checked the parking lot earlier that morning, the cave had not yet been opened to the public. The woman selling tickets looked carefully at the photo and said she remembered her buying some local guidebooks two or three days earlier.

"She spoke French like someone who hadn't lived here for a long time," the woman added. "It was perfect, but a bit old-fashioned, a bit stilted. And she had some American dollars in her purse along with the euros. I remember her because she asked if there was a path across the valley to Commarque, and I pointed it out to her. It's not easy to find through the trees. And I noticed she was wearing walking shoes and carrying a rucksack. She took it off to put the books inside."

Bruno made a note and thanked her before heading back to his van, telling Amélie he'd have to make sure all the hotels and campsites and rental agencies were shown the photo. "If she's a foreigner or a visitor from another country I'll have to get the foreign ministry to circulate her photo to the embassies. Tracking missing persons is about the most time-consuming job I know."

"Can't you use facial recognition software?" she asked. "I know there's a pilot scheme at the interior ministry trying to use the database of the photos on French ID cards, and you could try the Americans. If she had dollars in her purse, she may well have been to the U.S., and they'll have her photo on file."

Surprised to hear this, Bruno glanced sideways at her as he drove. "In all the tons of paperwork I get sent by the various ministries, there's never been anything about identifying unknown persons from the photos on their ID cards. It could be very useful. I don't think J-J knows about it; he's the chief detective for the *département*."

Amélie was already tapping at her phone, and Bruno noticed that she was doing so faster than he could type.

"Ever since the ISIS attack in Paris," she said, "there have been a lot of new projects to exploit the databases the state already controls—ID cards, driving licenses, passports, criminal records. It's a huge job, and I don't know how far they've gotten with it, but I'm sending the photo to a friend from law school who's working at the Ministry of the Interior. Maybe she can run it through their database and also send the request to Interpol. It's ridiculous that you haven't been informed of these new capabilities," she said as she finished texting. "That's exactly the kind of information I need to put in my report. How often do you see this J-J?"

"A lot. He'll check in with me about anything that comes up in this part of the *département.* I saw him this morning at Commarque after I called him about the dead woman. A suspicious death is his business. We work well together, and strictly speaking it's his job to identify her, but I'll always try to use our local contacts to help. Just because the Police Nationale and the gendarmes and I have three different employers, I don't think that stops us working together. We're all on the same side."

Bruno's phone began to play the first notes of "La Marseillaise," and he pulled onto the side of the road to answer. It was the man from the Templars' society, saying he did not recognize the woman and knew of no new reports about treasure at Commarque, but he'd circulate the photo among his fellow members.

"Do the letters *I-F-T-I* mean anything to you, some sort of Templar lore perhaps? I ask because the woman seemed to be trying to paint a word with these letters on the château wall."

"On the wall of Commarque? That's sacrilege; I wouldn't want to have anything to do with a member like that. But no, it means nothing to me. Again, I can ask around."

"And you think some Templar treasure might be at Commarque?"

"Who knows? Commarque is one of three thousand sites in France with Templar connections, but it was never a *commanderie,* or local administrative center. There are five or six in the *département* of the Dordogne. But if they wanted to hide treasure from the king, they probably would not have used a *commanderie.*"

"So they might have used a lesser site, like Commarque?"

"Possibly, but the king's searches were pretty thorough. He put a lot of resources into crushing the Templars, and he did it quickly. He sent out secret orders to all the bailiffs and seneschals across France for a single devastating strike to be carried out a month later. More than five thousand Templars were arrested in a single night, Friday, October the thirteenth, 1307. No French state could mount that kind of operation again until World War Two. Even Napoléon couldn't have done it. Just imagine the numbers of troops or police required, the cells to hold them, keeping the secret while the orders were transmitted around the country on horseback."

Bruno raised his eyebrows. He could imagine the scale of such an operation and would never have dreamed a medieval monarchy could have mounted something so efficient.

"Five thousand trained knights, all arrested at once. Did they go quietly?" he asked.

"No, the fighting knights were in Spain and Cyprus, facing the Saracens. In France, they were mainly old men, but even so, it was quite an operation. It shows the king's desperation to get their treasure."

"But he didn't get it?"

"He got their land and their castles and manors, which was good enough. And he'd already forced the Templars to make him some huge loans. But he never found the treasure."

"And you think it's still to be found?" Bruno asked.

"I think it was smuggled out across the sea, perhaps to Scotland because of the Masonic connections, perhaps even to Nova Scotia. There are various theories. I'm less interested in Commarque because there is so much archaeological work being done there. If there's anything to find, they'll find it, so the place has really dropped off our radar screen. But you say this woman fell to her death as she was climbing the wall of the *donjon*? That seems unlikely to me. The *donjon* has been rebuilt, restored, thoroughly searched. If there's any treasure to be found, it will be in those caves underneath the rock."

Bruno had his phone on speaker so Amélie could hear. When he ended the call, he said to her, "Imagine, five thousand men all across France, arrested on a single night. It wouldn't be easy to do that today."

"Just as well, when you think about it. Remember, it's the justice ministry I work for, not the Ministry of the Interior. I don't think I'd much like to work for a ministry that could do that." She showed him the screen of her phone.

"While you were talking, I was running a multilanguage search for those letters, *I-F-T-I*. The only hits I got were in Arabic, mainly names, unless the *T* could have been an *R*, and in that case it's 'Ifriqiya,' the old name for North Africa. And if the final letter was unfinished and the extra stroke was making it into an *A* we could get *iftar*, the meal Muslims eat after the Ramadan fast. I don't think anyone would want to paint that on a castle wall. There's another one, *iftikhar.* It means 'proud.'"

A very faint idea began to form and almost as quickly it went, too elusive to stay. He recognized these subterranean mental stirrings. Sometimes Bruno thought of them as hunches, and sometimes as an idea coming from a part of his brain that was not entirely his—a part formed of curiosity, experience and intuition—that kept churning, calculating and making hypotheses that would suddenly erupt as a breakthrough. He knew the components of this latest puzzle—an ancient château and an Arabic name, Crusaders and Templars, a modern woman falling or perhaps being pushed to her death—and at some point and in some mysterious way they would fall into a pattern that made sense to him.

Chapter 8

Bruno seldom paid much attention to the thirty-five-hour workweek he was supposed to respect, but wondered whether that might also be an item Amélie would be monitoring. He shrugged. The ministry could hardly complain if he worked longer hours of his own free will. There was something he needed to check, but perhaps she was watching her own hours.

"Are you prepared for one more job today?"

She checked her watch. "As long as I'm back at the hotel by seven. That gives us a couple of hours. I'm having dinner with some of the local Socialists tonight. I want to see if I can get them to launch a youth group. It's depressing how few of the local parties have one."

"Is that how you got interested in politics?"

"No, it began with my parents, who talked politics all the time. My mother's on the left and my dad's more of a Green. Later, when I was at school, there were the riots in the cities when kids burned all those cars. Then came the recession and it all became more serious, and now it's what I want to do."

Bruno drove out of St. Denis past Hubert's wine cave heading for Le Buisson where he could take the road that led to the Dordogne Valley. Making a mental note to introduce Amélie to the local wines, he turned off to the left to what he thought of as the suburb of St. Denis, homes built in the 1950s and 1960s, now extended with new tracts of housing meant for the growing numbers of retirees from northern and eastern France who preferred the kinder climate of the Périgord. Most of them were priced at around a hundred thousand euros, small houses with two bedrooms, a single bathroom and a garden large enough for a lawn, a vegetable patch and a terrace for outdoor meals. They looked as though they belonged in Provence rather than the Périgord, with walls of white stucco and roofs of semicircular tiles. Bruno stopped at one such structure at the corner of two roads. It was larger than the others, with more garden and a third bedroom in the upper story of the small tower that anchored the two wings of the house.

When the door opened, he was embraced by Dilla, the wife of Momu, the math teacher at the local *collège*. They were good friends, and he was fond of them both, and of Dilla's couscous and their annual *méchoui* feast, when they roasted a whole lamb for their friends. They were firmly irreligious, drank wine and spirits and always attended the town's rugby games to watch their son Karim, the team's star forward. His infant children helped to compensate for the loss of their adopted son, Sami, an autistic boy whose death they blamed on jihadists. Bruno introduced Amélie, and then Dilla bent down to greet Balzac as Momu emerged from the living room to embrace him in turn. From behind Momu came the sound of baroque music.

After a brief exchange, Bruno showed them a printout of the photo he'd taken of the letters. "The final letter could just be an accident, scrawled when the woman who painted it fell to her death. Mean anything to you?"

"Was this the unknown woman who died at Commarque?" Dilla asked. "It was just on the radio news, but there was nothing about any writing. It's so sad, at such a lovely place. I'll never visit it again without thinking of her."

"It was a fortress," Amélie said flatly. "A whole lot more people were probably killed there over the centuries."

"Yes, of course," Dilla replied, giving Amélie a sideways glance before leading them into the sitting room where Momu turned down the music and offered them a drink. Amélie asked for tea, and Bruno said that would be fine for him. Beside Momu's armchair was a pile of his pupils' homework and a glass of what looked like scotch. The room bore not a single trace of his Algerian heritage, and the bookcase seemed filled with books in French. A copy of the latest *Le Monde Diplomatique* lay on a coffee table.

"Why paint an Arabic word in roman letters?" Momu asked, studying the photo. He read them aloud and shrugged. "It could be *iftin*, which means 'light,' or *iftinan*, which means 'enchantment.' It could be a name, Iftikhar, not very common in the Arab world, but you find it in Sudan and in Pakistan and maybe Persia. There's a Pakistani poet, Iftikhar Arif."

"Does the name mean anything?"

" 'That which creates pride or a sense of worthiness,' so you could translate it as 'honor' or 'glory.' Nichan Iftikhar was the Order of Glory in the Ottoman Empire, a bit like our Légion d'Honneur."

"Could it be any other word?"

"Not that I can think of offhand. But if you like, I'll call a friend who's more of a literary scholar than I am."

Dilla came with a tray holding the tiny glasses for the tea and an old fat-bottomed silver teapot with a high neck and spout that she had inherited from her family. The room suddenly filled with the scent of mint, and Momu stood up to pour the heavily sweetened tea into the glasses from a great height, evidently proud of his skill. Bruno knew that custom required that he drink three glasses. Balzac nibbled contentedly at the biscuit Dilla had brought for him.

"Is it always this sweet?" Amélie asked, after emptying her glass.

"Always," said Dilla, solemnly. Amélie looked abashed.

Bruno thought he'd better change the subject. "This is the woman who fell to her death." He handed each of them a printout of the photo he'd taken.

"The poor woman," Momu murmured as he studied the face. Then he looked up. "She doesn't look Arabic or Pakistani. I'd have said she's European."

"She probably wasn't alone. Somebody took away the paint can and probably also the rope that we think they were using for the climb. I can leave you the printouts. It may help your literary friend."

Bruno finished his third glass of tea, thanked Dilla and rose. "My love to the grandchildren," he said as he left.

Bruno dropped his companion at the hotel, telling her he'd be patrolling the town market by eight the following morning. She bid Balzac goodbye with a kiss on his head, shook Bruno's hand, wished him a good evening and thanked him for an interesting day. He picked up a bottle of Château de la Jaubertie white wine at the cave before heading for Pamela's riding school and the ritual of the weekly dinner with his friends. It was the turn of Fabiola and her partner, Gilles, to cook, so Bruno's responsibility was wine and getting some water from the spring on Pamela's land.

But first there were the horses to be exercised, and he looked forward to all of it, the perfect way to end a working day. There was the apple to be given to Hector, the struggle to pull on his riding boots and stamp them down to fit. There was the welcoming scent of horses and fresh straw, the heft of the saddle in his arms and the regular game of Hector blowing out his stomach as Bruno tried to secure the saddle strap. Bruno would knee him gently in the belly to remind his horse that he knew this trick and then tighten the strap.

The stables were empty when he arrived. He was a little late, but Hector was waiting for him, and there was a note on Hector's door in Pamela's handwriting to say they had taken the ridge trail to Audrix. Bruno gave Hector his treat and lingered, enjoying the warm breath on the palm of his hand. He leaned his head forward to rest it against Hector's neck. Bruno stepped back and saw Hector lean down to nuzzle the dog he'd known since Balzac was a puppy. Bruno wondered whether Hector thought of the basset hound as a miniature horse and Balzac thought of the horse as a gigantic dog. No matter, the two animals were friends, evidently happy to see each other.

When Bruno put on the bridle, he noticed somebody had used saddle soap on the leather. That would have been Félix, transformed by Pamela's good sense and the experience of horses from a sullen young delinquent into a helpful and enthusiastic stableboy and a promising horseman.

With no other horses to slow him down, Hector could barely restrain himself until they were out of the paddock, heading past the house and up the ridge. Miranda, Pamela's partner in running the riding school, gave him a wave from the kitchen window as he passed, and then Hector was powering his way up the modest slope and onto the open ground ahead. Within moments he had gone from a canter to a steady run, not quite a gallop but a pace he could keep up for hours.

At the entrance to the bridle trail through the woods, Bruno slowed the horse and then turned him, waiting for Balzac to catch up. They trotted on, the three of them together, past a place where Bruno remembered seeing a nest of cèpe mushrooms the previous fall. Then the trees thinned, and he could see the small tower of Audrix church in the distance and a group of horses with their riders even farther off, maybe two kilometers ahead. He gave Hector his rein, and with other horses in sight Hector stretched into a gallop and Bruno narrowed his eyes against the wind.

"That looked like fun," said Gilles as Bruno joined them. He was riding Victoria, Pamela's elderly mare. Fabiola was on a well-mannered Selle Français that had come with the riding school, and Félix was riding the Andalusian. Pamela was on Primrose, the horse she had originally wanted to buy before deciding to make an offer for the whole riding school. Three more horses and a pony, all unsaddled, were on leading reins, just along for the exercise.

"It was glorious," Bruno replied, beaming with the pleasure of seeing his friends and the thrill of the ride. They trotted on, past Audrix and back by the shorter route, Pamela leading and Bruno bringing up the rear. It was a position Hector hated if his master was riding fast, but at this gentle pace, he seemed content to enjoy the outing. They came over the top of the ridge and stopped, still stunned despite its familiarity by the magnificence of the view. The whole of the double valley opened up below them, the oxbow curves of the River Vézère flowing into the Dordogne. The houses of the village of Limeuil seemed almost to be clambering up the steep slope to the latest of the many fortresses that had squatted on this hilltop for centuries, watching over the confluence of the two rivers and the trade and revenues they had brought.

Pamela turned her horse's head, and they rode on down the slope to come to the rear entrance of the riding school. Gilles and Fabiola left the horses still saddled and headed for the kitchen to start the meal going. Pamela gave Bruno a hug when they dis-

Scotland, even in Cyprus and the Middle East. And they certainly have been right here. Over the years their metal detectors must have gone over every inch of ground. Not that it stops such people. As somebody once said, when people cease to believe in God, the problem is not that they believe in nothing, it's that they are prepared to believe in absolutely anything."

The ground seemed to lurch beneath their feet as the great metal plate pounded again. Horst laughed as he staggered, just managing to keep his balance.

"If there is anything to be found, these seismic surveys and the ground-penetrating radar will find it," he said.

"What about you, Monsieur Dumesnil?" Bruno asked. "Do you believe there is something to be found?"

"I certainly hope so. What is significant is what we have not found here. There are many prehistoric remains, which medieval people must have seen and pondered. But they left us no similar remains except for the château itself—only paper records of charters and endless lawsuits between families. Why should that be? I suspect that if anything new turns up, it's more likely to belong to my period than to Horst's cavemen."

Chapter 11

Bruno stopped at the Maison de la Presse to scan the back pages of *Archéologie* for the account of the graffiti daubed on the ruined Crusader fortress and to make a note of the details. Once in his office, he searched the Internet for its name and found a news story in the English-language version of the Israeli newspaper *Haaretz*. A slogan had been painted in Hebrew a month earlier at a place in the Galilee called Beit She'an. The paper's translation was "The Testament of Iftikhar is a forgery."

" 'Iftikhar'—that fits with the letters at Commarque," he said to Amélie, but her fingers were already flying over the keyboard of her phone.

" 'Iftikhar ad-Daula, the Muslim governor of Jerusalem in the year 1099 when he surrendered the citadel of the city to the First Crusade in return for free passage for himself, his family and his guards,' " she said, reading aloud from a website she had found. "There's some controversy about it, since the Crusaders slaughtered just about everybody else in the city, Arabs, Jews and even Christians. So why would they let him go?"

"Interesting question," said Bruno. "But what is this testament?"

"Iftikhar supposedly wrote some statement as part of the deal to let him and his family go, declaring that Jerusalem was of no religious significance to Islam and therefore he and his troops could abandon it with a clear conscience."

"I thought the whole point about Jerusalem was that it was sacred to all three religions, to Jews, Christians and Muslims," said Bruno.

"Me too. But now it seems there's a whole controversy with Islamic scholars claiming that the Jews had nothing to do with Jerusalem and that the place was always inhabited by Arabs called Jebusites or Canaanites and that Solomon's Temple was built elsewhere. Jewish scholars are counterclaiming that the Arabs fabricated the claim that Muhammad in a dream visited Jerusalem at the place where the al-Aqsa Mosque now stands. And this Testament of Iftikhar is supposed to prove it."

Bruno felt his head spinning. "What has all this got to do with Commarque?"

"I have no idea, except that it now seems that the dead woman was Israeli. And we know Commarque had a Templar connection. This supposed Testament of Iftikhar, which had long since disappeared, had been in their keeping. The Templars' headquarters were on the Temple Mount, on which now stands the al-Aqsa Mosque. That's the golden dome you always see on TV news reports about Jerusalem."

"I think we'd better let J-J sort all this out," Bruno said and reached for his phone, which began ringing the moment before he touched it. A familiar voice was demanding, "Have you heard the news about the Muslims?"

"Bonjour, Yacov," said Bruno. "No, I haven't. What news?"

Yacov Kaufman was a Paris-based lawyer, grandson of the elderly lady who was paying for the new scout camp, as well as for a museum of the Périgord Resistance in World War II and the sanctuary the region had provided for Jewish children.

Bruno and Yacov had become friends when Bruno helped trace the family and the farm where Yacov's grandmother Maya had been sheltered.

"The Muslim scouts have backed out, they're withdrawing from the opening ceremony," Yacov said angrily. "They won't send any of their scouts for the opening week. They claim they just found out the camp is being financed by Israeli money."

"Are all the Protestants and Catholics still coming?"

"Yes, but the whole point was to make it an ecumenical camp," Yacov said.

As they spoke, Bruno quickly scrolled through that day's accumulated e-mails on his desktop computer. Mostly they contained negative replies from hotels, campsites and *gîte* owners in response to his queries about any rentals in the names of Leah Wolinsky or Leah Ben-Ari. Suddenly he paused, spotting the e-mail from the Jewish scouts that told him of the Muslim scouts' decision.

Bruno shook his head in frustration, thinking that only in France did they have four separate Boy Scouts—for the Catholics, Protestants, Jews and Muslims. The formal opening was to be the following weekend, the spring holiday for schools.

"Why not invite some German scouts instead? It makes for a good symbol of European reconciliation."

"That's not a bad idea," said Yacov. "I'll make some calls. But I also want to know if it's convenient for me to come down this weekend, just so I can reassure Maya that everything is in order. Then I'll come back to Paris, meet her at the airport when she flies in next week and bring her down for the opening."

"I'm going to be a bit tied up with a wedding for some friends of mine on Saturday, but you're always welcome, Yacov, and so is your grandma. I can't put you up, I'm afraid. Several of the wedding guests are staying at my place."

"That's no problem, I don't need babysitting. Who's getting married?"

"I don't know if you've met them, Clothilde Daumier from the museum in Les Eyzies is marrying Horst, a German archaeologist. They've been a couple for years and years, but they're finally tying the knot."

"I don't think I've met them. I'll try not to get in your way. Is Pamela still renting out her *gîtes*?"

"She is, but she's moved, taken over a nearby riding school. I'll ask if she has a place free, but I think she may be full with wedding guests. If so, I'll book you into a hotel. How many nights?"

Yacov said he'd stay just two nights, Friday and Saturday, confirmed the date, offered to buy Bruno and the mayor lunch on Friday and hung up.

"Who was that?" Amélie asked. "It sounded rather official, but he has a lovely voice."

"That was a lawyer friend from Paris, Yacov, you'll like him," Bruno began. He was about to tell her of the scouts' project but almost immediately the desktop phone rang again.

"Bonjour, Bruno, Jack Crimson here. About that daubed slogan you showed me last night. One of my old colleagues rang me back to say he thinks it's connected to similar graffiti painted recently on a castle in Israel."

"About the Testament of Iftikhar," said Bruno.

"You know about that? I'm impressed. But it seems there are some tricky political and diplomatic issues attached to all this, and I thought I should tip off our friend the brigadier that there may be more to this young woman than meets the eye. Unless, that is, you've already done so."

"No, we've just come across this connection," said Bruno. "And it's all thanks to a colleague from the justice ministry with a smartphone that she plays like a maestro. She's even come up with a name, or rather two, for our dead woman. She's an Israeli named Leah Ben-Ari, and she seems also to be a Frenchwoman named Leah Wolinsky. They may be one and the same. And she has a Palestinian boyfriend called al-Husayni. J-J is working on it. If you want to call the brigadier, go ahead. He'll probably take it more seriously from you."

The brigadier was a senior official in the interior ministry. Bruno had come under his command before and turned down an offer to join the brigadier's team in Paris on a permanent basis. Jack Crimson and the brigadier had worked together in the past, were on first-name terms and maintained friendly relations. Whenever both of them became involved in something, Bruno was aware that matters had reached far beyond his pay grade. The brigadier always observed the courtesies, asking the mayor of St. Denis for Bruno to be temporarily assigned to his staff at the ministry, but with a subtle threat to trigger Bruno's transfer from reserve status in the French army to active duty.

"Who is the brigadier?" Amélie asked. Bruno gave a suitably cautious explanation.

"Sounds like intelligence," she said, grinning at him. "This is getting to be fun."

"This is getting to the point where a country policeman like me bows out and lets the big boys take over."

"That's not what I hear."

Bruno gave her a stern look. "What do you mean by that?"

Amélie shrugged. "I already told you I wanted to follow you around on this job. There's some other intriguing stories told at the ministry about some of the cases you've been involved in—some rich American you broke out of jail, a shoot-out in a cave, that mysterious business with the young jihadist who made bombs in Afghanistan, the autistic one . . ." She paused. "Would he have had something to do with that friend of yours we met yesterday, Momu?"

He ignored the question. "This is a straightforward case of identifying a woman who fell to her death and best left in the hands of Commissaire Jalipeau and the Police Nationale. With any luck, our work on this is done."

"Oh yes?" Amélie's voice was mocking. "You have a scout camp being opened next week financed by a wealthy Jewish woman and the Muslim scouts have decided to boycott it. And at the same time you find an Israeli woman dead while painting something on the wall of your château that seems related to an Arab-Israeli dispute over Jerusalem. And you're telling me that all these things aren't linked?"

"I very much hope not. And it's not my château."

"I know it's not your damn château, Bruno, but that's not the point," she snapped at him. Then she sighed loudly and gazed at the ceiling as though willing herself to be calm. "There must be a connection here. We just have to find it."

"You may be right, but so far I don't see it," he said evenly. Bruno noted her use of the word "we." He accepted that Amélie was a gifted researcher who had saved him hours or even days of work. But she was not a policewoman, and he'd already bent some rules in letting her become so involved in the case.

"May I use your printer?" she asked.

"So long as it's official."

"It's some material about this Jerusalem controversy and the testament that I want to look at more carefully."

She looked at the printer and the cable that linked it to Bruno's desk computer and shook her head. "The first recommendation in my report will be to get all you municipal policemen up-to-date with technology. This printer must be ten years old. I'll have to e-mail you the documents and let you print them out."

To change the subject, he asked how her dinner with the local Socialists had gone. She glared at him for a moment, and then her face did not exactly relax, but it softened. Bruno had the impression that she was trying to focus on an object that was at the same time very close and yet far away.

"They were sweet and welcoming in a rather formal way, but not what I think of as political comrades," she said slowly, groping for the right words. "They actually talked of 'the workers,' here in a town without factories. When I asked them what they did, they were pharmacists, teachers, insurance agents or employees of the *mairie*. None was under forty and most were older. I didn't have the heart to tell them they were classic members of the petite bourgeoisie."

"I don't think they get many visitors from the national headquarters, even from its youth wing. How did they react to your idea for a youth section of the party?"

"They said it was a great idea but wanted to know what the youth section was meant to do, supposing they could actually start one. I think they expected me to give them a detailed plan and hold their hands while they got started."

Bruno nodded. He had not expected anything different. "Well, let's go and see one of our local youth projects that might interest you, although it's not political. I've got to go check on this scout camp that has to be ready by the end of this week. You'll need to change your shoes again."

"You mean the one that you don't think could possibly be linked to this Arab-Israeli business?" she asked him, a mocking tilt to her eyebrow.

"You don't have to come," he said.

"Yes, I do," she retorted, picking up her bag. "It's my job."

Chapter 12

At the hilltop village of Audrix, Bruno paused to show Amélie the view over the valley before turning off onto the plateau
where the springtime green was dazzling. He plunged down
what had once been a hidden turn into a deeply rutted country
lane flanked by bruised and broken vegetation that testified to
the passing of many heavy trucks. He made a mental note to
get some gravel laid here to fill the ruts before Yacov's inspec-
tion visit. He stopped the car as he came over a small rise. Below
them unfolded the hollow containing the old farm and the
restored barn, the roofs gleaming with new solar panels. A long
stretch of pasture sloped down to the stream and a bathing place
below the small waterfall. Beside the stream was a long stretch
of flat ground, with a net rigged for volleyball and two goalposts
installed to make a soccer field.

Two men were unloading army surplus tents from a truck.
Bruno caught the sound of an electric drill coming from inside
the farmhouse as he pulled up. The men with the tents stopped
to stare as Amélie climbed out of the van, followed by Balzac.
She waved at them and Bruno greeted them and went into the
farmhouse. He found Arnaud, a local carpenter, fitting cupboards and bookshelves into the alcoves on either side of the fire-

place in the room that was designed to be the office. The other room on the ground floor was a large kitchen and dining area, with a new bathroom installed in a lean-to at the rear. Upstairs was a bedroom for the caretaker and his wife and another across the landing for visitors.

"I'll be done before I leave this evening," said Arnaud, putting down the drill and shaking hands with the visitors. "The caretaker and his wife already moved in, they've just gone to do some shopping. If you want to take a look around, I'll put some coffee on."

Bruno went first to the old barn, which had been fitted out with tables and benches. A double sink occupied the rear wall with waist-high cupboards topped with work surfaces to one side and a large wood-fired stove and cooking range on the other. A staircase and an upper floor had been installed with more bunk beds, enough to sleep twenty or so people. Behind it stood a new barn for storage and a separate block for showers, rows of sinks and toilets. A long stretch of freshly turned earth showed where the array of septic tanks had been buried. With eight scouts to each of the big bell-shaped tents, the camp could house another hundred scouts and a dozen or more scoutmasters. There were stone fire pits for campfires, an old well that still functioned and a large terrace for outdoor eating that had a single basketball net at one end.

Amélie followed Bruno down to the stream and the swimming hole. She dabbled her hand in the waterfall, swiftly snatching it away, saying it was too cold for her. They strolled back, Balzac snuffling alongside them. Bruno pointed out the land that was intended to be turned into a vegetable garden by the first contingent of visiting scouts, to help feed their successors later in the summer.

"It's idyllic," said Amélie. "A pity that the Muslim scouts

aren't coming, but that's their loss. Does the place have to be restricted to the scout movement? Some of my youth groups in the party would love to have a place like this to visit."

"I don't know. We'll have to ask Yacov when he comes. But Girl Guides will be coming, too. You saw the double facility in the shower block. I think the terms of the trust that was established to run this place limit it to scouts. Maya, the woman who's funding all this, reckons the scouts saved her and her brother's lives in the war."

"Good for her," said Amélie. "I think this place is wonderful, a brilliant idea for a memorial. I just wish there was some way of making this available to all those kids in the high-rise ghettos around Paris."

"There is," said Bruno. "They simply have to volunteer to join the scouts."

"But I never see scouts in the *banlieues*."

"Now there's a project for your party's youth group. Don't you think it's better to get kids out in the fresh air of the countryside learning things than sitting in some hall talking politics?"

"Of course, but scouts are mainly all white, middle class."

"Not so. There are thirty million kids in the scout movement worldwide, and two-thirds of them are in the developing world. When this project got started, I thought I'd better find out something more about it. And did you miss what I said about scouts helping save Jewish kids in the war?"

"No, I got that. And now who's this?" She pointed to a car bumping along the rutted lane.

"That's Alain, the caretaker. He used to be a priest and left the Church to get married. He's been a scoutmaster in Bergerac, and he and his wife liked the idea of living here rent-free."

"Bonjour, Alain, madame," Bruno said, and introduced Amélie. "I gather you moved in already."

"It's a lovely place, and much better than the cramped apartment we had in Bergerac," Alain replied. "We have the chance to make a garden, maybe start a small vineyard on that south-facing slope. And the scouts will keep us busy once they start coming."

Alain was a slim, wiry man of about fifty with gray hair and a ready smile. His wife, Anne-Louise, a kind-looking woman with an air of quiet competence, looked to be the same age. Bruno could never see them without thinking of the passion that must have brought them together and taken Alain from his vows in the priesthood. She had been working as a nurse when they met and then volunteered as a cleaning woman in Alain's church.

"Did you see Dr. Stern at the clinic in St. Denis?" Bruno asked Anne-Louise. He'd suggested that Fabiola might find it useful to have a trained nurse available, and Anne-Louise might appreciate some extra money in the winter when no scouts were expected. And it was a bonus for the camp to have someone on hand with medical qualifications.

"Yes, thank you," she replied, and gave Bruno a warm smile that lit up her eyes and helped explain why Alain had fallen for her. "I'll be doing regular shifts at the clinic in winter, and other times I'll be on call if needed."

"Have you dealt with large numbers of teenage boys before?" Amélie asked. "They can be quite a handful."

"I'm accustomed to it, growing up in a church orphanage," she replied. "Just like you, Bruno."

"I was in Bergerac. Were you there?"

"No, at Mussidan, the place where all the fuss is."

"So you'll have talked to Commissaire Jalipeau about the inquiry?"

"No, just to one of his detectives. I told him I never knew of any sexual abuse, but one of the nuns was very cruel. She used to beat us with a bamboo cane." Anne-Louise raised her right arm and brought it down fast, saying, "Swoosh."

"You still get nightmares about it," said her husband, taking her hand.

"Which nun would that have been?" Bruno asked.

"The one who's making the allegations, the alcoholic. Looking back, I'm sure she was drunk when she beat us. It was the priest, Father Francis, who finally stopped her and got her into a nunnery where they treated her for the drinking. He's the same priest she's making the allegations about. I said all this to the detective, and I'm sure he didn't believe the dreadful stories she told about Father Francis. I can't believe this case is still going on."

Bruno nodded. "Another priest who knew him said he found the stories hard to believe. But Jalipeau is a good man, a fine policeman, you can count on him. He'll get to the bottom of it all."

An hour later, Bruno dropped Amélie at her hotel and drove to the riding school, stopping only to pick up some veal for dinner from the Oudinots' farm. At the stables, he noticed Jack Crimson's elderly Jaguar parked by the main house. He greeted Pamela in the office, said he'd join her shortly and then strolled up to see Crimson, who was sitting on the floor with his grandchildren, reading to them from an English book.

"I'm making sure they don't lose their British culture," he said as the kids broke away to pet Balzac. "Do you know Winnie the Pooh?"

"Of course, he's very popular in France. We call him Winnie l'Ourson. Did you speak to the brigadier?"

Crimson nodded. "He said he'd check it out and asked me to give you his regards. His first question was whether you were involved. You'll be hearing from him, I think."

"So he's taking it seriously? That's good."

"He was planning to ask the French embassy in Israel how serious this business about the Testament of Iftikhar might be. I had to say I'd never heard of it until now, but the camel I talked with thought this argument about Jerusalem had surged beyond the historians into current politics. The Arab League and the Palestinians have put out statements questioning the Jewish origins of the city."

"It's all a long way from the Périgord," Bruno replied. "Why on earth do we have to get involved?"

"First, because it's the Middle East. Second, because it's also the Holy Land. And third, because of the Sykes-Picot Agreement, named after a British and French diplomat who carved up the old Ottoman Empire in 1916. That was the year before Britain issued the Balfour Declaration promising to make Palestine a national homeland for the Jewish people. Between them, for better or worse, Balfour, Sykes and Picot created the map of the modern Middle East. We are now living with the consequences."

Bruno sighed and headed back to the stables, checking his watch. His guests were coming at seven. He could ride for maybe forty minutes. Miranda was not back with her pony trekkers, and Pamela said she was still busy with paperwork and he should exercise Hector alone. That was no hardship, thought Bruno as he saddled Hector and took him out through the paddock.

Bruno believed that he did his best thinking on horseback, his conscious mind on the route and the horse, but some part of his brain ticking away at whatever bothered him. Right now it was this strange mixture of Templars, Crusaders, Jerusalem in history and Arab-Israeli politics, all focused on an Israeli peace activist and a medieval castle. The pieces did not fit together in a way that made any sense. If the woman had wanted to make a stir with her graffiti, there were far more prominent and better-known castles with their own Templar or Crusader connections. There was the hilltop fortress town of Domme, where some of the Templars had been imprisoned and carved crosses on the walls of their dungeon. A message daubed on the town walls would have been seen by many more people and would not have involved a dangerous climb.

And the dead woman had been more than two months pregnant, so she might have known or at least suspected her condition. Would an amateur have embarked on a nighttime climb knowing that? Above all there was the missing partner, the person who took away the rope and the paint and also must have put that horn by her hand to echo the ancient pose of some prehistoric Venus figure. And what was the dead woman's motive? He chided himself for not calling her Leah; she was not just a body in the morgue, but a woman who had been alive, who had conceived a child. She deserved the respect of a name. But if Leah had been seeking publicity for some cause of Arab-Israeli peace, there were many better targets for her spray can.

Bruno knew no more of the intricacies of Arab-Israeli relations than anyone who read the papers and listened to the radio. He had heard of the Peace Now movement and knew it carried little political weight in Israel and that the supposed objective of a two-state solution for Israelis and Palestinians was further off now than it had been when Yitzhak Rabin and Yasir Arafat had shaken hands on the White House lawn. But that was about all he did know, except that there were various Palestinian factions, though he was far from clear about the difference between Hamas and Hezbollah.

Suddenly he was aware that Hector was shaking his head with impatience. Bruno had been so lost in thought that he'd slowed to a walk, and Hector wanted more than that. Bruno loosened the reins and gave Hector's sides a nudge with his heels.

His horse almost bounded forward through the trees to the open country ahead, stretching out in that glorious, even stride that horse and rider enjoyed so much. All too soon, the ridge narrowed, and a thick hedge squeezed him toward the trees until Bruno was forced to dismount and lead Hector and Balzac back to the riding school.

Chapter 13

Bruno took the cheese from his fridge, and from his freezer removed the stock for the fish soup, which he'd made with the discarded shells and heads of shrimp from an earlier meal. He peeled a half kilo of shallots from his garden and put them in a saucepan with a little butter. He did the same with a half kilo of button mushrooms he'd bought in the market. He cut the kilo of veal into cubes and put them into his largest saucepan, covered the meat with water and put it on to boil before peeling a medium-sized onion and pushing into it four cloves. He then jumped into the shower and changed into jeans and a sweater. He fed Balzac, put the frozen fish stock into the microwave to thaw and paused to consider. He planned fish soup, followed by *blanquette de veau* with rice, salad with cheese and pears poached in spiced wine for dessert. They would be four, since he'd invited Annette, the young magistrate based in Sarlat, to join them. She and Amélie would have a lot in common, and her presence would stop it feeling too much like a working dinner.

He put one bottle of sparkling Bergerac rosé from Château Haut Garrigue and another of Pierre Desmartis's white Bergerac Sec into the fridge and opened a bottle of Clos Montalbanie, a lighter red from Château de Tiregand that he thought would go well with the veal. The veal was starting to boil, so he turned down the heat, skimmed off the surface fat and then dropped in a chopped carrot, a rib of celery, the onion with its cloves and one of the bouquets garnis he made every few days. He adjusted the heat to let the meat simmer and then skimmed it again. Then he set the table, put out the champagne flutes, lit his woodstove and turned on the radio to hear how the local station was covering the events at Commarque. A reporter at the site was asking people what they knew about the place, and every answer he got was about the Templars and their treasure.

His fish stock had almost defrosted, so he cut the cod he'd bought into small cubes. He put two large spoons of duck fat into the bottom of his favorite flameproof casserole and put it onto the heat. Then he peeled two potatoes and half-a-dozen cloves of garlic. He diced the potatoes and crushed the garlic with the back of his knife, mixed them together and tossed them into the casserole. He let that cook on low heat while he went out to the garden to pick some salad, washed and chopped it and put it to one side while he added the cubes of cod, the fish stock and a can of tomatoes to the casserole. He poured a large glass from the five-liter box of simple white Bergerac that he kept in the pantry, added it to the fish, stirred and tasted. A touch more salt was needed, and he adjusted the heat to a very low simmer.

He checked his watch. Usually he would simmer the meat for as much as two hours to get it really tender, but this was Oudinot's veal, the best in the valley, from milk-fed calves raised with their mothers. The meat would be deliciously tender anyway, and his guests would be arriving within the next fifteen minutes. He cleaned up the kitchen, tidied the books and papers in his living room and brushed away the ashes from the tiles below his stove. Then he filled his electric kettle with water, set it to boil so it would be ready for the rice and took a pot of heavy cream from the fridge.

Finally from the freezer he took the vacuum bag with the last of the basil he'd picked last autumn. And when he saw Balzac's ears twitch and the dog move to the door, Bruno knew his guests were about to arrive. Balzac always heard the sound of an engine coming up the road a good half minute before his master. He opened the door so that Balzac could bound out and give the arrivals his usual noisy welcome. Before he followed Balzac, Bruno added another glass of white wine to the fish soup, tasted it and smiled to himself. It was good.

Sergeant Jules in uniform was driving his own car, with Yveline and Amélie in the rear and Annette in the front seat. Bruno shook Jules's hand, welcomed Annette and Yveline and helped Amélie extract herself from Balzac's obvious affections. This time she was wearing a bright yellow dress with a generous headdress of some coarse cloth in blue and yellow stripes. Yveline wore black slacks, a cream silk blouse and fitted tweed jacket. Annette was in jeans, a white cotton sweater and a knee-length cardigan in black cashmere. They were three striking women, each in her different way.

"Will you stay for a *p'tit apéro?*" Bruno asked Jules.

"Better not," Jules replied, with a glance at Yveline, his *commandante*. "I'm on duty this evening. But give me a call at the station when you're ready and I'll come back to pick them up."

"It made sense for us all to come together and go back together," said Yveline. "Annette is staying at my place tonight rather than drive back to Sarlat." She handed Bruno a bottle of chilled Monthuys champagne. Annette waved a paper-wrapped bottle at him, saying it was his favorite Château de Tiregand, and Amélie handed him a small glass jar of what looked like a greenish sauce.

"*Epice,* my mother's recipe," she said. "Ivan let me borrow his kitchen to make it. I gave him a jar, and this one's for you."

Once inside, the guests settled in his sitting room with glasses of champagne. Bruno excused himself and went into the kitchen to check on the food. He added some lemon juice to the fish and wondered how to serve some of Amélie's gift. She'd certainly be hoping that he'd find a way for them all to try it. He opened a can of his own venison pâté. It should go well with Amélie's *épice.*

"I thought we should try your *épice* right away," he said, returning to his guests.

"Not too much, it's pretty spicy until you're used to it," warned Amélie, casting Bruno a grateful look. He gave her a grin in return, one cook to another, as she spoke again. "This is the heart of Creole cooking."

It was hot, but not unpleasantly so, spicy rather than burning, and it went well with the venison. Bruno could imagine it working with chicken, but he recalled Amélie saying that rice and beans were a staple in Haiti, a dish of the poor, and the *épice* would add flavor to an otherwise bland but filling meal. Yveline fanned her mouth and asked for a glass of water, pleading that she wasn't accustomed to such fiery food. Annette, by contrast, added even more *épice* to her next slice, saying she had come to enjoy hot peppers when she'd worked for Médecins Sans Frontières in Madagascar.

"Do you know anybody who works for them in Palestine?" Bruno asked suddenly, with a quick glance at Amélie. "A friend you know well enough to call and ask about that dead woman at the château? Amélie managed to identify her, an Israeli woman who lives with a Palestinian boyfriend."

"Yes, I have a good friend who's a psychologist at a clinic in Hebron," Annette replied. "She works mainly with traumatized children. And I know another in East Jerusalem. Why?"

"Could you call them tomorrow and ask if they know any-thing about Leah Ben-Ari, or maybe Leah Wolinsky, and her guy, name of al-Husayni."

"Saïd al-Husayni, a historian at the university," Amélie interrupted.

Annette pulled out her mobile and began typing a text mes-sage. "Why wait till tomorrow? It's late there now, but I should get a reply tomorrow."

Bruno poured out the rest of the champagne, invited them to move to the table and went back to the kitchen to check the seasoning and toss some chopped parsley onto the fish soup. He opened the white wine and took it to the table, then brought in the tureen.

"If anyone wants to try adding some of Amélie's *épice* to the soup, that might be interesting," he said, handing around the bread and then pouring the wine.

"I'll wait and try it when I'm close to the end," said Annette. "This is really good, Bruno, rich and hearty."

"It's great," said Amélie, stirring a spoonful of her sauce into her bowl. "But since we're here to talk about policing, Yveline, what does a village cop like Bruno mean to you?"

"A lot more than I'd expected when I came here. A good local policeman is like a living archive of a community, a real resource of local history and knowledge. I'd be a fool to ignore it, which is why Bruno is now invited to my weekly planning meetings. In my future postings I'll do the same—but I might not find another village cop who can cook like this."

"It's the same for me as a magistrate," said Annette. She explained that when the *procureur* assigned her to a case to see whether a prosecution was warranted, she'd learned always to talk first to the municipal policeman in order to understand the background. In juvenile cases the local cop could describe the parents before she went to see them, give her a sense of the local context and degree of family support she might expect.

"I didn't start out like that," Annette added. "In fact I was very suspicious of Bruno as a hunter and rugby player. I thought of him as an old-fashioned male chauvinist, a rather sinister figure in a local Green-hating mafia that would block and frustrate me at every turn."

"It was hard for us locals to work out why they'd send a vegetarian feminist to be a magistrate in the Périgord," said Bruno, smiling. "That was before we learned you were a fearsome rally driver. Now I'm going to try this with the *épice*." He stirred in some of the green sauce with the last spoonfuls of soup in his bowl and tasted the result.

"Not bad," he said. "But I prefer it without, since I don't think this would work with *chabrol*."

"What's that?" asked Amélie.

"An old local tradition. Just watch," he said. He served the remainder of the soup, then he ate the last pieces of fish until only liquid remained in his bowl and then added perhaps half a glass of red wine and stirred it together. Then he put down the spoon, picked up the bowl with both hands, brought it to his lips and drank. He smacked his lips as he put it down and watched with satisfaction as Annette and Yveline followed suit.

Hesitantly, and with a doubtful glance at Bruno, Amélie did the same. "Interesting," she said, putting down the bowl. "It's good, might be better if the wine was heated. What's the story about this *chabrol*?"

"There are different explanations," said Bruno. "The one I like says it comes from the English soldiers who were here in the Hundred Years' War. There wasn't much meat around in winter when they were on garrison duty in the castles, so their staple food was pickled herring, brought from the coast in barrels. The

English term for a young herring is 'shad,' and their word for soup is 'broth.' Say them together a few times, and you'll see how the French could turn 'shad broth' into *chabrol.* And given the quality of the local wine the English could afford, it probably improved the wine as well as the herring."

He gathered up the bowls and went to the kitchen, stacking them in the sink and turning on the hot water. Then he tasted the veal and nodded; it was time to make the *blanquette.* He drained the sauce from the meat over a measuring cup and put the meat aside, removing the bouquet garni and the carrot and celery. He poured the sauce into a separate large saucepan and left it over a low flame. He put the rice into a separate saucepan with a tablespoon of duck fat, stirring until all the grains were coated and then added boiling water from his kettle, covered it and left the rice to cook.

Then he began to make his roux, using the saucepan in which the veal had cooked. He put three thick slices of butter into the pan and brought over his glass jar of ordinary flour. When the butter had melted, foamed and subsided, he reduced the heat a little and began sprinkling flour into it, stirring steadily with a whisk. Slowly, making sure the flour was fully absorbed, he added four tablespoons and then began to pour in the juice from the veal, continuing to whisk to ensure it was fully blended. He turned up the heat and brought it to a simmer, still stirring until it began to thicken. Then he added the veal, the shallots, the mushrooms and the pot of cream, stirring steadily until it returned to the boil. He turned down the heat to a simmer, checked the rice, adding half a cup more water, piled the dirty dishes into the sink and opened the bottle of red wine.

Quickly, he peeled the fat pears he had bought, put them into a saucepan and poured in red wine until they were just covered. He added two cloves, some cinnamon and some grated nutmeg.

Finally, he poured in half a glass of his own *vin de noix* and left it simmering.

"Five minutes," he said, returning to the table with the red wine and a bottle of mineral water. He shared out the last of the white wine and began to follow the conversation. It was clear that they had been talking about J-J's pedophilia investigation.

"But it's almost always the case that you only have the testimony of the victims to go on," Amélie was insisting. "The children hardly ever complain to other adults at the time, so there's no chance of physical evidence or DNA. That thirty years have passed since the kids were molested is typical. And when you get three kids saying the same thing about the same abusers, that to me is corroboration."

"But that's part of the problem," said Yveline. "When you get into detail, the kids are not saying the same thing."

"The real problem is this psychologist and her use of so-called recovered memories," said Annette. Both in Britain and in the United States, she noted, the medical authorities had treated such memories with great skepticism and warned against their being used as evidence without strong corroboration.

"There are several cases where these memories are now thought to have been suggested to the patient by the psychologist involved, often through the use of hypnosis. In this case that J-J is dealing with, hypnosis was used on all three," Annette went on. "As a magistrate, this is a case I would not want to take to court. The evidence is just too flimsy."

Bruno excused himself to bring in the *blanquette de veau* and the rice and was not surprised to find them still arguing about the case when he returned.

"You can't seriously argue that the reputations of these adults are as important as the lives of the kids that were destroyed," Amélie was saying fiercely. "What about their rights?"

"*Mon Dieu,* this is rich. I'm going to gain at least a kilo from this meal," Yveline interjected. Bruno threw her a grateful glance for changing the subject.

"This is a Pécharmant from one of my favorite vineyards," said Bruno, pouring out the red. "But it's light enough to go well with the veal. Still, if anyone would prefer to stay with white wine, I have some in the fridge."

"Let me pay you a compliment, Bruno," said Amélie. "I would not want to add any *épice* to this dish. It's perfect just as it is. But I suspect Yveline is right about the extra kilos we'll be putting on."

He offered second helpings of the veal, and despite her joke about gaining weight, Yveline was the first to proffer her plate. The others followed.

"There may be one more treat in store for us all this evening," Bruno said, bringing in the dessert, adding a scoop of vanilla ice cream and a splash of cognac to his poached pears. "We have a star among us, a singer who has recorded albums, and the moment I heard her I knew she was extraordinary." He turned to smile at Amélie. "I'm hoping that you'll grace our dinner table with a song. I promise not to join in."

Annette clapped her hands, and Yveline said, "Now that we know you're a singer we have to hear you—anything you like."

Amélie beamed at them and remained seated. "Well, now that I've gotten back into the habit since I've been driving around with Bruno, maybe you'd like a little Cole Porter, a favorite of mine that I learned by heart."

Tapping her finger gently on the table to keep time, she launched into "Just One of Those Things," a song of a love affair that flared suddenly and magnificently but then died away as quickly, that then merged into "Every Time We Say Goodbye."

It was a song that hit Bruno like a fist, a lament of lovers parting that he had listened to again and again after Isabelle had left him. He felt tears prick his eyes. It was a song she had loved, and she had written down the English words for him. He could never play it without wondering if Isabelle was alone in Paris, playing the same song and feeling the same regrets. Finally, sick of the melancholy it brought, he had put away the disc she had left him.

Chapter 14

The next morning Bruno drove with Balzac to the stables to exercise his horse and then joined Amélie at Fauquet's café, where she was enjoying her morning croissant. She raised her eyebrows at his dress, a tracksuit and tennis shoes rather than a uniform, before thanking him for dinner. He accepted her offer of coffee, and Balzac sat expectantly at her feet until she slipped him a corner of croissant and then a crust of baguette.

"Off duty today?" she asked.

"Depends what you mean by 'duty.' Teaching the kids to play tennis is not part of my job, but I think it's good for them, and I know it's good for my work."

"How come?"

"They grow up knowing me as something other than a policeman. It helps once they're old enough to get into mischief that could turn into something worse."

She pulled out her phone and began tapping in a note to herself. "Sounds like you're a social worker as much as a cop. Anything else? Soccer or basketball?"

"Rugby in the autumn and winter, tennis in spring and summer for boys and girls alike. Do you play any sports?"

She shook her head, which today was wrapped in a billowing

yellow headdress. She was wearing jeans with a yellow polo shirt, her leather jacket draped around her shoulders.

"I liked to play soccer, but my brothers always wanted me to be in goal, so I took up swimming. But you don't have a gym anywhere nearer than Bergerac."

"There's a yoga and Pilates club that meets at the *collège*. Yveline's a member, so if you're interested you could ask her. I've done some work today already. Annette forwarded me the e-mail she got from her friend in Hebron. Leah Wolinsky did some volunteer work for charities, but she was a historian and an archaeologist, so not many useful skills. Mainly she was known as a critic of Israel's behavior on the West Bank, got arrested a couple of times at demonstrations. Her boyfriend is apolitical but from a prominent family, landowners and politicians. I forwarded the e-mail to J-J."

He checked his watch. "The kids will be there by nine, so we'd better go."

The town tennis club boasted three open courts and one covered, all flanked by a modern clubhouse with a bar, changing rooms and a well-appointed kitchen, since it was a tradition that no communal activity could take place in St. Denis without there being food and wine involved. The main room was filled with long tables which could seat forty for lunches and dinners during the annual club tournament. The kitchen was in use most days, when regular quartets of doubles players would end their session by cooking their own lunch. This morning a group of seven-year-olds were getting changed, and several mothers sat on the courtside benches waiting to watch them play.

Bruno had learned from experience that in each class three or four children shone as natural tennis players, another dozen would show decent hand-eye coordination, and the remainder would need a lot of practice. He put one of the natural players in each of the three open courts with a basket of balls, and the others lined up in turn to hit balls back and forth until one went into the net and another player took his or her place. Eight of the better youngsters then went off to the covered court to play under the critical gaze of Montsouris, a train conductor who had taken advantage of the generous pension plan for his profession to retire at the age of fifty.

The only Communist on the town council, Montsouris spent his time hunting, fishing and helping the various sports clubs, an endless round of activity that kept him from spending too much time with his relentlessly radical wife, who found his politics far too tame for her own convictions. He was also in charge of the tennis club barbecue in summer. Bruno liked him and led Amélie across to the covered court where he introduced her to Montsouris and left them, no doubt to talk about politics.

"*Ça va, Bruno?*" one of the mothers called from a bench as he passed. "Who's the new girlfriend?"

He stopped to greet Giselle and her younger sister, Amandine, who had both been in his tennis classes only a few years earlier, and explained that Amélie was a colleague from Paris. Giselle was married to a local builder, had one child in the tennis class, two more in nursery school and another grinning toothlessly at Bruno from the carriage beside the bench. Amandine's official job was to spend four nights a week as a carer for old people in their homes, for which she earned the minimum wage, but she also worked unofficially as a housecleaner, which allowed her to own a small car.

"That dead woman in the paper, have you found out who she is yet?" Amandine asked.

"No, have you seen her before?"

"Not sure. There was someone like her, about a week ago, came into one of the *gîtes* I was cleaning on changeover day. She was there early. I couldn't swear it was her, but there was something about the hair. Was she tanned, this woman, as if she was just back from a vacation in the sun?"

"Yes, she was, unusually so for this time of year. Which *gîte* was this?"

"Over toward Sarlat, just after Meyrals on that back road. It's called La Bergerie, but I've never seen any sheep around there. You take the second left after that new art gallery, and it's about two kilometers up there on the right. The last five hundred meters is a dirt road."

"Who owns it?"

"A guy in Sarlat, that union guy who's in the papers. I forget his name."

"Vaugier, is that the one?"

"Yes. That's him. Funny that he's always going on about the law about shops opening on Sundays, but he pays me strictly cash, with no receipts, either."

Bruno made a mental note to check whether Vaugier had registered his *gîte* with the local *mairie*. "This woman, was there anything special about her? An accent, maybe?"

"She only spoke a few words, said hello and excused herself and asked what time she should come back, but she sounded Parisian to me. Have you got any better photos of her than the one in the paper?"

Bruno took out his phone and showed Amandine the pictures he'd taken, along with the visa photo Amélie had sent him.

"It could be her. I couldn't swear to it, but there's definitely a strong likeness."

Bruno took from her Vaugier's phone number and went off to supervise the rest of the tennis lesson until the next class arrived. This time it would be the nine-year-olds, most of them by now able to hit some sort of forehand and backhand drive and to place most of their serves into the right court. A new collection of mothers took their places on the benches.

When the tennis ended at noon, Bruno heated the soup he'd brought and Montsouris set out his own contribution, a big baguette with pâté and cheese. Amélie had learned from Montsouris that she could take red wine from the ten-liter box of Cuvée Cyrano behind the bar, leaving a euro for each glass in the old biscuit tin that served as a cashbox.

"Do you know this union guy, Vaugier?" Bruno asked Montsouris as they began to eat.

"I've met him a couple of times, but can't say I know him. He's not what you'd call one of the boys, doesn't follow rugby or go hunting. Comes from the north, Lille or somewhere. He was in the Socialist Party, but he moved to that new left-wing breakaway, the Parti de Gauche. He married a girl from Périgueux and moved down here when she inherited her parents' property. He's an ambitious guy, out to make a name for himself. Why do you ask?"

Bruno explained the court case in Sarlat and Montsouris nodded, adding that his cousin's son worked in one of Hugues's bakeries, liked the job and thought Hugues was a good employer. The three of them made coffee and washed up the dishes together. Bruno took his uniform from his van, changed out of his tracksuit and set off with Amélie for Vaugier's *gîte*. There was no singing on this ride; the mood was too serious.

The place was deserted, with no car to be seen and the key left in the door. Bruno put on a pair of evidence gloves, gave another pair to Amélie and let himself in. The place looked immaculate, as if it had been thoroughly cleaned. The pots and dishes had been washed and were stacked in the plastic drying rack. The refrigerator had been unplugged, the door open to reveal it was empty and gleaming. There was no washing machine, but bedding for several people had been washed, probably in a launderette, and piled onto the dining table in the big room. A bucket and mop stood in the corner, and there was a lingering scent of disinfectant.

"Whoever was here has made a very thorough job of cleaning up," said Amélie. "Not the way most tourists leave a holiday rental."

"It could be a way to get rid of fingerprints and DNA." Bruno began taking photos with his phone, including a close-up of the stove, fed by a bottle of Calor gas.

"Why are you taking a photo of that?" she asked.

"It's an old dodge to avoid paying the *taxe d'habitation*," he replied. "It's easily removed, and if there's no working stove to cook on, you can say the place is not fit for residence and avoid the tax. But now we've got a date-stamped photo to say the place is liable for tax, and it will be interesting to see if he's registered it as a rental property."

The barn was also left unlocked with the key in the door and newly laundered bedding piled onto each bed. The bathroom had been thoroughly cleaned, taps and porcelain shining. The waste bins in each kitchen had been emptied and so had the dustbins outside, all of them smelling of bleach. Bruno recalled seeing back at the road junction a group of big rubbish bins where the locals were supposed to leave their garbage in yellow sacks provided by the local council. They might not have been cleared yet.

Bruno called J-J to explain what he'd found. He was about to suggest a forensics team might find some trace of the inhabitants that had been overlooked in the cleaning, which was itself suspicious, when J-J interrupted.

"You'd better stay there until I arrive," he said. "I just had the brigadier on. The Israelis are getting excited. Apparently this woman was high up on their watch list, Jewish but a pro-Palestinian militant, lives with an Israeli Arab who's also on their list. They've asked for her DNA and any information we have on her movements."

"When you say 'they,' do you mean their embassy?" Bruno asked.

"Not anymore. It began with the embassy, but now it's Israel direct. I'll let the brigadier know about this *gîte* you've found and then come join you. Can you find out who owns this place? We'd better call them in."

Bruno supplied Vaugier's name and number, suggesting they tell Vaugier only that there had been an anonymous tip-off of a sighting of the dead woman. "It looks like this guy's main concern is to stay below the radar of the tax people," he added. "There's no sign of any Internet connection here, but there's a good cell-phone signal. You might want to get the phone records from the local tower."

By the time J-J and his forensics team arrived, Bruno had established from the *mairie* at Meyrals that the house was not registered as a holiday rental, and no *taxe d'habitation* had been paid on it. He'd also called Amandine, who confirmed that she had regularly cleaned the place between rentals the previous summer. He'd also found two clear sets of what looked like recent tire tracks on a patch of bare ground beside a nearby pigeon tower.

J-J arrived in convoy, his own car followed by the forensics van, which was in turn followed by a *gendarmerie* van from which a worried-looking Vaugier descended. The rear of the parade was brought up by a private car that contained the mayor of Meyrals and his town's treasurer.

Once the forensics crew had booted up and put on their "snowman" paper overalls, J-J took Vaugier and Bruno aside.

"Don't bother lying, you're in enough trouble already," he told Vaugier. "Who's been renting this place most recently?"

"A woman, middle-aged, sounded like a Parisian," Vaugier replied at once. "She answered the ad I have on Le Bon Coin, the website. I met her here at the *gîte* just over a week ago. She rented it for two weeks and paid cash, five hundred euros in fifties. She was driving a silver Peugeot. I took the number, just a precaution."

He took a notebook from his pocket and read out the number, adding that the *département* number was six-zero. That meant the Oise, but to Bruno and J-J that meant almost certainly the car had been rented, since the Oise was the cheapest *département* for registration, and most of the rental companies had a base there. J-J called over one of his detectives, handed him the registration number and asked him to track it down.

"Not a bad start, but you're lying about the money," said J-J, turning back to Vaugier. "This is a four-bedroom place, even out of season you wouldn't let this out for two-fifty a week, and you look to me like the kind of suspicious little bastard who'd want some security deposit against damages. So let's start again, shall we?"

"She gave me five hundred for the rental and then a deposit of five hundred, to be returned if she left early."

"Did she come here alone?"

"Yes, alone in the silver Peugeot."

"And you never dropped by to see how she was doing?"

Vaugier shook his head. "Never."

"Did she give you a name?"

"Marie Dubois. That's how she signed the rental agreement."

J-J snorted and Bruno could not repress a smile. That was so much the kind of common name an adulterous couple might use that it had become a cliché of TV comedies.

"It's not funny," Vaugier protested. "She even showed me an ID card with that name on it, and her photo."

Vaugier handed J-J an envelope containing a single-page rental contract with an indecipherable signature at the bottom, the name hand-printed below in neat capital letters, along with an address on avenue Leclerc in Paris, the Montparnasse district. Bruno took note of the address and called the security number for France-Télécom. He was not surprised to learn that the address did not exist.

"Chef," called out the detective who had been checking the rental cars. "It's a Europcar, a five-seater Peugeot Traveller rented at Gare de l'Est in Paris by a woman with the name of Marie Dubois. They took a photocopy of her license and ID card. She paid with a BNP Paribas credit card in the same name. I've got the account number, and I'll check it out. The ID card was also issued in Paris, so I'll check on that, too."

J-J and Bruno exchanged glances. Forgeries of ID cards and driving licenses were not difficult to obtain but indicated some familiarity with the criminal underworld or a connection to serious intelligence networks. Establishing a fake bank account and credit card was more difficult in these days of routine identity checks against money laundering.

"Did you see this woman again after that one time when she paid you?" J-J asked Vaugier.

"No, never."

"Did you ever hear from her, by phone or e-mail or note?"

"Again no, I did not have contact with her by any method. The only time I heard from her was when she called about the ad on the website and then when she paid me." He pulled out his phone and scrolled back through a week or so of calls to a number he read out. It began with 06, a cell phone.

Bruno called France-Télécom security again, gave the new

phone number and the reply came quickly. It was a pay-as-you-go phone bought at a store at the Gare de l'Est in Paris along with a prepaid phone card for forty euros. Because of the new regulations requiring all such phones to be registered, Bruno learned it was one of two such phones that had been bought by one Marie Dubois, and a photocopy of her ID card was on file.

"Did you ever see anyone else here?" J-J went on. "Maybe you just drove past it once or twice, just to keep an eye on the place?"

"No, I never came by," Vaugier insisted.

"So you were not at all concerned about your property?"

"It's not my property. It belongs to my wife."

"Did she come by, just checking that all was well?"

"Not to my knowledge."

"Right," said J-J. "You stay here and have a nice friendly chat with the mayor and the treasurer about your tax status until my forensic experts have checked the buildings, and then we'll walk you around and you can tell me if anything is missing or out of place. Then we'll take you to my headquarters in Périgueux where you can look through a lot of photographs of suspected terrorists."

"Terrorists?" Vaugier's voice went so high it was almost a shriek.

"Didn't I tell you?" J-J asked. "It must have slipped my mind. We're holding you under the emergency regulations on suspicion of aiding terrorists. You must be aware of your duty to register tenants of your property at the *mairie*. You'll have some explaining to do about your taxes, and since this property is in your wife's name, we'll have to bring her in as well. What's her name and where do I find her?"

"Marie-France. At her clinic in Périgueux, she's a psychologist, uses her maiden name, Duteiller."

J-J's eyebrows rose, and Bruno's head snapped around as he

heard the name. Marie-France Duteiller was the psychologist behind the allegations of pedophilia at the Mussidan church orphanage and the charge that J-J was dragging his feet in the inquiry.

"So she's your wife?" J-J said, a slow smile spreading over his face. "That's interesting. I've had the pleasure of meeting her in another context."

Chapter 15

Vaugier had been driven away with J-J, and Bruno was just apologizing to Amélie for abandoning her, when his phone rang. The special green light was glowing, which meant that it was someone on the brigadier's secure circuit.

"Bruno," came the familiar voice. "You seem to attract this sort of trouble."

"Yes, sir," Bruno replied, the safe and noncommittal reply that all soldiers learn within weeks of joining an army.

"Do you know the difference between Mossad and Shin Bet?"

"No, sir." That was not wholly accurate. He knew that Mossad was Israel's international intelligence service and Shin Bet dealt with domestic security, but that was all he recalled, so a confession of ignorance seemed in order.

"We've got them both on our necks thanks to your château-climbing woman. Which means I have our interior ministry and our foreign ministry and the Elysée all pressing me for information. Any developments?"

Bruno explained about Leah Wolinsky being seen at the *gîte,* the van hired at the station in Paris, the phones and the false ID and driver's license. J-J's forensics team was still at work, trying to work out exactly how many people had been staying at the *gîte.*

"I've faxed the usual letter to your mayor, so you'll be coming under my orders again, Bruno. What are your plans?"

"I'm going to start by searching the nearest garbage depository. The bins here are empty, so they must have dumped the contents. Then I was going to visit the Laundromats in the area to see if I can find who did the wash of all the bedding."

"Good man. Let me know if you need more manpower, and I'll get some gendarmes assigned to you."

"If they could handle the garbage, sir, I'll do the Laundromats. They may need to liaise with J-J's forensics team."

"Very well. I'll take care of that. Do you think this woman's associates are still in your area?"

"Hard to say, sir," Bruno replied. He was thinking that forged ID papers seemed extreme for simply daubing some graffiti on a château wall. "I think it would be safer to assume that whatever mission they came here to carry out might not yet be complete. The most obvious security concern will be the opening of Lascaux IV, but that's not expected until much later in the year."

"Right. It could have been a reconnaissance mission, but then why draw attention to themselves with this graffiti? When you can, draw me a timeline for this woman, when she first booked this *gîte*, when she hired the car, when she died and so on—whatever else you can scrape up. The Israelis have yet to tell me much about her. We don't even know when she left their country or who she was traveling with. There are how many bedrooms at this *gîte*?"

"Four, sir, all double bedrooms, but three of the beds only had one pillowcase, which suggests one couple and three singles. The car she hired was a five-seater, and J-J already has it on the priority watch list. Forensics should be able to tell us more, but so far we have no idea who the others might be other than the name of her Palestinian boyfriend, Husayni. Did you know she was pregnant?"

"Yes, J-J made sure I was aware of that detail, something that the Israelis did not know, so we were able to surprise them. That name Husayni could be useful. Anything else about her or her companions you can find out, let me know right away."

The brigadier hung up in his usual brusque way, and Amélie looked up from the cell phone to which she seemed umbilically attached.

"I'm going to need your printer again," she said. "I've found more material about this Wolinsky woman, stuff she wrote about the Palestinian issue but mainly her historical work. She got her master's at Nice in international studies and a doctorate from the Sorbonne on Islamic settlements in eighth-century France. I've downloaded a copy. She was fluent in Arabic."

"So she was a historian?"

"She wanted to be, but she had trouble getting a job in Israel. My friend from the Geneva peace conference said she was very bitter about it, claimed she was blacklisted because of her politics and could only make a living by working as an archaeologist. And Jenny, the American friend of Leah, has promised to send me some article Leah was writing."

Bruno dropped Amélie at the *mairie* and told the mayor's secretary that she would be using his office printer, and then began telephoning the region's Laundromats, asking about people bringing in a large number of towels and bedding on Monday. After calling the ones listed in the phone directory in Les Eyzies, Le Bugue and Sarlat, he found a place in St. Cyprien where the attendant recalled that a middle-aged Arab speaking what he called "educated French" had taken over four big washing machines on Monday morning. A second man, also looking to be Arab, had helped him carry in the load. And yes, came the answer to Bruno's query, the Laundromat was open late so they'd had a security camera installed.

He drove there at once with Amélie, calling J-J on the way, picked up the security tape and drove it directly to Périgueux. Within the hour, recognizable images of both men had been copied, digitalized and sent on to the brigadier, who in turn forwarded them to the Israelis. But first, the brigadier's team began running the images, along with Leah Wolinsky's photo, through the facial recognition program in the surveillance tapes that had been collected from the Gare de l'Est. Since the first terrorist attacks in Paris, there had been a crash program to install digitalized surveillance cameras in public buildings, sensitive areas and transport hubs around France.

By the time Bruno and Amélie returned to his office in St. Denis, Leah's arrival at the Paris station had been spotted on the tapes as she came up the stairs from the Métro. She had then spent an hour alone with a book at a café in the station until she was joined by the older man from the Laundromat tapes, who arrived on a train from Cologne. Her greeting was affectionate, and they held hands as they went to a different café in the big square outside the station, where they were later joined by the second man from the Laundromat. He was much younger and had arrived on another German train, this time from Frankfurt. Two more young men in hoodies then joined them.

Unknown to Bruno, a vast machine of international cooperation was then triggered into action as the images and travel dates of the targeted individuals were launched into a system of global databases that contained in total close to a million names. Many of them had no more connection to terrorism than a link through family, through school or places of study or through travel records that had been deemed interesting by the algorithms that had been programmed to track specific routes and patterns.

The databases included Palestinians, Syrians, Iraqis, Kurds, Turks, Uighurs, Moroccans, Algerians, Colombians, Chechens, Afghans, Pakistanis, Irishmen, Sikhs, Bangladeshis, Indonesians and now elderly Japanese, Germans and Italians from the various Red Army groups of the 1970s. The most recent additions to these expanding lists were an ever-increasing proportion of British, French, German and American citizens of Islamic origin.

The brigadier first made contact with his counterparts in Germany's BND, the Bundesnachrichtendienst, and asked them to track the movements of the men Leah Wolinsky had met and any associates they may have encountered. As a routine, the photos were then forwarded by the brigadier's staff to a series of organizations, beginning with the French joint antiterrorism center, and then to Europol, to the European Union's Intelligence Analysis Centre and to the office of the EU antiterrorism coordinator in Brussels. They went also to the British National Counter Terrorism Security Office, with whom the French worked closely, to the Global Counterterrorism Forum and to the National Counterterrorism Center in the United States. They also went to the Shin Bet liaison officer at the Israeli embassy in Paris.

There was too much data for any individual service to handle. The three thousand officers of Britain's MI5 and the thirty-five thousand staff of the FBI, let alone the handful of officials at the EU's various coordination centers, could not begin to trawl through the hundreds of thousands of data points that the computers logged each hour. Instead, the task was left to the algorithms to narrow down the mass to the significant, and from the significant to the seriously interesting. And at that point, a handful of extraordinary individuals took over.

One was a legendary woman in Paris, a veteran of the old Renseignements Généraux police intelligence service, who had a unique knack of recognizing a face from the shape of an ear and a hint of jawline. In Tel Aviv, an elderly Jewish man, who had been born in Poland and taken to Israel from a Cyprus refugee camp while a babe in arms, had a photographic memory for Arabs with terrorist connections. In London, a Chinese woman, formerly in the criminal intelligence section of the Hong Kong police, could even identify people from gestures and the way they walked. There were two brothers in Pullach, Germany, former members of the East German Stasi, who had an uncanny ability in facial and pattern recognition that allowed them to make connections between suspects. After years of coordination and meetings at conferences on counterterrorism, experts like these had developed their own informal networks to communicate with one another.

It was the elderly Israeli who identified the older man who had met Leah at the Gare de l'Est station as Saïd al-Husayni, a member of an influential and well-established Jerusalem family who had studied in Spain and was part of the Islamic history faculty at Birzeit University just outside Ramallah on the West Bank. The university, which had been closed by the Israeli occupying authorities for four years before the signing of the Oslo Accords, was closely watched by the Israelis. They had no record of Husayni having any political or radical links, though for the previous year he and Leah had been living together in Ramallah. Leah was on their watch list as a militant member of the Peace Now movement.

Yet for all the computer algorithms and surveillance powers of modern states, the most significant breakthrough came from Bruno's office in the St. Denis *mairie*. Working on her own smartphone, Amélie explained that she couldn't find anything in the usual databases about Marie Dubois using the date of birth on her ID card.

"What about health records, pharmacies?" Bruno asked when

he returned from delivering the surveillance tape. "If she's French, she should at least have a *carte vitale.*" Like every French citizen, he carried the small green card in his pocket that took care of most medical bills.

"I'll try it, but if she doesn't have an ID card . . ." Amélie sighed but began working her phone. After a few minutes she looked up.

"There's something interesting about this Marie Dubois woman. She's supposed to be in a psychiatric hospital in Paris, the Pitié-Salpêtrière."

She had tried the health ministry database, which was still under construction. But since Marie had been included in a ministry survey looking into the costs and causes of long-term residential care, her name and details were on file. She had been a patient at the hospital, one of the largest in Europe, for the previous six years.

"And two years ago our Leah Wolinsky was briefly a patient in the same hospital, under the same specialist, diagnosed with severe depression when she was finishing her doctorate," Amélie added. "Do you think she could somehow have stolen Marie's ID card? Maybe she claimed it had been lost and applied for a new one in Marie's name?"

Bruno called the brigadier at once to pass on the information and then sat back to read the printouts Amélie had collated from her research into Leah's academic work. Her thesis was on the Arab occupation of southern France in the eighth century, after the Muslim invasion of Spain in A.D. 711. Within five years, the Visigoth kingdom of Spain had been pushed back to the Pyrenees, and the Arab armies had then poured through the mountains to conquer the province of southern Gaul known as Septimania. Bruno sat up in surprise when he learned that for the next forty years they retained control of much of southern France from their base at the old Roman city of Narbonne.

"I had no idea they were in France for so long," Bruno murmured, almost to himself.

"Nor did I," said Amélie. "Did you get to the bit about the Arabic words that stayed in the language? I never knew that our *chemise* came from their *qamisa*. Nor that the town of Le Bugue, just up the river, came from the Arabic *al-buca*. Apparently it means 'station' or 'military post.'"

Bruno was skimming through the index and then recalled that someone had once told him that in any academic publication it was important to read the acknowledgments. Leah Wolinsky had mentioned "two scholars to whom I am indebted for their support and their comments on an early draft of this thesis, the historian of al-Andaluz, Saïd al-Husayni, and the French medievalist Auguste Dumesnil."

Horst had introduced Dumesnil, the man who followed the Benedictine rule who lived in nearby Sarlat. Bruno tried the number for him he found in the phone directory. When Dumesnil answered, he reminded him of their acquaintance and said he was trying to confirm the identity of a woman recently found dead who was thought to be a former pupil of his, Leah Wolinsky.

"Leah, dead?" came the startled reply. "But I saw her just last week and she looked in excellent health. And she wasn't my pupil, not in any formal sense."

"What day was that?" Bruno asked.

"Let me see, Friday afternoon, at a time when I had no classes. She came with Saïd Husayni, whom I was delighted to meet. I knew his work on the Moorish period in Spain, and of course his brilliant treatise on Avicenna. He speaks excellent French. But what happened to Leah? Was it some kind of accident?"

"She fell to her death from the wall of Commarque."

"What? But when she came we talked of Commarque and of my hopes from the new excavations. And of course about this latest nonsense about Iftikhar's famous testament. Leah was very worked up about that, and I must say I find it very hard to believe that it really exists. But are you sure this woman is Leah? You said the body was thought to be hers. *Mon Dieu,* Commarque—I was just there, when I met you."

"I know, I should have shown you the photo of the body then," said Bruno. "It was my mistake, I'm sorry. I should also have taken you beyond the château so you could see the letters we think Leah was painting on the wall when she fell. They were *I-F-T-I*, which could be the beginning of 'Iftikhar.' I need to pick your brains about that. At the time I had no idea you knew her, not until I read the reference to you in her thesis. Since you are the only person in this area who knew her, perhaps I could come and show you the photo and then take you to the morgue in Bergerac. We need someone who knew her formally to identify the body."

After a long moment of silence, Dumesnil agreed to see him that evening at seven, when his choir practice should have finished. He was teaching the cathedral choir to sing Gregorian chants. Bruno ended the call and immediately phoned J-J to say that he should be able to provide a definitive identification of Leah from someone who had known her. Then Bruno turned to Amélie.

"It will be after the workday, but if you're interested in meeting a medieval scholar who knew Leah, I'm going to see him in Sarlat at seven," he said. "You remember, we met him at Commarque. It seems that his expertise does not stop at the Templars. He also teaches Gregorian chant."

Amélie stared at him with an odd expression. He couldn't tell whether it was confusion or surprise.

"Gregorian chant? In Sarlat?" She paused, looking at him solemnly. "Yes, I'll certainly come. Meanwhile, I have a phone number for Leah's American friend. It turns out that she's another historian and she's currently in Paris, doing some research at the national archives. She's writing a book about Paris during the war."

Bruno dialed the number, and Jenny Shindler answered as she ate a sandwich lunch in a park just off the rue des Francs Bourgeois. Her initial surprise at his call was complicated by the need to finish chewing. He explained in English that he was following up on the death of her friend Leah.

"I saw it on social media," she replied in good French. "Some kind of climbing accident at a medieval château, which doesn't sound like Leah. Why call me? We weren't that close and we parted on bad terms."

"Her death looks suspicious. She was climbing with somebody who left her dead and took away the paint can and climbing rope she had with her," he replied. "I was hoping you might know something about her traveling companions."

"I didn't even know she was in France. She'd been living in Ramallah for some time with an Arab professor, Saïd Husayni, and I know they were hoping to have kids. I can't think who else she might have been with. Maybe someone from his family. Where was the château where she died?"

Bruno explained the location of Commarque and its Crusades and Templar connections, and the letters she had apparently been daubing.

"Oh, no," Shindler exclaimed. "Don't tell me she was still on that crazy trail. That's what we argued about just a few weeks ago. She wanted me to translate an article she'd written and get it into the American press, or at least circulated on social media, about the Testament of Iftikhar and Jerusalem. I told her it was just a distraction from the real issues of today. She sent me a very angry reply."

"Do you still have the article she sent you?" Bruno asked, trying to keep the excitement out of his voice.

"I never got it. She sent me an e-mail and I skimmed it and told her to forget it. I wasn't interested and no one else in the peace movement would give a damn. We're focused on what's going down today, not what happened a thousand years ago. I should still have her e-mail."

"Could you possibly forward it to me?" He gave her his e-mail address at the *mairie*.

"The least I can do, I guess. We got on pretty well until this Jerusalem business blew up. I'm looking for the e-mail now."

Bruno heard the sound of laptop keys being tapped and then her voice, "Coming through now."

"Would you have any photos of Leah you could send, or of her friend al-Husayni?"

"Leah and me, yes, from when she visited me in the States, but not of him. I'll send them. You might find more on her Facebook page; she used that a lot. Do you really think her fall was no accident?"

"You might help us establish what really happened," he said as his computer beeped with an incoming e-mail. He looked to be sure it was the right one and sent it to his printer. "I have the e-mail, thank you. I'll let you know what we conclude and thanks again for your help, mademoiselle."

"'Dear Jenny,'" he read, the words written in French.

I'm really depressed and worried about the way things are going here. The Peace Now movement is on the ropes, so many of the old stalwarts seem to have given up or been intimidated and now the academic row over Jerusalem has entered a new phase. I told you about the way that Israeli and Arab scholars have been arguing like a bunch

*of schoolkids about who first built Jerusalem and whether
it was really significant to the early Islamic faith. I can't
prove it yet but I'm pretty sure that there's some dirty work
around a long-lost document that we only know of at second
and third hand. Some people tried to sound a warning by
painting this graffiti, photo attached, on the walls of a castle
here that was linked to the Crusaders and to the Templars,
thinking with all the interest in the Templars it would be
sure to make a stir. Photos have been sent to newspapers and
history magazines around the world but so far it has been
virtually ignored. Perhaps you could help get the word out
in the U.S. I'm going to try again in France.*

*First, some background you'll need. Pro-Israeli scholars
(and see the link I attach to the article in* Middle East
Quarterly*) suggest that Jerusalem only became an issue
for Arabs when it had some special political status. After
all, Jerusalem is never mentioned in the Koran, but there
are some seven hundred references to the city in the Jewish
Bible, the one Christians call the Old Testament. The Dome
of the Rock mosque on the Temple Mount was built by the
Damascus-based Umayyad dynasty in the decade after* A.D.
*690 when they were faced with Zubayr's revolt in Mecca,
the holiest center of Islam. The Umayyads deliberately
built up Jerusalem as a rival, pouring in money for new
buildings in an attempt to give it equal standing with
Mecca. In the Koran 17:1 you will find the phrase referring
to Muhammad's famous night journey, or dream:*

*"Glory to He who took His servant by night from the
Sacred Mosque to the furthest mosque."*

*There is really no proof that this "al-Aqsa Mosque" (the
furthest mosque) refers to Jerusalem, where there was no
mosque in Muhammad's lifetime. But the Umayyads built*

*a mosque in Jerusalem and called it the al-Aqsa Mosque,
in a transparent attempt to make the direct connection with
the Prophet Muhammad. Once the Umayyad dynasty fell in
A.D. 750 and the center of the caliphate moved to Baghdad
under the Abassid dynasty, Jerusalem sank once more into
obscurity—until it was brought back into prominence in
1099 when the city was first captured by the Crusaders.*

*Iftikhar ad-Daula was the governor of Jerusalem when
the Crusaders took the city. Iftikhar retreated to the citadel
and negotiated freedom for himself, his family and his
personal guard—while the rest of the inhabitants were
slaughtered, Jews, Muslims and local Christians alike. The
brutality of the Crusaders was extraordinary; one of their
monks reported that their horses were up to their fetlocks in
blood. So it is all the more surprising that they agreed to let
the enemy commander and his family and his picked troops
all go free. Bribery alone can hardly explain it since the
Crusaders could have taken whatever gold or jewels he had.
He must have offered them something very special in return
for his life.*

*The agreement Iftikhar reached with the Crusaders was
written down, the celebrated Testament of Iftikhar, and
entrusted by Baldwin, the first Christian king of Jerusalem,
to the Templars. Iftikhar allegedly affirmed that the city was
of no religious significance to Islam, and that its reputation
had been an invention of the Umayyads to shore up their
religious and political credentials. The testament then
disappeared, if it ever existed.*

*You can imagine the political impact today if this
long-lost testament were to surface, which I believe is about
to happen. But I suspect it would be a very careful and
professional forgery. That is why the graffiti was painted*

*onto the castle and why honest historians have to do
something similar in Europe and the U.S., where such a
warning would not be ignored. Please feel free to show this
to any medieval scholars you know.*

*You know my own views. I seek a two-state solution, for
Israel and for Palestine, with a shared capital of Jerusalem,
and the old city itself under international control, open
to all and shared between all faiths, Jews, Muslims and
Christians—and Buddhists and Confucians as well, come
to that. I know some Jewish extremists accuse the Peace
Now movement of being traitors to Israel. This is untrue.
I love Israel, and love it so much that I think the only
way to ensure its future is to share it with our Palestinian
neighbors. Otherwise I fear that we will disappear, just like
the old Crusader kingdom. I'll do anything to prevent that
from happening. Yours in peace and love, Leah.*

Bruno reread the final paragraph and then looked across at
Amélie, who was reading the printout. "Leah strikes me as an
impressive woman and she could be right about the political
impact of this Testament of Iftikhar emerging now."

"I agree," said Amélie. "But what does this mean for these
other men who were with her at the *gîte*? Were they trying to
sound the same warning as Leah about this testament? Or is
something else going on?"

"We know Leah wasn't alone at Commarque when she fell,"
Bruno replied. "But who would want to stop her from painting
that graffiti?" He paused. "I'd better forward this to J-J and the
brigadier before we go see the historian in Sarlat."

"Dumesnil?" Her voice was clipped, and Bruno glanced up,
surprised.

"Do you know this guy?" he asked.

"I'm sorry. I didn't mean anything." She turned away and began putting her papers together. "What time should we leave?"

He ignored the question and decided to press her. "Have you come across this Dumesnil before, perhaps in another context?"

"It's not that. I'm just upset because of that e-mail from Leah, a voice from the grave." She snapped the catches of her bag shut and then looked at him, a challenge in her eyes.

Bruno was sure there was more to this than Amélie was prepared to admit. That reminded him to make the usual courtesy call to his colleagues in Sarlat to explain that he was coming onto their turf to see a possible witness. Then he forwarded Leah's e-mail to J-J and the brigadier, adding a brief note about its source.

Chapter 16

Bruno was deeply attached to the old town of Sarlat, thinking of it as one of those magical places, like Notre-Dame de Paris or Mont St. Michel or the battlefield of Verdun, where French history came immediately and thrillingly alive. It was not simply that the heart of the old town was virtually unchanged since the early seventeenth century. The narrow streets and crooked alleys, the ancient stone buildings with their Renaissance windows, all made him think of d'Artagnan and his fellow Musketeers, plumed hats and rapiers. Passing the house of the La Boétie family reminded him that Montaigne himself had strolled on these same ancient stones, cultivating the friendship that had inspired his immortal essays.

A link that went back much further, to the abbey from Charlemagne's time and the medieval tombs built into the walls of the town, intrigued Bruno even more, along with the strange cone-shaped stone building known as the Lantern of the Dead. It had been built to mark the visit of Bernard de Clairvaux, the Cistercian monk who had written the rules of the Templars and whose preaching had launched the Second Crusade. He recalled a carving on the Lantern's wall of a horse and two iron crosses, a traditional sign of the Templars. Odd, Bruno thought, how the theme of the Templars kept recurring.

"I've seen it," Amélie said curtly when Bruno offered to show her around in the ten minutes before his appointment. "My cousin lives here. She showed me round."

Sorry you weren't more impressed, Bruno thought, looking at her curiously. He'd grown accustomed to Amélie and her usually sunny nature and had developed a sense of respect verging on awe for her research skills with a computer. Something seemed to be upsetting her, and he hoped her testy moment would soon pass.

He took a roundabout path to Auguste Dumesnil's home on the rue des Consuls in order to pass by the cathedral, hoping that he'd still be rehearsing his choir. As they climbed the steps, the sound of a chant became audible, wholly fitting to the ambience of this ancient place. He and Amélie stood at the back of the church, moved by sacred music that was centuries old yet seemed to embody the very spirit of holiness. Then Amélie craned forward, staring at the choir. A moment later she moved to one side for a clearer view, apparently looking for someone. She bit her lip, took her phone from her bag and slipped outside the church.

Bruno edged back to the slightly open door to hear her say, "Is she there?" Then came a pause as Amélie listened to a reply. And then he heard her say: "You're watching her play basketball? Is she winning? Give her my love."

Bruno stepped back as the door opened, and Amélie came back inside the church, her phone disappearing into her handbag. They stood at the back of the church as the music swelled around them. Bruno was surprised to see the choirmaster was a woman. When the chant stopped, she thanked the singers before turning away, leaving the members of the choir to collect their bags and coats. Bruno followed her and asked where he might find Dumesnil. She simply shrugged and said he had failed to turn up.

Dumesnil lived on the second floor of an old building whose doorway was open, leading to a wide spiral staircase of stone. Bruno found a light switch and began climbing the steps. The door to Dumesnil's apartment was closed, and Bruno's knock brought no response. There was no sign of a bell. Amélie leaned across him and tried the door handle. It opened, and the now-familiar sound of a Gregorian chant seeped out from within. He called out Dumesnil's name, but there was no reply. Looking through the doorway he could see tumbled books and an overturned chair in the corridor.

"Police," he called out and went inside, telling Amélie to remain where she was. He located a light switch inside the apartment, but it wasn't working. He was instantly struck by the bitter scent of burned cooking along with something else, perhaps hair or cloth.

He opened each door he came to, but every room was dark except for one whose double doors were partly open, a faint light leaking out through them. Inside, a sputtering candelabra revealed more books scattered on the floor and furniture overturned. Bruno had a sudden sense of having stepped into another century. Walls that were not covered in bookshelves were draped in old tapestries, hanging in folds. The floor was bare wood, great planks almost a meter wide but smooth underfoot as if trodden by generations of feet.

Before one of the tapestries was a life-size wooden statue of a Madonna standing on a plinth, gazing down with one hand raised in blessing upon a prie-dieu which had an unlit candle at each corner. Bruno took the two long candles, lit them from the dying candelabra, left one in place and took the other to help him look around the room. The sound of chanting was coming from a stone archway whose ironbound wooden door was just ajar. Now the smell of burning was stronger, though there was no flickering light that a fire might give. He pushed the door open farther, calling out once more, "Police."

There he stepped into a room that captured the fire and torments of hell. A gagged and naked figure, head sunk down on his chest and his arms bound behind him, was slumped awkwardly and bent almost double on a wooden chair. The man's knees seemed almost as high as his head, his buttocks having fallen through what had been the woven cane seat of the chair. Bruno saw the stub of burned-out candle overturned beneath the chair and realized what had caused the smell of burning and how terribly Dumesnil must have suffered.

He could detect no pulse in the neck but used his pocketknife to cut through the strip of cloth that gagged the man. His mouth was stuffed with something. Bruno pulled out a sodden sock. Then he put his wristwatch under the man's nostrils and saw the faintest misting. The poor devil was still breathing.

"Call an ambulance now," he shouted to Amélie, turning to see that she had followed him and was standing in the doorway, her hand to her mouth and her eyes wide in horror. She seemed frozen in place.

He strode forward and pushed her out of the room. Then he used his own phone to call for the *urgences,* giving his name, rank and location and said the victim had very severe burns but was still alive. Once they had confirmed the address, he hung up and called Fabiola's cell phone to ask what he should do until the ambulance arrived.

"Third degree, flesh and some muscle looks as if it has been burned away," he said when she asked how it looked.

"Remove any constrictions like tight clothing, elevate the heart above the site of the burn and cover the burn with a cool, moist cloth," she replied. "If the victim's breathing is very faint, try mouth-to-mouth. Where's the burn?"

"Buttocks and genitals, mainly the backs of his thighs. I think he was tortured."

"*Mon Dieu*. You have to keep him breathing. I'll call a colleague at the hospital in Sarlat to warn them what's coming. There's a man there who is good with burns, and I'll get them to call him in."

Bruno returned to the room, slammed his boot into the crossbars of the chair and then pulled away the chair legs. It was the only way he could see to free the man. Only when the buttocks came free did the legs extend, and Bruno could see the horrific extent of the burns.

"Find the kitchen or bathroom and bring me a clean, cool, moist cloth," he shouted at Amélie. This time she complied. By the time Bruno had the victim draped facedown on a couch, his legs on the floor so the heart was elevated, she returned with the cloth and draped it over the burned area.

"Thanks, you're doing well," Bruno said. "Now can you help turn his head?"

She did so, saying, "There's a pool of fresh vomit on the kitchen floor." Bruno ignored her and began giving Dumesnil mouth-to-mouth resuscitation, rewarded after what seemed to be a long, long time with a faint groan and then a cough from the victim, followed at once by the thunder of booted feet climbing the stairs and a call of *"Urgences."*

"Keep his head up," Bruno said to Amélie as he went to the door to guide the ambulance men, explaining what he'd found and what he'd done.

"You did right," one of them said. He took one look at the victim and pulled a portable oxygen mask from his kit bag as well as a large lamp that lit up the room. A second man unrolled the stretcher he had brought with him. They applied the oxygen mask before checking the victim's blood pressure. Then they rolled him onto the stretcher, strapped him facedown and took him out and down the stairs. Bruno followed with the lamp and helped them to load the stretcher into the ambulance. He gave the driver his cell-phone number and asked to be kept informed of Dumesnil's condition.

He climbed back up the stairs and looked around the entrance hall of the apartment for the fuse box, opened it and shined his own flashlight onto the fuses. The orange master fuse had been turned off. So what was the source of the Gregorian chant he could hear? He turned on the fuse and a light came on in one of the side rooms. He tried the hall light switch, and it worked.

"Amélie?" he called. "Can you locate the source of the music?"

"In here," she replied, and he followed her voice into a room that might have been a monk's cell. The outer wall was stone, the others whitewashed. A single iron bed stood in a corner, topped by the thinnest mattress Bruno had ever seen. Above it hung an icon of a stylized female head surrounded by a golden halo. It looked antique. At first Bruno thought there was some kind of white carpet until he realized that sheafs of paper had been scattered over the floor, apparently from the single, waist-high bookcase, which must have held manuscripts rather than books. Perched atop the bookcase was a small tape recorder of the kind Philippe Delaron carried for his interviews. That was the source of the music.

"Battery driven," said Amélie, following his gaze. She was standing at a small table that seemed to be Dumesnil's desk. A fountain pen lay beside a thin pile of writing paper which looked handmade, the old-fashioned kind that was produced by one of the restored paper mills at Couze, Bruno thought.

"He was writing a letter to some professor at the Sorbonne about this Testament of Iftikhar," she said, gesturing to a page that was half filled with neat handwriting. "I haven't touched anything."

Bruno nodded, looked into the kitchen and placed a chair over the vomit to preserve it from careless feet, thinking that the forensics team might be able to identify its owner's DNA. He pulled out his phone to tell J-J of Dumesnil's fate. He was told to remain in the apartment until J-J arrived.

"We're going to be stuck here for some time," he told Amélie. "Do you want to call for a sandwich or a pizza to be delivered? We have to stay here until J-J gets here, half an hour or more, and then I may have to wait until the forensics team arrives."

"I couldn't eat, not after seeing that. What a terrible thing to do to someone, to anyone. I'd just like to stay here with you."

He nodded, thinking she didn't have much choice. He pulled out his phone again and called the commissariat of police in Sarlat to explain what had happened, thankful that he'd made the courtesy call to them earlier. The duty officer took down the details and promised to send a town cop to guard the entrance to Dumesnil's building.

"Any chance of starting some door-to-door inquiries?" Bruno asked. He was told that would need authorization by the town's police chief, a morose man named Messager who was a year or two from retirement. Bruno had Messager's mobile-phone number and found him at some mayoral reception where the background noise made it hard for Messager to hear what Bruno was saying. He waited until Messager had found somewhere quieter and then explained what had happened and that J-J would be taking over the case.

"Torture? Dumesnil? *Merde,* my wife's in his choir. She'll be distraught. It happened at his home, you say? We'll start the door-to-door inquiries right away. I'll be right there."

Bruno closed his phone and looked at Amélie. "Why not tell me what it was that was upsetting you about Dumesnil when you realized he wasn't at the church with the choir. I saw the expression on your face when you went out to use your phone."

"Why do you want to know?" Her voice was irritated rather than hostile.

"Do you know something about Dumesnil that I don't?"

She shook her head. "I was worried about something, but I think I was wrong. Let's leave it there."

"Sorry, this is a crime scene. I don't want to have to tell J-J that I think you're hiding something that could be relevant."

"*Merde*, Bruno. It's something personal, about my cousin's kid. She's fifteen and we're worried about her. She's had a sudden mood swing. Once she was always cheerful and bouncy, now she's silent and morose. Her mother is worried that she's a victim of something, maybe a pedophile. And since she's in Dumesnil's choir and he's such a weird guy . . ." She broke off and raised her hands in the air, an exaggerated shrug.

"Do you or her mother have any reason to suspect him, other than that he's fixated on the Middle Ages and seems to live like some fourteenth-century monk?" Bruno kept his voice calm and matter-of-fact.

She shook her head. "Not really."

"Don't you think your cousin's daughter is going through what sounds like a fairly typical adolescence?"

"It's not typical," she snapped. "I wasn't like that, nor was her mother, nor are other kids. It's as though Jojo suddenly fell into this deep depression. That's her name, Joséphine."

"Has your cousin asked Joséphine's teachers if her behavior has changed at school? Have her marks suddenly gotten worse?"

"Look, I don't know. And I accept that her mother and I have probably been making two and two add up to five, and after seeing what's just happened to Dumesnil I feel terrible about it. I'm sorry, all right?"

"The town's chief of police is on his way here. Do you want me to ask him, very discreetly, if there's any gossip about

Dumesnil? I doubt it, since I've just learned that his wife is in Dumesnil's choir, which wouldn't happen if there was any whiff of suspicion about him."

"No, let's drop it, okay?"

Amélie turned to leave, but Bruno said sharply, "You can't leave until the place is secure and you have given your statement. You work for the justice ministry, remember? We have to do this by the book."

She stopped, keeping her back turned to him, and let out a long, noisy sigh, as if her patience were being tried too far.

"Think about what just happened here," Bruno said. "You're missing the most important piece of evidence that might just support your suspicions. A man was tortured, but he was gagged so he couldn't speak. Why was that? Were his torturers not interested in what he might be able to tell them? So was the torture just a punishment, and an obviously sexual punishment, at that? Has some other relative of a young person jumped to conclusions and taken the law into his own hands?"

"The thought had crossed my mind." She turned to face him again.

"Well, it could also be that they were the same guys who met Leah in Paris. Perhaps they'd already questioned him, learned what they needed and then gagged him before leaving him to burn. Maybe they left the tape deck on to silence his screams, although I'd have thought he'd have been loud enough to bring a lot of attention. Why did they turn off the main fuse and do everything by candlelight? It looks to me as if they were making some kind of search, and I'd have thought that would be easier with the lights on. There are all sorts of odd things about this, as there often are at crime scenes. So we have a procedure. We try to build various scenarios that might explain what we've found, and then we look for further evidence to test those scenarios to see if they hold up. One scenario is that you could be right, that Dumesnil was a pervert and someone was determined to make him pay for it."

"The other scenario is that Leah was with some Middle Eastern terrorists who were desperate to learn something from him," she said.

"Exactly," said Bruno as voices from the hallway below and footsteps on the stairs signaled the arrival of Messager and others.

"A waiter in the restaurant on the corner was opening up just before six when he saw four strangers leaving this building," Messager began, slightly breathless from running up the stairs. "Three were wearing hoodies, and the bareheaded one looked like an Arab. Does that make any sense to you?"

"They could be the men we're looking for, connected to that woman who fell to her death at Commarque," Bruno said. He explained that the interior ministry had already launched an antiterrorism inquiry. Messager's office must have received photos that should be shown to the waiter downstairs as soon as possible.

"I thought this was about an attack on Dumesnil? What's he got to do with terrorism?"

"It's a long story," said Bruno, and explaining it took up the time before J-J's arrival. Halfway through, Bruno had a call from the ambulance driver: Dumesnil was in intensive care, but the doctor thought he'd live.

Chapter 17

"The trail has gone cold in Germany, at least for the moment," said the brigadier, his face enormous on the video screen. "We can't even track them from the stations where they boarded the trains. The Germans still have all sorts of legal limitations on security cameras and on storing the data. The good news is that we've identified one of the three unknown men. He's Mustaf al-Takriti, Iraqi, thirty-six years old and a serious threat. He's on the Americans' target list. Commissioner Perrault will explain."

The brigadier was in Paris, and Bruno was one of four men attending the videoconference in Périgueux. J-J was sitting on one side of a long table, flanked by Prunier, the police commissioner for the *département,* and by the regional general of the gendarmes. Bruno sat beside Prunier, feeling slightly dizzy, disconcerted by the way Brigadier Lannes's image kept jerking, slightly out of sync with his words coming out of the speaker. The brigadier adjusted something on the console before him, and the camera backed away from the close-up and revealed the others in the Paris studio.

Beside the brigadier was a saturnine, middle-aged man from France's joint antiterrorism center and an attractive and elegantly dressed young woman who made Bruno's heart turn over when he saw her on the screen. It was Isabelle, who, after leaving him and the Périgord, had worked first at the Ministry of the Interior in Paris, then at Eurojust in The Hague. She was introduced as the Eurojust official attached to the European Union's antiterrorism center, which sounded like another promotion for her.

Bruno kept his face impassive but his eyes were hungry for this sight of her. She was still too thin, as she had been since being shot in the thigh during an ambush of a shipload of illegal immigrants. There were dark shadows under her eyes, and her hair was longer, enough to be pulled back into a bun. Her outfit was plain, a black turtleneck sweater and a black leather jacket slung over the back of her chair. He wondered if she knew he was watching her, if the video screen at her end showed all four men at the table.

"Mustaf al-Takriti comes from Takrit, hometown of the late and unlamented Saddam Hussein, and is a member of his clan," Isabelle said. "He was a new recruit in the Mukhabarat, the Iraqi secret police, when Saddam was overthrown. His father, who was killed in the U.S. invasion in 2003, was a Mukhabarat general and close to Saddam. Somehow Mustaf became attached to the Sunni resistance movement against the Shia-dominated government in Baghdad. He's now part of ISIS."

Isabelle paused, and gently tapped two of her fingers against her lips as if thinking. Bruno sat bolt upright, and he felt his heart skip a beat. He knew that gesture. It had been her private signal to him when they were not alone that she wanted to be kissed. But was it for him? Did she even know he was there at the other end of the video link?

She went on to explain that ISIS was the Anglo-Saxon acronym for Islamic State of Iraq and Syria, but the jihadists called themselves Daesh. This was the Arabic acronym which asserted their claim to the whole of the Levant, which encompassed

Lebanon, Jordan, Palestine, including the territory of Israel, and North Africa, as well as Iraq and Syria. Daesh was committed to restoring the historic caliphate of the Ottoman Empire and ruling all Muslims around the world under strict Islamic law.

"Mustaf has been identified as a senior figure in the Daesh force that occupied Mosul and then took part in some of the mass executions that followed. There is a reliable British report that he was seen in Raqqa, Syria, three months ago. The Americans have circulated a photo that shows he was also present in Derna when that became the first Libyan town to declare allegiance to Daesh," Isabelle went on.

"The reason we have a good photo of Mustaf," said the saturnine Frenchman, "is that it comes from a mug shot taken by the Americans when they arrested him in Iraq in 2004. They put him in the Camp Bucca detention center. That was where he got to know all the other Daesh leaders. The Americans ran the place almost like a vacation resort, with first-class health care and the inmates were allowed to organize their own education and religious classes and even set up a soccer league, in which Mustaf was a star."

"Then the Americans decided to let them all go, when Washington switched tactics and began to back the Sunni resistance against the Shia," said the brigadier, poker-faced. These video-conferences were all recorded, Bruno knew, and the brigadier was being careful of the diplomatic etiquette. The Americans could be touchy about European colleagues criticizing their policy shifts in the Middle East.

He waved to Isabelle to continue, and she nodded coolly and spoke again without consulting her notes.

"Mustaf, as a member of the country's elite under Saddam Hussein, went to a special school in Baghdad where he learned English, so he is bilingual in that language. When he was a child, the family had a French-born nanny of Moroccan origin, who taught him French, subsequently returned to France when Mustaf went to university. She added that Mustaf also studied Russian at school. His French, she told us, was very good indeed.

"We know Mustaf has been with al-Husayni, the partner of the dead Israeli woman Leah Wolinsky, also known as Leah Ben-Ari. However, we are still trying to identify the other two members of the team," Isabelle went on. "The fact that the Israelis and the Americans don't have anything on these two may indicate that they are Europeans, either Muslim born or converts. We are checking, but our files on European sympathizers, even French nationals who went to fight with Daesh, are far from complete. I suggest we have to assume that they will be able to blend easily into European and possibly even into French society. So far, we know more than fifteen hundred French nationals who have gone to Iraq or Syria to join Daesh."

Isabelle stopped and turned to the brigadier. He nodded and said, "So Mustaf is a category one target for us. But he's a very skilled operator, fluent in our language and obviously dangerous. I'm sending down three teams of special forces, so you will have firepower on hand if you need it. We'll probably base them in Périgueux, Sarlat and Bergerac. Of course, we'd like to catch Mustaf alive. From now on we'll do these briefings daily, at eight in the morning with another, if required, at six in the evening. Any comments?"

Prunier raised his hand and asked about possible reinforcements for his police and for the gendarmes to help search for the vehicle Leah had rented. Whatever you need, the brigadier replied.

"This has now been formally listed as an antiterrorism inquiry," said the brigadier. "Someone from the specialist unit is drawing up a list of possible targets in your region, including nuclear power stations, chemical plants, dams and so on. I'll arrange for extra police from Bordeaux, Limoges and Toulouse. General, do you have space for them in your barracks?"

"We do. Commissaire Jalipeau has just reminded me to ask when can we expect the breakdown of calls from that cell-phone tower near the *gîte* where they stayed?"

"There's a team working on that and we should have something today," Isabelle replied. "I'll call J-J—I mean, Commissaire Jalipeau—as soon as it comes in. We also have a team going through all the other rail stations, ports and airports and entry points to see if we can find when and how those other two men in their hoodies came to France. Chef de Police Courrèges, I gather you will be coordinating the local search for whatever new base Mustaf has found. Will you need more staff?"

"Not immediately, Commissaire," Bruno replied, feeling slightly ridiculous at calling Isabelle by her rank when they had been lovers for a whole glorious summer. "If we do, I'll let you know. But we might want sniffer dogs on hand to detect explosives; that way they can patrol major tourist sites without arousing too much public concern. One other thing, this Testament of Iftikhar. I think we need to contact a medieval scholar who may be able to tell us more about its significance? There's a professor at the Sorbonne called Philippeau. It looks as though our Dumesnil was writing to him when Mustaf and his team came in to torture him. I can call Philippeau. May I suggest you liaise with the Israelis."

"I'll do it. I have an Israeli contact here," said the brigadier. "What do I tell them?"

"This so-called testament was obviously very important to Leah, and I can't think of a reason why they would want to torture Dumesnil except to try and learn more about that. Mustaf doesn't strike me as the scholarly type. Why else would Mustaf have this Palestinian history professor on a terrorist team? Imagine the political implications if this testament were to be found."

"Very well. Talk to the professor. We'll confer again tomorrow morning. By then, perhaps we can come up with some idea of what these men are after. Thank you, messieurs."

The screen went black, and the four men in Périgueux sat back in their chairs. J-J stood up, stretched and then opened the door to ask a secretary to arrange some coffee. He came back and sat at the head of the table.

"We can't talk if we're all lined up in a row like schoolkids," he said. "Come around where we can see each other so we can work out how to organize this."

"My gendarmes can take care of the road traffic watch, the garages and gas stations," said the general.

"My guys can handle the rail stations, hotels, restaurants and *gîtes* outside Bruno's turf," said Prunier with a grin as he glanced at Bruno. The two men had played on opposite sides of an army-versus-police rugby match more than ten years earlier and had become friends. "We all know Bruno has his own system in that valley of his. We'll also double-check all the Internet cafés and other public access points, as well as security cameras in supermarkets and ones covering mosques. We also have the telephone monitors on standby for all calls in Arabic. I'm briefing the media after this, so we'll have Mustaf's face on the front page of every newspaper and on TV. Am I missing anything?"

"Shops selling halal meat," said Bruno. "And motorbike and cycle rentals. They probably won't want to use that Peugeot Traveller they rented, unless they've already found a new set of wheels. They may be living rough, so we'd better check places selling sleeping bags and portable stoves."

"Is there any reason to believe they're still in the region?" asked J-J. "They had an hour and a half to get away from Sarlat before we could even ask for some roadblocks to be set up. They could be anywhere by now."

Prunier shook his head. "They came here to the Périgord

with this woman, Leah, for a reason. Maybe it had to do with the Iftikhar business, maybe not. But I think we can assume they went to see Dumesnil because they wanted to find out more about it from him. What I don't understand is why all four of them went and why they used torture. If al-Husayni had called on him alone, Dumesnil would have reason to welcome him as a scholar and fellow historian."

"Perhaps Mustaf doesn't trust al-Husayni out of his sight," said Bruno. "Al-Husayni doesn't seem to fit the usual profile of a Daesh militant."

"That could be right," said J-J. "But what's here in the Périgord that would attract a senior Daesh figure? This region is about food, wine, tourism, farming and historic monuments. The big opening of Lascaux IV is months away. That would be a target, but right now it isn't even the tourist season."

"To these guys, all monuments are targets," said Prunier. "Remember when the Taliban blew up those Buddha statues in Afghanistan, and then Daesh blew up the Roman temples in Palmyra and took pickaxes to the statues at Nineveh. They believe in destroying monuments and we've got plenty of those."

"Maybe they're here for more than one reason," J-J suggested. "There's something to do with the Iftikhar testament, certainly, but maybe while they're here they want to take the chance to attack or destroy something important to French culture. To me that spells the Lascaux Cave. Perhaps that's what the two unknown guys are for."

"There could be another target, the Boy Scout camp that we're opening outside St. Denis next week," said Bruno. "Maya Halévy will be there, the Israeli woman who paid for the place as a memorial. She and her brother were sheltered there from the Nazis during the war. It was going to be opened with contingents from all the scout groups, Catholic, Protestant, Jewish and Muslim, but the Muslims announced this week they were pulling out because of the Israeli connection. A hundred French youngsters and this Israeli philanthropist could be quite a target."

"We hadn't been thinking of arranging any special security but that could be a very bad mistake," said Prunier. "We can't leave them unguarded. Maybe we could use one of those special forces teams the brigadier mentioned."

"I can assign some of our *forces mobiles* with their own helicopters," said the general of gendarmes. "They aren't special forces, but they're very good, the ones we use to guard nuclear power stations. And I'll put in a request for GIGN."

Bruno nodded his approval—Groupe d' Intervention de la Gendarmerie Nationale was an elite unit—but he wondered how to steer the general away from the idea that all that was needed was firepower.

"I wonder whether just guarding the camp is the best approach," said Bruno. "These are kids. What are their parents going to say if anything goes wrong, and we knew there was a threat? They could accuse us of using their children as bait to set a trap. Perhaps we should consider postponing the opening." He paused, and looked at Prunier and the general. "If the politicians and the media start looking for scapegoats in the event of a disaster, they'll start with you two."

"Point taken," said Prunier.

The meeting broke up. Bruno pondered contacting Amélie. When Prunier had called him at dawn to attend the videoconference, he'd left a note at her hotel explaining that he had to attend a security meeting to which she would not be admitted and he'd call her when he could. He'd turned his phone off during the meeting, and when he turned it back on, he saw an urgent text from Horst that said simply, "Eureka. Join me at Commarque soonest."

Bruno grimaced. He wanted to get back to his office and start going through the e-mails from his network of people in the local tourist business after he launched the search for the four suspects. Commarque was out of his way. But Horst was a good friend, and about to get married. Bruno skimmed through the e-mails on his phone, saw nothing particularly urgent and set off for the château.

The crowds had gone, but the count was there with Horst, Clothilde and two more of the archaeologists from the museum. Another truck was parked beside the seismic sensor Bruno had seen on his last visit.

"That's the ground-penetrating radar," said Horst, who was shifting from one foot to the other in his excitement and clutching Clothilde's hand. "They've found another cave, at least one. And there's something inside it. From the blurred shape, which is all we can make out, it could be an altar or a tomb."

"Congratulations," said Bruno. He kissed Clothilde and shook hands with the count and the other archaeologists before asking, "Where is it?"

"The cave is quite deep, at least five meters below current ground level, at about the same depth as the cave where the equine engraving was found," said Clothilde, her eyes bright. "It seems to be quite close behind one of the troglodyte caves, one where we found animal bones, flints and pollen in the floor. They were dated between fifteen and eighteen thousand years old, Lascaux period."

"When you say it's behind a known cave, is it sealed off or is there a way into it?" asked Bruno.

"The technicians are in there at the moment, trying to map the new cave and look for others," Horst said. "The seismic investigation showed the whole hill to be honeycombed with caves and what look like courses of underground streams. Heaven knows what passages between the caves we might find. Remember how much lower the ground was that long ago."

There came a shout from the tower of the château, nearly a hundred meters above them. Looking up, Bruno saw three men, all waving down at them.

"You'll meet them this evening, the guests I told you about," said Horst. "Two colleagues from Germany and another from England, close friends of many years and very good archaeologists. One of the Germans is from Düsseldorf, and that is very significant for this region. Can you guess why?"

"I couldn't begin," said Bruno, smiling.

"Here at Les Eyzies is where the first Cro-Magnon skeletons were found. But before that was the discovery in 1856 of Neanderthal man near Düsseldorf. So we shall have here archaeologists from the two great sites of prehistory."

Horst threw up his hands with a flourish. "What could be more suitable for a marriage of archaeologists? And I'm delighted that our wedding is coinciding with this latest discovery at Commarque. Clothilde and I couldn't have had a better wedding present."

Bruno nodded, wished them luck, slapped Horst on the back and reminded him not to let the cave get in the way of his bachelor supper that evening. Bruno was in charge of the cooking, but the event was being hosted by the baron at his *chartreuse,* since they assumed Horst's German friends would prefer to dine in a historic building than in Bruno's modest home. The baron also had a much-bigger oven than Bruno, which would be needed for the dish Bruno had in mind. Ivan at the bistro had ordered a whole wild salmon of three kilos from his supplier, to be delivered to him at the restaurant fresh that day. Bruno was providing the herbs and new potatoes from his garden, and Fauquet was making the *tarte au citron* that was Horst's favorite dessert.

Marcel, who ran the finest vegetable stall at the local market, had promised Bruno two kilos of young green asparagus to begin, and Stéphane from the *fromagerie* was preparing one of his special cheese boards.

Jack Crimson and Gilles were providing the wine, and considerable thought had gone into the selection. To begin, they had three bottles of sparkling rosé wine from Château Feely, which would be the aperitif and could also accompany the asparagus. The white wine for the salmon would be a Cuvée Mirabelle from Château de la Jaubertie, but Hubert from the town's *cave des vins* had suggested they might like to try something unusual, a red wine that would go surprisingly well with the salmon, a Château Laulerie, made entirely of merlot grapes. Since Horst preferred to drink red wines when he could, and Bruno and the baron had tasted the wine and approved, they had three bottles, and two bottles of the honey-sweet Monbazillac from Château La Robertie for the dessert.

Bruno knew that his plans for the evening could be derailed by the hunt for Mustaf, but he hoped he could find some way to keep his commitments to Horst and Clothilde. He would need about an hour to cook the salmon and only a few minutes for the young asparagus, which he intended to serve only with butter. Young Edouard Lespinasse from the garage had agreed for twenty euros to pick them all up and drive them home at midnight. The English archaeologist was staying with Gilles, the two Germans with Bruno, and nobody lived more than four kilometers from the baron's *chartreuse*.

Chapter 18

As Bruno parked his van by the *mairie,* a woman called his name. He turned to see Amélie waving at him from a table on Fauquet's terrace. A copy of *Le Monde,* a notebook and her ever-present smartphone were in front of her, along with a cup of coffee. He went to join her, apologizing for abandoning her that morning.

"Where's Balzac?" she asked.

"At home. I couldn't take him to the security meeting. It was a videoconference with Paris." Even mentioning it brought Isabelle back into his head, a sudden memory of his undoing her hair from its bun and letting it trickle through his fingers. With an effort, he brought himself back to reality.

"Have you been here all morning?" he asked her.

"Fauquet has a good Internet connection, perfect croissants and excellent coffee, and I've been enjoying the sun, reading the paper, going over my notes and being surprised that there's nothing on any of the news feeds about the attack on Dumesnil." She gave a sudden shiver. "I didn't sleep too well, remembering what they'd done to that poor man."

"The hospital says he's in intensive care. There's nothing in the media because J-J wants to keep it quiet for the moment."

"I presume this security meeting was about him?"

"Let's not talk about that here. Are you ready for some lunch?"

"Always. Are we going to Ivan's again?"

"No, to my place, so I can pick up Balzac and make you an omelette you'll never get in Paris. It will be a light lunch because I have a big dinner tonight for Horst, the bridegroom at Saturday's wedding. It's his bachelor supper."

He picked up a baguette from Fauquet, and they drove out on the familiar road home to find Balzac, who made a point of greeting every car he heard. As Bruno expected, the basset hound was waiting for them at the end of the lane and giving a tuneful howl of greeting. Now that he could sound like a grown-up basset hound, Balzac had become appreciative of his own voice.

"*Mon Dieu,* they could hear that back in town," said Amélie, evidently impressed, as she bent down to greet the dog.

"That's a sign of a good hunting dog, so I'll know where to find him in the woods when he's on a trail. He'll never be fast, but he can run all day. That's how bassets hunt wild boar, they run and run until the boar collapses with exhaustion. I think it's nice enough to eat outdoors."

He left Amélie to set the table on the terrace while he went to his chicken coop and took out six new-laid eggs. He picked some roquette and parsley and used his pocketknife to collect tiny green buds of *pissenlit* that would eventually become the yellow dandelion flowers. But Bruno had a better use for them.

Once he'd collected about twenty of them, he went to the kitchen, opened a bottle of white wine and poured each of them a glass. Amélie leaned against the kitchen counter watching as he washed the salad and the buds, put a large knob of butter in his frying pan and broke the eggs into a bowl. Once the butter was half melted, he added the buds of *pissenlit* and began stirring them so they were well coated. He whisked the eggs together with half an eggshell of cold water, salt and pepper, and poured the eggs into the pan just as the melted butter began to foam. He left it cooking while he tossed walnut oil and a little cider vinegar with the roquette in a salad bowl, then returned to twirl the frying pan, folded the omelette and shredded the parsley on top before serving the food.

"I didn't know you could eat these," she said. "It's a very different taste, a little nutty, but it's wonderful to eat food so fresh."

With a fork in one hand and a chunk of baguette in the other, Bruno grinned at her. Amélie picked up the wine bottle to read the label; she looked surprised to see it came from St. Denis's own vineyard. She sipped at it approvingly and then attacked her omelette again. They ate in silence, feeling wholly comfortable in each other's company, occasionally breaking off to hand Balzac a piece of bread that had been wiped on their plates. When they were finished, Bruno took the plates back to the kitchen and brought out some Tomme d'Audrix cheese made by his friend Stéphane, explaining that it was made just up the road.

"Eat locally, that's you," she said, nodding in approval at the cheese. "Now, what can you tell me about the security meeting?"

"Not very much, but one of the men who attacked Dumesnil seems to be from Daesh, a man with a very bad reputation. We don't know how he got into the country, nor what he's planning to do, but Paris is taking it all very seriously. Police reinforcements are on the way, along with special security teams. I have another conference tomorrow morning, but it shouldn't take long. And this afternoon I have to work in my office, going through e-mails from my network."

"You mean your other local policemen?"

"Not just them, but all the hotels and rental agencies, campsites, restaurants, rental-car places, Internet cafés, *mairies,* tourist offices and supermarkets from Lalinde to Montignac. I have a list set up so I can contact all of them with one e-mail, and I've circulated the photos that we have of the four men and their car license plate. With any luck, I might have some replies by now, maybe even a sighting."

"You did that yourself?"

"Not a chance, that's way beyond my skills. The schoolkids did it for me as a club project. Do you want to drop in and take a look as we go back to the office? We're very proud of our school's computer club."

It was officially the spring holiday for schools, but since Florence was there to supervise, the computer room was half full when Bruno and Amélie arrived, her appearance exciting the usual stir. Florence seemed startled by their arrival, her hands fluttering to her hair and smoothing her dress before offering her cheeks to Bruno to be kissed. He introduced his companion to the others as a colleague from the ministry in Paris. Two small children who had been playing quietly with a tablet on a couch in the corner suddenly realized Bruno had arrived, and they scurried to him, to be lifted one in each of his arms.

"Bonjour, Dora; bonjour, Daniel," he said, kissing them both. "These are Florence's children and much better on computers than I am."

Amélie smiled at them and shook each small hand, although the pair looked not at all sure of this stranger. Amélie congratulated Florence on her children, but then her eyes widened as she looked around the room at the quality of the computers the youngsters were using.

"This is serious equipment." She looked back at Florence. "How did you afford these on a school budget?"

"The students can explain better than I can," said Florence. "It's their club."

"We earned them," said Maurice Cordet proudly. Son of a tree surgeon, he was in his final year at the *collège*. He explained that they had started with computers rescued from the town dump and then began building websites for local businesses. Later they developed a computer game and tried but failed to sell it. However, one of the games companies had liked their approach and donated their old computers to the *collège* when they upgraded.

"We do testing for them, telling them what we think about their new games, and they've invited two of us to their offices in Grenoble for an internship," Maurice added.

"What are you working on now?" Amélie asked two girls sitting side by side before a big screen. "And what are your names?"

"I'm Eglantine and this is Sylvie," said the taller of the two. "We're trying to build an interactive system to learn English, using songs and phrases and scenes from movies we all know. It starts with some fun, a karaoke session where you sing along, and then the computer gets you to make new sentences using the words you know. It's fine with our voices because it knows them, but it takes ages to recognize new ones."

"Impressive," said Amélie. "Which one of you set up Bruno's network for all his contacts up and down the valley?"

"We all did," said Sylvie. "It was just a data-entry chore." She glanced at Bruno. "He's a dinosaur on computers, hasn't got a clue about social media." It was said affectionately.

"I'm not extinct yet, and Amélie here has been showing me how it can help in my job, so I'll probably be back here for you all to give me some more lessons," said Bruno. "We'd better get going. Thank you, Florence, everybody."

Back in his office, Bruno called the hospital in Sarlat to ask about Dumesnil's condition. Stable, he was told, but still in intensive care. J-J had already asked to interview him when the doctors gave their approval. He forwarded to Amélie the photos of the two unknown young men from the Gare de l'Est, asking her to put them onto social media sites to see if anyone recognized them.

"No problem," she said. "Do you have Florence's number? I'd like to arrange to see her and ask how other schools might go about setting up similar clubs."

He gave her the school number, Florence's mobile and her e-mail. "You need a live wire like Florence to get it started. She's a great teacher and a good friend and does an impressive job of bringing up those two kids on her own."

Amélie gave him an enigmatic smile, then turned back to her phone and murmured, "She's an attractive woman. Great cheekbones. Is she one of those friends you dine with on Mondays?"

"Yes, and there's another young mother with children in the group. The other kids are English, so they're all becoming very fluent in each other's tongue."

"I suppose it makes up for not having children of your own," she said, her eyes on her phone as her fingers darted over its virtual keyboard.

What did she mean by that? Bruno wondered, before rising and saying he'd better brief the mayor about the security meeting. He was very fond of Dora and Daniel, but nothing really made up for not being a father. Nor could he say there was an important woman in his life. There was Martine, a businesswoman from the region who lived and worked in London and came to St. Denis every couple of months to see her parents and develop the project for a new rally for electric cars. They had lusty reunions together on her visits, but Martine made no secret of her other love affairs in London.

"How are matters working out with Mademoiselle Plessis?" the mayor asked as Bruno stood before his desk. He capped his fountain pen and pushed the letter he was writing aside.

"Better than expected. She's sensible, courteous and sings so well I'm hoping she'll perform at our concert evenings this summer. By the way, did you ever come across a medieval historian called Dumesnil who lives in Sarlat?"

"Yes, I know something about his work. The staff around the coffee machine this morning was talking about that horrible attack on him. Roberte has a sister who is a nurse at the hospital so word has got around. I hear he's stable. Are you involved in that as well as this business at Commarque?"

Bruno explained the whole affair, stressing Amélie's role in identifying Leah and the way Leah had managed to establish for herself a new identity and bank account. "I'm not sure that we'll be a target here in St. Denis, but I think we have to postpone the opening of the scout camp. Yacov Kaufman is coming down from Paris tomorrow to see the camp, and you and I are giving him lunch at Ivan's. It's in your diary. I think we have to be frank with him about the reasons for postponing."

"Very well. Are we still going ahead with Horst's bridegroom supper this evening, or has that been put off as well?"

"No, we're going ahead. It's at the baron's place, remember, and young Lespinasse will drive us all back afterward. I'll get there about seven to start cooking, and we'll serve drinks at eight. I think we'll be ten altogether."

"I'm looking forward to it and to officiating at the marriage. I presume you saw Horst's latest piece in *Archéologie*?"

"I did, and I'll be quoting from it in my wedding speech, if I ever get time to sit down and write it."

As he said this, a knock came at the door, and Amélie poked her head inside, excusing herself but saying that Bruno had just received a new e-mail that looked important. The mayor waved him out.

The e-mail had been sent from the Casino shop in Le Buisson. Best known in France for its giant hypermarkets, Casino also ran a chain of small local supermarkets in rural villages that were otherwise ill served for basic foods and supplies.

He called the manager as soon as he read that one of the men in Bruno's photos had just spent more than a hundred euros at the shop.

"Is he still there?" Bruno asked as he forwarded the e-mail to J-J, Prunier, Yveline and the brigadier.

"No, he left a couple of minutes ago in a white van, a Renault, no markings on the side. Somebody helped him load the bags, and then they drove off on the Sarlat road. I took down the license plate number and then e-mailed you."

"Thanks, give me the number and I'll be right there," he said, sending second e-mails to the same addresses with the latest details. Then he went to his safe, opened it and took out his gun, a PAMAS nine millimeter of the kind he'd used in the army. He checked that it was empty, loaded a magazine, attached the belt holster with its pouch for a spare magazine and settled the gun at his side.

"Amélie, you'd better stay here until I get back. Please take care of Balzac." He left, running down the *mairie* stairs and out to his car. As he got behind the wheel his phone rang. It was Yveline, asking if he wanted support, and indeed he did, asking her to call the Le Buisson *gendarmerie* and for her own team to join him at the shop. And could she arrange for roadblocks to be established at Siorac, Lalinde and outside Sarlat? No sooner had he closed his phone than it rang again, J-J calling this time.

"Have those special forces teams arrived yet?" asked Bruno.

"They just landed in Bordeaux, haven't been briefed yet."

"If they have their copter, better get them moving and see if you can brief them in flight. I'm on my way to Le Buisson, with two squads of gendarmes on the way. Yveline is asking for roadblocks."

"That's what I want you to do," said J-J. "No point in going to the shop if they've left, but could you set up a roadblock out-side St. Denis?"

"A roadblock? What with? I only have a handgun."

There was a pause before J-J replied, "You'll just have to do your best. I've got motorbike cops heading your way. Where do you plan your roadblock?"

"I'll do it at the turnoff to Limeuil and try to get Yveline's gendarmes to join me."

"I'll get her general to call her. Now get on with it."

Driving one handed as he tried to call the baron, Bruno navigated the sharp S-bend at the railway crossing and then drove on cautiously, watching the oncoming traffic for a white van.

"Baron," he said when the call was answered. "Can you come to the Limeuil turnoff on the road to Le Buisson with your hunting guns? Please call other hunters from our club and ask them to do the same. We've got an emergency, terrorists, probably armed. I'm setting up a roadblock there with my van."

"As soon as I can," the baron replied, a veteran who knew better than to waste time with questions. He'd been in the Algerian War, and despite his age he still played tennis, hunted regularly and was a fine shot.

At the Limeuil turnoff, Bruno stopped, his car across the center of the road. Leaving his blue light flashing, he pulled out the accident hazard–warning triangles from the back of his van and extended the blockade with them. He left only a narrow route through, part of it on a grass verge that bordered a ditch so any vehicle coming through would be forced to slow down. Then he put on a flak vest, left from a previous operation, over his uniform jacket.

The first vehicle that came was a tractor, driven by a farmer he knew, who stopped and eyed Bruno curiously.

"Emergency, Pierre," said Bruno, his eyes on the road behind the tractor. "There are some armed criminals on the loose. Sorry, but I have to commandeer your tractor. Could you use it to block the road where I've put the accident triangles. Then I'd like you to get in the ditch and stay there until reinforcements get here."

Pierre did as he was told, climbed down and asked, "Have you got another gun? I did my national service in the infantry."

"Thanks, but no, only my own weapon. Sorry, I'd use you if I could."

A small blue Ford driven by a middle-aged woman stopped at the roadblock, and Bruno waved her through. She was followed by an old Citroën he recognized, driven by Dr. Gelletreau.

"What's this, Bruno? I'm due to be at the clinic."

Bruno explained and asked the doctor to park his car behind the tractor, and then to stand by with his medical bag in case he was needed. Then from behind came the tooting of a horn and the baron's stately Citroën DS cruised up to join them. From the backseat he took a shotgun and two Verney-Carron hunting rifles, each with a bolt action. He handed one to Bruno with a magazine already loaded, left the shotgun resting on the roof of Bruno's van and then loaded his own rifle.

"What's this roadblock for?" he asked.

"I'm not supposed to tell you so keep it to yourself. There's an alert for a bunch of jihadist terrorists. Can Pierre borrow your shotgun?"

"Certainly. Jihadists, you say? I haven't hunted them since the Algerian War."

At this point, Bruno heard a siren and turned to see the *gendarmerie* van coming from St. Denis, Sergeant Jules at the wheel and Yveline in the passenger seat. Jules parked, leaving the siren blaring and his blue light flashing, and four more gendarmes piled out from the rear, each with a flak vest and a handgun at his belt.

"My general called," said Yveline. She was carrying an MPF submachine gun, the only one stored at the St. Denis *gendar-*

merie. "He says I'm under your orders until further notice." She looked at the rifle at his side and gestured behind her to where Sergeant Jules was pulling something from the back of the van. "Jules brought his hunting rifle."

"Good, I was feeling outgunned until the baron arrived. Another rifle could be just what we need. Other hunting friends should be arriving with more, but we probably won't need them. If the white van hasn't shown by now, they're probably taking another route."

His phone rang. It was J-J to say that the official registry recorded that white van's license plate should have been attached to a black Renault on a parking lot for used cars in Bergerac. Local police were checking.

Five minutes later, J-J called again. The *urgences* at St. Cyprien had been called to an incident. A motorcycle gendarme had been shot by the side of the road at Siorac, a crossroads about five kilometers beyond Le Buisson.

"The bastards could be anywhere," he said.

Chapter 19

Bruno drove over the bridge into the main square of St. Denis. Amélie was standing on the balcony outside his office, anticipating his return. He waved once he'd parked, slung the baron's rifle over his shoulder and broke open the shotgun he had borrowed. Entering the *mairie,* he heard the sound of her high heels clattering down the stairs to meet him.

Her eyes widened at the sight of the guns. "Did you catch them? Was there a fight?"

"They took another route, shot a gendarme who tried to flag them down and disappeared."

"Is he dead?"

"I don't know."

They mounted the stairs together, and the mayor was waiting for him along with Xavier, the *maire-adjoint,* some of the senior members of the town council and Fabiola. The mayor led the way into the council chamber and asked Bruno to brief them all on the potential danger to the town.

"We have four armed terrorists on the loose," he began, leaving the guns by the door. "Two of them were stocking up on supplies at the supermarket in Le Buisson and we had little time to organize roadblocks. They shot a gendarme at Siorac and disappeared. He's been taken to the hospital, but I don't know his condition. This is now a major antiterrorist operation being run by the Ministry of the Interior. We'll be getting serious firepower. Three special forces teams, including one from the elite GIGN group of the *gendarmerie,* are being deployed with helicopters."

One of the councillors tried to interrupt with a question, but Bruno waved him aside.

"Sorry, Michel, I don't have time for discussion," he said. "We know the identities of two of the group and have photos of the remaining two. Their leader appears to be an important man from ISIS. We know they assaulted and tortured a man in Sarlat, but we don't know their mission. It could involve Lascaux, since they like destroying monuments. It could be the planned opening of the new scout camp here, but that's being postponed. It could be something or somewhere else altogether. We'll be coordinating a search from the *gendarmerie* here in town because it has good and secure communications."

He was interrupted by a flurry of questions but held up a hand until they were silent.

"That's all I know and probably more than I should tell you. Please don't speak of this outside this room, and above all do not mention ISIS. We don't want people to panic. I know the mayor and I can count on you. And now, excuse me, I have to get to the *gendarmerie.*"

He went to his office to say hello to Balzac and check his e-mails. Amélie followed him, and he said she should stay; she would not be allowed into the command post being set up at the *gendarmerie.*

"I understand. I'll stay with Balzac," she said. "While you were away I was working on a couple of things. First, remember I used my phone to photograph that letter on Dumesnil's desk? Here's the number of the historian at the Sorbonne he was writing to."

She handed him a piece of notepaper. "And I was looking again at Leah's false ID. It was set up over a year ago, so how long had she been planning this? Was the bank account opened at the same time? I put the details on the paper with the name and phone number. And here's a copy of the printout from the till at Casino of the supplies they bought. The manager e-mailed it to you."

He began to thank her, but she interrupted.

"I'll stay here and answer your phone. This evening I'm having dinner with your friend Florence to talk about computer clubs. If you need me, just call my mobile. Take care." She gave him a quick hug as he thanked her and left.

The parking lot on the old parade ground in front of the *gendarmerie* had been closed to the public and was now occupied by three gendarme vans and a mobile communications unit. Bruno recognized J-J's car parked beside it. Three gendarmes with flak vests and submachine guns were standing by the roadblock formed by another van. Inside the building, J-J and the gendarme general were already installed in Yveline's office, each of them talking on his phone, and Yveline was talking to a video link on her laptop. She was the first to finish.

"We're rebasing the helicopters at the Belvès airfield because it's closest," she said. "The brigadier is on his way down here with some antiterrorist staff, and we've taken over the Royal Hotel to house people. They should arrive late tonight, and we all meet here tomorrow morning at eight."

"Talking of housing people, the bad guys are equipped to feed themselves for a week," Bruno said, giving her the copy of the Casino bill. "Rice, eggs, bread, milk, noodles, olive oil, cheese, tomato paste, vegetables, fruit and fruit juice, a lot of coffee, sugar and jam, chocolate and nothing frozen. And no meat, presumably because they couldn't be sure it would be halal."

"That sounds as though they have access to a kitchen with

saucepans and crockery, which suggests to me that they've found a vacant house."

"You know how many thousands of vacation homes we have around here, all closed up and waiting for the tourist season. It would take months to search them all."

J-J finished his call and broke in. "Isabelle sent me the breakdown from the cell-phone tower near Vaugier's place. We've got two numbers that we think must be theirs, with very heavy Internet use. So France-Télécom is now watching for those numbers on every cell tower in the *département*. But they seem to know what they're doing, using a VPN and proxy servers along with Tor encryption."

"What does that mean?" Bruno asked.

"A virtual private network using proxy servers is a way to hide your identity and location," said Yveline. "'Tor' stands for 'the Onion Router,' a way of encrypting data that's done in layers, like an onion. So while we might be able to track where they are, we can't read what they're up to."

"And if they're that sophisticated, they won't be using their phones anywhere near where they're staying now that they know we're hunting them," said J-J. "They'll probably want new throwaway phones, so we're checking on all smartphone thefts and all new sales. But maybe they brought extra phones with them."

"It's possible one of them just panicked when he saw a cop waving them down and shot him," Bruno replied. "So now they're panicking even more. They'll want to get new wheels, unless they already have them. Maybe they could do an amateur paint job on the van."

"The problem is we can't block all the roads." Yveline turned to the large map of the *département* on the wall by the door. "So we're doing the usual blocks, all autoroute access points and all national road intersections. Even with the extra manpower, we can't do much more than that."

"We know when they were at Siorac, and presumably heading back to their base. We also know that at that time we had motorbike cops at the obvious choke points—on the main road below Belvès, at Beynac, outside Sarlat, at Les Eyzies and your own block at the Limeuil turnoff. I think we have to work on the assumption that they're in this area—they'd have to know the back roads to get out of that net."

"It's still four or five hundred square kilometers, and full of vacant *gîtes*," J-J said.

"Yes, but with all the major roads blocked and helicopters cruising the minor ones, we'll at least have them pinned down," Yveline replied.

Behind them, the general slammed the phone down. "They say it can't be done, not with their current technology. Still, it was a good thought. Well done, Lieutenant." He gave Yveline a quick smile and explained to Bruno that Yveline had wondered if the electricity network could pinpoint houses that had suddenly started using power after a week without.

Bruno excused himself to find a quiet space to make some calls, but the squad room was full of gendarmes being briefed and issued local maps. He told Sergeant Jules that he'd be in the bar across the road. Once there, he ordered a coffee and called the number of Professor Philippeau in Paris. He explained himself, said that Dumesnil was in the hospital without explaining why, but that he had been writing to the professor about the Testament of Iftikhar. What could the professor tell him about it?

"This is very odd. I hadn't heard of that supposed document for twenty years, but this is the fifth or sixth time it has come up in the last couple of months."

He explained that it started at the recent annual meeting of the American Historical Association in January. He had given a paper on Outremer, the Christian kingdom that was established around Jerusalem after the First Crusade. Afterward, one of the

American scholars came up to ask whether he thought Iftikhar's testament was genuine.

"A lot of historians are very dubious about it, me included. And then another scholar, who had been at some conference in Israel, said he'd heard a rumor there that it had been tracked down, and some intensive tests were under way to establish whether it was genuine, the parchment and ink and so on. Of course, I questioned him, but it all seemed very vague, told to him by someone he didn't know talking about it in a group at a bar after a dinner, but then shutting up when he realized he might have said too much. It's very political, you understand, this document. If it's genuine."

"How did Dumesnil come into it?" Bruno asked.

"He was my pupil, and I'm fond of him, a brilliant man. So what's this about being in the hospital? Nothing serious, I trust."

"They say his condition is stable. When I spoke to him about it, he sounded very skeptical about this document, like you."

"Yes, I called him and we discussed the rumor, of which he had heard nothing. But it's possible, because with all the chaos in the Arab world in recent years museums and archives have been looted and destroyed."

"Would that include documents?"

"Oh, certainly. There's a flood of Middle Eastern antiques and ancient books and documents on the world market, some priceless old Arabic calligraphy from the Baghdad museum. More has been reaching the market from Aleppo and more recently items from Nineveh and Mosul and Palmyra that Daesh looted and sold. It's tragic that these collections have been broken up, but I'm on a committee at the Institut du Monde Arabe here in Paris that advises on acquisitions. We're deluged with offers of material that a few years ago we'd have paid a fortune to have, but now they're being offered for a pittance."

"So it's entirely possible that this long-lost testament could suddenly have surfaced. But wouldn't the Arab museums have known what it was?"

"You wouldn't believe the state of some of these national museums, even before the Iraq War and the Arab Spring. They were underfunded, understaffed, too many jobs given as political patronage rather than to real scholars. The Arab curators were just as distressed, but even when the region was stable they had little influence."

"So they might not have known what they had, what was there?"

"That's right. And we don't know what happened to the archives of King Baldwin other than that they were entrusted to the Templars. When Jerusalem fell to the Arabs in October 1187, Saladin was merciful. He allowed all the Christians to leave if they paid a ransom, and there was a lot of haggling over the terms. Finally the Templars and the Hospitallers agreed to pay the ransom of those without money, in return for being allowed to take with them their holy relics and ornaments. Heraclius, the Roman Christian patriarch of Jerusalem, left with wagons containing treasure and the relics from the Holy Sepulchre. The Templars led one of the refugee columns to Tyre, which was still in Christian hands, and they took their own treasure with them."

"And that could have included the testament?"

"Yes, it was supposedly shown to Richard Lionheart in Acre, when the Templars established themselves there. But after the rest of the Holy Land fell in 1291, except for a tiny offshore island that later fell to the Mamluks, the Templars fled to Limassol in Cyprus, and the trail goes cold. Whether it was lost in Acre, in Limassol or at the base they established on the island of Arwad, we don't know. We do know that at this time the Templars had negotiated an alliance with the Mongols, who were ravaging Muslim lands from the east. And of course it could have been lost when Constantinople fell to the Ottomans in 1453."

"So you think it's possible that the testament was captured from the Templars, stored in some Muslim or Mamluk archive and has now reappeared in the chaos of the Arab world?"

"Yes, but it may be a fake. I joined one group in Baghdad a few years ago, with funds raised from charity to buy precious relics and bring them back to France for safekeeping. I was offered two holy shrouds, several pieces of the true cross, nails from the Crucifixion and several swords of Saladin."

"But you are hearing of the Testament of Iftikhar only now?"

"Yes, and as I said I keep hearing about it, most recently from a British colleague, who said that somebody from the British Museum had been invited to Israel to help verify the document. And then two days ago I had a call about it from a reporter at the *New York Times,* so word seems to be spreading. But until I see it and can examine the original myself, I'm reserving judgment."

"Do you have the name of this reporter and this British colleague?"

"The colleague is named Keenan, a medievalist at Merton College, Oxford, and the reporter is—let me check—yes, Jackson, Bill Jackson."

Bruno thanked him, adding that he'd keep him informed about Dumesnil. Bruno then called Amélie to relate what he'd learned and to say he needed her excellent research skills. He gave the names of the professor's two contacts and asked if she could track down their phone numbers.

"No problem," she said. "I think my English is better than yours, so do you want me to talk to them? I assume you're trying to find the origin of these rumors about the testament. And there are no new e-mails from your network—you left your e-mail up on your screen. Do you want me to close it?"

"No, keep monitoring it. We're trying to organize a proper roadblock and search system. Thanks, Amélie."

He sat back, reflecting on this remarkable young woman who'd entered his life. No, he wouldn't put it that way. Amélie was striking in her way, but not in any sense that stirred him. He respected her intelligence, her judgment and her readiness to help, and he admired her ambition. If he cultivated the relationship, they could become good friends, and he resolved to try to do so. As he was paying for his coffee, his phone rang. It was Philippe Delaron, asking about the shooting of a gendarme at Siorac and Bruno's sudden roadblock earlier that day.

"Call the police spokesman in Périgueux, Philippe. I'm not saying a word."

"Nor is she, that's why I'm calling you. A cop shot, a teacher in Sarlat hospital who's been tortured, gendarme helicopters and reinforcements, and then you set up an impromptu roadblock outside Le Buisson. It's a manhunt for those guys whose photos you gave us. We can help, Bruno, if you could tell us a little more. I can put word out on the radio and in the paper."

"I can put word out myself, Philippe, and when I can say more, I will."

"Is it terrorists? Arabs? ISIS?"

"Sorry, Philippe." He closed his phone and instantly it rang again.

"I just called the news desk at the *New York Times*," said Amélie. "They have no reporter by the name of Bill Jackson, and there is no freelancer of that name on their books. But they told me that it wouldn't be the first time someone tried to impersonate one of their reporters. It may be significant that your professor got a fake media call, almost as if somebody is trying to spread the news. Now I'll start looking for the guy at Oxford."

"Wait, don't hang up. You mean that there could be a deliberate attempt to spread a rumor about this testament?"

"Absolutely. Something about this has triggered my suspicious little mind. After all, this all started with Leah's fall at Commarque, and she was trying to paint something about it, and then that e-mail of hers warning that somebody was trying to make a forgery. Why bother to make a forgery that could be disproved when you can make this document into a virtual reality by rumors?"

Bruno frowned, not sure he was following her meaning. "Why would anyone want to do that?"

"There's one obvious suspect, and the strategy is smart: first the historians, some anonymous guy in a bar at a conference, then the newspapers start asking questions. Pretty soon I'll bet it's going to be on Twitter and then there'll be an Internet meme. It doesn't have to exist in reality as long as people give it a kind of reality by talking and writing and arguing about it."

Bruno understood. "I get it. You and I had never heard any suggestion that Jerusalem was not really a holy site for Islam. But now we have. And as that word spreads, fed by rumor and hearsay, Israel's right to Jerusalem becomes stronger and the Arab claim weaker, even if this document never existed."

"Exactly. You can't prove a negative. And that makes me wonder about what Leah was really up to."

"On the face of it, she was sending a warning. But you're suggesting that she was trying to build this rumor, this myth of the existence of the Testament?"

"It fits, Bruno. Remember what you told me about trying to solve a crime—you start by building a hypothesis and then try to disprove it. This hypothesis of mine holds up. Assume for a moment that this is all some subtle Israeli intelligence ploy and that Leah, despite being known as a peace activist, was really working for Israeli intelligence. That might explain why she died. If the Arabs found out, they'd have killed her for sure. It would also explain why she had set up a false French identity card and bank account over a year ago, long before all this started."

"You've been reading too many spy stories."

"Maybe you haven't been reading enough. I'll ask the British Museum if they really sent some expert scholar to Israel to examine a long-lost document from the siege of Jerusalem. I'll bet they didn't."

Chapter 20

Bruno had learned in the army that there were few more point-less exercises than to hang around a headquarters getting in the way when nothing was happening. In those days he had taken such opportunities to catch up on his sleep, knowing that when something serious occurred sleep would be hard to come by.

So with the roadblocks in place, the helicopters cruising and competent gendarmes manning the communications, there was nothing useful for Bruno to do. Rather than sleep, he needed the exercise and mental relaxation that he found on horseback. He collected Balzac and drove out, whistling, to Pamela's riding school with his dog, smelling faintly of Amélie's perfume, sitting alert beside him.

Breathing hard after a gallop with Hector along the ridge, Bruno looked down on his town as it nestled in the valley he knew so well. In the afternoon sun, the honey-colored stone of the buildings and the arched bridge glowed all the more richly. The stone and the red-tile roofs and the fresh green of springtime in the trees and gardens were all reflected in the river's smoothly flowing surface. He gazed, enjoying the scene until he heard the familiar panting of Balzac finally catching up with his master and his horse.

How strange and offensive that such a picturesque and peaceful scene should be under the threat of terrorists who had already destroyed towns and communities in their own parts of the world. He had seen the newspaper photos and TV images of Aleppo and Homs. How could anyone seek deliberately to eradicate the monuments and the history of their own people? He felt sure they must fail. The past could never be wiped away with the arrogant sweep of a violent hand; the past always survived because memories remained and children grew up hearing their parents' tales of them.

He knew that St. Denis had known war within living memory. For centuries of the English occupation it had lived through war, and then suffered another century of France's own religious wars. And yet it had survived and prospered with its essence intact, the geography of the river and the rolling landscape shaping its character as a trading point, the fertile land and temperate climate making it a region that could feed far more than its inhabitants. But even as it attracted invaders and soldiers, it could always hold out, endure, adapt and, if need be, rebuild. Like their people, towns were resilient.

He nudged Hector with his knees, loosening the reins, and they set off down the trail through the woods at a gentle trot so that Balzac could keep up. When the woods thinned and the trail became a hunter's path, he increased the pace to the kind of canter that Hector could keep up for hours. Then, struck by an idea, he turned up another trail that led to the cabin used by the hunting club of St. Cyprien, mostly formed of men he knew. Two of them were skinning rabbits on the big tree stump outside the cabin when he arrived.

"You can't be going hunting with that," said one of them, pointing at the gun on Bruno's belt. He was a man whose face Bruno knew, but he'd forgotten his name. Bruno shook his head, laughing.

"Seen any strangers around here?" he asked, after shaking

hands and accepting a small glass of wine from an unlabeled bottle. He'd have preferred water, but wine was the custom. "You may have heard, a gendarme got shot at Siorac by two guys in a white van, and you'll see a lot of helicopters and roadblocks, but this time the cops won't be stopping you to check if you've been drinking. We think they've tried to hole up somewhere in the area. They're armed and dangerous, so don't get close, don't confront them, but let me know and we'll check the place."

The two men shook their heads but said they'd pass on the word to let him know. Bruno shooed Balzac away from the pile of rabbit guts, mounted Hector once more and trotted back to the stables at the riding school. Back at his office he began calling all the hunting clubs in the area. Mostly, he had to leave a message, but usually he knew someone in each club and could track them down. He asked them all to let him know if any strangers were spotted, or a white van, or if any remote vacation home or *gîte* suddenly seemed to be inhabited.

"Networking the hunting clubs sounds like a good idea for other village policemen," Amélie said, writing in her notebook. "That's another recommendation for my report, like your e-mail system to all the local hotels and campsites."

"I'm afraid your report has been overtaken by events," he said, smiling at her.

"I wouldn't have missed it for the world. It's been really interesting, giving me an insight into police work that I'd never usually get to see." She bent down to stroke Balzac, who was nuzzling at her knee. "I hope I've been useful."

"More than useful, you've been a godsend," he said. "You've got a gift for this, not routine police work but tackling this kind of emergency. I know you're planning on becoming a magistrate and building a political career, but I think you might find detective work more congenial."

"How do you mean?"

"An English friend once told me of some statesman who said that all political careers were doomed to end in disappointment and usually in defeat. I imagine all politicians start off as idealists, hoping to achieve something, but politics is a rough game. I think you're impatient to achieve things, but you're likely to be endlessly frustrated. You must have thought about that."

"Of course I have. But with a legal qualification, I'd have a second string to my bow if politics didn't work for me. And I think I have a talent for it."

"No question, but you also have a talent for police work, for detection, or even for security, intelligence."

"That's not me," she said firmly.

"Maybe not, but I'm sure you've realized that we in Europe are in for a long struggle. London, Madrid, Paris—they've all been attacked. This isn't going to stop, and we're going to need a better, more subtle kind of security to defend ourselves against it, fresh minds, new thinking, people like you. It's your country, too."

"Are you sure about that, Bruno? One reason why I think politics makes sense for me is that it's one career where the color of my skin works in my favor. They need people like me because a lot of us have votes. Would I be as desirable to a police force? To an intelligence agency? To a bunch of detectives who find it hard enough to accept female colleagues, let alone a black one?"

"I can't challenge that, but have you felt the slightest whiff of racism here in St. Denis?"

"No, but St. Denis is unusual, you have a good mayor and it's a small town. Believe me, it's not like this in Paris or Marseille."

"But you accept the possibility that it could be if we do things right."

"Yes, I do accept the possibility, but I think I can do more to bring that about through politics than I ever could in the security services."

"You could be right, but it's their loss."

"Thank you, I'll take that as a compliment. And don't forget I have another week to follow you around and watch you work." She grinned. "You may have changed your mind about me by then."

He grinned back. "We'll see. Now I'd better head off. I have to cook Horst's bachelor dinner and then be back at the *gendarmerie* at eight tomorrow morning for another security meeting. I'll see you here when I'm done." He handed her a spare set of keys to the *mairie* and his office. "And enjoy your dinner with Florence. Give her and the children my love."

He collected the salmon from Ivan, who had kindly gutted it and removed the scales, picked up the young asparagus and lemons from Marcel and the *tarte au citron* from Fauquet. He drove home to feed his chickens and to collect his cooking knives, the new potatoes and some herbs from his greenhouse and mâche from the garden. Then he headed with Balzac for the baron's house, where the red wines had been decanted and the table had been set for ten. Jack Crimson and the baron were already drinking champagne in the kitchen, where Bruno unwrapped the fresh salmon and invited the two men to admire it.

"Do you want to use that for the salmon?" the baron asked, pointing to the top of the wall cabinets where a meter-long copper poaching pan for fish had been gathering dust, unused for years.

"No, thanks. I'm planning to bake it." He began to wipe the inside and the skin of the salmon dry with a paper towel.

"I don't have a roasting pan big enough."

"I'm going to do it on a rack, wrapped in foil. And I'll put more foil on the bottom of your oven to catch any drippings."

He chopped the tarragon and parsley and mixed the herbs with the zest of three lemons, a head of finely chopped garlic, a tablespoon of olive oil and salt and pepper. He used his favorite knife to score eight deep slashes into each side of the fish, stuffing a generous portion of his herb paste into each slash. He then sliced two of the lemons and used them along with half of the herb paste to stuff the salmon's stomach cavity. He spread a thin film of Dijon mustard over the top of the salmon and then added the remainder of the herb paste and squeezed the juice of two lemons on top.

"Okay, that's it," he said as he finished wrapping the fish in foil. "When the guests arrive, I'll put it into a very hot oven for about fifteen minutes, then turn it down to medium heat while we eat our asparagus and cook the new potatoes. Now I just have to prepare the asparagus and the salad and make a vinaigrette."

"The chef deserves a drink; champagne, scotch or wine?" Crimson asked.

"A glass of champagne, please," Bruno replied. "Do you know all the men who are coming?"

"All the locals, of course, and Horst, and I've also run across another of his guests, an English friend named Manners. He's a former soldier like you, retired as a colonel and now a bursar at one of the Oxford colleges." Crimson poured out a glass of Monthuys for Bruno and refilled his own and the baron's.

"I knew his father as well, also a soldier, who served around here with the Resistance during the war, on one of the Jedburgh teams," Crimson went on. "They were dropped into France before D-day to organize parachute drops of weapons and to train the Resistance fighters."

"Was that when that second important cave was found?" Bruno asked.

"I think so. They also got caught up in some of the infighting between the Communists and the Gaullists in the Resistance. It was a difficult time. But you'll like Manners, and his American wife, Lydia, who was with him when they and Horst found the new cave. She's a stunner, now also at Oxford, a curator at the Ashmolean Museum."

"So with you and me, Horst and the baron, Gilles and the mayor and Manners, that makes seven. Who are the other three?"

"One British and two German archaeologists," the baron replied. "I think the two Germans arrived today, the ones who will be staying at your place. The British one is staying with Crimson, a Professor Barrymore. He's upstairs changing. He got here about an hour ago, very excited about this new cave the seismic experts have found at Commarque. He said Horst was so enthusiastic about it he wasn't sure he'd get here in time for dinner."

"He'd better," came a voice from the kitchen door. It was Gilles, carrying a big cheese platter in both hands. He greeted his friends and accepted a glass of scotch.

Bruno began washing the asparagus while the baron trimmed it, bending the stem of each one until it snapped naturally. Gilles washed and chopped the salad, all of them working companionably side by side as they had done often before at hunting feasts and their own dinners.

By the time the mayor arrived and Barrymore came down to join them, the salad and vinaigrette had been prepared along with the bowl of ice water that Bruno would use to blanch the asparagus once it had boiled for three minutes. Crimson was opening a bottle of sparkling rosé wine as young Lespinasse dropped off Horst, Manners and the two Germans. Bruno set the oven to 250 degrees C for the fish, checked his watch and put the kettle on to boil for the asparagus.

Even without being told, Bruno would have known that

Manners had been a professional solider. He stood erect but relaxed, a half smile playing on his face as he strove to be pleasant to a group composed mainly of strangers. He watched and listened carefully to the others and thought before he spoke. When he did say something, it was short, to the point and in good French. He also seemed comfortable talking German to Horst's friends. In Bosnia Bruno had come into contact with British officers forged in a similar mold, or perhaps a similar school. They were invariably polite to their men, attentive to their sergeants and usually ready to take responsibility. But then, he thought, the British had ended conscription and returned to its tradition of a small professional army before Bruno had been born. The French army by contrast still retained the heritage of the *levée en masse* that went back before Napoléon to the revolutionary wars.

The conversation ebbed and flowed as the meal unfolded, the fresh asparagus in melted butter, the salmon and new potatoes with the Jaubertie white wine. The mayor, Horst and the baron chose the merlot from Château Laulerie instead. Horst had decreed that the language of the evening would be French, and the St. Denis contingent was entertained by reminiscences of archaeological digs in Scotland, Germany, France and the Holy Land until Bruno cleared the plates and brought in the salad. The cheese board circulated as the mayor asked about the impact of DNA upon their profession.

"I recall your lecture at the museum in Les Eyzies, on the way the DNA had proved there had been interbreeding between the Neanderthals and their Cro-Magnon successors," the mayor said to Horst. "Have there been new developments?"

"Tell them of Professor Sykes, your Oxford colleague," Horst said to Barrymore. He was small and dapper with curly red hair, brushed into order with hair oil. He had slipped into a pocket the tie he had been wearing until seeing that the others were all casually dressed.

Bryan Sykes was a genetics professor at Oxford, Barrymore explained, one of the world experts in the field who had worked on the five-thousand-year-old DNA of the so-called Iceman found frozen in the Alps, and had traced a direct descendant, a woman living in modern Britain. He had also used DNA to prove that the bodies found in Ekaterinburg in 1991 were indeed those of the czar of Russia and his family, slaughtered by the Bolsheviks. More recently, he had explored the mitochondrial DNA through the female line back to the original Eve.

"Not Adam's consort of the Bible," Barrymore added. "This Eve was an African woman who had lived between one hundred thousand and two hundred thousand years ago and was our most recent common ancestor, the woman from whom all known human beings are descended. Sykes explored the DNA further to establish seven subgroups from whom almost all modern Europeans are descended and called them 'the seven daughters of Eve.' The most important, whom he called Helena and who had lived in this very region of southwestern France, was the direct ancestor of around forty-five percent of modern Europeans.

"The next-most-important ancestress had been named Jasmine; she came from modern-day Syria or Israel and was ancestress to around seventeen percent of modern Europeans," Barrymore added. He raised his eyebrows and looked around the table mischievously. "I suppose I should write a letter to the *Times* suggesting that this could mean lots of those poor Syrian refugees are simply rejoining their family members long ensconced in Europe."

Bruno was charmed by the idea that almost half of Europe's population came from a single woman who had lived in his part of France. But why name her Helena? he wondered. It sounded

Greek to him. Why not name her Francette or Marianne, or even Europa?

"Is there any map or graphic that could give some indication of where Helena's and Jasmine's descendants had spread?" Bruno asked. He had long considered the various wars of the twentieth and earlier centuries as so many civil wars between the various European tribes. Even more than that, he thought, the conflicts were family quarrels!

"You'll find various attempts on the Internet," said Barrymore. "One of my postgraduate students is trying to do something more detailed. And I know our friend Horst, after his latest work on the Venus figurines, is wondering whether there is any connection between our great ancestress Helena and her sisters."

"I've been looking in particular at two rare examples of Venus found near here," Horst said. "One comes from the cave of Laugerie Basse. She was dubbed by her finder La Vénus Impudique, or 'the Immodest Venus,' since unlike most of the classic Greek Venus figures, she made no effort to conceal her breasts and vulva with her hands. She's slim and athletic, a striking contrast to the overblown matrons being carved in the same period. The other was also a slim young woman, whom I know to be a particular favorite of Bruno, carved at a time about midway through her pregnancy. Known as the Venus of Abri Pataud, she came from the cliff behind Les Eyzies, where she was found in 1958, so named because Pataud had been the family that owned the land."

"There's a recent book, very popular in Germany, *French Women Don't Get Fat,* so that indicates that your Helena was one of these slim Venus figures," said Horst's friend from the valley of the Neanderthal.

"What a wonderful wedding gift from Clio," said Manners, "to present you with this new cave at Commarque."

Bruno was wondering who this Clio person might be, when Barrymore raised his glass and declared, "A toast, to Clio, goddess of history, daughter of Zeus and Muse of historians."

"Clio, the cruel goddess, who rides her chariot over heaps of the dead," intoned Manners, raising his glass in turn.

"Clio, she who has the power to make men famous," added one of the Germans, and the others raised their glasses in turn. Bruno followed suit, smiling to himself that learned professors and academics could make just as much fools of themselves as anyone else when the wine had been flowing. A short buzz came from the phone at his waist to signal an incoming message. Discreetly, he checked it. Isabelle had texted him that the gendarme who had been shot at Siorac would live.

Chapter 21

Thankful that the quality of the wine and his deliberate avoid-
ance of Crimson's whiskey had spared him a hangover, Bruno
entered the *gendarmerie* shortly before eight the following morning. He had spent the previous thirty minutes in his office,
checking e-mails and messages from his networks. At one point
he had risen from his desk in excitement to study the map on
his wall. On the way to the briefing he stopped at the Maison de
la Presse to buy copies of the detailed local maps used by hikers
and marked each of them with his latest findings. Pleased that
he had something significant to contribute, he greeted Prunier
and J-J as their car pulled up. Despite the cardboard coffee cups
each man carried, they looked tired and solemn. Bruno's bright
mood did not last long after J-J looked at him grimly and asked,
"Heard the news?"

"Not yet. What's up?"

"That ex-nun in my pedophile case, the alcoholic. She committed suicide yesterday, pills and a bottle of gin. The problem is
she phoned Madame Duteiller, the psychologist, who happened
to be giving her statement at the commissariat at the time, on
this tax-evasion charge. So Duteiller didn't get the message, and
now she's saying that it was just a cry for help, and the ex-nun

would still be alive if she'd been able to take the call. She says the nun told her she was going to end it all because there would be no justice for the innocent victims of Mussidan."

"Did the nun leave a suicide note?"

"Yes, saying exactly the same thing and adding that she blamed me in particular and the police in general for not getting the evidence to sustain her story. Duteiller is now all over the radio saying the police are responsible for the nun's death. If it weren't for this case, I'd be on the mat in front of the prefect right now."

"Is the radio also saying that Duteiller was in the police station because she was being charged with tax evasion?"

"We'll see whether the commune wants to press those charges after they listen to the local news. I'm not getting my hopes up. Right now, the nun is a victim of police neglect, and Duteiller is the saintly angel of mercy seeking to bring justice to molested kids."

Prunier shook his head. "Don't worry, J-J. I'll give a statement to the radio as soon as this is over and straighten things out. And I'll make sure the commune files charges against Madame Duteiller."

Sergeant Jules showed the three of them into Yveline's office, and Bruno almost stopped in his tracks when he saw the brigadier and Isabelle seated behind the desk, frowning at their laptops. She was the last person he'd expected to see back in St. Denis. At least she hadn't seen his surprise, and probably would not detect the way his pulse was racing at the sight of her.

"Bonjour, messieurs," the brigadier greeted them, hastily adding, "and you, mademoiselle," when he noticed Yveline slipping into the room. "I believe you all know Commissaire Perrault, whose local knowledge and European connections I thought would be useful."

Isabelle smiled politely and then rose to be heartily kissed by J-J, her former boss when she had been stationed in the Périgord. Prunier was greeted with a cool, "Bonjour, monsieur," while Bruno received only a courteous nod and a handshake that lingered just a moment too long. Half expecting this, he returned a beaming smile, and she raised an eyebrow in return, an ironic facial gesture he recalled fondly, before asking after Balzac. She was looking well, if a little tired, but her eyes were bright. The thrill of the chase had always inspired her.

"I have to brief the minister at nine before he goes to the Elysée to report to the president," the brigadier went on, "and so far there's nothing new to tell him, except that the overtime bills will be going through the roof. I'm hoping you gentlemen can improve that."

Nobody spoke. J-J made a gesture of deference to Prunier, who grimaced and said, "Nothing new to report, sir, except that our roadblocks have all been manned throughout the night and minor roads patrolled by helicopters with searchlights. It looks as though these terrorists have found somewhere to hole up, eating the food they bought. Once they break cover, which we assume they will have to do, we should get them."

"We're checking all known associates in France of this woman Leah and the scholar al-Husayni but have found no such connection yet for Mustaf. The other two remain unknown to us or to our European neighbors," said J-J. "We're running their photos through various databases but no hits yet. Sir, has the antiterrorist team completed the list of possible targets?"

"We are adding to it all the time," intervened Isabelle. She mentioned two possible human targets, a former French prime minister who lived in the region and a former foreign minister who lived near Sarlat. The foreign minister had been in office at the time of Iraq's invasion of Kuwait, when French troops had joined the Americans and British in liberating the oil-rich sheikhdom.

"There's also your neighbor Monsieur Crimson, former head of Britain's Joint Intelligence Committee at the time of the Iraq War, the one we did not see fit to join," the brigadier added. "He's authorized to keep a weapon for self-defense, but I've arranged for a guard to be assigned. Bruno, do you have anything for us?"

"Yes, sir, we may have something. As you know, my local network gave us the first sighting at the Casino store yesterday, and now a second network, of local hunting clubs, has come up with three rural houses which were certainly unoccupied a week ago but which now have signs of occupation. We're fortunate that the hunting season is not quite ended. The hunters noticed fresh tire tracks, chimney smoke and, in one case, a crack of light showing where curtains had not been properly closed. I'm checking the records to see if we can identify the owners and plan to call each of them as soon as we're done here. Meanwhile, here's a copy of a detailed local map, and I've marked each building, assuming you'll want to brief the helicopter teams."

"Well, thank the Lord somebody seems to know what he's doing. Don't let us keep you," the brigadier said. He handed Bruno a small, square enamel badge, about the size of a thumbnail, formed of a blue and a white oblong inside a red border. He saw that the brigadier and Isabelle were wearing the same badges. "Keep that on at all times. Everybody briefed for this operation will know that it means you're on my staff. And now, track down those owners as soon as you can and call me or Isabelle with the results."

"Yes, sir," Bruno said, then saluted and left. He had one owner's name already, of what looked like an old *fermette,* a small family farm in the sprawling rural commune of Urval. The owner of the second house, in the woods beyond St. Cyprien, would have to be checked by the local policeman. The third house was in a commune too small to have its own local policeman, but the mayor of St. Denis was tracking down his colleague to open the tiny *mairie* early and check the map and tax records. As Bruno approached the *mairie,* he spotted Amélie, who waved and called out a greeting from Fauquet's terrace. He tapped his watch in return, signaling he had no time to talk.

"No, wait," she called, jumping up from the café table and coming across to him at a perilous pace in her customary high heels. "This is important. Those photos from Gare de l'Est. Did you notice they all smoked when they were on the terrace of the balcony on the square? Smokers need their fix. So I made a list for you of all the licensed *tabacs* in the area, with e-mails and phone numbers and loaded it onto your computer yesterday."

"Many thanks," he said, embracing her. Then he darted up the steps of the *mairie* to send out the e-mail to all the *tabacs* with photos of the four suspects attached.

Once he had received the name of the property owners from the St. Cyprien colleague and from the mayor, he checked the *annuaire* for the three phone listings and began calling the houses his hunting contacts had identified. The first phone was answered sleepily by someone speaking what sounded like Dutch. The man said in halting French that he and his family had recently arrived from Rotterdam for a spring vacation. There was no reply from the house near Urval, and he could find no phone listing for the name of the owner in the tiny commune of Castels. Those houses would have to be searched. He e-mailed the details to Isabelle and the brigadier. He then sent the e-mail with photos attached to Amélie's list of tobacco shops and went back down the stairs for a coffee and croissant with Amélie.

"You really are very good at this," he said. "I wish you'd think again about what I said."

"Forget it," she said sharply. "Any more thoughts about the

target? I was looking through the local paper to see if there were any long-planned events that might attract them, like the big soccer match in Paris. I don't think local rugby games are what the jihadists have in mind. Nor this new cave at Commarque. Your friendly local reporter has used it to write about the Templars again."

"I'm not surprised. He has to sell papers. How was your evening with Florence?"

"Great, I really liked her, once she stopped singing your praises. It was almost embarrassing, until she said she sang in the choir and then we started doing duets. She has a great voice. She said you'd gotten her the job at the *collège*."

He shook his head. "I just heard that the old science teacher was retiring, and she's a trained chemist with a university diploma, which meant she was much better qualified than most of the science teachers we tend to get around here. She's getting her teaching qualification while working."

"Yes, she told me that. And how she went about starting the computer club. And her kids are great."

"I'm glad you got to know them. She's a wonderful woman, a real asset to the town. I expect she'll be elected to the council before long and become one of my bosses." He paused, looking at his watch. "I'd better get back to the *gendarmerie* to see if they have work for me. Meanwhile, I'd be grateful if you can track down these two property owners and see why their houses suddenly show signs of life." He handed her the short list and said the first one had been checked, a Dutchman he'd woken up when he called him.

"If he's Dutch, why is his name de Villiers?"

"It's a fairly common Dutch name, from the Huguenot Protestants who fled there in our wars of religion." He paused, reflecting. "Maybe we should double-check."

Leaving Balzac with Amélie, Bruno headed for the café to ask Fauquet if there'd been any Hollanders in today, but he shook his head. He began looking through his phone for the number of Willem, a Dutch friend from the tennis club, but as he returned to the terrace he heard Amélie on her phone. She seemed to be asking someone to call a number to see if whoever answered was really Dutch and then call her back. She paused and laughed in response to something and closed her phone.

"What was the joke?"

"A friend in Amsterdam who is going to call them now. She said if there was any doubt she might ask them to say 'Schevenin-gen.'" She stumbled as she tried to say it. "It's the name of a town on the coast that only a Hollander can pronounce. Apparently it was how they identified Germans in the war."

"First rule of policing," said Bruno. "Make sure you have friends everywhere."

Amélie waited, watching her phone as if willing it to ring. But Bruno's phone rang first, the one he'd been given by the brigadier during a previous case. Along with the special ringtone came a telltale green light that showed the caller was someone else connected to the special security network. It was Isabelle.

"Where are you?" she asked, her voice brisk as if to tell him that this was official. Bruno wondered why she bothered. Every call on this network was automatically recorded.

"Just leaving my office and heading back to the *gendarmerie*," he said, in a tone as official as hers. Damn it, he thought to himself, we know each other too well for that. And allowing his voice to convey the affection he felt for her, he added, "Shall I bring Balzac along? He'd love to see you."

There was a pause, and then he heard a nonverbal sound that seemed friendly; in a cat, it would have been a purr. "I'd love to see him, but it's not a good idea. I'll try to see him later. We've got a helicopter on the way to the house near Castels, and then it will check on St. Cyprien—"

"Wait a moment," Bruno interrupted, seeing Amélie answering her own phone and gesturing at him. "Another report is coming in."

"No reply?" Amélie was saying into her phone. "Are you sure? Somebody answered just a few minutes ago. Could you try it one more time? It's really important."

Bruno spoke to Isabelle: "We're checking on the house where I spoke to someone, apparently a Dutchman. We're now trying to confirm his nationality with a native Dutch speaker, and now the phone's not answering. I'll call you back."

As soon as he closed his phone, it rang again, and an unfamiliar male voice asked, "Is that Chef de Police Courrèges?"

"Yes, speaking. Who is this?"

"My name is Laurier, I run the *tabac* on the main street in St. Cyprien and got the e-mail you sent. A man has just been in my shop who was the spitting image of the older man in your photos. I took a good look at him because he bought two cartons, that's four hundred cigarettes. Marlboros, and we don't often sell cartons here. A hundred and forty euros, it was, and he wanted a new lighter, some chocolate bars and mints. He gave me three new fifties, and I let him have a lighter for free and a plastic bag to put it all in."

"How long ago was this?"

"Five or ten minutes. I served him and afterward I was looking at the news on my tablet. My wife gave it to me for my birthday. Anyway, after I'd looked at the headlines I checked the e-mails and saw your message."

"What was he wearing?"

"I didn't really notice. Jeans, I think, and a turtleneck sweater and a leather jacket. I remember he was wearing a baseball cap."

"Was he on foot or did he have a car?"

"I think he was on foot, but I wasn't really looking, sorry. He might have had a car further down the street. Is this a criminal thing? Not forged banknotes, I hope."

"No, it's just routine, not about forgery. But thank you, Monsieur Laurier. Could you just take a look outside and see if he's still in sight?"

"No sign of him," said Laurier after a brief pause, and Bruno thanked him again, ended the call and turned to look at Amélie.

"No reply the second time my friend called."

"Right, I have to go," he said. "That was one of your *tabac* men. He just sold two cartons of Marlboros to al-Husayni in St. Cyprien. Thanks, Amélie, and well done. Could you keep trying that number where there was no reply? It strikes me as suspicious. I'll call you from the *gendarmerie*."

He called Isabelle as he trotted along the rue St. Denis.

"We have a sighting," he said. "It happened minutes ago in the *tabac* in St. Cyprien, within walking distance of that house with the suspect Dutchman. The shopkeeper identified al-Husayni."

"But how—" she began.

Bruno interrupted her. "I sent photos to all the *tabacs* and this one just called me. But you'd better warn the helicopter team that they may have a hot landing zone and see if you can arrange extra backup."

"Right, got it." Before she hung up he heard her shout, "Stop, everybody, emergency . . ."

Minutes later when he entered Yveline's office, he caught the mood of controlled urgency that he remembered from military operations rooms when a serious mission was under way. Isabelle smiled at him, put her hand over the mouthpiece of the phone she was holding and said, "The GIGN helicopter is heading for St. Cyprien, touching down in about fifteen minutes. Another one is on the way and we're rerouting all the motorbike cops to seal off the town."

"There's more," said Bruno, and the room fell silent, the brigadier, Prunier and J-J all turning from their phones to look at him expectantly. Yveline stopped putting pins into the big map on the wall and turned to listen.

"About twenty minutes ago I called the house outside St. Cyprien. A male voice answered claiming to be Dutch and to have just arrived at his vacation home. When I got a native Dutch speaker to call him, just ten minutes later, there was no reply. The house is marked on the map I gave you. Then I got the call from the *tabac* owner. He said that al-Husayni was carrying a plastic bag containing two cartons of cigarettes and chocolate bars," Bruno said, and described the clothes he'd been wearing. "This is the scholarly one, not a trained soldier."

"Understood," said the brigadier and turned back to speak into his phone. "We have a possible location. Please route gendarme helicopter call sign Angel Two to a house two kilometers northwest of St. Cyprien, map reference seven-four-one-two-two-six. Land the combat team to observe only, and then I want that helicopter circling overhead until we can get reinforcements there. I want the other helicopters to head for St. Cyprien and await instructions."

Prunier was barking out orders for police units to converge on St. Cyprien and start door-to-door inquiries with the photographs while J-J was telling his forensics team to head for the *gendarmerie* at St. Cyprien and call him when they were about to arrive. And now we wait, thought Bruno, to learn the fate of the men we are sending into danger.

"Right," said the brigadier. "Time for me to talk to Paris, so I'll be grateful if you'd let me have the room for a few minutes. Carry on, everybody, and remember we want to get these men alive."

J-J went out to the *gendarmerie* steps to smoke a cigarette.

Yveline reloaded the coffee machine in the squad room, and Isabelle asked for the ladies' room. Yveline gave her a key.

"Use my apartment. It's on the ground floor, to the right." She pointed the way across the yard to the small apartment block, known inevitably as *la caserne,* the barracks where the gendarmes lived. "The budget didn't provide a second bathroom for women in the *gendarmerie.* So we use my place."

Prunier took Bruno's arm and said, "Tell me about these networks of yours. How do they work, exactly?"

Bruno explained how he'd organized the first list as a way for far-flung members of the *police municipale* to keep in regular contact, then how he'd added the tourist offices, hotels and restaurants and recently the hunting clubs.

"The credit should go to this young woman from the justice ministry who's following me around to do a report on the future of the *police municipale.* Apparently her minister likes the idea of beefing up what she calls the *police de proximité,* closer to the public. She's a brilliant researcher, and she realized I hadn't taken advantage of the Internet to bring together all my local contacts. It was she who had the idea of adding the *tabacs.* I'd never have thought of it, and she set up the listserv system so I can reach all of them with one e-mail. She's been extraordinary, using social media to identify Leah and then researching her background. We'd never have picked up on this Testament of Iftikhar without her."

"What else do you know about her?"

"She's a rising star in the Socialist Party, on the executive board of their youth wing, sits on their international committees and plans to go into politics. It's a shame. She'd be a brilliant detective, or in intelligence."

"What did she study?"

Bruno explained what he knew, adding as Yveline joined

them with a pot of fresh coffee that Amélie had also graduated from magistrates' school.

"I had dinner with her at Bruno's place," Yveline said. "She's very smart, I liked her, and she sings like an angel."

Bruno wondered whether he should mention Amélie's concern about her cousin's daughter, but J-J returned, still talking on his phone. Isabelle came in through the rear door, and Prunier's phone then rang, followed instantly by Yveline's.

"They've got him? Brilliant," Yveline said and gave Bruno a thumbs-up as she replied to whoever was on the other end of her phone. Then her face fell as she put the phone down.

"*Merde,* he's been shot, but not by us. The brigadier's on the phone with the minister in Paris. I'd better go in and tell him. A gendarme van found al-Husayni. Apparently he was shot on the street while walking out of town, but he's alive," she told Bruno, her hand knocking on the door of her own office. Before she slipped inside to tell the brigadier, she added, "The gendarmes said they would bring him straight here to the clinic in St. Denis."

"Which direction was he walking?" Bruno asked her, looking at the map.

"The gendarmes' van had come through Les Eyzies and Meyrals," Yveline replied before disappearing.

"That's the direction of the Dutchman's house," said Isabelle, wearing a single headphone and sitting by the main radio set. "The GIGN helicopter is on the way."

"It's no more than twenty minutes since I called that house," Bruno said. "If they decided to flee at that point and abandon al-Husayni, they won't have gone far."

"The roadblocks are still in place. We should have them."

The brigadier came out of Yveline's office. "One down, three to go. Do we have a holding charge we can use to arrest this al-

Husayni? I'd rather not use the antiterror legislation at this stage. We'd never keep that from the media."

"Leaving the scene of an accident, Leah's fall," said Bruno. "Suspicion of being an accomplice to her murder and maybe breaking into the de Villiers' house, if that's where he was coming from."

The brigadier turned to Isabelle. "Any word from the GIGN team?"

"Just that they're on the way, they have the new coordinates," she said, the headphone pressed tightly to her ear.

"Right, no point in sitting around waiting for news," the brigadier said. "Who's going to interrogate al-Husayni when he gets here?"

"I'll do it with Bruno," said J-J.

"Do we need an Arabic translator?"

"No," said Bruno. "Dumesnil met him with Leah and told me that al-Husayni speaks good French. We might want to begin on the assumption that he may not be a hostile witness."

The brigadier gave Bruno a skeptical glance, and then Yveline interrupted.

"The GIGN team has landed, taking positions and watching, as ordered, sir. They report no signs of life at the house, and the front door is open."

"Send them in," said the brigadier. "And make sure all the roadblocks are on top alert."

Chapter 22

Saïd al-Husayni was a bespectacled man in his forties, looking pale and exhausted in the hospital bed in the St. Denis clinic. His left arm and shoulder were swathed in bandages, and his face was bruised and scraped. An intravenous drip was taped into his other arm.

"He's a lucky man," said Fabiola as Bruno and J-J came into the room. "One bullet through the upper arm and another just below the shoulder that then glanced off a rib. He won't lose the arm, but he won't have much use of it for a while. We don't have an anesthetist here, so I had to use a local anesthetic. You can have ten minutes, but if I tell you to stop the interview, you stop. Is that clear? He's lost a lot of blood."

"Thank you for letting us see him," said J-J. Like Bruno, he was now wearing one of the brigadier's identifying badges. "We'll do as you say."

J-J greeted al-Husayni politely by name, preceding it with "Monsieur," introduced himself and Bruno and asked if he would like some water or anything else.

"Might I have some coffee, please," came the reply. Al-Husayni looked bemused by the courtesy of his reception. "And could I have a cigarette? They took my bag from me."

J-J took out a pack of his own Royale filters, but Fabiola shook her head. "You can have water, but we're out of coffee, and we don't allow cigarettes in this clinic."

"How were you shot?" J-J asked.

"They all wanted cigarettes, so I was told to go and buy some, but they didn't trust me alone so I was driven to the town by Sadiq, given money and told to buy two cartons. When I came out of the shop and walked back to the car, Sadiq had turned the car around. He had the phone to his ear, and when I opened the passenger door he shot me in cold blood, *snap-snap,* just like that."

"Did he use a silencer?"

"I don't know, it was a very long barrel. Not very noisy, but I heard it clearly."

"Were you with Mustaf of your own free will?" J-J asked in an affable way. He had taken a chair beside al-Husayni's bed. Bruno was in his shirtsleeves and leaning casually against the wall by the window after putting a tape recorder on the bedside cabinet and turning it on.

"The last time I was a free man was when I was studying in Spain," said al-Husayni, taking a deep breath as if he were sucking on a cigarette. "I have family in Ramallah, and Mustaf told me they would be killed if I didn't do what he ordered. You don't know what these men are capable of."

"We know what they did to Dumesnil," said Bruno.

"They are animals. They made me question him, a kindly, harmless man like that. It made me ill. Have you arrested them all?"

"Let's begin at the beginning," said J-J. "Were you there at Commarque when Leah died?"

"Died? She was killed." Al-Husayni almost spat the world. "Mustaf hated her. He despised women, and she was a Jew. He only tolerated her as long as he did because of me. He wanted me to tell him of the history of the caliphate and the time of Arab rule in Spain. That was what he dreamed of, that such times would come again. He made me tell it again and again, that Arabs had once ruled here in this part of France."

"How was Leah killed?"

"Mustaf cut her rope and pushed her off the wall when she insisted on painting her slogan. I was waiting below with the Belgian and saw her fall."

Who might the Belgian be? Bruno wondered, exchanging glances with J-J.

"Ah, yes. The Belgian," J-J said easily and opened a manila file on his knee, leafing through to a random page as though knowing what he was looking for and finding it significant. The file looked to Bruno like Yveline's duty roster for her gendarmes. J-J looked up from the file. "And what name was he using with you?"

"Ahmed, but he spoke bad Arabic, very crude, with an Algerian accent. His French was better, and he also spoke Dutch, or maybe it was Flemish. I think he came from Antwerp."

J-J held up the photographs from the Gare de l'Est. "You can see we've had you all under surveillance since you arrived."

"Yes, that's Ahmed and Mustaf and me with Leah," al-Husayni said. "And that's Sadiq, of course." He pointed with his good arm at the remaining man. "He's French, a convert originally from Normandy, never told me his original name. Ahmed and Sadiq had both been fighting in Syria and were very proud that Mustaf chose them for this mission."

"How long ago was that, when they were chosen?" Bruno asked, thinking how long it had been since Leah set up her false ID and bank account.

Al-Husayni tried to shrug, but a spasm of pain crossed his face. "They never said."

"How about you? When did they force you to join them?"

"A month ago. I was smuggled out through Sinai, then from Cairo to Spain on a forged Spanish passport. They knew I spoke Spanish well. From Barcelona I was told to fly to Frankfurt and then go by train to Paris."

"What about Leah? When did she leave?"

"The same time as me, but being Israeli she could fly out to Cyprus and then to Paris. They told each of us the other would be killed if we did not do as we were told."

"Did you know Leah had earlier set up a false identity?" J-J asked.

"Yes, of course. That was our plan. She told me that she'd done that so that she and I could be together in France as we felt we could never be in Palestine, or in Israel. We were waiting for a medieval history conference in Seville. We knew I'd receive a formal invitation there. That would allow me to get a visa to leave Israel."

"Why would you need a false identity in France?" Bruno asked.

"Because I feared these people would look for me and demand that I work for them, once I was out."

"It is not illegal for a Palestinian to marry an Israeli and live in Israel," J-J said.

"Oh yes it is," said al-Husayni, bridling. "An amendment to the Nationality Act of 2003 barred a Palestinian from living with an Israeli spouse inside Israel. And Israel's Supreme Court ruled in 2006 that this did not violate rights under the constitution, which they call the Basic Laws. Even if it did, the court said, this erosion of family unification was outweighed by security concerns."

"I didn't know that," J-J said.

"We wanted to be married, to start a family." He took a sip of water. "Leah was worried that time was running out for her."

"I'm sorry to ask this, but did you know that Leah was over two months pregnant when she died?" J-J could sound very sympathetic when he chose, Bruno observed. He was more accustomed to seeing the big detective in bullying mode during interrogations.

The Palestinian rolled his head back to stare unseeing at the ceiling. J-J remained silent, waiting for him to react. The seconds stretched out and then finally came the single word, "Leah." It was more like a sigh than a statement.

"She said she thought she might be. We hoped—we had dreamed—that she was. But once we were in France with Mustaf, it was impossible to go to a doctor to confirm it. That would simply have given Mustaf even more of a hold over us."

"When Leah died, do you remember seeing a cow's horn?" Bruno asked gently.

Al-Husayni nodded. "I tripped over it in the woods on our way to the castle, and when I saw Leah was dead, I left it by her side. Something about the way she lay, it reminded me of a piece of prehistoric art she loved. She had a postcard of it on the wall of our bedroom in Ramallah."

"The Venus of Laussel," said Bruno.

Al-Husayni smiled at him. "That's the one."

"Why did Mustaf want you along?" Bruno asked, hoping to steer the talk toward Mustaf's mission. "You're not a jihadi, not a fighting man."

"Leah had been talking openly about this Testament of Iftikhar and the rumor that it was being verified and was about to emerge. She suspected it would be a very clever forgery and that this would have to be exposed by Western scholars whose criticisms would have far more weight than anything Arab scholars could muster. Some Islamic scholars took this very seriously and so did some influential imams. They alerted their contacts among the jihadists, and we found ourselves conscripted."

"Why would a jihadist operation in France compromise itself by bringing along two amateurs like you?"

"My younger brother is a jihadi," said al-Husayni. "He knew of our plans to get out of the country to live in France and knew that Leah had managed to set up an identity and bank account here. They thought that would be useful to them, and they would be able to keep a watch on us. I don't think Mustaf had much interest in the testament. A clean bank account and French identity that he could use to rent cars and accommodations were much more important to him."

"How did you find the second house?" Bruno asked.

"As soon as we got into the first place, Mustaf told the other two to look around for alternatives in case we had to leave in a hurry."

"You mean Ahmed and Sadiq?"

"No, the other two, new ones, Frenchmen who joined us later. They had Arab origins but were born and raised here. I only saw them once, when they took us to this place near St. Cyprien. It's a pretty town."

J-J scribbled a note, passed it to Bruno and asked him to give the news to the brigadier. As he left, Bruno heard J-J ask, "Did these two Frenchmen have names?"

Bruno called the *gendarmerie,* but the brigadier was on his phone again, so Bruno dictated J-J's note to Sergeant Jules and asked him to take it to the brigadier and hold it up before his eyes. Within seconds, Bruno's phone rang.

"Two new ones, just what we need," said the brigadier. "No names, no ID?"

"Not yet, but he's being very cooperative. We'll probably need an artist to do some sketches with him. What about the house?"

"The birds had flown, and now we've lost them again. The coffee on the table was still hot. They left in a hurry, leaving some papers, a lot of prints. We're working on those now."

"I'd better go back in," said Bruno.

"Tell me about this car the other two guys were using," J-J was saying.

Al-Husayni shrugged and then winced. "I don't know much about cars. It was smaller than the van we had, darker in color. It had a shiny badge on the front, like the Greek letter omega. When I first saw them, the two men were very neatly dressed, jackets and ties, like businessmen. They could almost have been twins. Then last night when they came they were dressed casually, jeans and sweaters, khaki jackets like hunters."

Fabiola called a halt, insisting that al-Husayni should rest.

"One moment," al-Husayni said. "Can I go and see Auguste Dumesnil? I must apologize for what was done to him."

"You'll be better before he is," said Fabiola. "But now, this interview must end."

"It was because Mustaf thought Dumesnil was the very image of a Crusader, a Christian militant," al-Husayni went on urgently, ignoring her. "All those religious images in Dumesnil's apartment infuriated him."

"That's enough," Fabiola spoke sharply, and Bruno and J-J left reluctantly, knowing there was more to be mined from al-Husayni. Back in the squad room at the *gendarmerie,* the search and roadblock routine had been relaunched. Sergeant Jules was fielding calls from the media asking for a comment from J-J on the suicide of the ex-nun. Philippe Delaron, who had set up camp outside the *gendarmerie,* was brushed aside by J-J without a word. The place felt as if it were under siege. Bruno sensed the energy leaking away as the excitement of the chase gave way to frustration and routine.

This was a time, Bruno knew, when a team needed leadership, not the drive of a bully but something more refined, someone with the ability to change and lift a mood. He was curious to see whether the brigadier or Isabelle had such skills, running a complex operation that included police, gendarmes, elite mobile teams, traffic patrols and military units, all the while keeping the politicians happy. Bruno wondered what he would do in such circumstances to revive morale. It would need something different, a new focus for the search. Perhaps it was time to lift the search altogether, regroup and focus the armed units on a different mission, guarding the most obvious target points. It would be a risk to let the quarry run free, but they might have a better chance of catching them if they did. And they needed to focus on the new dimension, the two strangers.

No sooner had he thought the words than Yveline turned from her phone and called, "We have a match, fingerprints from the house fit an ex-con called Abd-el-Kader Demirci. He did two years in Fresnes for drug trafficking."

Where he was radicalized, thought Bruno, like so many other young men from immigrant families. Two-thirds of France's prison inmates were Muslim, and more and more of them were fervent jihadis by the time they came out.

Yveline darted across the room to the printer, where Demirci's prison mug shot was spooling from the roller, followed by his personal file and prison record. Yveline took the photo to the clinic, to see if Fabiola would allow her to show it to al-Husayni.

Bruno leafed through the other papers that came from the printer. Demirci came from a family that had been part of the Turkish minority in Algeria, descendants of the Turkish officials who ran North Africa in the era of Ottoman power. Mainly police, military and administrators, they had long been loyal to France during the Algerian War of Independence, and many of them were persecuted after the French left and the war was won. Demirci had three brothers, and remembering what al-Husayni had said about the two men looking like twins, he asked Yveline to see if there were any files, photos or criminal records for the brothers. Then he began thinking about the implications of there being two terrorist combat teams in the area, able to hit two separate targets at the same time.

"Yves is at the scene," said J-J, referring to the head of the forensics team. "He's found the bullets that hit al-Husayni. It was a small gun, and he's sure it was fired from a Manurhin with a silencer fitted. It's a French copy of the Walther 5.56 millimeter, the caliber the Anglo-Saxons call a two-two."

A small bullet and slowed by the silencer, thought Bruno. A bigger gun could have blown Husayni's arm off. But why would they want to kill him? Had he lost his usefulness? And the shooter had been talking on his phone, presumably back to his base. Perhaps Mustaf had panicked after Bruno's phone call, despite the way the Flemish-speaking Ahmed had sounded like a Dutchman. They must have called al-Husayni's driver and told him they were leaving and to get out fast and kill the now-useless al-Husayni. That call could be traced and the numbers monitored as they triggered each new cell tower that came into range.

He called the familiar number at France-Télécom and asked for an emergency review of the calls logged by the St. Cyprien cell towers for the thirty minutes after the *tabac* owner's call to him. They should send the breakdown to Yveline's e-mail address at the *gendarmerie,* he said. Then he told J-J and Yveline that they might be getting some useful phone numbers and then that he had to leave for an appointment with the mayor.

"Anything that you'd like me to say to Delaron about this ex-nun?" he asked J-J. "He's camped outside, desperate for some comment from you. He probably also wants something on the helicopters, maybe the shooting."

"There's nothing I can say," J-J replied tiredly. "I'm sorry the woman committed suicide, but we interviewed her several times, followed it all up and found nobody who corroborated her allegations. Tell him to get some statement from the police spokesman. I'm not saying a word."

"Can I tell him anything about this latest development with al-Husayni?" Bruno said. "It might help. Every lead we've had has been because some member of the public has called us with information. And visible roadblocks, helicopters cruising overhead, a shooting in St. Cyprien—we can't keep this secret."

"We have to," interrupted the brigadier. "The minister wants this wrapped up quietly, no publicity, no panic. He's given us all the resources we need. It's now up to us to settle this."

Bruno shrugged, picked up his képi and left, thinking to himself that to live in a democracy was a wonderful thing, except for the politicians. Outside, Philippe was leaning against his car, camera at the ready.

"What's this about a shooting in St. Cyprien?" he demanded.

"I'm not allowed to say a word to the press," Bruno replied. "And J-J says any comment on the ex-nun's suicide will have to come from the official police spokesman, sorry."

"Can you tell me if this is linked to those photos you asked us to run, the woman who died at Commarque?"

Bruno raised an eyebrow, grinned and walked on.

"You know the psychologist, Duteiller, is saying that J-J was morally responsible for the suicide."

"Don't tell me you believe that. Bye, Philippe."

"Come on, Bruno. How about some give-and-take? I help you when I can." Philippe tried to look appealing. It didn't suit him.

Bruno stopped and tapped him on the chest. "You know the wonderful thing about living in a country with a free press?"

Philippe sighed. "Okay, tell me."

"It means I'm also free not to have to talk to you."

"But you're a public employee. We pay your salary."

"Quite true, Philippe, and I'm glad you brought that up. My salary has been frozen for two years, even with my promotion. May I have a raise this year, please?"

"Very funny."

"I do have one lead for you, on this ex-nun who committed suicide. You know she was an alcoholic?"

Philippe nodded. "That's old news."

"Here's something new. If you go up to the scout camp you might talk to the couple who are the caretakers, Alain and Anne-Louise."

"The priest who left the Church and got married to his housecleaner?"

"She's a nurse. She was only cleaning the church as a volunteer. She's an orphan and she was at the Mussidan orphanage. Ask her about this ex-nun. She's talked to the police, but nobody else has heard her version yet."

Chapter 23

Yacov and the mayor were already installed in Ivan's bistro when Bruno arrived, to be greeted with a hug from Yacov and a wave from Ivan behind the counter, who called out, "You're getting the *menu du jour* like everybody else."

"It's been too long," said Yacov.

"I don't see Bruno much these days, either," said the mayor, drily. "I presume you know something about all the helicopters and the armed camp that has sprung up around our *gendarmerie*."

"And I'm under orders to say nothing about them," Bruno replied. "But since we have to inform Yacov that security concerns require us to postpone the formal opening of the scout camp, I'm sure he'll put two and two together."

"That's what I just told him," the mayor said. "I also told him what you told the council and swore him to secrecy."

Bruno nodded as Ivan placed a tureen of vegetable soup on the table along with a basket full of bread. He returned with a bottle of the house white wine and a carafe of water.

"All sorts of rumors are swirling around town," said Ivan. "Dead nuns, Arab terrorists, and now Fabiola performing some emergency operation in the clinic and a mysterious patient with a gendarme with a machine gun guarding his door."

Ivan's eyes swiveled across the dining room to where Dr. Gelletreau was lunching with his wife, the pharmacist. The two of them studiously avoided Bruno's eye. He waved a greeting at them anyway. There was no way to keep secrets in a town like St. Denis.

"I think I understand why the formal opening of the camp can't go ahead," said Yacov. "I even heard some rumors at the embassy in Paris."

Bruno was not surprised. He knew that Yacov's law firm did a lot of work with the Israeli embassy, and Yacov, although a French citizen, had chosen to do military service in Israel and was still in the Israeli naval reserve.

"What were they saying?" he asked.

"Arab terrorists, something about a medieval document and the Arab claim to Jerusalem, plus a dead Israeli woman who was a Palestinian sympathizer."

"Does Maya know about this yet?" Bruno asked.

"Yes, I called her, but she's coming to Paris anyway. There's a meeting of the family trust and I have to deliver a report on the camp's progress. And she wants to come down and see you and say hello to Pamela and the mayor and all the schoolkids who did the design for the museum. She'll travel incognito, but she definitely wants to come and see the camp for herself."

"We can probably arrange that," said the mayor. "And we three can visit it this afternoon, if Bruno's other duties allow him an hour or so to join us."

Bruno nodded and poured some wine into the last of his soup. "I can do that." He picked up the bowl and drank.

"*Chabrol,*" said Yacov, smiling. "I remember that." He put a little more soup into his bowl, added wine and drank it down.

Ivan brought plates of pâté and pickles and said in a low voice to Yacov, "The pâté is venison, is that okay for you? That green bowl with the pickles is our special new sauce, Haitian *épice,* a friend of Bruno taught me how to make it and now it has become very popular, spicy but I think you'll like it. *Poulet chasseur* to follow."

"That's fine, thank you. I'm not kosher. Venison is great and so is chicken. What's the dessert today?"

"Apple tart. You've eaten that here before, the last time you were here. Red wine coming up. Bon appétit."

"Ivan never forgets a face of anyone who's eaten here," said the mayor. "I'd be delighted to welcome your grandmother here again, so long as the security question is resolved. When is she coming to France?"

"Monday. She'll rest for a day, hold the trust meeting Wednesday afternoon and was planning to come down here for the opening next weekend, but we can delay that until you're sure it's safe."

The mayor sighed and sipped his wine, and they began to eat. After a while the mayor spoke.

"I hate to say this, but after what happened in Paris, I'm not sure we can say that anywhere is safe these days. Not even St. Denis."

"The question is whether we can ever bring over some Israeli scouts to stay at this camp. As you'll understand, that is something that Maya very much wants to happen. And we'd also hope that scouts from this region would come to camp in Israel as our guests."

"We have no problem with that," said the mayor.

"When your scouts come, I'm sure the mayor would agree that I should move in and stay with them," said Bruno. "And we'll have every member of my hunting club patrolling the grounds while they stay. Around here, we take our obligations to guests very seriously. Your grandmother has done a lot for this town, and we're prepared to do the same for her."

Yacov raised his glass, and Bruno and the mayor clinked theirs against it.

"Celebrating?" asked Ivan as he cleared the plates.

"You could say that," said the mayor.

"If you're celebrating, where's the lovely Amélie?" Ivan asked, sending a stab of guilt through Bruno. He hadn't called to say he'd been held up. Despite all her help, he hadn't even thought about inviting her to lunch.

"She's tied up in the office working on the report she has to write," he said smoothly, chiding himself for being so glib. "But we're visiting the new camp after lunch, and she'll be joining us for that." He explained her role and presence to Yacov, adding how useful she had been.

"I told you she'd be useful," said the mayor. "I know you've been tied up with this security business, but I'm surprised you didn't invite her to join us for lunch."

Feeling ashamed of himself, Bruno pulled out his phone. "You're right, I should have done," he said as he dialed.

"Sorry, Bruno," Amélie answered. "But I'm enjoying a perfect homemade quiche with Monsieur and Madame Fauquet in their apartment above the café. It's such a treat and they're very kind. Perhaps I could join you later for coffee."

Bruno felt stunned, and the mayor was equally surprised when Bruno explained. While the very soul of hospitality in their café, Fauquet and his wife guarded carefully the privacy of their home.

"I've never been invited up there for a quiche," said Bruno.

"Nor me," said the mayor. "And she's barely been here a week."

"She sounds like quite a woman," said Yacov.

Over the apple pie, they agreed that they would take the mayor's car, which could seat four in comfort, unlike Bruno's van. When the mayor left to get it, Bruno took Yacov to Fauquet's for coffee and called to ask Amélie if she would like to join them. She should be ready to wear the rubber boots again, he warned her. He then called Alain at the camp to tell him they were coming.

Yacov stood, smiling appreciatively as Amélie approached their table. Bruno had grown accustomed to her colorful style of dress, but Yacov seemed captivated by the combination of her bright yellow jeans and matching headdress, along with an even-brighter red polo shirt. And Yacov's height with his slim, athletic build and dark good looks seemed to be having an equal effect on Amélie. She held out her hand to be kissed rather than shaken, and she treated Yacov to one of her beaming smiles as he brushed her fingers with his lips.

Bruno made the introductions, and Yacov and Amélie quickly discovered that they had been to the same law school in Paris and began trading stories about professors they had known. When the mayor rejoined them, he asked how the quiche had been.

"Perfect," Amélie replied, almost casually. "The pastry was as light as a feather." She turned to Yacov, resuming their reminiscences of law school.

It had become a perfect spring afternoon, bright sunshine with scattered clouds like white puffballs and a gentle breeze that set the young green leaves of the willows by the river quivering so that the trees seemed almost to dance on the water. Mother ducks paddled serenely, each with a row of tiny ducklings behind her like warships in line of battle. An angler standing in the shallows was casting his fly in a long, flickering curve that just kissed the surface of the river.

"I'm falling for this place," Bruno heard Amélie say from the backseat. "I've barely been here a week, but it's so green and the landscape so gentle. In Paris you forget that France is like this."

The mayor took a slightly roundabout route to pass Oudinot's farm, where half the hillside was filled with golden daffodils and the other half with grazing cattle. As the road climbed they saw ewes, their fleece gray after the winter, with their snowy-white young lambs. Picking their way along the skyline was a line of children riding ponies, and it looked like Pamela was leading them. Bruno rolled down a window to call and wave, but they were too far away to hear him. Then to his delight came the unmistakable double note of a cuckoo, the first he'd heard that year.

"That's it," he cried, turning to see Yacov and Amélie craning their necks and almost cheek to cheek as they stared out of her window to try to see the bird. "The cuckoo makes it official. Spring is here."

Bruno turned back to face ahead and saw the mayor give him a wink; he'd obviously been watching Yacov and Amélie in his rearview mirror. What an extraordinary gift it was, thought Bruno, this mystery of human attraction. What was it that made the current pass between two people? And why was it—he thought of Isabelle—that its power could endure so long?

There were women who were not conventionally pretty or striking to whom he felt powerfully drawn, and there were stunningly beautiful women who left him cold. There were women he liked, and whom he acknowledged to be attractive and alluring, like Amélie, but who did not stir him that way. And yet Yacov and Amélie had responded to each other almost at once. He wondered what might come of it. And the miracle of human attraction had little to do with age. Horst and Clothilde were in their sixties, had enjoyed an on-again, off-again affair for most of the last three decades, and now they were marrying. Would that ever happen to him? A woman whom he could commit his life to, have children with, grow happily old with as they waited for the coming of grandchildren?

"We're here," said the mayor, bringing the car to a halt as it crested the last hill.

The rutted track was no more, filled in with freshly rolled gravel, and the sunlight warmed the honey-colored stones of the farmhouse and gleamed from the solar panels on the barn roof. The bell-shaped tents reminded Bruno of the wigwams from American Western movies, or were they called tepees? Recent rains in the hills swelled the small waterfall into a tumbling foam. The bright new grass on the long slope down to the stream looked smoother than a carpet, and the whole valley seemed blessed with an air of welcome and peace.

"It looks better than I could have dreamed," said Yacov as the mayor drove on and parked beside the farmhouse.

The small piles of builders' rubble had been cleared away, and half-a-dozen chickens were clucking as they pecked at the earth and explored the territory of the coop that had been built since Bruno's last visit. Alain and his wife were waiting for them at a large wooden table on the terrace before the old farmhouse that was their home and office. Young geranium plants peeked through the potting soil in four big terra-cotta urns that flanked the terrace.

"*T'as fait chabrol?*" asked Anne-Louise as the mayor shook Alain's hand. Have you had your *chabrol*? It was the old Périgord form of the traditional peasant greeting, inquiring whether a guest had yet eaten.

"We've had lunch, thank you, and what a pleasure to see you settled in and the place looking so well," the mayor said. He introduced Yacov. Alain led the way to the barn, but Anne-Louise put her hand on Bruno's arm to keep him back and murmured that she had spoken to Philippe Delaron about her time at the children's home in Mussidan.

"If that old bitch could blacken the name of a good priest after his death, I thought it was only fair to do the same to her. She was a cruel woman, cruel and vicious. She enjoyed beating us, you could see it in her eyes. And as she hit us she would always tell us it was for our own good, that she was teaching us to avoid the flames of hell. Children are so helpless."

Bruno nodded. "You and Alain will make the youngsters who come here very happy. It looks homely."

She looked fondly toward Alain who was pointing out to Yacov the places for the planned vegetable garden, the basketball court and sports field.

"He's happy here," she said. "He feels he has a purpose in life again. It was hard for him, leaving the priesthood, and I felt a lot of pressure on me to make him feel that what we had together was worth the sacrifice he'd made."

"Is he still a believer?"

"We both are, but not in a way the Church would recognize. I've never thought God had much to do with buildings, or with priests. I think the God we believe in is closer to us here in this little valley. It's a place touched with grace."

"I can understand that," said Bruno. "The shelter it gave to two Jewish children in the war makes it blessed. Did you know they were Protestants, the farmer and his wife who lived here?"

"Yes, Alain told me." She paused, then looked him in the eye. "I am glad you sent Philippe to see me. It's something I've long wanted to get off my chest, but I thought the Church would just ignore it, sour grapes from a woman who lured a priest away from his vows. But it wasn't like that, Bruno. Alain was so unhappy, torn not between me and the Church but between himself and his own faith and what he felt the Church had become, a kind of obstacle between him and God."

"It must have been a great trial for him."

"He's found peace now. Let's go and join them."

Alain and Yacov were upstairs in the barn, and the mayor and Amélie were exploring the kitchen area, Amélie using her phone to take photographs as the mayor looked into the cupboards and then opened the fire door of the wood-burning stove to see how big it was inside. Alain had already chopped a supply of firewood and kindling that was stacked neatly against the barn wall.

"It's great," Yacov called down from upstairs. "Better than I hoped for."

"Have you got the package?" the mayor asked Bruno. "I put it in the trunk of my car."

Bruno went to fetch a parcel wrapped in brown paper and tied with string. It wasn't heavy, the thickness of a large book and about half a meter square. He handed the package to Yacov and suggested he open it. Two blue enamel plaques emerged, ordered by the mayor from the same firm in Périgueux that made street signs for all the communes in the region. The first said, in capital letters, CAMP DAVID. Beneath, in lowercase, was written: THIS CAMP IS NAMED IN RESPECTFUL MEMORY OF PROFESSOR DAVID HALÉVY, WHO WITH HIS SISTER, MAYA, FOUND REFUGE HERE IN 1943–44.

The second sign said simply: HERE LIVED MICHEL AND SYLVIE DESBORDES, WHO PROTECTED TWO JEWISH CHILDREN FROM THE STORMS OF WAR IN THEIR SIMPLE HOME, AND WHO WERE KILLED BY ENEMY FIRE IN JUNE 1944 WHILE TRYING TO RETURN THE CHILDREN TO THEIR PARENTS.

Yacov stared at the plaques for a long moment, and then said a simple thank you and shook the hand of the mayor, Bruno and Alain. Amélie was weeping and trying to take photographs at the same time.

"We thought we'd put the Camp David sign above the barn

doors," said the mayor. "The other one for the Desbordes will go above the front door of the farmhouse."

"That's great," said Yacov. "You've given me an idea. Maybe we could make a third sign, to put by the waterfall at that place where you and I went swimming, Bruno. We could call it Maya's Pool."

Chapter 24

There ought to be a collective noun for a group of archaeologists, thought Bruno as he entered the cave beneath the ruined château of Commarque. Before him was an excited throng of the friends of Horst and Clothilde, all jostling to see the image on the small laptop screen. Horst stood at one corner, perched perilously atop a rocking boulder. His arm was plunged into a gap in the cave wall, and a long cable snaked beneath his arm and down to the laptop. Clothilde was trying to hold the boulder stable with one foot while one arm was pressed supportively against Horst's back and her head was craned to catch a glimpse of whatever was on the screen.

Clothilde's call had come as the mayor drove from the camp, asking Bruno and the other passengers to join them at Commarque at once. And with triumph in her voice she had added, "Eureka!"

A "dig" of archaeologists, he thought suddenly. That would fit. He could identify Barrymore from Oxford, Manners, the former soldier from England, and the German from the Neanderthal valley. There was one unknown woman in the scrum of scholars around the laptop, who must be Lydia, Clothilde's friend from Oxford. Conflicting orders were being shouted in German, French and English for Horst to move the lens this way or that and shine the lamp left or right, up or down.

"It's so exciting," said the count, extricating himself to greet the newcomers. "They can look inside the cavity with that device, and they've found what seems to be a tomb."

"How does it work?" asked the mayor.

"It's a much-bigger version of the cameras doctors use to see inside the body. It lets us look into the cave behind the wall," the count explained. "One of the Germans brought it as a wedding present for Horst, and once they realized this was a false wall they drilled through."

"Wouldn't it be easier if you raised the laptop so that Horst could see which way he's pointing the cable with the camera lens?" asked Amélie, pulling out her smartphone and diving into her handbag for a small case that contained a selection of cables. "Wait, I think I've got a solution."

She burrowed her way through the throng of people, smartphone in hand, and reemerged at the back of the laptop, examining the cables. A chorus of protests arose as the laptop screen went black, but then the ghostly gray image reemerged while a second image appeared on the screen of her phone. Amélie handed her phone to the count.

"You're the tallest guy here," she said. "Hold the phone so Horst can see the screen and then he'll know where he's pointing the cable."

"That's better," said Horst as the count did as she suggested. The protests from the archaeologists gave way to murmurs of appreciation and a tumble of competing interjections, from which Bruno made out the words "medieval" and "tomb," followed by "Crusader" and "thirteenth century," and finally he heard the unknown female voice declare "Templar."

The count handed Amélie's phone to Manners and left the

archaeologists to it. Once out in the open air, the count then explained that the seismic survey and the ground-penetrating radar had between them defined the dimensions of the cavity that lay hidden behind the one in which the archaeologists now stood. The cavity, which seemed to have no entrance or exit or connecting passage, was six meters deep and four meters wide and tapering from three meters in height down to a single meter the farther it went back into the hill beneath the château. But this cavity appeared to be protected by an almost-impenetrable wall, two meters thick, of solid stone.

Lydia Manners had then observed that she had never before seen anything quite like the strange geology of the cave they were standing in. She'd examined the face of solid rock that stood between them and the cavity. "I've never seen limestone do that before," she had said, pointing to the way the rock seemed to change in color and texture, the chalky limestone running in almost geometrical streaks.

Then another of the archaeologists, the count explained, had telephoned a geologist friend and e-mailed to him photographs taken with his phone of the rock, the surrounding limestone and the streaks of white calcareous stone. The geologist had confirmed it looked like a schist boulder, possibly brought by glacial action. By this time, Lydia Manners and her husband were scraping gently at the calcareous stone and pronouncing it to be pure chalk. Clothilde commented that it reminded her of the hidden caves in Cappadocia, Turkey, where caves and passages had been concealed behind false walls formed of large boulders mortared into place, the joins covered by moistened chalk dust which was left to dry.

"At that point there was no stopping them," the count continued. The archaeologists had begun to measure the outer cave and agreed that the boulder could have been rolled in to block access to the deeper part of the cave and thus form the hidden cavity. The boulder had then been sealed into place with smaller stones and chalk. At the top of the boulder, they found the chalk was only a thin layer. Scraping it away, they realized they could get a light and a mirror inside to get some sense of what the cavity contained. Horst's German friend from the Neanderthal valley then said he could do even better. The cable with its lens and light was brought and inserted through the thin gap in the chalk, and that was how they had been able to see the tomb. At which point Clothilde had called Bruno.

"So the cave was deliberately hidden by bringing in that boulder," said Bruno. "But it must weigh tons."

"They could have brought it by rolling it over logs of wood as they did building the Pyramids of Egypt," the count replied. "And now they have found the tomb, which I imagine contains the remains of one of my ancestors, and who knows what else. Clothilde called the ministry in Paris," he went on. "They'll have to authorize a full opening of the cave. It will be quite a job, drilling around the boulder. But now that we know there's a tomb there, it should be just a formality. Usually when the ministry gets such a request they consult the experts at the Musée National, which is Clothilde. And I'm the landowner, and I suppose I'll have to agree."

"You don't sound too happy about it," said Yacov. "Is there a problem?"

"It's certainly a medieval tomb. There's an effigy of a knight above the sepulcher with crossed feet, which is usually the sign of a Crusader, and a cross on his shield which looks like a Templar sign, which is interesting but a mixed blessing. It means we'll be overrun with Templar enthusiasts looking for lost treasure."

Bruno nodded, remembering the crowd of cars and sightseers that had thronged this place after Philippe Delaron's story in *Sud Ouest*.

"Look over there," the count said, pointing across the valley to where a knot of people was staring at them with binoculars. "I closed the château today, but we can't stop them walking through the valley, so they've set up camp to watch what we're doing. The moment we leave they'll be clambering all over this spot."

"You could fence off the access to this cave," said Amélie.

"That won't stop them," the count said glumly. "We'd need a security guard around the clock and probably have to fence off the valley itself, which I'd hate to do, and it would cost money."

"We might be able to help with that," said the mayor. "I think we could find some money in the Conseil Régional budget."

"And think of the publicity," said Yacov. "Commarque will become one of the hottest tourist attractions in the region."

"And as you said, who knows what you might discover inside that tomb?" said Amélie. "Maybe you'll even unearth this long-lost Testament of Iftikhar. You know the Templar legends, you could find the Holy Grail, the Ark of the Covenant. It's going to be huge."

"Sorry to interrupt, but I have to get back to St. Denis," said Bruno, looking at his watch. "I just need to speak with Clothilde before I leave."

He headed back to the cave, and Amélie followed to exchange her phone for one belonging to Lydia Manners, checking that she had recorded the images of the tomb. The archaeologists were still clustered around the laptop.

"I'm heading off," he said, addressing Clothilde's back as she peered at the screen. "We'll see you at Laugerie Basse at seven-thirty."

"We might be late," she said, not shifting her gaze from the screen. "It looks like we could have some Paleolithic engravings on the wall inside this cave. I'm pretty sure that's a horse's head, and there are some of those mysterious marks you see at Lascaux."

"It's your wedding, and they're opening the inner cave just for us so all your archaeologists can say they've dined in a cave that contains a prehistoric grave," said Bruno. "You can't be late."

"Don't be silly, Bruno. All the guests are right here, and the wedding itself isn't until tomorrow afternoon. That's the important bit."

"For tonight, Clothilde, the food is the important bit, and you know better than to mess around with a chef."

She gave no reply. Bruno shrugged and headed back to the car, phoning J-J to say he was on his way back to St. Denis.

"Sorry we can't take better care of you this evening," he said to Yacov, turning around from the front passenger seat.

"You already told me about the wedding, so I've invited Amélie to join me for dinner." Yacov and Amélie exchanged the kind of glance that Pamela would have described as significant.

"He's taking me to the Vieux Logis," she said. "But I really like weddings. Would it be okay if we waited at the *mairie* tomorrow and threw rice and confetti?"

"You'd be very welcome," he said. "Clothilde couldn't be happier. It looks like they've found some prehistoric engravings as well as the tomb."

Amélie was fiddling with her phone. "I'm just e-mailing you some of the images from the tomb so you'll have them for your media friends."

Back at the *gendarmerie* in St. Denis, Bruno was greeted by the brigadier with a testy "Where the hell have you been?"

Startled, since he'd already explained his plans to Isabelle that morning, Bruno reminded the brigadier that he'd been with the mayor and one of the trustees of the scout camp to arrange the postponement of the formal opening. Evidently under intense pressure from Paris, the brigadier grunted a reluctant assent.

Fortunately, J-J was waiting to haul Bruno across the road

to the Bar des Amateurs for a beer, saying he couldn't stand the atmosphere of frustration around the *gendarmerie* for another minute. They took a seat on the small terrace with their drinks, and J-J drank half of his glass before speaking.

"No news on the search for Mustaf," he said. "Isabelle thinks they'd already prepared some backup accommodations, maybe even a camper. The road patrols are now stopping all vans and trucks for proper searches, but we can't keep up the current level of manpower much longer. The overtime bill is going through the roof, and there are no new leads, unless your hunters and hoteliers come up with something."

Bruno shook his head. He'd already checked his phone for messages.

"And we've had to arrange a guard for some Professor Philip-peau in Paris," J-J added. "The damn doctor forgot to pass on Dumesnil's message that he'd had to give them the man's name. Apparently it was the first thing Dumesnil said when he was able to speak. Thank heavens the nurse remembered. And it looks like they'll let us interview him at the hospital first thing tomorrow morning, so we'd better meet here at the *gendarmerie* at seven sharp. There's one bit of unrelated news which I personally found very welcome. We had a team searching through the records at the psychiatric hospital to find how Leah got the fake ID card from the patient, and an interesting name came up. Want to guess?"

"No idea."

"Madame Duteiller, the psychologist who's been giving me such grief over the pedophile case. She used to work there, but they asked her to leave, citing professional differences. When pressed, one of her colleagues said they found her work, I quote, 'less than reliable and not very helpful.'"

"So she was fired?"

"And walked right into a new job down here, where we provincial dummies don't know any better. Anyway, it gives me a bit more ammunition when the magistrate and prefect's wife start nagging at me again. In the meantime, we've asked the head of her clinic in Périgueux whether they checked her professional credentials with the Paris hospital."

"You're playing rough," Bruno said. "Isn't there some proverb about never taking a sledgehammer to crack a nut?"

"I've barely started. One of my sergeants has a friend on the news desk at France Bleu Périgord, and he's leaked what her Paris colleagues think of Duteiller." He glanced briefly at Bruno. "And I hear your friend Delaron from *Sud Ouest* has been making inquiries about this ex-nun beating the kids in her care. So if Duteiller thinks she can use the media to embarrass me, she's about to learn what it's like to be on the receiving end. You want to play with the big boys, you play by their rules."

"Is she going to be charged with tax evasion on that *gîte* she was renting out?"

"Officially that's up to the *procureur,* but he'll be reluctant to go ahead unless he knows the mayor of the commune wants a formal prosecution, since it involves local taxes rather than national. But Prunier has been helping the mayor understand the benefits of justice being seen to be done, particularly when it comes to renting to terrorists."

J-J finished his beer, slammed his empty glass on the table between them and looked Bruno squarely in the eye.

"I worked that case as hard as I could, interviewed everybody, checked dates and time, ran cross-referencing on every single allegation and looked into the background of everyone who was said to have abused the kids. At the end of all that, we had no more real evidence than we did at the beginning—these recovered memories from hypnosis and the unsupported claims of the embittered ex-nun. What would you have done?"

"Laid it all out to the investigating magistrate and said if she wanted to bring in another investigative team, she was free to persuade Prunier to spend even more of his budget on a case that was going nowhere."

"I knew Prunier would back me up, in spite of the prefect's wife. But that wasn't the point. What I wanted to do was to come out and say the allegations were unfounded, that these people had been wrongly accused. And the magistrate wouldn't let me do that. She was content to let those allegations hang around the necks of those men, one dead, one senile and one too old to defend himself, rather than come out openly and say she'd been wrong. It makes me sick."

Bruno turned down J-J's suggestion of a second beer, reminding him that he had a wedding rehearsal dinner to attend. He knew J-J, who had become friendly with Horst and Clothilde after meeting them during another case, had been invited to the wedding itself on the following day—if the manhunt gave him time to attend.

Bruno drove home, planning to feed his chickens and take Balzac for a brisk walk through the woods. And while he was not greatly surprised to find no sign of the two archaeologists who were staying with him, there was a strange car, a rental, in his driveway. And there was no sign of his dog. He whistled and heard an answering bark from behind his house, and a familiar voice called out, "We're here."

Isabelle, lit by the evening sun, was seated on the grass before the barn, Balzac looking ecstatic as he lay in her lap having his tummy scratched. There was a glass of white wine on a tray beside her and a bottle, nearly half empty, of Château des Eyssards, a dry Bergerac wine he liked. She knew where he kept a spare key for those rare times when he locked the house and felt sufficiently at home to help herself. The thought gave him a little thrill of pleasure.

"I thought you were going to the wedding dinner," she said. "But I really wanted to see him."

"I just came back to walk him, feed the chickens and change before going out," Bruno replied, noting wryly that it was Balzac she had wanted to see rather than him. Could he possibly be jealous of his own dog? "It's good to see the two of you together. And congratulations on your new job."

"It's mostly boring bureaucracy and politics so it's a relief when something real like this comes up," she said. "And every time I come back it always makes me wonder why I ever left the Périgord."

A younger Bruno would have seized on that to suggest she stay. But he'd been hurt too often by Isabelle on her occasional forays to the region. She always left again. Her career was her priority. Sometimes he thought that Balzac was the only chink in her armor. But Balzac loved her in return. It was only for Isabelle that his dog would not have come to welcome him.

"You change and go. I'll walk him and I'll feed your chickens and I'll lock up again when I leave. Have a good evening." She blew him a kiss.

He went inside and checked his watch. He'd have time for a quick shower. But first he called Clothilde, who was still at Commarque, full of apologies and saying she'd lost track of the time. He told her that Edouard Lespinasse would drop him at the restaurant, and Edouard would then drive on to Commarque to pick them all up, and he'd drive them home later. He'd see her and her other guests at the restaurant. Then he showered and listened to the local radio news while dressing in a clean shirt, khaki slacks and his blazer.

The first item on the local news was a report on what was described as "an antiterrorist training exercise" involving helicopters and roadblocks, and Commissaire Prunier gave a brief interview saying that any disruption was regretted, but he was confident that the public would understand the need for such training. The second item, which came just as Edouard drove into his driveway, made Bruno pause to listen.

The pedophile case in Mussidan has taken a new turn, with inquiries now being made into the professional credentials of the psychologist Marie-France Duteiller, who treated the three people bringing the allegations that they had been abused at the orphanage. The director of the clinic where she works announced today that she had been suspended after he consulted her former colleagues at the mental hospital in Paris on her qualifications. Madame Duteiller used the controversial technique of hypnosis to recover the supposedly lost memories of the three accusers who claimed to have been abused. One of them today told our reporter that she was no longer sure of what she recalled.

It was a thoughtful Bruno who climbed into Edouard's vehicle for the short drive past St. Cirq to Laugerie Basse. Madame Duteiller was indeed learning what it was like to play by what J-J had called big boys' rules.

For Bruno there were few sights more impressive in the Périgord than the great sweep of the Grand Roc, a sheer cliff more than fifty meters high and nearly a kilometer in length, sweeping down the flank of the River Vézère as it flowed toward Les Eyzies. Almost halfway up this limestone wall was a long horizontal slash in the rock, an overhang that had created a *gisement,* or shelter, up to fifteen meters deep, in which humans had lived for some fifteen thousand years. They had left behind the richest and most impressive relics of the culture of the prehistoric peoples, their arrowheads and spearpoints of flint; their tools and barbed harpoons; their marvelously carved spear-throwers engraved with animals and hunters; their needles and knives, stone saws and scrapers; the awls they made to pierce reindeer hides so they could use sinews to sew garments together.

He would always be grateful to Horst and Clothilde for the way they had encouraged him to probe a little deeper than the cave paintings of Lascaux and Font de Gaume and to see their creators as humans much like himself, responding with courage and invention to the harsh realities of their day. How would he have survived, Bruno often wondered, with only flint tools and a hunter's skill to feed and clothe and warm himself and a family in such a desperately challenging environment?

But looking up at the Grand Roc with the eyes of a modern man, Bruno always smiled to himself at the readiness of the people of the Périgord to learn from their ancestors. Tucked into the long horizontal slice of rock where the cave people had found shelter was a cluster of more modern buildings, taking advantage of the way the rock spared them the need to build rear walls and complete roofs. There were dwellings, a small museum and a ticket office for access to the *gisement* and enough space for half-a-dozen cars to park. He climbed out at the foot of the steps and sent Edouard on to Commarque.

It was to one of these buildings built into the rock that he made his way, a local family-run restaurant that had become one of his favorites, serving plain but classic meals at reasonable sums. He and his fellow hunters lunched here weekly, enjoying the *menu du jour* of soup, pâté, *confit de canard,* salad and dessert for thirteen euros. In summer, he would eat on the terrace, the towering rock above him and the river flowing below. But this evening was a special occasion, arranged by Clothilde. The rear cave, containing the grave of a prehistoric man who had been buried in an upright crouch, clutching his knees, was very seldom opened to the public. The skeleton had long since been removed to a museum, but the damp chill of the cave and the sense of an ancient death made the place inviting only to archaeologists. The waiters crossed themselves before entering.

Tonight for Clothilde's prewedding dinner a long table had been laid inside and a special menu prepared by Madame Jugie, the owner. Bruno kissed her in greeting and left her to welcome the other guests who had arrived, Gilles and Fabiola, Pamela and the baron, Jack Crimson and his daughter, and Bruno's own guest for the evening, Florence, from the *collège*. Clothilde and Horst and the other archaeologists had yet to arrive, but Manners and his wife, Lydia, were already enjoying a glass of champagne at the bar with the count and his daughter.

Then Raquelle, one of the artists who had helped paint the copy of the Lascaux cave that visiting tourists now saw, arrived with Professor Barrymore and the German archaeologists. She explained that Clothilde had insisted on going home to change. Another bottle of champagne was opened and then almost finished when the bride-to-be arrived with her future husband. Clothilde looked stunning in a green silk dress that set off her red hair and had Lydia whispering "Armani" to Florence. Horst looked as if he'd dressed in a hurry, his shirt buttons in the wrong buttonholes, and one of his shoelaces undone. But his guests were indulgent, warmed by the glow of pleasure on his face as he saw his friends assembled and called for more champagne. Bruno felt that he'd been right to arrange once more for the taxi services of Edouard.

They went through the special door at the back of the restaurant and down the steps into the inner cave, ducking slightly beneath the low roof to take their places at the long table, lit only by candlelight. Clothilde sat at the far end of the table, and Horst stood at the place nearest the steps to give some formal words of welcome, and to tip a drop of champagne from his glass onto the place where the skeleton had been found.

"A libation to our ancestors," he declared. "And what better place for a marriage of archaeologists than this wondrous Grand Roc that has revealed to us so much of the life of early humankind. And what a day of discovery we have shared together at Commarque, which I take as a sign from the gods of their approval of our wedding."

The candles suddenly flickered and Bruno crossed his fingers under the table. He thought of himself as only occasionally superstitious, but to invoke the gods and assume their benevolence in a cave such as this where the sense of the past was so palpable struck him as playing with fire. And looking around the table at the raised eyebrows and the nervous glances being exchanged and then noticing the discreet gestures that Pamela, Florence and Fabiola were making to touch the wood of their chairs, he knew he was not the only one so alarmed.

"To Clothilde and Horst and the friendship that has brought us all here together," he exclaimed, raising his glass. And to his great relief, Madame Jugie chose that moment to descend the steps with a cheerful smile and a tureen of soup. Its scents of garlic and wholesome bouillon drove away his sudden mood of dread and replaced it with hunger and good fellowship.

Chapter 25

Bruno had risen at six, drunk two glasses of water with aspirin and then forced himself into a brisk run through the woods with Balzac before taking a shower that he ran first hot and then cold. He fed his chickens, made coffee, boiled an egg and shared his toast with Balzac before driving down to meet J-J.

"I heard on the news about Madame Duteiller's suspension," he began as they set off for the hospital in Sarlat.

"Then you only know the half of it," said J-J, jerking his thumb at the backseat where that morning's *Sud Ouest* had been opened to an inside page. Bruno reached to pick it up. Philippe Delaron's story of his interview with Anne-Louise from the scout camp and her account of being beaten by the nun ran under a subheadline that read "I Don't Believe a Word of It." She said that in all her years at the orphanage she'd never heard a word about sexual abuse, just the endless physical punishments by the sadistic nun.

"Do you think this psychologist had any idea what a storm she was raising with this business?"

"I don't know and I don't care. What I do know is that with the news on the radio and in the paper, her mayor is going to have to file the tax charges against her and probably against her husband as accessory. He was the one who took the cash, and they file a joint tax return, so he's liable."

Bruno nodded, thinking that after what he'd done to Hugues, there was a rough kind of justice in Vaugier facing a stiff fine for tax evasion.

"So it looks as though the case will now go away?" he asked.

"Not until I can get some form of official statement that the inquiry is over and that the allegations were groundless. I want to repair what these fanciful tales did to those poor old men who spent years of their lives helping kids. If the magistrate doesn't have the guts to do it, I'll make my own statement even if it costs me my job. I'm close enough to retirement as it is."

"Have you talked to Prunier about this?" Bruno asked. As overall head of the police in the *département,* Prunier was J-J's boss.

"He always backs me up. The problem is the prefect, or rather his wife. It turns out she's the daughter of a cabinet minister, so her wish is our prefect's command." J-J levered his bulk out of the car and stomped into the hospital.

Auguste Dumesnil had been moved from intensive care into a room that usually contained two beds. He was alone, lying facedown, reading a book that had been placed on a low table beside the bed. His legs were covered by a sheet and blanket that had been raised on some kind of cradle so the cloth did not touch his flesh.

The doctor had said he would be moved within the next two days to Bordeaux for a series of skin grafts on his thighs and buttocks. But he might have to undergo a further operation to ensure that he would be able to urinate normally. Bruno swallowed hard when he heard this, and then tried to make sure his face looked normal when he greeted the armed gendarme at the door and was shown into Dumesnil's room.

"The doctors tell me you're doing well, which is good news, and I may have something to help cheer you up even more," said Bruno. "I was at Commarque yesterday. They've found a hidden cave containing a medieval tomb. I've got some images on my phone." He handed it to Dumesnil.

"Thank you." He took it gingerly, careful not to move anything but his head and arms. "It's not very clear, but that's a tomb of a Crusader, probably a Templar, late thirteenth or early fourteenth century, I'd say. And it looks like marble, which means somebody rich. I presume it hasn't been opened?"

"They can't even get into the cave yet. It was deliberately blocked with a big boulder and sealed. Those photos come from a remote camera that they were able to poke inside."

"So with any luck, I might even be there when it's opened. That's something to look forward to."

"Excuse my interruption, but we only have limited time with you and I need to ask about your attackers," said J-J.

"I expected that so I made a tape recording. The cassette is on the cabinet by the bed. I could identify only one of them, Saïd al-Husayni, obviously acting under compulsion. The big one, whose name I think was Mustaf, was twisting his arm to make Saïd translate their questions and my answers. Then Saïd collapsed and I heard him being ill and then another one took over the translation. He had an accent, maybe Dutch or Flemish. I told them everything I knew, which wasn't much, mainly what I'd already said to Saïd when he came to see me with Leah. Have you confirmed that hers was the body you found?"

"I'm afraid so. It seems both Leah and al-Husayni were being forced to work for the others."

"I'm sorry about that. She was a very promising scholar and I liked her. Never did I dream that something as tame and remote as medieval studies would leave her dead and me hurt like this."

"Are you still in great pain?"

"I wouldn't call it great, more a constant stinging. They gave me morphine, but I'm afraid of becoming addicted, so I've asked them to stop. They say they're steadily reducing the dose and then they'll give me other painkillers. Since they told me I wasn't going to die, I've felt much better, but it's difficult to make sense of it all. I'm hoping you can help me there."

"It seems to be Middle Eastern politics, with some Arabs determined for obvious reasons to suppress or destroy this Testament of Iftikhar," said Bruno. "If it exists."

Dumesnil rolled his eyes. "If it exists, indeed. I still have my doubts. And now it hardly seems to matter if the document is genuine or not. It would appear to have assumed a political life of its own."

"Was that the only reason why they were torturing you?" J-J asked. "Did they question you about anything else?"

"No, it was all about the testament. I thought that by telling them everything I knew they wouldn't hurt me. But they kept wanting more, as if certain that I knew where the testament was, maybe that I even had the original or at least a copy. Perhaps if I had lied, or not told them everything at first, it might have stopped them hurting me, but I think Mustaf took pleasure in it."

"Did you hear any other names?" J-J asked.

"No, and I'm not sure about Mustaf. It was when the phone rang in the other room, and the big one was hitting Saïd when he started to be sick. Someone shouted a question from another room, and I'm sure he said 'Mustaf,' well, almost sure, as much as one can be at such a time."

"Then what happened?"

"I'm not sure, I was passing out and then coming to. They threw water in my face a couple of times. But I think it was then or soon after that they left in a hurry. I remember trying to shift the chair so I could knock over the candle."

"You succeeded," said Bruno. "It was what saved your life."

"I was told that it was the policeman who first arrived who saved my life, with a black woman."

"That was Bruno here," said J-J. "He gave you mouth-to-mouth until the ambulance came."

"Thank you. I'm in your debt."

"Not in the least, I'm just sorry I didn't get there sooner, except that men like that would probably have killed you as soon as they saw my uniform."

"Have you caught them?"

"No, but we have Saïd al-Husayni. We'd tracked down where they were hiding and had helicopters looking for them, but they left, leaving al-Husayni behind. They shot him before they fled, probably thinking he'd outlived his usefulness. He's okay, in another hospital. And he's very worried about you and whether you're alive."

"I am, as you can see, after a fashion. The doctor says I'll need three months in hospitals and another three months to convalesce before I can walk again and get back to my normal life."

"Could you identify any of the men from these photos?" J-J asked, showing Auguste the surveillance photos from the Gare de l'Est. He put them down, one by one, on top of the book Dumesnil had been reading.

Dumesnil studied them carefully in turn. "This big one was the man I think they called Mustaf. He only took his scarf down from his face during the interrogation, but that nose and mouth are striking. And I think the one standing while Leah is sitting at the café table is the one who spoke with the Dutch accent."

"Did they begin torturing you at once?"

"No, they came in and hit me in the stomach and then slapped my face several times, and al-Husayni and Mustaf began questioning me while the others searched the apartment. It was only when I said I had told them everything that they stripped me and tied me onto the chair."

"What did they ask you?"

"All about the testament, what I knew, where it was, who else might have it, what the link with Commarque was. When I said I knew of no link with Commarque they became angry and started slapping me again. They seemed to think these new excavations with that seismic machine were searching for the testament."

"They knew about that?" Bruno asked.

"They thrust a copy of *Sud Ouest* into my face with a photo of Horst at the site."

"How long was it before they put you into the chair?" J-J interrupted.

"Ten, maybe fifteen minutes. I can't be sure. But I know when they arrived. It was shortly before five. I was about to leave for choir practice."

"Did they talk among themselves?"

"Yes, but not in any way I could understand. My Arabic is classical, mainly for reading. Modern Arabic speech is very different. I could make out some words, some of them about whether I was lying, whether they should gag me and how they'd be unable to hear what I had to say if they did. That was all. There were some words about a Jewish farm and another group they called the soldiers."

A knock came on the door, and a nurse entered to tell them their time was up. When Dumesnil said he was fine and could continue, she took his pulse, checked the drip in his arm and then wrapped the black bandage around his arm to measure his blood pressure.

"Were you the nurse who remembered to tell us about warning the professor in Paris?" Bruno asked.

She nodded. "I'm sorry I didn't check sooner that the doctor had passed on the message. Is he all right?"

"He's been under guard since about ten minutes after you spoke to us," J-J said. "And thank you for doing so."

"The patient's pulse is fast and I'm not happy about his blood pressure," she said. "Just one or two more questions and then you'd better go."

"Okay," said J-J and turned back to Dumesnil. "Did they say anything at all that might give an indication of where they were staying, any place-name or road directions?"

"Not that I recall, except for the phrase about the Jewish farm," said Auguste. "Please convey my profound regrets to Horst and Clothilde that I cannot make the wedding and give them my best wishes."

"Of course," Bruno said. "When they showed you the newspaper, did they seem to know who Horst was?"

"Well, yes. I'd talked about Horst and Clothilde and their dig at Commarque when Leah and al-Husayni had come to see me earlier. I even told them about the wedding because I said they might need to talk to them before they went off on their honeymoon. Do you think I might have put them in danger?"

"That's enough," said the nurse. "He's getting upset."

Outside the hospital, which perched on one of the hills that surrounded Sarlat, J-J paused to gaze around the countryside. Bruno assumed that his friend was thinking of the vastness of this region and the thousands of empty farms and ruined barns, the great mass of vacation homes and rental properties that were closed up waiting for the tourist season. It was a great place for terrorists to go to ground. And with much of the countryside thickly wooded, the helicopters would have trouble seeing through the spring foliage that grew thicker each day.

"During the war, the Germans brought in an entire division of troops who'd learned about fighting a guerrilla war in Yugoslavia, against Tito's partisans," Bruno said. "They were experts, but they still couldn't find the Resistance fighters. It's easy country to hide in."

"What on earth are they doing here?" J-J said quietly, as if speaking to himself. "Whatever can be their target? This is a big operation for them and I just can't see what makes it worthwhile. Not even in symbolic terms."

"There was nothing symbolic about those cafés and restaurants, and the nightclub the jihadists shot up in Paris," said Bruno.

"Yes, but it was the night of that big soccer match, France against Germany. There's nothing like that here, except maybe Lascaux, and that's now well guarded. They even have sniffer dogs in the parking lot."

"Just as well," said Bruno. "Horst and Clothilde have arranged a special visit there for their wedding guests this morning. Raquelle is going to be the guide and explain how they did the painting."

"Come on, I need a coffee and a croissant," said J-J, leading the way to his car. They drove down into Sarlat, parking on the boulevard Eugène le Roy and strolling down to one of the cafés on the rue de la République. J-J ordered a double espresso, a croissant and a *pain au chocolat*. Bruno took a simple coffee.

"If it was me, I'd send suicide bombers or gunmen into Notre-Dame," said J-J. "Or into the lines of people waiting to go into the Louvre or into Galeries Lafayette or the place du Tertre in Montmartre, somewhere where they could be sure to hit lots of tourists. Or one of the big train stations or airports or even the Métro. Remember they killed eight people that way in Paris back in 'ninety-five and look what they did at the airport in Brussels.

Those are what I'd call targets. I just can't make sense of their being down here, torturing harmless historians and asking about archaeology."

Bruno's mobile rang. It was just after eight-thirty. He answered and heard the count's voice.

"Sorry to bother you, Bruno. I've just heard from the château. I'm on my way there, my daughter driving me. There's somebody standing on the battlements and threatening to throw himself off. He says he wants to talk to the police officer in charge of the pedophile case, so I called you to find out where I could reach him."

"He's right here with me," said Bruno, handing over the phone, gulping his coffee and putting down a five-euro note to pay the bill. J-J listened, rose, finished his coffee and stuffed the remainder of the *pain au chocolat* into his mouth, picked up the croissant with the other hand and began walking quickly back to the car, grunting occasionally into the phone.

Within fifteen minutes they were at the château, J-J risking the suspension of his car by driving too fast down the rutted road, past the bridge over the stream that fed into the River Beune. He parked, and Jean-Philippe, the kiosk worker, ran down the wooden steps from the big wooden gate to the château, shouting, "This way."

From the main gate, he led the way through the gatehouse, then left past the ruined chapel, up the slope to the barbican, right to skirt the ditch and past the main living quarters into the stone tower of the *donjon*. As they raced, Bruno considered the military cunning of the medieval builders, forcing any attacker to turn, double back and then remain in a killing ground for archers before they could get to the defended core of the building.

The tower was now occupied by a single figure, a man dressed in a gray suit.

He stood on the highest possible point, a gap between two of the battlements, a hand resting on the stone to each side of him. He turned to see Bruno, the first arrival, panting his way up the stairs. J-J was some way behind, and Bruno could hear his friend's labored breathing as J-J paused to rest before attacking the final steps.

"You might have to wait a bit. The commissioner is not a young man anymore," he told the man on the tower. "The poor guy is racing up here. He might have a heart attack."

"I'm sorry," said the man in the suit. He turned and Bruno could see he was wearing a white shirt and a wide dark tie that Bruno recognized as the fashion of the 1980s. The trouser legs were two or three centimeters too short, and the jacket had been made for a much-slimmer man.

"I see you've dressed up for this," Bruno said. "That's your best suit. You take care of your clothes."

"I always have, the nuns taught us that," the man said in a local accent. He turned back to look across the valley. "Put your trousers under the mattress to keep the crease and say your prayers before you sleep."

"I remember," said Bruno. "I was brought up the same way. I still hang my clothes up before I go to bed."

The man turned at that to look at him.

"You must be the policeman from St. Denis, the one called Bruno. I suppose you're here because you think you can rescue me."

"If you'd been a kid, maybe," said Bruno, desperately trying to recall some item of paperwork he'd received, notes on dealing with suicide attempts. "But you're a grown man. If you want to end it all, then as far as I'm concerned you have a right to do so. I'm just worried for the *pompiers,* the guys who'll have to scrape away what's left of you once you hit the ground below. They're volunteers, you know, not really trained for it. They won't be able to sleep for weeks."

"I don't want to be a bother. I've already caused a great deal of trouble to people."

"How do you mean?" Bruno used his question to climb two of the last steps, but the man wasn't even looking at him anymore. He was staring across the valley again.

"I've brought shame and guilt onto innocent people who never did me any harm," he said.

"You mean the people at the orphanage?" Bruno took the last step onto the floor of the tower. The wind was strong up here, shifting direction and coming in sudden, unpredictable gusts, some of them fierce enough to blur the man's words but not quite strong enough to make a full-grown adult lose his footing. He was in his forties with thinning brown hair and was freshly shaved.

"That's right. The Mussidan orphanage. I was at Mussidan until I was sixteen, and then they found me a job in an office, dealing with bills and invoices. I was good at that. At least the nuns taught me to read and do math."

"What's your name?" Bruno spoke the question loudly while waving J-J to stay back. The brochure on dealing with would-be suicides said that only one person should establish contact and should then try to maintain the emotional link that might enable him to talk the person down.

"Francis. They named me after the saint. I was left in a basket outside the orphanage soon after I was born."

"Just like me. I was left at a church," said Bruno. Making sure that Francis was still looking away, Bruno pulled out his phone and turned on its recording function.

"I just stayed there, year after year, watching other children going away to foster families. I suppose I was an ugly child. Nobody ever wanted to take me."

"Maybe the nuns thought you were too useful, Francis," Bruno said, recalling that the brochure had recommended using the person's name to establish personal contact. "You probably helped with the younger kids."

"I don't know. I don't trust my memories anymore. I don't trust any memories, not after I heard the radio this morning. And now I don't trust Madame Duteiller."

"Are you still working at the office, Francis?" The brochure had said to change the subject whenever the victim began to focus on the reason for taking his own life.

"I was at Gaz de France before I got sick. But they're very good, they kept me on for quite a while. Thanks to them I have a disability pension."

"I didn't know you'd been ill, Francis. Was that recent?"

"Two or three years ago now. It was after I'd wanted to get married. I was a bit lonely, and somebody told me to try the Internet and I found this nice woman, at least I thought she was nice. She was from Ukraine, but she wrote very good French. We corresponded for a while and then I sent her money to come to France to join me, but then she had this problem with the father of her child. He wanted money before he'd sign the papers to let his daughter leave Ukraine."

The poor, innocent bastard, thought Bruno, falling for that old trick.

"Then her mother fell ill and needed money for the operation, and I sent that, but that was all I had. I never heard from her again. That was when I got my depression and they sent me to the clinic where I met Dr. Duteiller."

"What happened then, Francis?" Bruno knew he had to keep repeating the man's name.

"She said the hypnosis would help in cases like mine, and she tape-recorded what happened when I went under, her questions about the orphanage and my replies. Then she brought me around, she played it all back, and I was very surprised at the way my voice sounded."

"How often did this happen, Francis?"

"Twice a week, sometimes more. She said we were really making progress. I remember thinking that I knew from her questions what she wanted me to say and I wanted to please her because she was very nice, like a friend. So I said all those things that I was supposed to remember, but I didn't, not really."

"You made it up to please her?"

"She was the first person who'd ever taken much interest in me. But now I know it was all pretending. Once I'd heard on the tape recorder the things I'd said, I couldn't back down. She said they were real memories, but they weren't. And then it all began, the police coming, the questions and the statements, the court case. Then she played me recordings of what the others had said, and she brought in the terrible old woman who'd been a nun at the home, the one who used to beat me when I wet the bed."

"It wasn't your fault, Francis," said Bruno, advancing quietly toward the battlements. "She wasn't a very good doctor, and she did some bad things."

"I know that now, but I said all these dreadful things about the priest and the director, she had them on tape. She played the tapes back to me and insisted that what I'd said was the truth and if I tried to deny them I'd be guilty of perjury and go to jail."

"She was wrong, it wasn't your fault, Francis." Bruno was almost close enough. Two more steps and he'd be able to grab the man.

"But it was my fault that those men were accused. I couldn't look at the old director when Madame Duteiller brought him in. It was so I could confront him with the truth, she said. But that awful old nun was there and I couldn't say a word. I wet my trousers when I saw her. I was so ashamed."

He raised his hand to his eyes, and Bruno leaped forward.

He caught Francis above the knees, twisted so that his back and shoulder bounced off the stone battlement and then fell backward to bring Francis tumbling down onto him, the wide tie flapping into Bruno's mouth. Then J-J was there and they were secure.

Chapter 26

The brigadier was in a better mood when J-J and Bruno returned from the hospital after entrusting Francis to the psychiatric wing. Despite the pain in his shoulder, Bruno drove so that J-J could dictate his notes of the interview with Dumesnil and his statement on the attempted suicide and e-mail the sound file to Isabelle, with a copy to his secretary back in Périgueux to be typed up. They had then changed roles so Bruno could do the same. Once in the *gendarmerie,* they saw on the desk before the brigadier a thick sheaf of printouts of photographs. Two of them had been extracted and were now being pinned by Isabelle to the corkboard on the wall.

"Isabelle's hunch paid off," the brigadier said by way of greeting. "She thought the second of the two unknowns that al-Husayni mentioned might have done time in prison, since that's where most of them seem to get radicalized these days. So she downloaded prison mug shots of all Muslims released over the past couple of years and persuaded al-Husayni to look through them. There they are."

The first portrait posted on the wall was of Demirci, the man identified from his fingerprints. The caption to the second portrait listed his name as Idris Lounis, born in Paris, released after serving three years of a five-year sentence for armed robbery. He had been in Fleury-Mérogis, Europe's largest prison, where two-thirds of the four thousand inmates were now Muslim. Most of France's terrorists had served time and been radicalized there, including the Kouachi brothers, who had attacked the Charlie Hebdo offices; Amedy Coulibaly, who killed four hostages and a policewoman in the siege at the Porte de Vincennes; and Djamel Beghal, who served ten years for his part in an attempt to bomb the U.S. embassy in Paris.

"How in hell do we let this happen in our prisons?" J-J said bitterly. "They commit crimes, we arrest them, they go to jail, and they come out as terrorists. We're doing something wrong here."

"We're working on it," said the brigadier, tiredly.

Isabelle rolled her eyes and then explained that all relatives and known associates of the two men were now being questioned, and their phones and credit card records were being checked. Their photos were now being run through a new facial recognition search engine that was processing dozens of digital surveillance cameras of the kind found increasingly in banks, gas stations and shopping malls. All that was routine, but they had one promising lead. One man Demirci had known in prison, who now lived in Limoges and ran a used-car business, was also being questioned, and his inventory of vehicles and bank accounts had been examined.

"Two cars that were logged into his books when he bought them are no longer on his premises, and there is no evidence of any sale, so we are circulating their details," she added.

"Have you checked for any robberies of *tabacs*?" Bruno asked. "They wanted cigarettes, and they didn't get the ones al-Husayni bought."

"Good idea, I'll get onto it," said J-J, tapping the screen of his phone.

"I'm waiting for prison mug shots from the Belgian police," Isabelle said. "Yveline is printing out French prison photos for men released the previous year; we'll show them to al-Husayni, as well."

She then explained that they had some traces on phones from cell-tower analysis that might belong to the terrorists. But Mustaf's team was highly disciplined, usually keeping their phones turned off and batteries removed. They only turned their phones on for brief periods and usually when they were moving between two and three cell towers in dense areas, so they had become hard to track.

"That means they are still mobile, so we are concentrating on these new vehicles we think they got from this old prison contact in Limoges," she added. "But they could be using motorbikes or even mountain bikes. That's all we have at this moment."

While listening to Isabelle, one part of Bruno's mind was thinking that she was skilled at this, keeping calm while coordinating a complex operation and bringing together different strands of information, never letting the routine stop her from thinking of new ways to drive the process forward. She was good with people and with keeping up morale, brisk without being brusque, efficient without being cold. Curious, he thought, to have at once an impersonal admiration for a female colleague, while at the same time mourning the end of their affair and knowing that his love for her was not just dormant but eager at the slightest encouragement to blaze into flame again.

"Did you get anything out of al-Husayni about possible targets?" J-J asked, looking up from his phone. "He told us Mustaf and the others didn't trust him or Leah and refused to discuss anything about their mission."

"He said the same to me," Isabelle replied. "And I think he's genuinely trying to be helpful, as he was with the photos."

"Getting shot by your supposed colleagues would tend to have that effect," said the brigadier, raising his eyes from a sheaf of cell-phone traffic reports.

"The big news was that he told us about their weapons. Demirci brought a cache of weapons with him, AK-47s, a box of what may be grenades and lots of explosives. They also have gas masks," Isabelle said, brushing her hand over her short hair in a way Bruno remembered. It meant she was tired. "So now Paris is getting worried about the use of biological weapons or nerve gas.

"Al-Husayni also said that Mustaf was contemptuous of Leah and her focus on this testament, even though her efforts had the backing of some influential imams," Isabelle went on. "Apparently Mustaf referred to Leah as a 'Jewish spy' and accused al-Husayni of being a traitor to his people and his faith by living with her. Mustaf's only use for her was to get access to her bank account and her ability to rent cars and lodgings with a French ID. Al-Husayni said he'd tried to persuade Mustaf of the importance of the testament, but he's full of guilt about that because the only result was the torture session with Dumesnil. By the way, J-J, I got your notes of your interview with him, thank you."

"You must have picked up on Dumesnil's reference to hearing them talk about a Jewish farm," J-J replied. "Bruno and I assume that was a reference to the scout camp. Maybe Mustaf and his boys don't know the event has been postponed, but I'll bet they know that the Muslim scouts have backed out. Maybe they even had something to do with that."

"It was going to be next weekend," said Bruno.

"Maybe we could set a trap, see if Mustaf's killers turn up, even though they know we're looking for them."

Bruno shrugged. If they were still searching for Mustaf's gang the following weekend, the brigadier would probably be out of a job. Isabelle turned to look at him, but the brigadier was on his phone to Paris again. "I'll ask him later. It might be worth a try. We have to do something."

"You know I have to attend a wedding this afternoon and the dinner this evening," Bruno told her. "You remember Horst, the German archaeologist who got kidnapped by the Basques? He's getting married to another archaeologist. The guests are getting a special tour of Lascaux this morning."

"Might they be eminent enough to be a target?" Isabelle asked. "Al-Husayni told me that to try and protect Leah, he'd stressed to Mustaf how important archaeologists were in France, and that Lascaux was like a national shrine."

"Only if you're an archaeologist," said the brigadier, putting down his phone. "And Lascaux is now well guarded by a gendarme mobile unit. What time are your archaeologists going there?"

"Their trip is booked for eleven-thirty," said Bruno, looking at his watch. It was just past ten. "I could join them, if you think it's worth it. Then they're having lunch in Montignac and supposed to get back to St. Denis at four for the wedding in the *mairie.*"

"Why not? I have nothing else for you to do except to keep on monitoring those networks of yours, and you can check for any holes in the security cordon the gendarmes have set up," said the brigadier. "Make sure you're armed."

Bruno called Amélie and found her still in her hotel room, and it did not sound as if she was alone. Yacov was supposed to be returning to Paris this morning but maybe not. "How was your dinner last night?" he asked.

"Sublime, that's the only word for it." There was a joyous lilt in her voice that suggested the pleasures of the evening had not ended at the dinner table. "Is there something you need me to do?"

"Not really. I just need to keep an eye on the incoming messages, just in case the networks throw something up. But I can get those on my mobile and I'm calling to ask if you've ever seen the Lascaux cave? There's a special tour for the wedding party, and all the gods of Périgord would curse me forever if I didn't make sure you saw the cave while you're here. I can pick you up in about fifteen minutes."

"I'd love to see it and there's no problem about picking me up. Is there room for Yacov to come, too? We'll wait for you outside my hotel. Do I need your rubber boots again?"

"Sneakers will do. And certainly Yacov can join us. Make sure he brings his identity card."

Bruno went to his office in the *mairie* but saw nothing urgent on his computer. He unlocked the safe to take out his personal weapon. Even unloaded, it was heavy, just over a kilo, but it fit his grip like the handshake of an old friend. He cleaned it as he had so many times before, focusing on the task to dispel the somber knowledge that he held the lives of as many as fifteen people in his hands. He loaded it, checked that the safety catch was on and donned his holster with its spare magazines. Then he picked up Amélie and Yacov and saw to his surprise that Yacov was wearing one of the brigadier's special badges in his lapel. He pondered what that might imply about Yacov's status. It was not something he could raise in Amélie's presence, but he thought about Yacov as they drove out through Les Eyzies toward Montignac and the Lascaux cave.

It was a route he knew well, and on the way he tried to explain to his passengers why the cave was so important to him. Bruno now visited Lascaux at least once a year, since his friendship with Horst had deepened his interest in the rich prehistory of the region. The whole valley had been designated by UNESCO as a special zone of World Heritage, with one hundred forty-seven separate sites of importance and twenty-five painted caves, Lascaux prime among them. Bruno had now visited sixteen of the caves, many of them with Horst and Clothilde. He'd collected a small library of books on the caves and the culture that produced them, regularly attended lectures at Clothilde's museum and at SHAP, the Société Historique et Archéologique du Périgord.

Lascaux was special, Bruno explained, a great gushing torrent of art and color that snatched his breath away each time he entered the dark cave and saw the tumult of painted life above. It was an effort to keep his eyes still as his gaze was drawn in turn to the horses prancing around the great and looming bulls with the raw power of their shoulders and menace of their horns. He had learned to look for the artists' special touches, the gap between leg and body that gave them movement, the suggestion of perspective that made the beasts seem about to wheel and charge. And then his eye would be caught by the sudden hints of other life, a bear, the twin horns of an ibex, the antlers of a red stag, a parade of ponies, some with the shaggy hair of their winter coat, so different from the plump brown horses with their dark manes.

It must have been a great leap, Bruno said, for hunter-gatherers struggling to stay alive and warm to suddenly blossom and explode into such artistry, such an act of creation, and in so remarkable a communal effort to which they must have devoted years of their lives, perhaps whole lifetimes. It was not just the first flowering of human art but equally an unmistakable act of worship and of kinship with the painted animals they had made eternal.

Amélie was a good listener, leaning back against the passenger door so she could watch Bruno as he tried to convey his passion for Lascaux and all that it represented. Yacov was leaning forward from the rear seat, perhaps as much from a desire to stay close to her as to catch everything Bruno said.

What Bruno didn't tell them was his private thought that if his early life had been different, with better teachers in an upbringing that encouraged learning and kept books in the home, he might have passed his baccalaureate and gone to university and become a teacher or even an archaeologist. A decade or so earlier his regret had been that his schooling couldn't help him master the math and science required to join the air force as a pilot. Maybe in a few years' time he'd have other regrets, not being a chef or a winemaker, or not having children.

He crossed the old stone bridge in Montignac and, knowing that Horst and Clothilde had made special arrangements for their group, he drove past the ticket office and out through town toward the hill that housed the caves. As he approached the vast building site of the new Lascaux IV museum, he came to the first roadblock. Two gendarmes wearing flak jackets and helmets waved him down while two more stood, rifles ready, at each side of the road. Another twenty yards farther a Berliet VXB armored car was parked, engine running, and another gendarme in the open turret with a machine gun.

He slowed his police van and waited for them to come to him and see his uniform and the brigadier's special badge. When one of the gendarmes looked through the car window, casting an appreciative eye at the young woman beside him, Bruno said that he was armed and heading to join the archaeologists on the visit to Lascaux. Amélie showed her justice ministry pass, Yacov showed his ID card, and they were waved through, the gendarme saying the archaeologists' van had passed less than five minutes earlier.

"I'll tell the guards farther up to expect the three of you," the gendarme said, keying the button on his lapel radio.

On the final curve of the road that climbed to the cave they came to another roadblock with the same complement of gendarmes and armored car but with a sniffer dog attached to the unit. Bruno was waved through and parked under the trees, noting that there were fewer tourists than he'd have expected. He saw Clothilde and Horst and their friends standing under the shelter where groups waited to enter the cave in turn.

Chapter 27

Raquelle was standing on a small stool, apparently giving the guests a lecture. The guests kept darting nervous glances at the armored car parked by the entrance to the bookshop, and at the watchful gendarme in flak jacket and helmet manning the car's machine gun. There were usually about thirty visitors in each group, all the cave could hold, and the stewards tried to steer them through every fifteen minutes, rotating French guides with ones speaking English, German, Spanish and Japanese. There was room for at most a few hundred people per day to pass through the main cave and narrow axial chamber. Since more than two million tourists came to the region each year, mostly in summer, only a fraction of them could get tickets for Lascaux. That was why the new Lascaux IV museum was being built, to allow more people to appreciate the art and genius of their distant forebears.

Ahead of Clothilde's party were more armed gendarmes, all carrying FAMAS assault rifles, known affectionately as *le clairon,* the bugle, from its modernistic design. Another sniffer dog was checking everyone in line. Bruno went up to the sergeant in charge to introduce himself and his guests. Amélie showed her official ID again with its red, white and blue stripes of la

République, and Bruno asked where he could find the officer in command.

The sergeant saluted, evidently recognizing the badges Bruno and Yacov wore, and reported that the officer was moving back and forth between posts. There was another team covering the rear approach and patrolling the scrub and woodland.

"What about the original cave?" Bruno asked. "You know this one's just a copy."

"I don't know anything about that, we've just been flown in from Bordeaux. The only map we have is a tourist guide," the sergeant said. He pointed to the microphone attached to his helmet. "I'll ask the captain to join us."

The captain arrived a few minutes later, a tall, rangy man of about thirty. He was carrying a Heckler & Koch UMP9, a submachine gun favored by special forces, and wearing grenades on his chest webbing. Yacov seemed unconcerned with the high level of security and was looking around at the placement of guards and the weapons with what seemed to Bruno like a very professional eye. Bruno asked the captain if there was also security at the original cave. He pointed. "It's about two hundred meters due east along that track with the signpost pointing to Le Regourdou."

"What's that, a farm?"

"It used to be, it's now a tourist attraction, a site where the oldest Neanderthal skeleton was found. Weren't you briefed?"

"Yes, but very hastily. We were told Lascaux contained very important cave art, attracted lots of tourists, and we should start antiterrorist patrols and check visitors but not stop the public visiting the cave. We're here until further notice, twelve hours on and twelve hours off."

"You have one squadron, twenty troops?"

"Twenty-four, two armored cars and a scout helicopter on

call, and we're guarding the new museum, too." He glanced down at Bruno's chest, noting the ribbon of the Croix de Guerre on his uniform jacket that the mayor insisted he wear. "When were you in the military?"

"Over ten years ago, combat engineers, *sergent-chef.*"

"And where did you win that?"

"Sarajevo, I was attached to the UN peacekeepers."

"In that case, we're very glad to have you here. Have you heard anything new about the threat?"

"Just that their phone discipline seems remarkably good. At least three of them have been through ISIS training camps and they have AK-47s. These guys aren't amateurs, they'll watch for your patrols and they'll attack another way. Keep your eyes peeled on the woods to the south. Maybe you could get your chopper to do patrols from the air. Do you have access to dogs?"

"Only a sniffer dog for explosives," the captain said, adding that he'd ask his commander about the helicopter.

"I'll see what I can do," said Bruno, shaking his hand. "Good luck."

Bruno called Isabelle to pass on his concern about the lack of briefing and suggested she ask Commissioner Prunier if there was a police canine unit that could help search the woods. Then he joined Clothilde's group, where Amélie was already chatting with Florence, and Pamela was asking Yacov if his grandmother was returning soon to St. Denis. Pamela looked pointedly at Bruno's sidearm and said the so-called security exercise looked much more serious than she'd thought.

"Fabiola told me about the man she treated yesterday, the one who'd been shot," Pamela added. "Are we in any danger?"

"Not much more than anybody else in France these days," he replied, aware that he was being evasive but determined not to cause alarm. "Let's leave it there. I don't want to worry the guests."

"Too late for that. Once they saw the armored cars they've been talking of little else."

In fact, Raquelle had been talking of Max Raphael when Bruno had arrived. He had heard her speak of him before. Raphael was a German Jew, a Marxist scholar who had taken refuge in France in the 1930s. She and Horst maintained that he had been the most significant art historian and theorist of his time. Raphael had said the importance of the cave paintings and the tumult of animal life was that it represented the first time humans had seen themselves as distinct from the animal world, the moment we became conscious of ourselves as human beings.

Raquelle explained to the group how Raphael had taken detailed measurements and found to his astonishment that the prehistoric cave artists had used exactly the ratio that the Greeks of the classical age and the Old Masters of the Renaissance had defined as the golden mean, a ratio of 2:3 to 3:5. Euclid had studied it, Leonardo had sworn by it, the Renaissance scholar Pacioli had called it the Divine Proportion, and modern mathematicians had related it to the Fibonacci sequence of numbers. Raphael's theory was that this sense of proportion was innate and emerged from the shape and proportions of the outspread human hand.

"I had no idea," Florence murmured into Bruno's ear as they went into the cave. "I must look into this and get the *collège* students to work on it. It seems like an imaginative way to teach mathematics."

She stood close to him in the anteroom to the great chamber, where Clothilde explained the tools and pigments the artists had used. At one point Florence edged back to give the others more space and her hip brushed against Bruno's gun. She looked down, saw his holster, and her eyes widened. He put his finger to his lips and stepped back slightly.

Then, one by one, they each stepped into the almost-dark

Hall of the Bulls. The last lights were extinguished, and they were all inside a darkness more complete than most of them had ever known. It lasted perhaps ten seconds, long enough to realize just how far they were belowground and how accustomed they were to the comfort of at least some gleam of light.

Then the lights blazed on, and a collective gasp of surprise and then of enchantment followed as the roof and upper walls above them exploded with life. As their eyes adjusted from darkness to light, the great bulls seemed to quiver, almost to move, so confidently had they been depicted in their power. And then their vision shifted to the horses and smaller animals, their grace and delicacy balancing the size and the might of the bulls.

From somewhere, a hand reached out to grasp Bruno's right arm. It was Florence. He smiled to himself, understanding the reflexive need for human touch in a place so infused with animal strength. He felt her lean against him. Ahead he could see Horst and Clothilde, who each knew the cave well, standing entwined, their arms around each other, their faces lifted to the compelling display above them. In here, he thought, we all become infants again, feeling the innocent awe and delight of children at this moment of intense connection with the humans who made this place sacred some seventeen thousand years ago.

"The great historian Abbé Breuil, one of the first men of our own time to see this place, called it the Sistine Chapel of prehistoric man," Raquelle said, and let the thought sink in. "We don't know why they painted here, why they felt inspired to invest so much collective time and effort on this cave, whether it had a spiritual meaning or something more prosaic, a display of wealth and grandeur to impress other tribes and clans. We do not know what kind of society had developed that could produce this great work of art. We know only that we people of modern times respond instantly to this ancient masterpiece and recognize that it came from people recognizably like us, with the same aesthetic sense, the same response to beauty."

"Oh, Bruno," murmured Florence, still leaning against him, her face turning toward his.

A burst of distant gunfire cut her off. It stopped for a few seconds, then started again in short but slower bursts of four or five rounds. It sounded to Bruno like two separate weapons.

"Stay here," Bruno shouted and darted for the exit and up the stairs into the open air. The sergeant was on his radio, crouching behind the armored car. The machine gunner in the turret, his weapon now cocked, was looking nervously toward the woodlands to the south, and a group of tourists waiting their turn to go into the cave was huddled in the shelter of the steps down to the cave entrance.

"Captain is on his way," the sergeant shouted to Bruno as another long burst of gunfire provoked a chorus of wails from the tourists. "Patrol in the woods saw something, then came under fire."

"Where's that chopper of yours?" Bruno asked.

"Don't know. They're not on this net."

Bruno called Isabelle to report what was happening and asked if reinforcements were available, if the roadblock outside Montignac could hold back any tourist groups heading for Lascaux until there was an all clear. He heard her conferring, and then she came back to say tourists would be stopped and that a squad of army troops would be deployed by helicopter from Brive. Where should they land?

"On the access road, as near as they can get to the cave. The parking lot is too covered by trees for them to land. Do you have an ETA?"

"At least thirty minutes. They have to be rounded up, briefed on the mission, issued ammunition, and there's fifteen minutes of flight time."

Bruno ended the call as the captain arrived at a jog. "At least two of them," he panted. "One fired at a patrol and now another one has started shooting at our chopper on the ground. I asked for orders and was told to stand by."

"I've just been on to the command post," said Bruno. "A squad of army reinforcements is coming by chopper in about half an hour. Right now the priority is protecting these civilians, one group is already in the cave, the other is taking cover by the steps. I'll get them into the cave and your armored car should stay here to protect them. Your men at the roadblock will be getting orders to stop all further tourists. Can your chopper fly?"

"I'm waiting for a report. We have one man down in the patrol."

"You'd better stay here in command. Once we have these civilians under cover, may I take your sergeant to see what's happening with your helicopter? We can try to bring back the wounded man."

"Good plan."

Almost all the tourists, mainly Dutch and German, were only too happy to be steered into the shelter of the cave, crowding in with Raquelle's group. One of them, however, shouldered his way to the steps to face Bruno. It was Horst's English friend, the former soldier called Manners.

"Let me know if I can help, Bruno. You seem a bit short of manpower."

"Not yet, but thank you. It would useful if you could keep them all in order down here. We don't want any panic. Tell them that army reinforcements are on the way."

"Leave it to me."

The sergeant handed Bruno a FAMAS rifle from a rack in the rear of the armored car and a belt with pouches containing extra magazines. Keeping a good ten meters apart, they set off leapfrogging through the trees, one moving and one remaining still. After a hundred meters or so, the sergeant called out, "Fougières."

From ahead, someone called back, "Gallois." Bruno recognized it as a standard password and response among gendarmes, a combination only they were likely to know. Gallois de Fougières had been the first-known gendarme to die in battle, and his remains were buried beneath the gendarme memorial in Versailles.

Bruno and the sergeant moved up, cautiously, to find one gendarme on watch from behind a tree while close by another one was tying a tourniquet around the leg of a third. One field dressing, sodden with blood, lay beside the wounded man. Another had been applied to a thigh wound.

"He's all right, Sarge, not an artery."

In the small clearing ahead stood an unarmed and immobile Fennec helicopter with air force markings. There was a row of bullet holes across the bulbous glass nose and a large pool of oil or fuel spreading beneath it. From the position of the holes, the shooter had been to the east, somewhere to Bruno's left.

"How many are they?" Bruno asked the man on watch.

"Don't know. I heard only one gun that wasn't ours, but it came from different directions. Could be two shooters, could be one doing fire and movement."

"Where's the crew of the chopper?"

"Don't know, they're air force, nothing to do with us."

Frustrated, Bruno turned aside and called his colleague, Louis, the municipal policeman of Montignac, to ask where he was and what was he doing. He replied glumly that the mayor had told him to report to the gendarmes for orders and he'd been assigned to traffic duties.

"Are your *braques* at home, Louis?" Bruno asked. The *braque de Gascogne* was one of the best hunting dogs in France, able to deal with any type of game "from fur to feathers," as the hunters put it. They were excellent gun dogs but also good in the chase. Bruno explained where he was, what he wanted the dogs to do and assured Louis that by the time he reached Le Regourdou Bruno would have arranged new orders from the gendarme general.

He then called Isabelle, shared his thoughts, and within the minute she came back on the line with the general's authorization. Bruno asked her to repeat that for the sergeant of gendarmes at his side. After a brisk "Yes, sir—ma'am," the phone came back to Bruno. The man on watch and the gendarme who had applied the tourniquet then carried the wounded man back to the armored car. Bruno explained to the sergeant exactly what he expected to happen and what he intended to do.

Shortly thereafter came the sound of baying dogs in the woods to Bruno's left, but it sounded like considerably more than the two *braques* he had expected. Then the sound changed, from the bay of the hunt to the sharp bark that means the game had been found. Bruno tucked the FAMAS into his shoulder.

A sudden burst of gunfire erupted, then a second, followed by the yelping of a dog in pain, then more barking. On the far-left side of the clearing about two hundred meters away, a blurred shape emerged from the scrubland beneath the trees and began running, crouched low, branches that had been tucked into his jacket for camouflage bouncing around the figure's head. Bracing his arm against a tree trunk, Bruno sighted carefully and fired two bursts of three shots into the man's hips and thighs. The sergeant beside him followed suit.

The man fell and then a large brown-and-white dog emerged from the trees, crept forward, low to the ground, and then pounced onto the fallen man's chest and began to growl with menace. The man raised his arm, a strange gesture, as if pulling at something rather than trying to fend off the hound. And with that came a sudden flare of brilliant white light, the boom and instant echo of an explosion and then a fountain of dark smoke from which clods of earth rose almost lazily before scattering around the clearing and spattering the shot-up helicopter. Of man and dog, there was not a single sign.

"Mon Dieu," Bruno murmured to himself: a suicide bomber. Why didn't I think of that?

Some instinct made him look at his watch. *"Mon Dieu,"* he repeated. The wedding!

Chapter 28

Clothilde was looking marvelous as she descended gracefully from the hired Rolls-Royce in a beautifully cut dress of heavy cream silk. It hung just below the knee, and the flared sleeves came down almost to her wrists, just revealing a heavy bracelet of silver on one arm. She wore a necklace of the same metal in spirals that Horst had given her, a copy of a piece found in a Neolithic grave in Ireland. Her red hair was piled high on her head, and she carried a springtime bouquet of white and yellow daffodils and lily of the valley, the leaves matching the bright green silk scarf at her throat. She smiled broadly as she saw the mayor in his red, white and blue sash of office and Bruno, hastily showered and dressed in his only civilian suit, waiting to greet her. He forced his face into a welcoming smile, firmly repressing the memory of that blinding flash of the explosion and Louis's stricken features at the loss of his best hunting dog.

Lydia Manners, her matron of honor, had already climbed from the car, and she was quickly joined by Pamela and Florence, her bridesmaids. Florence's two toddlers, Dora and Daniel, dressed in white, were staring wide eyed at the bride. A small cheer arose from the gathering crowd of St. Denis folk as the mayor escorted Clothilde and Lydia to the elevator. Bruno waited to do the same for the bridesmaids and the children. Because of the old custom that bride and groom should not be together before the ceremony, Horst and his archaeologist friends had already taken the stairs before the bride's arrival, discussing how many centuries of feet had been required to carve such grooves into the old stone steps. Bruno made polite conversation while waiting, but spotted from the corner of his eye Yveline and Isabelle, taking time off from their duties at the *gendarmerie* to watch the show.

Ever alert to her surroundings, Pamela noted his quick glance at the two women in the crowd and asked, "Who's that woman with the short, dark hair standing beside Yveline?"

"Commissaire Isabelle Perrault, from Eurojust in The Hague," he said, keeping his voice neutral. He was pretty sure that Pamela had known who she was all along. He remembered her being furious when she had been told by some local busybody that Isabelle and Bruno had been spotted together at a hotel in Bordeaux. It had been during an operation against a ring smuggling illegal immigrants into France. They had each been on duty and nothing had happened between them. Isabelle had been shot in the thigh that day, leading the team arresting the smugglers and their cargo of Chinese.

"*That* Isabelle? Your old flame?" Pamela drawled, ice chips in her voice. Florence's eyes widened at her tone. Pamela turned away so as not to be caught staring and looked at him fiercely. "What brings her down here this time, more of your so-called security exercise?"

"She's here with the brigadier, based at the *gendarmerie*," said Bruno, coolly.

Isabelle and Pamela knew of each other but to his knowledge had never met until now. He had loved each of them and a part of him always would. But why did Pamela seem to think she still had some claim on him after breaking off their affair for what she had insisted was his own good? He damped down the surge of irritation, knowing how he'd feel if he found himself confronting some new lover of Isabelle's or a new beau for Pamela. Bruno remembered how shaken he'd been when he'd mistakenly thought Pamela had begun an affair with Jack Crimson.

Bruno shook his head to clear it of such thoughts. His role now was to officiate at a wedding, and he was uncomfortably aware of the shoulder holster he was wearing beneath his suit. The jacket was sagging with the weight of two extra magazines in each side pocket. The brigadier had insisted that he remain armed, despite the wedding. At least the jacket hung loosely enough to leave no obvious bulge. He'd have to tell Florence's children they were getting too big for his usual trick of picking them both up at the same time.

The elevator came, and Bruno led the way to the council chamber, from which the chairs had been removed and the ancient table pushed against the wall and covered with flowers. The mayor's secretary steered Clothilde and Lydia to a nearby waiting room. Bruno turned as he always did in this chamber to the long window to enjoy one of the finest views of St. Denis, the wide curve of the river and the old stone bridge, the quayside with its anglers and the gentle stirring of the willow branches as their tips kissed the surface of the water.

The room filled quickly behind him with the wedding guests. The baron and Raquelle stood to one side of Gilles and Fabiola, Jack Crimson and his daughter on the other. The visitors from Germany and Britain had somehow been steered by Pamela into the front row. He saw the tall figure of the count toward the rear among the staff of Clothilde's museum, along with various well-wishers from St. Denis and the surrounding communes. Wearing an enormous hat was Horst's neighbor, a plump and motherly type who did his cleaning. Beside her stood Sergeant Jules and Yveline, both in uniform.

Of Isabelle there was no sign. Philippe Delaron was crouched in a corner, two cameras around his neck. In the doorway Bruno spotted Yacov and Amélie holding hands as they made way for the mayor, leading in the soon-to-be-married couple. Amélie winked at him. Bruno suspected that she, too, was looking forward to the little surprise they had arranged between them.

Bruno checked that he had the ring in his pocket and took his place behind the groom as Horst and Clothilde came in separately to stand in front of the mayor to take their vows. There were no religious vows, though, in this civil ceremony, where the mayor announced under the powers conferred upon him by *la République française* and according to Article 212 of the civil code he was prepared to solemnize this union under the law.

First Clothilde and then Horst declared that they consented to take the other as spouse, the mayor pronounced them to be united as one in marriage, and they signed the register. Bruno and Lydia Manners then signed as *témoins,* the witnesses the law required, followed by Barrymore and Raquelle. Bruno and Lydia brought out the rings for the couple to slide onto each other's finger. Horst was formally handed the *livret de famille,* the mayor took his usual bonus of being first to kiss the bride, and the deed was done.

And at that point, pure and high, Amélie's voice rang out in that most beloved of French songs of love, Edith Piaf's "La Vie en Rose." Clothilde turned to see, a wide smile spreading across her features. Horst clapped his hands in delight until Clothilde took him in her arms and they began a slow, affectionate dance to the music of the song. It was, Bruno realized, their first act together as a married couple.

"*Mon Dieu,* that's delightful," murmured the mayor to Bruno as the song came to an end and the storm of applause died away. "She has a marvelous voice and we must certainly have her at our concerts this summer. You see, Bruno, I know you hated the idea at first, but I was right to bring the two of you together. I presume you and she worked out this little musical interlude?"

Before Bruno could reply, Clothilde was at his side, clutching Amélie with one hand, and hugging him with her other and announcing what a lovely idea the song had been and that Amélie and her escort must come along to the museum for the reception. They would fit them in somehow.

Bruno knew that while only the wedding party would attend the dinner inside the museum's biggest room of exhibits, there was to be a much-larger reception with drinks and snacks on the terrace where the huge statue of Cro-Magnon man stared out over the town. There would be plenty of room there.

On a ledge in the tall cliff that dominated Les Eyzies, the terrace was reached from the top floor of the new museum, along a cobbled path to the old ruined château that had occupied the ledge since the Middle Ages. The ruins had been bought by the state in 1913 and converted into the first museum of prehistory, a cramped, dark space, now used as offices. The original stone archway to the old château now led the way across cobblestones to the terrace and the statue. It was, Bruno knew, a splendid place for a party with room for a hundred or more people, and Clothilde had invited all the museum staff as well as the wedding guests.

"Do you think we could ask you to sing again at the reception?" Clothilde asked Amélie, still clutching her hand.

"I couldn't refuse a bride, and you look glorious, madame, and such a handsome husband," Amélie replied. "I'm glad you enjoyed our little surprise. It was Bruno's idea, but I was thrilled when you decided to dance."

"Thank you, we'll talk at the reception, but right now I have to circulate." Impulsively Clothilde kissed her cheek and set off around the council chamber, being kissed by everyone. She stopped at Florence's children and cried, "Our lovely little page and flower girl," and bent to kiss them both.

"I'm glad it worked," Amélie said to Bruno. "I wasn't sure if it was quite the right song for a wedding."

"It was perfect," he replied. "And you passed the audition. The mayor tells me I have to get you for our summer concerts, so tomorrow I'll introduce you to the guitarist who runs the local bookshop, the garage owner who plays drums and our choirmaster who plays piano and keyboard. They're pretty good, and I know they'll be delighted to accompany you."

"Maybe I can get Florence to sing duets with me."

"You're going to be adopted by St. Denis at this rate." He smiled and held out his hand to Yacov, who approached, kissed Amélie on the lips and then gripped Bruno's hand with both his own.

"A lovely wedding, Bruno, I'm glad to have been here for it. But I have to take you away for a moment. The brigadier wants to talk with you, urgently. There's been a development."

As they pushed their way through the crowd, most of whose members wanted either to shake Bruno's hand or to kiss him in the general mood of celebration, Bruno was jostled against Yacov. He felt something hard and solid under Yacov's left armpit. The man was armed. He glanced at his friend sharply. Yacov put a finger to his lips and murmured, "The brigadier gave it to me."

"What the hell is this?" Bruno asked, grabbing Yacov's arm when they were on the staircase. "Since when does a Paris lawyer get given a gun by a senior official of the interior ministry?"

"You'd better ask him," Yacov replied, gently removing Bruno's hand from his arm. "He's waiting downstairs."

A small crowd had gathered outside the *mairie* waiting for the wedding party to emerge, but the brigadier and Isabelle were standing at the far side of the road, and the brigadier beckoned to him.

"So, you were right about Lascaux," the brigadier said when Bruno arrived. "They found the remnants of his gun, one of those AK-forty-sevens that flooded into Europe after the Balkan wars. The problem is that after a very thorough sweep by the army reinforcements, it turns out there was only one of them. The other four are still at large, and they may have joined up with others."

Standing beside him, Yacov suddenly pulled out a phone and turned away, and after saying "Sync now," he pressed a button on his keypad, which to Bruno meant that Yacov was using a scrambler. He began speaking in a language Bruno couldn't recognize. He assumed it must be Hebrew and wondered why he hadn't realized earlier that Yacov was something more than the patent lawyer he claimed to be. Firearms were not handed out by the interior ministry to just anyone. Could Yacov be the official Israeli contact that the brigadier had mentioned in the videoconference?

"We have to assume they are on the loose, still active and possibly with another target." The brigadier broke off to shake hands with Jack Crimson who had joined them, his daughter Miranda at his side. Bruno could see no bulge under Crimson's armpit but remembered that the brigadier had authorized him to be armed.

Bruno felt a moment of outrage. St. Denis was his town, its safety his responsibility, but suddenly people were being armed as if this were the Wild West. He hated it on those rare moments when he had to wear his own weapon, but now Yacov, Crimson and no doubt the brigadier and Isabelle were all carrying sidearms.

"I gather you authorized a weapon for Maître Kaufman here,

sir," Bruno said. "Have you some reason to believe a civilian, a Parisian lawyer, might be in any danger?"

"Yes, and don't ask. It's my decision."

"I talked to Saïd al-Husayni again," said Isabelle. "That comment he made about the farm that we thought might refer to the scout camp—it came in the context of a diatribe against Jews. So we concluded that the scout camp was indeed a target, and that makes Yacov Kaufman a potential victim. He's got military training, he knows his way around weapons."

"Would he be the Israeli contact you referred to, sir?" asked Bruno.

The brigadier looked at him coldly. "Again, Bruno, don't ask."

At that point, the wedding party emerged from the *mairie,* Horst and Clothilde in the lead, the mayor and Lydia behind them and then the rest, all being showered with rice and confetti by the crowd. Philippe Delaron walked backward before them, his camera to his eye, taking photo after photo. Horst caught Bruno's eye, waved, nudged Clothilde, and they came across.

"I remember you," said Clothilde to Isabelle. "When Horst was kidnapped, you were part of the team that rescued him, so thank you for my new husband."

"I'm glad to see you both happy," said Isabelle. "Please accept my congratulations and best wishes." She gestured to the brigadier beside her. "My colleague here, General Lannes, led that particular inquiry, so he's the one who deserves your thanks."

Horst shook their hands. "Perhaps you would do us the honor of joining us at Les Eyzies for a glass of champagne at our reception. It seems this wedding would not have taken place without the two of you and, of course, Bruno."

"We're still involved in this exercise, but if we can . . . ," Isabelle began to say when Delaron came up, phone in hand.

"What's this about a shoot-out at Lascaux, Bruno? The news desk just called to ask if I can get there right away."

"You can't leave. We booked you specially to take the photos at our reception and dinner," Clothilde objected. "And we've all just come from Lascaux. There was an explosion and some shooting, but it's all over. They evacuated us and gave us the all clear."

"Gunfire heard and an explosion, the place now sealed off and surrounded by troops and cops, that's all I know," Philippe said into the phone. "Unless these types can tell me more."

He held out his hand to Isabelle. "I remember you from when you worked around here. I know you have some high-powered job in Paris. What do you know about this?"

"Even if I knew, I couldn't tell you," Isabelle replied without looking at the reporter. "Sorry."

"That's not good enough . . . ," the mayor began.

"The incident is over, none of our people were hurt, and Lascaux is undamaged," said the brigadier, turning away. "That's all I can say. Anything more will have to come from the police spokesman."

By now, people were picking up the news on their mobile phones, clustering together and talking in hushed tones. Some began to gather around Bruno and Philippe, hungry for more information or some detail of the attack on a place that symbolized so much of their region and its long history.

Florence declared that she was taking the children home and added, without much conviction, that she might join them later if she could find a babysitter. Pamela demanded, politely but firmly, if Bruno had anything to add to the news flash. Only that Lascaux was safe, he replied. She pressed him, asking whether they would all be safe at Les Eyzies. Bruno could only shrug and say that he was going there, when he saw a figure suddenly sinking down to sit on one of the stone bollards, her head in her hands. It was Raquelle, looking stunned, a handkerchief to her mouth. She had seemed fine in the cave and when they were escorted down to their bus. But she had given ten years of her life to reproducing the bulls and horses on the copy of the cave the tourists now saw. Shock must be setting in.

"Who is that senior-looking guy with Isabelle?" Philippe asked as Isabelle left with Yacov and the brigadier. "Is he down here for this?"

By now Gilles had joined them, notebook poised, Fabiola at his side but holding a phone to her ear, probably trying to check whether there had been an emergency call for doctors. They had seen the Lascaux cave before and so had not joined the visiting party. Gilles had taken early retirement from *Paris Match,* but he still freelanced for them. The old newshound was back on the scent, Bruno thought.

Mon Dieu, how could he deal with all these people with their questions and their worries? They were giving him no time to think. He felt he was being pulled in different directions: the emotional needs of his friends, his duty to the mayor and people of St. Denis, his obligation to the orders and official status of the brigadier, the threat to Lascaux, the unknown new danger of trained and violent men on the loose. With an effort, he resisted the temptation to reach into his shoulder holster and touch his gun to reassure himself.

"I thought all this was supposed to be a training exercise," Gilles said. "It looks as though the guards at Lascaux were on alert, almost as if they suspected some sort of attack was coming. Is that so? And is this incident linked to that dead woman at Commarque and the gendarme who was shot at Siorac?"

"You can call him a senior official at the interior ministry," Bruno replied to Philippe, ignoring Gilles's questions. "You heard

the man, there's no damage done to Lascaux, and this is Clothilde's wedding day."

Bruno left Philippe and Gilles and went to Raquelle to put
an arm around her and whisper reassurance that all was well at
Lascaux and that her cave had been untouched.

"What is it? Terrorists? Arabs?" she asked dumbly, her hair
awry from the distracted way she had been running her hands
through it. She gazed up at him. "*Mon Dieu,* will this ever stop?"
He remembered that Raquelle's mother had been Israeli.

"We're not sure yet what happened," he said as Amélie joined
them, looking bereft at Yacov's departure.

"Come on," he said, taking Raquelle by the hand. "Let's all
get to Les Eyzies, have a drink and celebrate with Clothilde and
Horst."

Chapter 29

By the time Bruno and his carload arrived at the National Museum of Prehistory, extra glasses had been borrowed from the nearby café, and Hubert had dashed back to his cave to bring two more cases of champagne. The sound of the party grew louder as they climbed the last spiral and came out into sunlight and conviviality. The guests had already overflowed from the terrace on the roof of the museum. Some of them were drifting through the stone archway of the old château that was tucked into the vast rocky overhang and spreading out on the longer terrace beyond the statue of prehistoric man.

The only access to these terraces was through the new museum, either by a small elevator for the disabled or by climbing a wide spiral staircase whose walls featured two-meter-tall reconstructions of the layers of archaeological excavations. Climbing past the entrance to the lower gallery, visitors could see at the end of one alcove a reconstruction of a giant stag, its antlers five meters wide.

Bruno often wondered at the courage of those ancestors, taking on such beasts armed only with spears and flint axes. In the upper gallery was a reconstruction of a hunter from around the time of Lascaux, seventeen thousand years earlier, aiming a slim spear with a point made from a reindeer's antler. In neighboring showcases were examples of spear-throwers, hooked sticks that extended the reach and flex of the human arm and endowed the spears with far-greater force. Bruno had tried throwing a spear with one at a site upriver called Pech Merle, where the family that owned the land had set up archery targets backed by thick straw. A good throw, Bruno had found, could penetrate through the straw from a range of thirty meters. No wonder humans had ended up on top of the food chain.

Raquelle had repaired her makeup in the car. She took a glass of champagne and went to join the archaeologists. Amélie was jolly by now, swigging half her champagne, and was then surrounded by a ring of people telling her how much they had enjoyed her singing. Bruno went to the bar and greeted the two barmen, one of them a former pupil of his rugby classes. He got a glass of champagne for Pamela, another for himself and escorted her through the tunnel of the stone gateway to raise a toast to the statue of prehistoric man. Horst and Clothilde were standing beneath it as their friends took snapshots of them on their phones.

The terrace had been decorated with some of the spare life-size wax models of Neanderthal people from the museum's storage room. There was a life-size model of a seated man in furs talking to a naked child as he worked on a flint tool, two women scraping furs, and a standing hunter, a spear poised in his hand.

"I think they'll be very happy," Pamela said to Bruno. "It certainly took them long enough before deciding to tie the knot. Clothilde told me they first became lovers thirty years ago, and they knew all of the other's bad habits, but they'd grown so used to one another there seemed little point in not marrying. You know she's selling her house here in Les Eyzies? Apparently Horst's place won because of that amazing new bathroom he installed. I often wanted to try it, all those nozzles in the shower to spray you all over."

"I'm sure she'd be delighted to let you enjoy it."

Bruno felt a little on edge. He had not spent much time alone with Pamela since she had ended their affair. They had met often enough, at the Monday dinners with their friends, at the stables, in the market, but he'd been startled by the bitterness in her tone when she saw Isabelle outside the *mairie*. He'd never found Pamela easy to read, despite her almost-perfect French. She remained an Englishwoman, or rather Scottish, not quite familiar with all the unspoken assumptions about life and love and la République that most French people unconsciously shared. He had found it charming, the way she believed that a cup of tea solved most problems or at least made them seem less formidable, her passion for English crosswords and listening to the BBC on her laptop as she did her household chores. He still did, Bruno admitted to himself, and on impulse he took her hand and squeezed it.

"Don't tell me you're letting this wedding carry you away, Bruno," she said, gently extracting her hand from his. "I wonder if anything will change for the happy couple? Whether Clothilde will still want to come over for a girls' evening with Fabiola and me?"

"Isn't Miranda also part of your girls' evenings?" he asked. "You share a house with her."

"She is once she's put the children to bed, like Florence. But there's a difference between women like Clothilde and me and those with small children, particularly when there's no man to share the upbringing. I must say, I rather enjoy having the little ones around—so long as they belong to somebody else." She fished in her bag for her phone. "I should call Florence and tell her she can leave the kids at our place. Félix the stable lad is there looking after Miranda's children."

A cheer went up from the other terrace as Hubert arrived with more champagne and people rushed for refills. Jack Crimson and Miranda were among the first to emerge from the scrum and came through the tunnel to join them, each carrying two full glasses. As Crimson put the two extras on the ledge beside Bruno and Pamela, Bruno's phone vibrated.

"We've had patrols and choppers with infrared sensors beating those woods and they're empty," Isabelle said. "The guy who blew himself up at Lascaux was alone, which makes it look like a diversion while Mustaf's team is still going for their main target. That means him and three more on the loose."

"Unless the diversion was to let Mustaf and his men get away from this area, maybe head for Paris. They must be feeling trapped."

"Another person feeling trapped is the brigadier," she said. "Can you imagine how much pressure he's under from Paris after all the resources they've plunged into this? And I can tell you he's made a lot of enemies in this job who are just waiting for it all to go wrong."

"Have the *mobiles* found any sign of the transport the bomber used to get to Lascaux? If not, that could mean he was dropped off."

"They're scouring the area now. Got to go."

"Wait," he said. "I presume this means you can't make the reception. Would that apply for J-J and Yacov?"

"Yacov left here some time ago and said he was joining you. J-J has gone to Lascaux. And I'll stay in touch. Sorry we can't make the reception." She rang off.

Bruno noticed more and more people coming through the tunnel to this larger terrace, away from the crowd around the bar serving champagne. Hubert was among them, carrying a bottle of champagne and chatting with Amélie. Suddenly Yacov emerged from the tunnel and Amélie's face lit up when she saw him.

"How's my old friend Yossi?" Crimson asked Yacov jovially, holding out his glass for Hubert to refill it. "Still running marathons?"

"No idea," Yacov replied, looking uncomfortable and turning to Bruno to ask if there was any news. Bruno put down his glass and took Crimson's and Yacov's glasses and put them alongside his own on the ledge. Then he led Crimson and Yacov aside, toward the farther end of the terrace until they were well out of earshot.

"I know you've both been authorized to carry weapons, which makes three of us. So let's stop drinking, just in case anything goes wrong here." He explained what he'd heard from Isabelle and that the four most dangerous men were still on the loose. "I suggest we go through the tunnel to the smaller terrace, since that's the only way to get up here."

"You don't think they could be coming here?" Crimson asked.

"I have no reason to think so, but let's not take any chances. And what was that crack of yours about Yossi? Who's he?"

"Yossi Cohen, head of Mossad, an old friend of mine," Crimson said. "We worked together when he was sabotaging Iran's nuclear program. And he does run marathons." He paused and looked at Yacov. "Don't try to tell me you don't work for him."

"I think Bruno just gave us some good advice," Yacov replied neutrally. "Let's go through to the other terrace. We can talk about old friends later."

"What are you carrying?" Bruno asked.

"Glock seventeen," said Yacov, and Crimson nodded. "Same here."

"Spare magazines?"

Yacov said one; Crimson shook his head.

"I'm carrying a PAMAS nine millimeter, with two spare mags," Bruno said. "That's about ninety rounds between us. If trouble comes this way, I'll hold the head of the staircase, you two get everybody else through the tunnel and hold them off there."

"You're serious about this?" Crimson asked as Bruno led the way back.

"I'm serious about taking intelligent precautions." At the bar, he asked for three glasses of mineral water, then installed himself at a corner where he could look down over the rooftops to the street and the entrance to the museum. He took out his phone to call Isabelle but kept watching.

"Remember in J-J's notes of the interview with Dumesnil, he told us that he'd talked to Leah and al-Husayni about Horst and Clothilde and about their wedding?" he said.

"I don't recall that being in J-J's notes," she replied.

"*Putain,* well he certainly told us that, and that when he was being interrogated he even had a copy of the paper thrust at him with a picture of Horst and that seismic machine at Commarque."

"Yes, I remember about the paper being pushed in his face, but I didn't make the connection. Do you think Horst is in danger?"

"I think it's possible this wedding reception could be a target. Can you get some reinforcements here right away? We've got more than a hundred people at the museum here."

"I'll get on it." She hung up.

In the street below, he saw a figure in a police cap emerge from the museum entrance and start patrolling the street. It was Louise Varenne, the town policewoman. He called her number and saw her pull her phone from the case on her belt.

"Louise, it's me, Bruno. This is urgent. Make sure you're armed and come up to the roof terrace of the museum. We may have trouble brewing. And wear your flak vest." As he spoke he

recalled that the ones issued to the police were said to give protection against handguns but would not stop a round from an
AK-47.

"I'll have to go to the *mairie*. My weapon's in the safe there.
What's up?"

"I'll tell you when you get here. Now move, as fast as you can,
and bring all your spare magazines."

They hung up, and he saw her trot across the street to the
small *mairie* and fish out a key to let herself in at the locked front
door. He looked up and down the street, filled with the parked
cars of the reception guests. There was no other traffic.

"You seem very serious about a security risk at this wedding,"
said Yacov, suddenly appearing at Bruno's side. "Is there a special
reason for that?"

"All this seems to have begun with a sudden spate of rumors
about the Testament of Iftikhar and the fall to her death of an
Israeli woman called Leah Wolinsky," said Bruno, his eyes on the
street.

"You may know her as Leah Ben-Ari, supposed to be a Peace
Now activist who was living with a Palestinian historian called
Saïd al-Husayni." Bruno's tone was thoughtful, not accusing.
"The two of them were blackmailed or threatened to join Mustaf and his group in France, and somehow she believed that the
testament was connected to Commarque. She and al-Husayni
went to interview her old teacher, a medieval scholar who was
later tortured by Mustaf's gang, just as Horst was starting his
excavations at Commarque. And there's a story in this morning's
paper about the new cave and secret tomb Horst and his team
have found there. I've been slow about putting all this together,
but now I'm worried enough to have called Isabelle to send us
some reinforcements. And I've been very slow about you, Yacov.
I should have realized when the brigadier authorized you to carry

a weapon. And now Jack Crimson just confirmed it. You're with Mossad."

Yacov shrugged. "If you're right about Mustaf's gang coming here, maybe we should move that table and glasses into the tunnel. We'll need everything we can to slow them down."

"Good idea," said Bruno, turning to the two barmen. He told them to start moving the bar under Yacov's direction before resuming his watch. Across the street, the *mairie* door opened, and Louise reappeared wearing her flak vest, her holster now around her waist. Bruno and she had done the annual firearms refresher course at the Périgueux range together, and he knew she was a competent shot. Louise paused, looking up the street where a white van had come into view and drove slowly down toward the museum. On the side of the van was the logo of one of the local catering firms. Of course, he thought, they would be preparing the wedding dinner.

Louise stepped into the center of the road and put up her hand, then pointed to the turnoff to the entrance to the museum. Then she seemed to start in surprise and began to reach for her gun. The man in the passenger seat was faster, put a long-barreled gun out of the window and fired twice, two soft coughs that were lost in the sound of chatter and clinking glasses on the balcony.

Chapter 30

Bruno craned over the railing and saw a face inside the van look up in his direction and at the crowd of people against the balcony railings. The van accelerated up the short lane and over the shallow steps that led to the glass frontage of the museum and then drove straight through it, the sound of breaking glass at last alerting the crowd on the terrace that something was wrong. As the van jerked and stalled, trying to push its way through the tangle of glass and metal, its rear doors opened. Two black-clad figures wearing headbands jumped out carrying what looked like Kalashnikovs and darted into the museum. They looked bulky, as if wearing flak jackets, and they were carrying something else slung around their necks that he couldn't identify. Bruno recalled that another two men, one at the wheel and the other who had shot Louise, had been in the driver's cabin.

The distance was too far for his handgun, so Bruno shouted an alert to Yacov and Crimson, quickly phoned Isabelle and said, "They're here and have already shot a cop. We need help now and an ambulance."

"Emergency!" he shouted, closing his phone. "Everybody back through the tunnel. Right now."

Yacov and Crimson were trying to struggle back toward him

through the crowd blocking the tunnel, the space even more cramped with the table and glasses. A tall figure emerged and began bringing order out of chaos, guiding people through the gap and pushing them forward, and then began examining the wooden doors folded back to the tunnel sides.

"I presume you'd want these closed," he called to Bruno. It was Manners. Bruno took up a position, sheltered by the wall, from where he could fire at anyone coming up the final spiral of the staircase. Now Yacov was by his side.

"Empty champagne bottles," he said. "Toss them into the well of the stairs there, it could slow them, trip them up."

"Go ahead," said Bruno, keeping his position as Yacov threw bottles. "I think they're wearing flak jackets. We might have to get them with head shots."

"Merde," grunted Yacov. "This is a new gun for me."

Then Crimson arrived, panting, his weapon drawn. "Keep an eye on that elevator doorway," Bruno told him, pointing to the two metal doors. "Put your ear to it and you'll hear if it starts working. Shoot anyone who comes out."

"Everybody's on the rear terrace," Manners called from the tunnel mouth, now almost closed by the wooden doors. "Have you a spare gun for me?"

"Not unless someone else there has a weapon. Can you lock those tunnel doors?"

"Not that I can see. We'll try to barricade it with the bar table. Perhaps one of you three with guns could wait behind the doors. You'll need cover, Bruno, if you have to run back."

"We'll try to stop them here," Bruno shouted back. He turned to Yacov. "We'll hit them from here with a volley, and when I say go, you retreat to the tunnel doors and give me cover when I join you."

"Any sound from the elevator?" he called to Crimson, whose ear was pressed against its metal doors.

"Not yet. Maybe they don't know about it."

Now Bruno could hear footsteps on the staircase and shouted commands in Arabic.

"They're coming up the stairs," he called to Crimson. "Leave the elevator, get back into the tunnel and, as soon as Yacov and I come in, be ready to hold the doors. If we go down, seal the tunnel anyway and hold as long as you can. Help is on the way."

Mon Dieu, he thought as Crimson ran back, if they break through they'll have a hundred hostages. Then he heard voices again, much closer, the sound of a bottle being kicked aside and then a gun barrel was poked out from the side of the spiral stairs and sprayed three quick bursts of automatic gunfire, shockingly loud. The shots went wild.

Another longer burst followed, and two figures jumped out from cover and began climbing the stairs, firing as they came.

Bruno fired two snap shots at the first figure, but too low, hitting only the chest, and then two more a little higher, and the man went down, falling into the second figure who then lost his footing on an empty bottle and tumbled back down the stairs. An arm snaked out and pulled him to safety. Then the arm reappeared, tossing something up to the terrace.

"Grenade," Bruno shouted, and ducked behind the wall. But there was no explosion, just a hissing, and Bruno suddenly understood that what they had been wearing around their necks were gas masks.

"They've got gas," he called to Yacov. "Get back to the tunnel and give me cover."

Bruno fired two more shots down into the well of the staircase, seeing the sprawled figure of the man he had shot. He was moving, sliding back down the steps, but he'd dropped his gun. Bruno, getting the first acrid taste of tear gas, fired twice more into the man's hips, beneath the protective flak vest. Then he fired twice again to keep the others' heads down, held his breath and ran back to slip through the gap in the double doors. Ten shots fired, he told himself, counting automatically.

Manners slammed them closed, and Bruno and Yacov pushed the bar table onto its side as a barricade for the wooden doors. Bruno sniffed the air, which was clear, and took a deep breath.

"I've got people trying to topple that stone statue to help block the door, but it's too firmly fixed," Manners said. He kicked a thick shard of glass from a broken bottle under the bottom of the door to help jam it in place.

"See if you can break into that storage house at the end of the terrace," Bruno said, crouching low. As Manners left, Bruno shouted after him, "Ask Clothilde if there's anything in there we can use for a barricade. Any furniture would be good, old chairs piled upside down, or if you find any flints, stuff them into any sacks or boxes you find."

"Better keep down low, below the table," said Yacov. "Do you want to hold them here at the doors or from the far end of the tunnel?"

"The far end; the tunnel makes a natural killing ground and they won't see much for the glare."

"But they can throw more tear gas down here and force us back, then rush us in the smoke," Yacov said.

Bruno was about to reply that Yacov was right when a burst of gunfire hit the thick wooden doors above them, and half-a-dozen little holes began leaking sunshine into the tunnel. Soon there would be gas seeping through.

"Can you get us a couple of wet napkins to cover our faces against the tear gas?" Yacov called back to Crimson as Manners appeared with Gilles, the count and the baron and some other men, pushing and dragging something heavy along the ground.

"The warehouse had these boxes filled with flints, good protection," Manners announced, ducking behind them and starting to push them up against the wooden door as two more bursts of gunfire opened more holes in the doors, much lower this time.

"No, leave them at the tunnel entrance," Bruno called. "These doors won't hold long." Then to Yacov, "Go back and help place those boxes, they'll give us good cover. Leave gaps for us to shoot through when we take shelter behind them. Then look for another position further back."

Horst and one of his German friends appeared, and to Bruno's disbelief he saw they had lost their trousers and were carrying bone-tipped spears. "It's a treasure trove in that storage house," Horst said. "We've got the rest of the men bringing more boxes of flints to build a barricade. We've got flint knives, axes." Horst's eyes were bright and he looked almost cheerful.

"What about your trousers?" Bruno asked.

"Clothilde, Pamela and Amélie have the women tying trouser legs together and ripping up shirts to make a rope they can climb down onto the rooftops below and get away," Horst replied. Despite the situation, Bruno grinned and nodded approval, knowing he should have thought of that.

At the far end of the tunnel, behind the boxes of flints, Bruno saw Barrymore manhandling into place the wax model of a Stone Age hunter with his spear poised to launch. Bruno approved. It would be the first thing Mustaf would see when he broke into the tunnel and would be the first target to attract his fire.

Something heavy slammed into the wooden doors above Bruno's head, some kind of battering ram Mustaf must have found in the museum. It slammed in again, and a crack opened as the glass shard beneath the door shrieked against the cobblestones. Bruno fired three quick shots through the door at waist height. There was no cry of pain, but the battering stopped. Bruno knew it was time to go. He crawled back along the floor to join Yacov and Crimson behind the boxes of flints, ejected his old magazine and slipped in a new one.

"Where do those steps go?" Yacov asked, pointing to his left.

"Up to the next floor of the old château, where the rooms used to house exhibits for the old museum," said Bruno, remembering that there were windows overlooking the terrace where Mustaf was now planning his next move.

"Thanks for reminding me. You hold on here, and I'll go up and try for a quick shot."

The steps were guarded by a locked iron gate, but Bruno holstered his gun and climbed over it and up the steps. The door into the exhibit rooms was locked, but he leaned back and kicked hard at the lock. The wood beside the door lock cracked but didn't give. He tried again and it swung open, revealing an empty room, full of dust that caught the light from the mullioned windows.

Bruno crept forward, staying in cover behind the stone wall and then peeking out to see three figures at the wooden doors below. He pushed his gun through one of the tiny panes and fired twice. He saw one of the men go down, twisting and pointing his weapon to shoot back, but Bruno had already ducked away. By the time a burst of automatic fire came through the window Bruno had moved to the next window in line and fired again twice. The return fire stopped.

Four bullets gone, eleven remaining and one full magazine. In the silence Bruno heard the distant sound of a helicopter. Help must be on the way.

For the first time, Bruno began to think they might just survive this as he went back down the stairs to the barricade of boxes where Yacov waited alone, crouching behind a box of flints.

"Where's Crimson?"

Yacov jerked his thumb back. "See that little stone turret, like a pulpit on the corner. He's in there. There's a small hole in the stone, just big enough to aim and shoot through. The women have started going down the rope."

To Bruno's left, just behind the angle where the tunnel opened out, Manners was standing, a spear in his hand. He gave Bruno a grin.

"The Seventh Cavalry appears to be on their way," he said, pointing down the valley where the clattering sound of a helicopter was growing louder, but it could not yet be seen, maybe hidden by the overhang.

"Whose idea was it to make the rope?" Bruno asked.

"Pamela, Clothilde, my wife, that black girl who sang—they just began to organize everybody back there. I thought at first it was just something for them to do to fend off panic, but the rope line seems to be working."

A helicopter swooped into sight about fifty yards away from the rock overhang and hovered, a machine gun pointing menacingly from the open side door. Bruno stood to give a thumbs-up just as Mustaf fired again. Ducking hastily, Bruno pointed to the far side of the tunnel, and the chopper backed away, rose and then moved gingerly forward and swooped again, its gun chattering.

That was when Mustaf came through the door, very low, two gas grenades preceding him, followed by a second man crouching and giving covering fire. Pushing the table before him for cover and firing short bursts the length of the tunnel, Mustaf kept coming despite Bruno's and Yacov's fire.

Bruno spun away with a yelp of pain as something hit his forehead. He clapped his hand to it and it came away bloody, but he was still conscious. It couldn't have been a bullet, maybe a chip from one of the boxes of flints. Blood was flooding into his left eye and his right eye was watering so much from the tear gas that he couldn't see. He felt rather than saw the box of flints being pushed back into him, a volley of shots spraying just above the level of the box. He heard a cry and felt Yacov crumple against his legs. He lost his balance and fell to the floor.

He half rose, lifted his gun above the box and began firing blindly, hoping for a hit. The automatic fire stopped. Mustaf must be changing magazines. Bruno began to rise when he sensed a movement to his left where Manners had been standing. Dimly through his tears he saw the Englishman lunge forward. And then the menacing figure before him, one hand on his gun and the other on his fresh magazine, jerked and screamed in pain as the long bone point of the spear ripped into his neck.

Mustaf dropped his gun and put his hands to the spear to pull it out. Barely able to see, Bruno jammed the muzzle of his own weapon hard into Mustaf's gas mask and fired.

Epilogue

The bandage around Bruno's forehead had been replaced with a small Band-Aid, just big enough to cover the stitches that would be removed later in the week. Horst and Clothilde stood before him, hand in hand, and Amélie had come down from Paris especially for the opening of the cave. The count stood beside the American cameraman from the Discovery Channel as the engineers checked the tension of the hawsers. Finally they were ready, and with a wave from the project director to the operator the giant winch engaged, the steel hawsers tightened and the great boulder began to move.

They stopped the winch at once, checking the impact of the boulder's movement on the roof and side walls, and then one of the engineers signaled again to the winch operator. This time the boulder moved perhaps five centimeters before they stopped again to use the camera on the end of the flexible cable to check the roof inside the cave. Once more they checked the walls and the position of the rollers that would help the giant stone to be inched out from the cave it had sealed for centuries.

Engineers held Horst and Clothilde back as they tried to be the first in. The project director used the remote camera again and then sent in the workmen with the hydraulic props that would reinforce the roof. He then went in himself, tapping gently with a small hammer on the walls and roof before he pronounced it safe. The cameraman went in first to record the moment when Horst, Clothilde and the count entered the cave and began looking around them in wonder.

"I can't wait," Amélie squeaked, gripping the count's arm. "When are they going to open the tomb?"

She had come down from Paris for the opening, but she had also come each weekend to visit Yacov, still in hospital in Sarlat after taking two bullets in his chest and another in his shoulder. His arm had been saved, but he would not have much use of it in the future. Bruno had been to see him three times, but only during the third visit had Yacov recovered sufficiently to talk and ask about the final moments of the attack after he was gunned down. Bruno explained that none of the wedding guests had been hurt. And by the time the French commandos had landed from the helicopter and reached them, all the women had escaped down the rope of clothes.

On the cupboards on each side of Yacov's hospital bed were two large bouquets of flowers. Bruno had looked at the cards. One was from Maya, Yacov's grandmother. The other was signed simply, "Well done, Yossi."

"Yossi Cohen?" Bruno had asked. "I presume he's your boss."

Yacov did not reply. Bruno continued, "I've been wondering whether Mustaf had been right about Leah when he called her an Israeli spy. I can see why you'd want to have someone planted inside Peace Now, someone close enough to the Palestinians that a lot of them trusted her. And I can't work out why else she'd have wanted to set up a fake identity and bank account. But it was a lovely operation that Leah ran, helping circulate that rumor about the Testament of Iftikhar, panicking the jihadists and running the scheme all the way to Commarque. I hope Yossi sent some flowers to Saïd al-Husayni."

"Thanks for coming to see me, Bruno," Yacov replied. "We are friends, but I'm not talking about this." He had then turned his face away and, although Bruno waited, he said not another word.

"We're doing the opening of the scout camp next month," Bruno told him after a long silence. "The doctors say you should be able to attend by then. And the Muslim scouts are coming this time."

"Good," said Yacov, closing his eyes. "I'll look forward to seeing you there, Bruno."

Bruno had gone to the room next door where Louise, the policewoman of Les Eyzies, was recovering well from two shots in her right lung. She faced six months of rehabilitation, but the doctors said she should then have a good prospect of returning to her job. Bruno suspected she'd retire, take her pension and then find a less perilous profession.

And now standing under the great overhang of the cliff at Commarque, Bruno was giving a blow-by-blow account of the opening over the phone to Auguste Dumesnil. He was still convalescing but eager to learn what secrets the cave contained.

"Horst and Clothilde are looking at the walls and taking photos of the engravings, but I can't see them yet from where I am," Bruno told him. "I don't see any paintings. The count is studying the tomb, just touching the lid with one finger, not trying to move it yet."

The opening of the tomb would be the crucial moment for which the TV channel had agreed to finance the whole operation. But permission had come only after much haggling with the Ministry of Culture for its approval to open the cave, and a great deal of research. Much of it had been done by Dumesnil from his hospital bed, with legwork by Horst and Clothilde. Then in Paris some crucial political strings had been pulled, first

by Isabelle and the brigadier and then by the minister of justice, Amélie's friend, and the cultural bureaucracy had grumpily
agreed.

Isabelle, back in Paris, had found the librarians who could
track Leah's earlier research at the national archive in Paris. Leah
had been looking for any traces of a Crusader named Gérard de
Commarque, an ancestor of the count, and for another known
only as Velos. She had apparently found very little and expressed
her frustration to the archivists. But she did establish that Gérard
and Velos had been French Crusaders who had been appointed
constables of Beit She'an when it was briefly a royal domain.
When it was later granted to Adam de Bessan of the powerful
Béthune family, Gérard and Velos had joined the Templars.

Leah had also asked for directions to the Chapel of St. Martin, built in the Vézère Valley by King Henry II of England in
penance for the murder of Archbishop Thomas à Becket in his
cathedral of Canterbury in A.D. 1170. Becket's assassins were
four knights who interpreted the king's angry outburst "Who
will rid me of this turbulent priest?" as an order for his execution.
After murdering Becket they traveled to Jerusalem and joined
the Templar Knights. Tradition says their tombs are located by
the entrance to the Temple Mount in Jerusalem.

Intrigued by her research, Isabelle had taken the early morning flight to Bergerac to attend the opening. She stood apart
from the others, on the small bridge that spanned the stream
trickling down to the River Beune, gazing up at the soaring
stones of the fortress tower. Bruno had not seen her since those
last moments of the fight above the museum when she'd come up
with the medics after the commando team had given the all clear
and she'd held his hand as his head wound had been dressed.
After the medic had cleaned the blood from his face and flushed
his eyes, her face had been the first thing Bruno had seen. Once

assured by the medics that Bruno was in no danger, she had left to return to the command center and begin drafting her report. He would never forget that she had been there.

Leah's instincts had been sound in coming to Commarque. For when the top of the tomb with its sculpture of a recumbent Knight Templar was levered aside, it was not entirely empty. Inside lay a skeleton, crushed almost into dust by the weight of chain mail and rusted armor. Heaviest of all was the great iron sword whose handle contained a small ingot of gold, which almost entirely covered a sliver of ancient wood.

Engraved into the crosspiece of the sword were the words in Latin: ECCE VERA ET SANCTA CRUX, "Behold the true and holy cross."

"A piece of the holy cross," breathed the TV producer beside Bruno in what sounded like reverence. Bruno had learned from the count that the Crusaders had bought from the cunning merchants of Jerusalem enough supposed pieces of the true cross of the Crucifixion to build a galleon, and enough of the nails supposedly hammered into it to build a modern ironclad.

From the intact skull, it was evident that the body had been bareheaded when it was buried. Behind the skull stood an ornate helmet, tall and topped with a dome and almost complete. Only the visor had fallen and crumbled away. Through the gap where the visor had been, something glinted.

"I can't get the camera in low enough," said the cameraman, and the producer brought in the flexible lens that had been used to look inside the cave when it was still sealed.

"Jesus Christ," said the cameraman. "It's a bowl on a stand, maybe a cup. And I think it might be gold. A golden chalice."

"Could this be the Holy Grail?" said the producer.

"Mon Dieu," said Amélie, crossing herself.

"What? What?" cried Dumesnil over the phone.

"I can't see yet," said Bruno, exchanging glances with the count, who gave a massive shrug and rolled his eyes.

Bruno lifted his gaze to Horst and Clothilde, knowing they were even more aware than he of the large number of fake relics. They had turned their backs on the tomb and were staring in wonder and delight, hand in hand, at the prehistoric engraving of a giant mammoth with enormous tusks carved into the rock of the cave. Clothilde turned and beckoned her friends to join them. The count led the way, Amélie still clinging to his arm. Bruno began to follow and was suddenly aware of Isabelle at his side and taking his hand, her eyes on the great mammoth ahead.

"May I stay for lunch?" she asked. "At your place."

Acknowledgments

This is a work of fiction, and all the characters and situations are inventions, except that some owe a little more to reality than others. My friend the count, Hubert de Commarque, showed me around his wondrous ruined château of Commarque and sparked something in my imagination that led to this novel. The magnificent castle was built by the French upon the rock that contains the prehistoric caves and engravings. It was entrusted to the Templars when Gérard de Commarque went on Crusade and was briefly captured by the English in the Hundred Years' War, embracing in one place and building much of the region's fabled past. I hope that many readers will feel inspired to visit this amazing place, rich in tens of thousands of years of history, and share my admiration for the heroic efforts the count has made to bring it back to life. If the Holy Grail were to exist, it could have few more imposing resting places. I warmly recommend the short films of this most noble of ruined castles that may be found on the website http://www.commarque.com/#!filmjp/c1qjf.

One of the indulgences an author can enjoy is to revive old characters from previous books. My first novel about the region, *The Caves of Périgord,* introduced two fictional archaeologists, the German professor Horst Vogelstern and Clothilde Daumier, a French curator from the National Museum of Prehistory in Les Eyzies. I have resuscitated them in previous books, but their two friends and colleagues in that adventure, the American art historian Lydia Dean and the English officer Jack Manners, have lain dormant until now. It has been a pleasure to bring them back to literary life.

I have also enjoyed making the link between Les Eyzies, the home of the Cro-Magnon people, and the excellent museum by the River Düssel in Germany, where the first bones of Neanderthal man were identified after being unearthed in 1868. I am indebted to Sara Willwerth and friends at Buchhandlung Weber in Erkrath-Hochdahl who showed me around the museum and the historic valley named for a seventeenth-century German pastor, Joachim Neander.

Almost all that is written in this novel about the genetics of prehistoric people, about the Venus figurines and the marvelous cave of Lascaux is as true as modern research can establish. The Testament of Iftikhar from the fall of Jerusalem to the First Crusade in 1099 is an old and disputed legend, whose veracity may not match the explosive political potential of such a document in today's Middle East. Anyone interested in pursuing this vexed argument between Jewish and Arab scholars over the history of Jerusalem might start with Daniel Pipes's seminal essay "The Muslim Claim to Jerusalem," published in the *Middle East Quarterly*, September 2001.

I am grateful to the staff of the Musée National de Préhistoire in Les Eyzies for the many interesting and informative hours spent attending their lectures and, among the exhibits, watching their videos of modern artisans making flint tools, bone harpoons and prehistoric paints and brushes. They deserve better than the carnage I have inflicted upon their terraces in this novel, but I suspect they might enjoy the image of a modern terrorist laid low by a Cro-Magnon spear.

As always, this novel owes a great deal to my friends and neighbors in the Périgord, to the warmth of their welcome, the quality of their food and wines and their generosity in introducing me and my family to the splendid way of life they have inherited from their ancestors and maintained to this day. It is a privilege to live among them, to eat and drink with them and hear their stories and to share something of their profound sense of the history they inhabit.

My wife, Julia, coauthor of the Bruno cookbook, and our daughters, Kate and Fanny, are always the first readers of my drafts and my helpful and supportive critics, and Kate is the custodian of the website brunochiefofpolice.com. Jane and Caroline Wood in Britain, Jonathan Segal in New York and Anna von Planta in Zurich do wonders with my raw manuscripts, and I am most grateful to them all. And our dear basset hound, Benson, is now very old and too lame for walks, but remains a great comfort and companion, sleeping beneath the desk and warming my feet as I write.

A NOTE ABOUT THE AUTHOR

Martin Walker served as foreign correspondent for *The Guardian* in Africa, the Soviet Union, the United States and Europe and was the editor of United Press International. He is a senior scholar of the Woodrow Wilson Center and directed the Global Policy Council, both in Washington, D.C. He now lives mainly in the Périgord region of France, where he writes, chairs the jury of the Prix Ragueneau cooking prize and is a chevalier of the Confrérie du Pâté de Périgueux. This is his tenth novel featuring Bruno, chief of police.

A NOTE ON THE TYPE

This book was set in Adobe Garamond. Designed for the Adobe Corporation by Robert Slimbach, the fonts are based on types first cut by Claude Garamond (ca. 1480–1561). Garamond was a pupil of Geoffroy Tory and is believed to have followed the Venetian models, although he introduced a number of important differences, and it is to him that we owe the letters we now know as "old style." He gave to his letters a certain elegance and feeling of movement that won their creator an immediate reputation and the patronage of Francis I of France.

Typeset by Scribe,
Philadelphia, Pennsylvania

Printed and bound by Berryville Graphics,
Berryville, Virginia